THE
Heirloom
BRIDES
COLLECTION

Treasured Items Bring Couples Together
in Four Historical Romances

THE
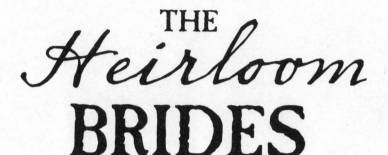
BRIDES
COLLECTION

—————◆—————

Kim Vogel Sawyer
Tracey Bateman, Joanne Bischof,
Mona Hodgson

BARBOUR BOOKS
An Imprint of Barbour Publishing, Inc.

Contents

Something Old

Tracey Bateman

Chapter One

Tucker's Creek, Kansas
October 1880

The horses pulling Betsy Lowell's wagon swayed toward the right side of the road as she tried to hang on to the reins with one hand and tightened her scarf about her neck with the other. The temperature had dropped at least ten degrees in the past hour since she and her grandpa left the cabin for town, and the morning's steady rain had frozen to icy pellets, driven by a gusty wind. Why they had waited until the end of October to get their winter supplies in the first place was beyond Betsy. She'd been after her grandpa for a month to get it done, but Pops always said there was plenty of time before the weather set in. Much as she'd like to point out that she'd been right, she thought better of it. No need to get him up in arms when he was trying to keep his horse upright.

"Mercy, Pops," she said, eyeing her grandfather, who rode his own horse next to the wagon. "You likely should've settled for the wagon instead of riding Job. Looks like we're in for some nasty weather, and you know how crazy that horse gets." But Pops never was one for wagon-sitting. He preferred the feel of the saddle, the strain of the bit. And Job, the four-year-old stallion, was about the strainingest-at-the-bit horse Betsy had ever seen. And ornery. You couldn't feed the animal a peppermint candy without him taking a nip at your fingers.

Predictably, Pops gave a snort. "Ain't never seen a horse yet I can't handle." He nodded at the two horses veering toward the woods. "You best worry about keeping the wagon on the road and don't concern yourself about me."

With a heavy sigh, Betsy added her other hand to the reins and righted the horses.

For once, Pops gave Job a yank, holding him back. "Now listen here,

Betsy. There's something I got to say to you before we get to town. I reckon I ought to have told you this awhile back." He cleared his throat and paused for so long Betsy cut him a glance. He had a faraway look in his eyes that meant he was getting the words in his head, and she knew better than to press. He'd come out with it in his own good time. And from the way Job was pulling against the biting wind and stinging ice, Pops would need all of his concentration to keep the dumb animal from tossing him to the ground again.

They approached town in silence as the ice picked up in intensity. "Pops?"

"We're almost to the general store now. No time to talk. We'll get to it."

A frown creased Betsy's brow. The only time Pops had ever seemed this nervous about talking with her was the day he'd told her about her parents' accident and that she was going to come live with him from now on. If the news he was clearly avoiding was even half as bad, she wasn't sure she wanted to know.

Surprisingly, the weather hadn't deterred the folks of Tucker's Creek from getting out and about. She passed patrons going in and out of Miss Annie's restaurant, noted the seamstress working at her machine through the window, and had to pass Fields' General Store by a good six wagons down to find a place to stop.

"Careful getting down, Pops," she said as she set the brake and carefully negotiated the slick road up to the boardwalk. She watched him and noted with some pride that, for a man his age, he got around pretty well. In front of folks, anyway. Back at the cabin was another story, but she and Pops kept their business to themselves. And hardly anyone ever came to visit, so no one needed to know the state of the place.

Warmth from the stove greeted them as they entered the store. She smiled at a few familiar faces. Rather than the friendly greetings she was accustomed to on their rare trips to town, folks gave her tentative smiles and looked away. Everyone just seemed nervous. Betsy chalked it up to the weather and didn't take it personally.

The store was busier than usual, and Betsy loosened her scarf and unbuttoned her coat, figuring it might be awhile before Mrs. Fields or her high-and-mighty son, Stuart, was able to fill their order for new supplies. She retreated to a corner and watched as Pops beelined for the other side of the store, close to the stove where three other codgers sat jawing—more to keep warm, she figured, than adding to the Fieldses' pockets. The old-timers greeted him loudly as he helped himself to the pot of coffee staying warm on top of the woodstove.

Mr. Mahoney, the former blacksmith and owner of the livery stable before his son took over the business, moved over and offered Pops a seat next to him on a roughly hewn wooden bench. "What are you doing bringing that little girl out on a day like this? Don't you know it ain't fit out there for the likes of her?"

"A little cold ain't gonna hurt nobody," Pops said, waving away the comment. "My Betsy might be little, but she's as sturdy as old Job, out there."

The pride in his voice brought a smile to Betsy's lips. Pops might never admit she was a grown woman of nearly twenty years old, but he had never been one to coddle her just because she was a girl. She reckoned it was just too much for him to think about the day she would find a man and settle down. Of course, she'd never marry a man who didn't understand she came as a pair. Her and Pops. He hadn't abandoned her after her parents had died, and she'd never leave him on his own.

Their conversation faded into the background as Betsy roamed the aisles, looking over the ribbons and store-bought dresses she'd never have the courage to ask Pops for. Mama had taught her to sew as early as she could remember, and she'd always had a knack for it, so as young as she was when her parents died seven years ago, Betsy had the skills to make her own clothes and keep Pops' trousers free of holes and his shirts with a full set of buttons.

Reaching out, she allowed herself a moment to indulge, fingering a silken, red ribbon between her thumb and forefinger. She imagined herself with the ribbon braided into her dark hair and twisted atop her head as she danced with a tall, handsome gentleman. A smile touched her lips at the thought.

"That would be lovely on you."

Betsy jumped and dropped the ribbon. "Mrs. Fields," she said, pressing her palm to her stomach. "I–I'm sorry. My hands are clean. I didn't hurt it."

The older woman smiled, her brown eyes filled with kindness. "Of course you didn't hurt it." She reached out and pulled the ribbon from the bin, then held it against Betsy's cheek. "This is the perfect color for you. Shall I wrap it up?"

Betsy darted a gaze toward Pops, feeling guilty for coveting what he called "women's foolishness." "No, ma'am. Pops and I don't go in for such things."

At the disappointment in the storekeep's eyes, Betsy reached out and touched Mrs. Fields' arm. "But I thank you for your kind words. Perhaps I'll look at the red when it's time for next year's dress."

She knew that wouldn't be possible. Pops wouldn't stand for such a bold color on her. She would eye the beautiful blues and reds and even yellows, but ultimately, Pops would insist she pick up a sensible brown, perhaps a blue—if it was dark enough—but never, ever a red. And never any embellishments such as lace or a pretty scalloped collar. Pops wasn't harsh; he just wanted her decent. And Betsy would never give him any reason to be ashamed of her.

"Well if I can't interest you in a ribbon, what can I help you and your grandfather with today?"

With a last glance at the bin of ribbons, she reached into the reticule tied around her wrist and pulled out the list of supplies. "We're out of just about everything. Pops said we best stock up before winter sets in or he won't get his biscuits." She smiled, but Mrs. Fields frowned.

"So, you've found a new place?"

"No, ma'am. It's the same old cabin as always. Pops and I did put up a new fence by the barn last month. The calf kept getting out. He made Pops so mad I thought he was going to bust a vein."

"That's not what I—"

"About time you got around to waiting on us." Pops' voice filled the room. "Thought we was gonna have to head down to Rex's store if you didn't want our business."

Stuart gave a loud snort from behind the counter. Betsy knew exactly what he was thinking. Their account was embarrassing and long past due, but he didn't have to remind them in such a rude manner.

Heat seared Betsy's neck and cheeks as all eyes turned toward them. "Pops, they have other customers." She sent her grandfather a scowl that said everything she couldn't say out loud about what she thought of his rudeness. "It doesn't hurt us to wait our turn."

Mrs. Fields smiled and gave her a passing pat on the shoulder as she walked to the counter. Betsy noted with some concern that the older woman moved a little slower than usual and seemed to be favoring one side of her body. She wanted to ask if everything was okay but didn't want to pry.

Mrs. Fields set the lengthy list on the counter and turned toward the shelves behind her. A sense of unease twisted Betsy's gut as Stuart walked toward the counter, glanced at the paper, and frowned. He turned his back, leaned over, and said something to his mother. She spoke right back, equally quiet, lifting a ten-pound bag of flour from the shelf and dropping it firmly into Stuart's arms. Anger and humiliation shot through Betsy as Stuart turned and practically slammed the bag down. His gaze landed first on Pops, then drifted to her. Their eyes met.

Stuart Fields might have been just about the handsomest boy in their schoolroom, growing up, and he might still be the handsomest man in town, but Betsy didn't find anything attractive in that haughty look. She narrowed her gaze at him to show him she couldn't care less what he thought. Noting with more than a little satisfaction that his face turned red and he averted his gaze, she raised her eyebrows and gave herself back to looking at the dresses and ribbons.

Stuart squirmed a little as he turned away from Betsy Lowell's haughty gaze. "Have you seen the ledger lately? Mr. Lowell owes for the last two years."

Predictably, his ma's lips pressed together, and she raised her eyebrows as she pointed to the sugar sack. "Three of those," she said firmly.

Stuart rolled his eyes but did as Ma commanded. "Fifteen pounds of sugar. Where do they plan to store it?"

"Keep your voice down. I don't think Betsy knows."

"Knows what?" He ventured a quick glance at the pretty brunette who at this moment stood, arms folded across her chest, shooting daggers with her blue eyes. He didn't begrudge her the anger she directed his way. He had been unforgivably rude.

"About the bank."

Shock shot through him. "You mean she doesn't know Old Joe lost their land?" How could her grandfather have done that to her?

"That's exactly what I mean. That girl has no idea that tomorrow it'll all be gone. So don't be so unkind."

Stuart wasn't without a heart. Compassion tugged at him as he imagined her taking supplies home and setting up for the winter only to discover she was out in the cold. "Ma, where will they live?"

"That's for this community to help work out for them. We can't see them without a roof over their heads with winter coming on."

"You two gonna jaw all day, or you gonna finish up my order?"

Stuart stiffened his spine at the sound of Old Joe's voice. You'd think a man living on the charity of others would show a little more humility than the cross old man. It wasn't too difficult to see where Betsy's pride came from. Stuart would have liked nothing more than to mention the fact to Mr. Lowell, but Ma would dress him down good if he showed disrespect to any customer—especially an old man—and, though he couldn't fathom the reason, to this old man in particular. His pa had been the same way about Mr. Lowell. But Stuart had never understood the devotion.

Stuart pulled a crate from beneath the counter and began boxing up the supplies. "Almost finished."

"Don't forget the peppermints. My horse has a hankering for them."

"Yes, sir."

Ma sent him an approving nod as he bit back the words he wanted to say and chose to be polite instead.

By the time the order was complete, Stuart had filled two large crates. He glanced at Betsy and noted with some surprise that she was focused on the ribbons in the bins next to the dresses Ma had ordered from Topeka. In his mind's eye, he could see her at eight or nine years old, long, dark braids tied with ribbons, but he couldn't remember anytime in the recent years when she'd worn anything but a dark dress, a man's coat, and a man's hat. Like today. The absence of any sort of feminine enhancements in no way detracted from her beauty. She might not be all that pleasant when she opened her mouth to speak, but only a blind man wouldn't recognize that Betsy Lowell was and always had been the prettiest girl in town.

"Get your eyes back in your head, son." Mr. Lowell's gravelly voice jerked Stuart from his thoughts, and he felt his ears warm as Betsy looked up at her grandfather's words just in time to catch Stuart staring at her. Her eyes grew wide, then narrowed. Clearly she didn't appreciate his admiration.

A low, almost indiscernible chuckle came from his mother. Stuart cleared his throat and grabbed one of the heavy crates from the counter. "I'll just take these out to your wagon," he said, needing to get out of there fast. Without pausing for his hat and coat, he carried the crate to the door and stepped out onto the boardwalk. He cringed a little, regretting his hasty exit. He knew his mother would pounce on his actions later, insisting he was sweet on Betsy—as she had insisted since he was a child and put worms on the little girl's desk or dipped her braids in his inkwell. And perhaps, as a boy, he'd had a particular admiration for her, but she certainly wasn't the sort of woman he was looking to wed.

He stepped carefully, noting the slick spots starting to form from the still-falling ice. He squirmed inside, kicking himself for staring at Betsy so openly that Old Joe and Ma had both noticed. Even if he'd had a schoolboy crush, he certainly didn't anymore. There were no less than half-a-dozen suitable young women he could court right here in town if he so chose. Young women without haughty eyes and sharp tongues. No, Betsy Lowell might be an uncommonly beautiful girl, but beauty was vain. He'd rather marry a homely girl—as long as she wasn't too homely—who had a quiet spirit and gentle words. Heaven help the man who got himself saddled with the likes of Betsy Lowell.

Chapter Two

Betsy followed behind Stuart and Pops as the younger man carried the last crate to the wagon. Pops was clearly miffed and didn't even thank Stuart, which embarrassed her more than a little. She maneuvered carefully on slick boots as she walked around the horses and reached for the seat to grab on to while she hoisted herself up. "Can I help?"

She turned, surprised to find Stuart at her side, holding out his hand. Her stomach did a leap, and she swallowed hard. She was about to accept his assistance when Pops nudged Stuart out of the way. "Best you go see to your customers and stop trying to take liberties with my granddaughter."

"Liberties?" Stuart's tone clearly conveyed his outrage. Betsy didn't blame him one bit.

"Honestly, Pops." She took his hand. She couldn't remember the last time Pops had helped her into a wagon or held open a door for her. Even now his grip was so loose she would have felt more secure holding on to the wagon seat and getting up on her own. She turned purposely to Stuart. "Thank you for carrying out the supplies, Mr. Fields. We appreciate it."

Pops gave a humph but fortunately didn't say anything else insulting. "My pleasure, Miss Lowell."

Pops snorted and stayed planted next to the wagon, staring hard at Stuart. "Well?"

"Yes, sir. I'm going." His gaze met Betsy's, and he offered her a wry grin. "Be careful. Looks like ice is making things slick."

"I will," Betsy said, nodding as she clutched the reins and released the brake.

Pops glared after Stuart as he walked back toward the store. "Don't be getting any ideas about that one."

"A girl's got to marry someone, Pops." Betsy grinned at her own teasing. Pops could be intimidating to folks who didn't know his gruffness covered a heart of gold. She'd figured it out when she was barely more than an infant, toddling around his cabin.

"You ain't marrying no fella with hands like a woman's. That boy ain't done a man's work a day in his life. My girl's gonna marry someone who can take care of her."

"Well, this girl is going to marry whomever I choose, and that's not going to be for a very long time." Even as she said the words, her heart sank a little. She wasn't exactly a spring chicken. Before long, she'd be so old no one would want her anyway.

"Leo Blakely would marry you in a second, and he's plenty set to take care of a wife."

"Yes, and he's old enough to be my pa." Not to mention that when he looked at her, she felt undressed. "Besides, I know you ran him off the place a few weeks ago." And much to Betsy's relief the man hadn't been back since. She'd assumed Pops had finally told him to stop coming around, trying to get Betsy to marry him. So why was he bringing up the old bachelor now?

She pulled her scarf tighter. "Pops, we best get going if we're going to get home tonight. Stuart's right. The roads are going to start getting too slick for the horses if we don't get a move on."

"We ain't going home tonight."

Betsy frowned. "What do you mean? Where are we going?"

"Over to the boardinghouse."

"The boardinghouse! And just how are we going to pay Mrs. Stone?"

"You let me worry about that. Drive on over to the livery. We'll board the horses and walk over to the boardinghouse."

Betsy didn't protest, but she couldn't help but wonder if Pops was beginning to lose his mind. It was one thing to buy their goods on account. Everyone did that. But she knew for a fact that Mrs. Stone was cash on the barrel. The woman wasn't going to let them stay in her home without payment. Mr. Mahoney's son owned the livery, and he and Pops had always been friends, so Betsy figured he wouldn't refuse them. But she had a feeling they'd be bedding down with the horses tonight.

She backed the wagon into the street while Pops walked to Job. It took him three tries before the horse allowed him to mount. She shook her head. The already cantankerous animal was clearly even more annoyed than ever after standing in the cold and wet for the past forty-five minutes. She followed as Pops rode toward the livery. She held her breath every time Job slipped, then gained his footing. "Pops. Maybe you ought to come ride in the wagon."

Pops waved, then reached into his pocket. "He's fine." Leaning forward, he spoke low to the horse. Betsy had seen him offer the animal treats from the saddle before and had always thought it dangerous for a man his age, but she sat helpless as Job took the treat, then immediately twisted his neck around for another, nipping at Pops' leg. Intent on the treat, the horse stepped down without looking where he was going and slipped, nearly taking Betsy's breath. "Pops, make Job mind you before he—"

Too late. Pops spoke harshly to the horse and smacked his neck, just as Job slipped again.

Helpless, Betsy bit back a scream as his attempts to right himself failed. Horse and rider went down as one, with Pops taking the brunt of the fall, landing beneath the horse's body.

Betsy's breath stopped as she yanked on the reins so hard her horses' front legs nearly came off the ground as the wagon rolled to a stop.

Job pulled himself up and limped away, his reins dragging the ground. "You stupid horse!" she screamed after him, running toward Pops, who lay on the ground, still as death.

Junior Mahoney appeared from the livery door and ran into the street just as she dropped to Pops' side. She heard the sound of boots running on the boardwalk behind her, but her mind spun as she looked at the still form next to her. "Pops!" She grabbed his hand. Blood trickled from his mouth, and she noted his other arm was twisted in a dreadful, broken manner. Her head swam as she looked slowly down his form and tried to make sense of what had just happened.

Junior Mahoney dropped to her side and nudged her. "Move away, Betsy."

She shook her head. "Pops? Can you answer me?"

Someone took her arm and pulled her to her feet. She spun and found herself in Stuart Fields' arms.

"Let me be!" She thrashed about, trying to get loose, but he held her tighter, seemingly without effort.

He held her out at arm's length. "Betsy, calm down. We need to get your grandfather over to Doc Avery. Do you understand?"

His brown eyes held her gaze, and she found her breath as his words began to make sense. She nodded. If they were in a rush to get him to the doc, then Pops wasn't dead. "Hurry," she said, her voice barely above a whisper.

He released her, and he and Junior gathered up the frail, twisted body. The sound of her grandfather's groan nearly took the small amount of strength still keeping her upright. They settled him as carefully as possible into the wagon bed. Betsy hurried to the seat and scrambled up. Before she could gather the reins, Stuart was next to her in the seat. "I'm driving you."

Nodding, she released the reins to his hands. Her mind raced back to what Pops had said about Stuart and his soft hands, but as she watched him guide the horses, all Betsy could think was that they seemed very strong and capable. And she was grateful that he had taken over.

She turned in the seat to check on Pops. Junior was in the wagon sitting next to him. Gratitude welled up inside of her. She'd had no idea the liveryman had climbed into the wagon after him. They reached the doctor's office in only a couple of minutes. Doc Avery was a middle-aged man who had only come to Tucker's Creek five years before. Until then, they'd relied on midwives for birthing and did the best they could in emergencies. Right now, Betsy was beyond grateful the doctor had come to town.

He rushed outside as Stuart pulled up and wrapped the horses' reins around the brake.

Doc was already rolling up his sleeves as he looked at Old Joe lying broken in the back of the wagon. "Get him in, quick. But be careful. What happened?"

"His horse slipped on the ice and landed on him." Junior held Pops's arms while Stuart took his legs. The doctor stabilized his middle, and the three men carried him into the house, which doubled as the doctor's office. "Where do you want him, Doc?" Stuart asked.

"Don't bother with the examining room. He won't be going anywhere for a while. Just take him in there." He pointed to a bedroom on the opposite side of the house as Mrs. Avery appeared in the doorway. She slipped her arm around Betsy's shoulders. "Come with me, dear."

"I can't leave Pops."

"It'll be best if you let the men get him undressed and let my husband examine him in private."

Stubbornly, Betsy shook her head.

"Honey," the woman said, keeping her arm firmly around Betsy, her other hand on Betsy's arm. "Do you think your grandfather would want you to see him undressed?"

Finally Mrs. Avery's meaning sank in. Betsy gasped. Pops would be madder than all get-out if he thought for a second she stayed in the room when they were about to strip him down. She allowed Mrs. Avery to escort her from the room. "Here, honey. Let me take your coat and hat."

Numb, Betsy surrendered as the doctor's wife slipped her out of her coat and hung it on the peg board next to the door. She led Betsy into the kitchen and pulled out a wooden chair. "You sit here and let me get you some coffee. I was just about to have some lunch. Are you hungry?"

Betsy shook her head, annoyed that the woman could even suggest food at a time like this.

Mrs. Avery set a steaming cup in front of her. "At least drink this. It'll warm you up." Instinctively, Betsy reached out and cradled the cup between her palms, allowing the warmth to seep into her ice-cold hands. She shuddered from somewhere deep inside of her. Her hands shook at the memory of Pops lying in the street, his body twisted and broken. Tears welled in her eyes and rolled down her cheeks. What would she do without Pops?

"Now, don't worry about a thing," Mrs. Avery said as though

reading her mind. The other woman handed her a dish towel. "Wipe your face, hon. The doctor will do his very best." She smiled. "And that is very good."

Nodding, Betsy grabbed the towel and swiped her face and nose. She knew Mrs. Avery was being kind, but as much as she appreciated it, she couldn't bear just sitting here, drinking coffee, when Pops was lying in the other room, maybe dying. Maybe even dead already.

"Was your grandfather's horse hurt in the accident?"

The words jarred Betsy from her maudlin thoughts and brought a swift jolt of anger. "If he wasn't, he will be."

When no response was forthcoming, Betsy ventured a glance to the woman. She stared back at her from across the table. "I see. You'll take your revenge on the animal, then?"

Betsy recognized a hint of admonishment, but she didn't care. With a jerk of her chin, she looked away. "Yes, ma'am. I sure will. That horse has been nothing but a thorn in Pops' side since the day he was born. Ornery as all get-out, and I say good riddance."

"Oh, the horse did it on purpose?"

Betsy's lips twisted. "Well, no. He didn't make himself slip on the ice."

Mrs. Avery set her coffee on the table and walked to the stove. "Are you sure I can't interest you in some stew, hon? The venison is fresh. George just shot him day before last."

"No, thank you." Her stomach twisted at the very thought of food. Although it did smell awfully good. She gathered a breath. "The fact is, if that ornery horse hadn't tried nipping at Pops to get another piece of peppermint, this never would have happened. So in a way, he did do it on purpose."

There was no real reason to care one way or another what anyone else thought about what she did with her own property. But Betsy couldn't seem to let it go until this woman understood. How could anyone not want to punish the animal that just got up and walked away?

"Do you think that's what Old Joe would want?"

Betsy sent her a scowl as she dipped stew into a bowl for herself and brought it to the table. She gave a short laugh. "Pops would probably be the first one to brush him down, give him a peppermint to soothe him, and rub liniment on his leg."

"Liniment? Was the horse injured, too?"

Betsy shrugged. "He limped a little when he walked off after nearly killing my pops. And I vow, if Pops dies—"

"Don't think about that. We are going to sit here and trust God to guide my husband's hands, and if it's His will, your grandfather will pull through good as new."

"But what if it's not God's will? What good does it do to pray if God wants to take Pops to heaven?" Like He had her parents. Was God's will for her to be completely alone?

"Honey, we don't know the heart and mind of God. All we can do is trust He knows better than we do."

Betsy knew better than to argue with a person's faith. And it wasn't as though she didn't believe in God; she just wasn't so sure He was very nice. If she had all that power, she wouldn't govern humans at her whim. This one dies, that one lives. What right had He to play with people's lives that way? She knew she ought to be more careful with her thoughts. Usually when she thought about her parents dying when she still needed them and anger against God burned fierce and sharp in her chest, she said a hasty prayer of repentance and tried to be sincere. But right now, she couldn't drum up even the slightest bit of remorse toward the Almighty.

"So tell me, why do folks in Tucker's Creek call your grandfather Old Joe?"

Betsy shrugged. "Because he's old and his name is Joe."

Mrs. Avery smiled. "That's it? What did they call him when he was young? I hear he was one of three men who founded Tucker's Creek way back fifty years ago."

Betsy knew the doc's wife was just trying to get her mind off the accident, but she wasn't in the mood for small talk. Still, given this woman's kindness, she didn't want to be rude. "My pa was named after Pops, so when he started at the school, everyone called him Joe-Joe and Pops became Old Joe."

She lifted her cup to her lips. By the time she set it back on the table, she heard footsteps and shoved up from her chair. Stuart stood in the doorway, face white and visibly shaken.

"Is he dead?"

He shook his head, and Betsy's legs went weak with relief. She grabbed on to the back of her chair to keep from dropping to the floor. "You look like he is."

"No, I'm sorry. Just. . .I never was one for this kind of thing."

"Come and sit down, Stuart," Mrs. Avery said with the gentleness of a mother. "You look like you're about to pass out."

Stuart gave her a wry grin. "Thanks for not saying *faint*." He practically stumbled to the chair and sat hard in the seat. Without asking, Mrs. Avery poured him some coffee. Betsy rolled her eyes. What would Pops think about a man who practically fainted at the sight of blood?

The doctor's wife patted him on the shoulder. "Buck up, and tell us about Mr. Lowell. How is he?"

Betsy broke in before he could say anything. "Can I go see him?"

Stuart shook his head. "Doc said to tell you to stay put while they're setting his bones."

With a heavy sigh, Betsy sat back down. "I could've helped since you clearly faint at the sight of blood."

A flash of anger brought back Stuart's color. "I don't—"

Mrs. Avery clicked her tongue. "There's no point in throwing stones, you two." She patted Stuart again. "Are you hungry? I have some venison stew warming on the stove."

"Thank you, ma'am, but I best get back over to the store. This kind of weather brings folks out for supplies, and Ma's going to need my help."

"Well, we're mighty glad you were there to help out with Old Joe, aren't we, Betsy?"

Betsy nodded and sipped her own coffee to avoid having to say something.

He stood. "Thank you for the coffee, ma'am."

"You're welcome." Mrs. Avery stood as well, grabbing his cup from the table. She walked to the sink to rinse it out. "Betsy, honey, can you walk Stuart out? I need to stir this stew before it scorches."

There was no way to avoid doing the polite thing. "Yes, ma'am."

With a sigh, Betsy followed him into the foyer as he retrieved his coat and hat from the peg board by the door.

Awkward silence filled the space between them as he stood there, his hand on the doorknob, looking down at her. "Betsy, I'm sorry about your grandfather."

Fighting back tears, Betsy nodded. Mrs. Avery was right. Stuart had been a godsend. "Thank you for your help. I—I don't know what I'd have done without you."

"Unfortunately, I've never been much help in these sorts of situations." He released a heavy breath and jammed his hat on his head. "I wish I could have done more."

"You were there when we needed you." Swallowing hard, she suddenly had a twinge of conscience about her outburst a few minutes ago. "I apologize for the fainting comment." She wanted to offer an excuse. Something about how worried she was and that was the reason she chose those insulting words. But she knew that wouldn't be a true apology, and after all, Stuart had been right there to help get Pops to Doc Avery's.

Stuart's face softened, and he reached out for just a second and touched her arm. "I'm glad I was here to help. If you need anything, please let us know." He touched his hat and walked out the door, leaving Betsy speechless at the uncommon gentleness from him.

She stared at the closed door. Had she misjudged Stuart Fields all these years?

Chapter Three

Still shaken from the twisted body he'd been forced to witness, Stuart walked into the store amid a jumble of activity. His ma glanced up from filling an order, and her face softened with relief. "Thank heaven you're back." Stuart grabbed his apron from the peg at the end of the shelves and tied it on with shaky fingers. "How's Old Joe?"

"Not good, Ma." He kept his voice low. "I don't see how he can survive, but Doc Avery and Junior Mahoney are doing everything they can."

"I hope you didn't come back here just for me. It doesn't hurt folks to wait a little while when there's a crisis."

"There wasn't much I could do to help the doc. Junior was there, so I felt like I was more in the way."

His mother nodded. Stuart appreciated her discretion in not mentioning his aversion to the sight of blood and broken bodies. Just the memory of Old Joe's injuries brought on a bout of dizziness.

"I can't imagine what poor Betsy will do if Old Joe doesn't pull through." A heavy sigh accompanied her words, and she shook her head.

"I told her to let us know if we could do anything to help out."

Ma's graying eyebrows rose. "That was. . .kind."

Fortunately, a woman carrying a pair of men's trousers approached the counter just then. She ordered several goods from behind the counter, and by the time she had paid for her purchases, Ma was occupied with another customer, so Stuart didn't have to continue the conversation. They remained busy for the next four hours until closing. At five o'clock, Stuart locked up with a deep sense of relief that the day was finally over.

Ma tucked a loose strand of gray hair behind her ear and dropped onto the bench next to the stove. "Gracious. What a day." She offered him a weary smile. "I'm getting too far along in age to keep up on days like this."

Stuart grabbed the broom and began the nightly cleanup. "You just sit and rest, and I'll tidy up. Then we can go over to Miss Annie's for supper before we go home."

"Annie's. The prices she charges are highway robbery." Ma gave a snort. "And the food isn't even that good."

A smile touched Stuart's lips. "You know, Ma," he said, swiping at the floor with the broom. "Eventually, you're going to have to forgive Annie."

"Forgive? What on earth are you talking about? I have nothing against that woman except for her ridiculous prices and overcooked roast."

Not to mention the fact that thirty years ago, Miss Annie had invited Pa to the Sadie Hawkins dance before Ma had drummed up the courage to do so. Of course, Ma hadn't confided this fact to him. Pa had. As much as he'd love to force her into an admission, he knew better. When Ma set her mind to something, there was no convincing her of anything else.

She sat by the fire, staring out at the front window. "You know, I've been thinking."

"About what, Ma?" He collected the dust he'd just swept and walked toward the door to throw it outside where dirt belonged. He noted with some relief that the ice had stopped falling. He'd still have to help Ma cross the street to the restaurant, but the wagons going back and forth all day had helped melt some of the ice, so there were places to step. He closed the door and carried the broom back, leaning it against the wall behind the counter.

"Are you listening?" Ma's voice sounded testy, and he realized he hadn't heard the last thing she'd said.

"Sorry, Ma. I am now."

"Even if Old Joe pulls through, he'll likely be off his feet for quite some time, wouldn't you agree?"

"No doubt about it. He'll be indisposed for weeks if not months." If he made it at all. Stuart wasn't very optimistic that the old-timer would regain consciousness, let alone return to his former strength.

"I'm guessing Betsy still doesn't know about losing the farm."

"Not unless Mrs. Avery told her. I still can't understand why Old Joe didn't let her know. It doesn't seem right to leave her in the dark. Especially now when he's unconscious and Betsy's going to learn about it from someone else."

"Do you have any idea where Betsy is planning to stay while her grandfather is recovering?"

Stuart shook his head. Truth be told, the thought hadn't occurred to him. "I can't imagine she has the money to stay at the boardinghouse. The Averys will likely put her up for a while at least."

"Of course they won't throw her out in the street. But she's going to have to plan long term. I wonder what Old Joe had in mind for them."

If the old-timer even had a plan. The thought of Betsy's ignorance over the situation annoyed Stuart more than a little. It didn't seem fair to her. "What's on your mind, Ma?"

"I think we should offer Betsy your sister's old room."

The very idea sent waves of horror through Stuart. "Ma—"

She held up her hand. "I don't know what you have against her. I have my suspicions, but this is my decision."

"I don't have anything against Betsy Lowell, Ma. But what will people say about an unattached man and woman living under the same roof? Do you think it might hurt Betsy's reputation?"

Ma scowled, waving away his concern. "Heavens, I'll be right there as chaperone. And you can move down to your father's study so that you're not sleeping on the same floor of the house."

"You're kicking me out of my room to give Betsy a home?" He grinned. They'd been discussing his moving downstairs for a while.

Shaking his head, he grabbed their coats from the storeroom. When he returned, Ma was working her way to her feet. "You're not doing so well today. That hip giving you trouble?"

"No, it's fine. I'm fine. Don't fret, and don't change the subject." She slipped her arms into the coat he held out. "Now, about Betsy—"

"Do what you think is best. I'll move my things downstairs tonight."

If he knew Betsy Lowell, she'd never accept the room. She was even more stubborn than his ma.

———— ◆ ————

Betsy sat next to her grandpa's bed, grateful for each shallow rise and fall of his chest. Despite Mrs. Avery's insistence that she take the other bedroom in this vast house, Betsy refused to leave his side. But two nights of sitting in the chair at his side was beginning to wear on her. Doc had come into the room several times through the night, as he had the night before, and now as the sun began to rise, she heard his familiar footsteps on the stairs. A moment later, the door opened, and he walked in.

"Good morning, Betsy."

Betsy nodded, too weary and worried for pleasantries. "He made it through another night. That's a good sign, right?"

The doc shushed her and listened to his patient's heart. He straightened up with a sigh. "His heart isn't as strong as I'd like to hear it, but as you said, he made it through the night again. Your grandfather is nothing if not a fighter."

The words did little to comfort Betsy. "Is he going to make it, Doc?" Her voice broke with the question.

Doc Avery looked at her with kind, sympathetic eyes. "Only God knows that. But I can promise I'll do my very best with the abilities He's given me. The rest is up to Him. But you need to prepare yourself just in case it's Old Joe's time. The cracked ribs, the broken bones, a weak heart. We'll have to watch for pneumonia."

He'd said all this to her before. "I know. I'm not closing my mind to what might happen. It's just. . ." She wanted to give in to the threatening tears, wanted to beg the doctor for more reassurance than he was able to give. But if Pops died, she'd be all alone. At least she'd have the cabin and the stock. Pops had taught her everything she would need to know. She could cut her own wood for the fire, fix a fence, put a new roof on the cabin. She'd been doing most of the work around the place for the last two years anyway. But without Pops, she had no family, no one to talk to at night. She would miss him dreadfully if God chose to take him. Swallowing hard, she squared her shoulders and faced the doctor. "It's just we can't leave the stock alone much longer. I'm going to have to go home today and take care of them. I might not make it back for a couple days."

The doctor frowned. "Betsy, there's something you should know. I can't imagine why Old Joe hasn't said anything. . . ."

Betsy frowned. Was there even more wrong with Pops than the doc was letting on? Before she could question him, Mrs. Avery came into the room, bringing with her the scent of coffee brewing and ham frying. "How's he doing this morning?" she asked, a little cheerier than Betsy had the stomach for this early.

"Not much different than last night," Betsy said.

Doc Avery patted Betsy's arm. "But I'm hopeful he will wake up today."

"Well, I have breakfast cooking." Mrs. Avery looked at Betsy. "Honey, why don't you go and wash your face and then come eat something?"

Betsy nodded. As much as she'd love to stay by her grandpa's bedside until he awoke, she had to keep up her strength in order to take care of him once he came to.

When she entered the kitchen a few minutes later, feeling better but still more weary than she could remember, Doc and Mrs. Avery stopped their conversation abruptly. Betsy could only surmise they were discussing either her or Pops, but she didn't pry. Mrs. Avery stood and went to the stove. "Have a seat, Betsy. I'll get your breakfast."

"You don't have to wait on me, ma'am. I can get my own."

"Nonsense. You look about dead on your feet. Let me pamper you a little."

Grateful, Betsy dropped into her chair. "Doc, I appreciate everything you're doing for Pops. I don't know how we'll pay you, but I promise it'll get done. Even if I have to sell off stock to settle up."

The doctor looked away and picked up his cup.

Mrs. Avery spared him an answer as she set a plate and cup in front of Betsy. She patted Betsy's shoulder. "There's plenty of time to worry about that. You just eat your breakfast and let's concentrate on getting Old Joe back on his feet."

Betsy frowned. "I don't want you to think I'm not going to pay my bills." Unlike Pops. Guilt worked through her like a cord at the very thought of being so disloyal to Pops. But he was as cheap as they came, and he hadn't plowed or harvested in two years, leaving the fields fallow and wasted. Until then, Pops had worked hard every day. The change in him had confused and angered her, but he wouldn't tell her a thing. Betsy had tried to rouse him. Had tried to do the farming herself. But it had been an impossible task for one woman, what with all the other work to do. And no harvest meant no cash money coming in, so of course they had basically lived off the charity of the town.

"Doc, do you think Pops is going notional?"

Doc Avery sat back and touched his chin. He drew and released a full breath. "It's possible. He's more than seventy years old. Why do you ask?"

Betsy shrugged. "He's been different the last couple years."

"I wouldn't add worry to worry," he said. "Let's just take one day at a time."

"But there has to be a reason he just stopped working a couple years back."

The doctor's eyes met hers as though scrutinizing her.

"If you know something, please tell me."

"He should have told you long ago, but he came to me complaining of pains in his chest and shortness of breath."

"When?" But she already knew the answer.

"Two years ago, Betsy. His heart was weak even then, and I'm not positive he hadn't already had a heart attack. I suggested he hire someone to help in the fields and stop doing the hard work."

"He did stop working, but he never told me why and wouldn't hire anyone." Placing her elbow on the table, Betsy rested her chin in her palm. "I don't know what I'm supposed to do with the farm now that it's gone so long without planting."

Mrs. Avery shoved the basket of biscuits toward her. "There's nothing for you to do for now except let me take care of you while you watch over your grandfather." She smiled. "Now, eat up. Tomorrow will take care of itself, and the day after tomorrow, and so on."

"Thank you both." Betsy dug into her ham and eggs and biscuits.

She barely heard a word either of the Averys said during the meal. When it was finished, Mrs. Avery waved away her attempt to clean up.

She checked on Pops, who remained exactly the way she'd left him before breakfast. The doctor had gone to make his daily rounds, and she heard Mrs. Avery humming as she washed the breakfast dishes. Not wanting to bother the kind woman, she quietly slipped into her coat and hat and walked out onto a wet, muddy road. The ice had melted under a bright sun, and the temperature seemed to have risen at least ten degrees above freezing. Betsy made her way to the livery, where Junior Mahoney had kindly offered to board the horses. The sweet smell of hay combined with the more pungent smell of horses greeted her when she entered.

"Morning, Junior."

The liveryman looked up from scooping out one of the stalls. "Hey there, Betsy. How's Old Joe today?"

"About the same."

"Well, don't you worry none. He's about as stubborn as they come. Doc'll pull him through." He set down the shovel and wiped his hand with a towel as he walked toward her. "What can I help you with?"

"I just need to collect my wagon and horses."

Junior frowned. "Going somewhere?"

Obviously. Betsy tucked back the sarcasm and nodded. "I have to get the supplies home and check on the animals. We missed chores the last two nights, the cow alone is probably about to burst."

"But don't you know what went on there yesterday?"

Betsy gave a short laugh. "Not much considering we've been in town."

"Listen, I don't know why no one has told you the truth." He scowled. "I especially don't understand why Old Joe left you in the dark about it."

Betsy reached up and rubbed Ginger's nose. "What are you talking about?"

"The bank called in your grandpa's note."

All the air left the room as Betsy turned and stared at the liveryman. "Wh—what note?"

"Old Joe took on a mortgage over a year ago. But he. . .uh. . .never paid it back. Now, I tried to loan him money from time to time, but he wouldn't take it."

Head spinning, Betsy leaned against Ginger's stall. "I can't believe Pops didn't tell me. I could have found a position somewhere to help. Or taken in sewing and ironing. I could have done *something*."

"I don't know what he was thinking."

"This must've been what Pops was trying to tell me." And why he couldn't bring himself to say it.

She gathered a breath. "I'll have to go to the bank and see what's to be done. I can sell off most of the stock. And Leo Blakely's been trying to buy the back ten acres that connect with his land for as long as I can remember. Do you think that might be enough to hold things off until Pops is back on his feet?"

"Honey, that might have worked six months ago."

"I don't understand."

He scratched at his beard and gave her a look of such dread Betsy's stomach turned over. She held up her hand as he opened his mouth to speak. "You don't have to say it. That's why Pops wanted to get to town day before yesterday. Why he said we weren't going home that night."

Junior's nod confirmed her words. "The auction was yesterday."

Fear leaped inside of Betsy. "What auction?"

"The bank sold off the whole thing. Lock, stock, and barrel."

"They just sold it? Just like that?"

"Didn't you understand what I said? The bank called in the note. Then they gave Old Joe a little time to move out, then they set an auction date. That was yesterday."

"But what about my books and pots and pans? They can't have the things that belong to me, can they?" Ma's treasured iron skillet that Betsy had cooked more meals in than she could count.

"I reckon if your grandpa had packed up and brought those things into town, there'd be nothing the bank could do about it. But I'm sorry to say, it's all gone now."

Old Joe's watch! Where was his watch? She hadn't seen it in his clothes when she emptied his pockets so Mrs. Avery could toss them. They were ripped too badly from the fall to be fixed.

"Junior, did you find Pops' watch in the street? You know the one. It's gold and fit in his pocket." The watch had been given to the oldest Lowell son on his wedding day since her grandpa's own pa had been a groom. When Betsy's pa died, Pops had taken the watch back, promising to give it to Betsy on her wedding day. It was her promise from Pops, the hope that she would inherit something from her pa and pass it down to a son.

Junior shook his head. "I know the watch you're describing. Everyone has seen Old Joe looking at it, but I didn't see it in the street."

Betsy's stomach sank. Pops had been vain enough about his prized possession to display it often when they were in town, so she was sure someone had paid a pretty penny for it.

She sighed. "I suppose Mr. Blakely ended up with the place?"

"That's what I heard."

Anger ignited inside her. Most likely the greedy neighbor had her watch, too.

"All the stock is gone? Everything?"

"Lock, stock, and barrel. I'm really sorry, Betsy. The missus and I can't offer you a place to stay, but we can pay for a few nights at the boardinghouse."

Betsy shook her head. "What about the horses and wagon? D–do I get to keep them?"

He shrugged. "No one's come for them, so I assume so. And there's Job, too."

Following his pointing finger, Betsy saw the culprit standing fat as he pleased in a stall, chomping on hay. She stomped over to him. "What's he doing here? Why didn't someone shoot him?"

"His leg wasn't that bad. He ain't even limping anymore."

"I don't mean because he was hurt, I mean because he hurt Pops!" Glancing around, she noted Junior's shotgun hanging next to the office door. She headed straight for it, but the liveryman got there first. "Now, Betsy, I can't let you shoot Old Joe's horse. You wouldn't want to if you were in your right mind, anyhow."

"I am in my right mind. That horse is going to pay for what he did to Pops."

"Now listen, gal. Think about what you're saying." He remained planted in front of the shotgun, so there was no way Betsy could get it. Frustrated, she stomped her foot.

"That horse has been nothing but a mean, hateful animal since the day he was born. But Pops treats him like a baby. And look what that got him? Practically dead. If he'd ever taught that animal to mind, he wouldn't be lying abed about to die."

"Seems to me, you might be madder at Old Joe than the horse."

Gulping back her tears, Betsy swiped at her wet face. "I told him not to ride on the ice. Then he had to go and feed that greedy, dumb animal a peppermint. A peppermint!" Besides, Junior was dead wrong. She was equally mad at them both.

"I'll tell you what. I've been eyeing Job for some time, and your stubborn Pops won't even hear about selling him. But seems to me, that's your decision right now."

Betsy frowned. "What are you getting at?"

"There's no point in putting that horse down. With a little discipline, he'll be a fine animal, and I'm willing to take him off your hands."

A gasp worked its way through her, and she stared wide-eyed. "And you call yourself Pops' friend." She spun around and walked back to Job's stall, folded her arms, and widened her stance. "I'm not letting anyone take this horse. Why, it'd break Pops' heart."

Junior nodded and smiled. "You're likely right. The offer'll still be there if you change your mind."

"Don't count on it."

She lifted Job's saddle from its stand and opened the stall. Job stomped when he saw her, likely looking for a peppermint—which as far as Betsy was concerned, he could just forget about. He had an awful lot of making up to do if he ever wanted another treat.

"Still planning on going somewhere?"

Junior took the saddle from her and slung it over the horse's back.

"This horse needs to be ridden regularly. Otherwise he gets particularly cantankerous."

The liveryman's eyebrows rose. "Sure you can handle him?"

Betsy sent him a withering look. "There's not a horse alive I can't handle." Just because she didn't care much for this horse didn't mean she hadn't exercised him plenty when Pops was too tired or lazy to do it. Well, not lazy, she supposed. After her talk with Doc, she realized that Pops had been sick the past two years. If he'd just told her, she wouldn't have gotten so mad at him all the time.

"Take it easy out there, and don't ride him too hard. The ground's still soft from the melting." He cinched the saddle straps and led Job out of the stall. After a full day and a half of being cooped up, Job stamped with nervous energy. Betsy knew she'd have her hands full trying to control him. But the image of Pops lying so still and pale and broken gave her confidence she wouldn't be taking any of Job's business.

Outside the barn, she held his reins with a determined grip and climbed into the saddle, adjusting her skirts for decency as she didn't have her sidesaddle. Heaviness descended on her chest at the thought. Pops had bought her sidesaddle for her fifteenth birthday. "It ain't decent for you to be straddling the saddle," he'd said. Betsy nudged Job and gave him his head, despite Junior's warning about the soft ground. Her sidesaddle, along with everything else, was likely gone. She had nothing left of her parents.

As Job raced through town, she realized where he was heading and where she'd intended to go all along. They were going home.

Chapter Four

Stuart held the broom tight and pressed hard on the boardwalk outside the store, sending mud flying with strong steady swipes. Ma had been complaining about the mud-tracked floor since yesterday. Better to take the time to sweep than listen to her fuss for another day. Just as he was turning to go back inside, a blur of horse and rider galloped by. He gaped as he realized Betsy was riding the horse that had thrown Old Joe. Knowing Betsy's temper, he'd figured she'd shoot the horse or at the very least sell him to the highest bidder.

Shaking his head, he stepped inside and set the broom against the wall, his mind remaining on the image of Betsy flying through Tucker's Creek on that wretched horse. Where'd she think she was going?

"Was that Betsy riding through town like a band of Indians was behind her?"

He nodded. Frowned. "You reckon she still doesn't know about the auction?"

"What's on your mind, Stuart? Are you worried that's where she's going?"

The more he thought on it, the more certain he was that the cabin was exactly where Betsy was heading. What would she find when she got there? He'd gone to the auction yesterday, surprised at how many folks had turned out to capitalize on their neighbor's bad luck. He squirmed a little at the thought. After all, he'd known exactly why he was going to the auction—though Ma had been against it. He'd bid on the item he'd gone for and won, although he'd had to go a bit higher than he'd intended.

The gold watch burned against his chest as he reached up and patted his shirt pocket. He pulled it out and flipped it open. Then shook his head. "Still isn't keeping time."

"Good. It serves you right, coveting poor Old Joe's prized possession."

"Someone was going to buy it." He couldn't resist the urge to defend himself, though he didn't see why Ma was so dead set against the purchase.

"What others do is between them and their Maker. What you do is. . .well, that's God's business, too." She scowled. "And mine. I don't know where I went wrong with you. Acting like all the other vultures in this town, wanting to pick away at that poor man's bones."

"That's a little—"

She held up her hand. "And think of poor Betsy. What on earth is she going to do? Old Joe has kept her all to himself out on that farm with absolutely no prospects, forcing her to dress practically like an old widow. I don't believe he ever intended for her to get married."

Stuart hadn't even thought of Betsy getting married. So Ma was likely right. He glanced toward the door, the thought of Betsy's image riding past still playing on his mind.

Ma swiped the feather duster across the counter. "Well?"

Stuart blinked. "Well, what?"

"Are you going to go after that girl, or is she going to have to find the cabin gone over and emptied out all by herself?"

"I suppose I should."

"I'd think so."

Stuart grabbed his hat and coat and headed toward the door. Then hesitated, pulled the watch from his pocket once more, and placed it in the money drawer behind the counter.

Ma snorted. "Coward."

Heat burned his face. "I just see no point in carrying a broken watch. I'll likely have to send it off to get it fixed."

"Lie to yourself all you want, but you can't fool me, young man." Ma's voice held a firm admonishment. "You are ashamed, as you most certainly should be, and you don't want to chance Betsy catching a glimpse of her grandfather's watch in your possession."

That was ridiculous, but he wasn't about to argue with Ma once she got something into her head.

"Sure you can take care of things by yourself?"

Her hand swept empty the room. "Surely," she said with a wry smile. "I'll be back as soon as I can."

"Be kind. And remember, she's just had a devastating loss. It's possible she'll be angry and possibly sharp tongued."

Stuart gave a one-sided smile of his own. "When isn't she?"

"Don't judge the girl too harshly. She has her crosses to bear."

Stuart made his way to the livery where he boarded his horse. Since Pa had built their home in the center of town, he and Mr. Mahoney had bartered their services to each other. Pa boarded his horses, and the liveryman received a certain amount of store goods each month for free. Once Junior took over, they'd kept the arrangement, and again, after Pa's death, Stuart and Ma had seen no reason to discontinue.

Junior glanced up, surprise evident in his face. Stuart didn't blame him. He rarely rode the horse through the week. Junior exercised the chestnut mare more than Stuart did. "Something I can do for you, Stuart?"

"I need to take Red out for a while."

"Going somewhere in particular?" Junior moved as he spoke, going to Red's stall and grabbing the horse blanket. Without asking Stuart, he started saddling the horse.

Stuart wasn't about to settle the man's obvious curiosity and let loose a swarm of idle town gossip that he was sweet on Betsy Lowell. He shrugged. "Just for a ride."

"Store's slow today?"

"Yep. Everyone came in for supplies during the storm. Guess they were afraid winter came early and meant to stay."

"I see." Junior cleared his throat and tightened the straps under Red's overfed belly. "You know, Betsy Lowell was in a bit ago. She took Job for a ride."

Treading lightly, Stuart weighed his words so as not to lie, while not giving anything away. "That so?"

"Yessiree. She was mad as all get-out when she stormed in here, ready to put a bullet between that horse's eyes. I talked her out of it."

"That's good. Although I can see why she'd blame the horse. Old

Joe spoils him so much, he thinks he's the master and everyone else is his to command."

A chuckle left the liveryman as he handed Stuart the reins. "Never seen anyone take on over an animal the way Old Joe did that one."

"Most likely to his detriment."

The thought sobered both men. "It's been two days, and he's still not awake." Junior scrubbed his hand across his chin.

Stuart cringed at the image of Old Joe the way they'd placed him in the bed at Doc Avery's. Short of a miracle, he didn't see how the old-timer could come back from such an awful accident, but then, he believed in miracles if God so chose. For Betsy's sake, he prayed her grandfather would pull through. Although she'd likely have plenty to say to him once he woke up.

"You going after Betsy?"

Stuart scowled at the way Junior had worked Betsy back into the conversation. "Ma figured she shouldn't face the empty place by herself. Old Joe never told her what was going to happen."

"She knows now."

"You told her?"

Junior nodded. "I figured she had the right to know, and no one else was telling her."

Relief washed over Stuart that he wouldn't have to be the one to explain what happened. Still, she'd likely be in a state.

"She shouldn't be alone out there."

"Likely not."

Stuart mounted Red, inclining his head to the liveryman as he headed out.

⸻

Betsy reined in Job on the hill just above the vacant cabin. The land looked so still, so lonesome, that it was difficult to hold back the tears. But she refused to cry. She preferred anger over sadness. Anger spurred her to action. Sadness made her weary. So weary she wanted to crawl into her bed—not her bed any longer—and sleep until Pops was well again and everything went back to the way it was before.

Though there was certainly no reason to go any closer to the cabin,

Betsy couldn't help herself. Job had grown antsy and was beginning to pull toward home. Despite her desire to show him who was boss, for once, she and the horse were of the same mind. She allowed him his head, and they cantered down the grassy hill and reached the cabin in minutes. Dismounting, she let Job roam. Slowly, she made her way into the empty cabin.

A heavy sigh left her. She had played at her grandfather's feet as a child when Ma and Pa would take her to visit, and she'd always dreamed of the day her own children would lift their chubby little hands and take his as he led them into the yard and showed them how to feed the chickens and milk the cow. A lump formed in her throat at the thought of what might have been. If Pops had informed her of the trouble they were in, she could have taken in sewing or, heaven help her, even married Mr. Blakely, though the very idea made her skin crawl.

"What are you doing here?"

Betsy spun around at the man's voice, coming face-to-face with Leo Blakely. She scowled. "So it was you."

He grinned and nodded. "Yep. I bought the place. Got it at a robber's price, too."

"That's fitting. Considering you're nothing but a low-down thief, snatching Pops' place out from under him."

Leo's gaze narrowed, and his eyes darkened with a danger Betsy had never seen before. Instinctively she stepped back. "I bought the place fair and square. It ain't my fault Old Joe didn't keep up his payments. If anyone's a thief, he is, living here a whole year without paying the bank. Reckon that makes you a thief, too."

Betsy snatched back the words on the edge of her tongue for fear that look in his eyes might turn into something more violent. "I didn't know anything about that."

"I didn't reckon you did. I've been telling Old Joe for months I'd settle up with the bank if you'd agree to marry me. But he wouldn't do it. I guess he's regretting that now."

Horror filled Betsy's being. He had suggested that Old Joe sell her? Of course, only moments earlier she had been thinking close to the same thing. But to hear it put so blatantly curled her stomach.

Especially since he'd obviously taken her silence to mean she wished Old Joe had done it. He moved closer, slinking forward like a mountain lion with its prey in sight.

"Say the word right now, and Old Joe will have this place for the rest of his life."

"You mean you'd sign it back over to him?"

"No," he said curtly, reaching out and gripping her arms.

"Then what do you mean?"

"I mean, once you're in my house, he can live out the rest of his days in this cabin. But it will always belong to me."

Pops would never go for it. Not in a thousand and one years. She gave a snort and tried to shake off his sweaty hands. "He'd rather shoot you right between the eyes."

He tightened his grip and pulled her closer. "Is that so? And what about you? Are you going to see your grandpa out in the cold with winter coming?"

Fear settled over her like a thick cloud, but Betsy knew she couldn't cower before this man. "Better that than marrying the likes of you. Now turn me loose this instant."

"Better do as the lady says."

Betsy nearly fainted in relief as Stuart walked into the cabin.

Mr. Blakely scowled. "Mind your own business, Fields." His voice held the edge of a threat, but fortunately, he did as Stuart said and turned her loose.

Despite the two inches and forty pounds Leo Blakely had on Stuart, her defender didn't back down. He might be sickened at the sight of blood, but he wasn't afraid of the likes of this bully. The thought raised Betsy's estimation of Stuart by more than a little.

He stepped closer and reached for Betsy. Without thought, she took his hand and allowed him to lead her to a spot behind him, where his body shielded hers.

"I'd say the sight of a lady in distress is my business."

"I'd say the two of you are trespassing on my property, and I'll thank you to get on out of here."

"Gladly." Barely holding back a shudder that would expose her fear of the man, Betsy stepped out from behind Stuart and faced Leo squarely, then backed toward the door. On shaky legs, she reached the exit, aware that Stuart's steely gaze never left Mr. Blakely's as he followed her out. She noted gratefully that Job had joined Stuart's horse and both stood close by, eating the dead grass.

Stuart cupped her elbow as they walked toward the horses, neither of them speaking until they were clear of the angry man whose nefarious plans had clearly been thwarted by Stuart's sudden and, as far as Betsy was concerned, divinely directed appearance.

Job refused to stay still as she tried to mount him. Stuart grabbed his halter and gave him a sharp command, and Betsy was able to climb into the saddle on the second try.

As they rode away toward town, Betsy gathered in a deep breath. "I don't know what might have happened if you hadn't been there."

But she did know, and so did Stuart, though neither of them spoke it aloud. "I'm just glad I was."

"What were you doing there anyway?"

"We saw you riding out of town." He hesitated. "Ma was worried how you'd take finding the place empty like that. We weren't sure you'd been told about the auction."

A sigh slid through her lips. "Just awhile ago. Junior Mahoney told me." She shook her head. "That's what Blakely was all about back there. He had the audacity to offer Pops the cabin to live in."

Stuart gave a snort. "I take it there were strings attached?"

Betsy nodded. "He's been trying to get me to marry him since the day I turned fifteen."

The day that just a few moments ago had gone gray and awful was beginning to brighten. Not only with the sun shining down and warming things up, but Stuart's timely appearance had spared Betsy from unthinkable horrors. She cut him a glance. Maybe he wasn't so bad after all.

Chapter Five

Stuart rode next to Betsy, feeling more guilty than ever for buying that watch at the auction. He needed to tell her what he'd done. But if he knew Betsy, she would insist he give it back. Probably wouldn't even offer to pay for it. It held sentimental value for her, but he, too, had memories tied to the timepiece.

She sighed as they approached town. He turned at the sound. "You okay?"

She nodded, but the worry etched her face.

Stuart didn't push, but he had a feeling he understood. She had just lost everything dear to her, and the whole town knew about it. With Old Joe hurt, she would have to find a position somewhere to take care of them and a place to live. She looked so weary, and his heart twisted with sympathy.

"Don't worry, Betsy," he said. "We'll find you a place to live. You won't be alone." He would've told her about Ma's offer but figured it wasn't all that proper for a man to offer a young woman a place to live.

Besides, far from the reaction of gratitude he expected, Betsy turned brilliant, flashing blue eyes on him. "I don't need your charity, Stuart Fields. I have two hands and I'll find my own place to live."

"Fine. Sorry for trying to help."

"I don't want your help." The catch in her throat revealed fear and uncertainty. Stuart tried to understand. To not get up in arms over her stubbornness. "I don't mean to sound ungrateful for what you did back there. Obviously, I needed help. But when it comes to working and finding a place to live, I'm capable of taking care of Pops and me."

Stuart couldn't help the pride he felt because he'd saved her from

47

that scoundrel back at the cabin. To his surprise, all he wanted to do was ease her load. If only she would let him.

Betsy left Job in Junior Mahoney's capable hands and headed straight for Miss Annie's restaurant. The heavenly smells of cooking meat assaulted her stomach and caused her mouth to water. But the absence of money in her reticule made the idea of a meal impossible. Besides, that's not what she'd come for. Miss Annie met her at the door with a tentative smile. "The dining room isn't quite open for business. You know we close down between lunch and dinner."

"Yes, ma'am. I mean no. I'm not here to eat, and I knew you'd be closed to customers."

The woman searched her face with a slight frown. Then her eyes widened and she lifted her chin. "You're looking for a position, I take it?"

Heat suffused Betsy's face. "If you don't have one available, I understand. I'm not asking for a handout."

Miss Annie waved her words aside. "And I don't give them. As it happens, I'm in need for someone to help serve food and drinks to the customers and clean. Is that what you had in mind?"

Besty had never eaten in a restaurant, so she had no idea what she had in mind except for honest work and enough wages to secure a place to sleep and to cover Doc's fee. And she'd need to eat from time to time. "Yes, ma'am. That's what I had in mind."

"Good, then. I understand you have some troubles. But don't think this is a charitable position. I'll expect you to do your fair share of the work, and trust me, it's not going to be easy. I've let go almost as many girls as I've hired over the past ten years." She eyed Betsy. "But I think you're made of stronger stuff than those others."

Relieved to hear her say those things, Betsy didn't withhold her smile. "Thank you, Miss Annie. Can I just ask. . .that is. . ."

"How much am I paying you?"

"I'm sorry to ask."

She snorted. "Don't be sorry. You deserve to know what you're working for. The pay is seven dollars a week. One meal per day included. I'll expect you here at four thirty each morning, Monday through

Saturday. You'll leave when everything is spick-and-span. That's usually around seven each evening. Sundays are the Lord's day, and I observe that without fail. I'll expect to see you at service each week. I can't have an employee who doesn't go to church."

The wages were more generous than Betsy had dared hope. The work and hours were going to take some getting used to, but she knew she could do it. The only thing that gave her pause was attending church services every week on her only day off. "Miss Annie, the thing about Sunday. . ."

The older woman's eyebrows went up. "Yes?"

"It's just that I need to go see Pops on Sundays. I'm just not sure how long he'll be in the doc's care. And after that I'll be taking care of him."

Clearly unmoved by Betsy's very reasonable explanation, Miss Annie scowled. "I'm sure your pops can wait until you've kept the Sabbath holy. I'm sorry, Betsy Lowell. But those are my rules. I have very few. Be good to the customers. Deliver hot food and make sure drinks are full. Oh, and never, ever talk back to a customer."

"Never?" Not even if one was rude to her?

"Ironclad rule and grounds for immediate dismissal. Even so much as a sour face would be grounds for dismissal."

So she had to hold her tongue and her face? This position might be more difficult than she originally expected.

"We all set, then?" Miss Annie asked. "Or should I look for someone else?"

"No, ma'am. No need to look any further. When would you like for me to start?"

"In the morning. Four thirty sharp. Do you have a place to stay?"

"Not yet. I was thinking of asking Mr. Mahoney if I could bed down in my wagon at the livery."

"Nonsense. I have an extra room just over the kitchen. It'll be comfortable in winter but does get rather warm in the summer with the heat from the kitchen. It's very small, and the cot isn't too comfortable, but you may have it for two dollars a week, and I'll throw in one more meal a day. Which I think is very generous."

Calculating what she knew to be the rates at the boardinghouse,

Betsy figured she'd save a dollar a week if she took the room over the kitchen.

"Thank you, ma'am. May I move in now?"

"Yes. I'm not without generosity. Tonight you'll be my guest. Your rates for the room will begin tomorrow when you begin working."

"I appreciate it."

"Just keep that attitude, and we'll get on just fine. You can get into the room from the stairs behind the building. Go gather your belongings and move into the room at your convenience. I expect you to be in by eight each evening, including this one, and although it should be obvious, you mustn't have gentleman callers at any time, day or night."

"Of course!"

"I know you're a good girl. But it had to be spoken aloud so there's no misunderstanding."

Betsy nodded. "Thank you for everything. I'm going to go check on Pops, and I'll be back later."

Betsy walked into Doc's with her head high, pleased that she had secured a position and a home in less than twenty minutes. Pops would be relieved to hear she was taking care of herself. She met Mrs. Avery in the foyer. "How's he doing?"

"No change, I'm afraid."

Betsy's heart sank. She'd held out a large amount of hope that just the act of her leaving and coming back hours later might somehow make him come around. "None?"

"Not yet. But his breathing is steady. Doc says it's a good sign that he's still hanging in there. Sometimes staying unconscious is the body's way of healing itself. We've certainly seen people wake up after days like this and be as right as rain."

Her words brought a measure of relief, though she couldn't help but wish Pops would snap out of it. Of course, his bones needed to heal, so it might be a mercy he was staying asleep. Awake, he'd likely be insisting on getting up. Or doing something equally foolish to slow his recovery.

"Are you hungry?" Mrs. Avery asked. "I have some ham slices still warm from lunch and some potatoes fried with salt pork."

"Yes, ma'am. Thank you. Just let me go and sit with Pops for a few minutes."

A bright smile lit Mrs. Avery's face. "Good to see you getting your appetite back." She slid her arm around Betsy's shoulders and gave her a quick squeeze. "You go on in and sit with your grandpa, and I'll bring your lunch to you."

Betsy tapped lightly on the door, but of course Pops didn't answer. Feeling foolish, she turned the knob and stepped inside. "Hey, Pops," she said. "I sure wish you'd wake up. And don't worry, I'm not too mad about the mortgage and losing the farm." She flopped onto the chair next to the bed. "Except if you'd told me," she said, anger beginning to build, "I could've helped do something about it. You know? You didn't have to lie to me all this time. I mean, mercy! You know who bought the farm out from under us? Leo Blakely. And today, he tried to take liberties. Oh! And your watch is gone. I mean, really, Pops. The one time you forget the watch and they sell it. And the worst part is I don't know who has it. Any decent person will know that was a mistake, and maybe I can buy it back."

A knock at the door interrupted her, and Betsy sat back, folding her arms. "Come in, Mrs. Avery," she called.

The door opened, and the older woman appeared, juggling a tray in one hand, a pitcher of water in the other. Betsy hopped up and hurried to help before the whole thing ended up on the floor.

"Thank you, dear." Mrs. Avery smiled. "I brought Old Joe's soup, too. I'll try to get some nourishment down him while you get some in your own body."

Betsy set the tray on the table next to the bed and grabbed her plate. She attacked the ham and potatoes as though she hadn't eaten in a month.

Mrs. Avery nodded in approval. "It's good to see you've gotten your appetite back. You've got to keep up your strength."

"Yes, ma'am," she replied around her last bite. "Especially starting tomorrow." Just the description of what her days were going to be like from now on was exhausting.

"What do you mean?"

"I'm going to start working at Miss Annie's restaurant tomorrow."

A frown creased Mrs. Avery's brow; then she nodded. "I suppose it's the sensible thing to do."

"Miss Annie is letting me rent a room over the restaurant."

"Oh, honey. You didn't have to leave here. We have plenty of room. And you can keep your money."

"I appreciate it, but we don't take charity. I don't know how much Pops' doctoring is going to cost, but I can start paying three dollars a week for now. And I'm thinking of selling the horses and wagon before the bank decides it owns those, too—except for Job."

"Don't you worry yourself about paying the doctor." Mrs. Avery spooned some thin soup into Pops' mouth and wiped away a dribble from his chin. "We're just praying for your grandfather's recovery."

Had the woman not heard her say she wasn't one for charity? Or was it something else? "Do you think Pops isn't going to make it? Is that why you don't want me to pay?"

Setting the half-empty bowl on the table, Mrs. Avery turned to her. "I couldn't begin to guess what God has in mind, but my husband was put on this earth to doctor folks. When patients are unable to pay, God always does."

Betsy lifted her chin. "This patient can pay. It might take awhile for me to earn the whole fee, but God won't be paying our bill."

A moan from the bed stopped them both. Betsy set down the plate and reached for her grandpa's hand. "Pops? You awake?"

A mumble came from his lips. Betsy's heart raced. *Oh, please, God. Let him be waking up.*

Mrs. Avery stood. "I'll go for the doctor. He's in his office patching up little Kate Frazier's bloody knee."

"Pops?" Betsy leaned over close to his ear. "Can you hear me?"

"I ain't deaf," came a weak but rough reply.

Tears sprang to Betsy's eyes. "Oh, Pops. I'm so glad you're awake. I was so worried."

Pops tried to open his eyes, but each time they opened a crack, he shut them again immediately. "How long?"

"Since you've been unconscious?"

He gave a barely perceptible nod.

"Two days."

"That long? What happened?"

"Job slipped on the ice and fell on top of you."

Dr. and Mrs. Avery walked in before she could tell him more. The doctor's face lit with a smile. "Well, look who woke up."

His eyes finally opened. "What's wrong with my leg and arm, Doc?"

"Are you in pain?"

"I don't believe I've ever hurt so bad in my whole life. When can I get back on my feet?"

A laugh rumbled the doctor's chest. "First things first." He listened to his patient's heart. Looked at his eyes. "Does your head hurt?"

Pops shook his head. "Not so's you'd notice."

Doc nodded. "That's good."

"But how long till I get out of this bed?"

"Your leg was badly broken in more than one place," the doctor explained. "And your arm isn't much better. If you were a young man, I would guess two to three months. But our bones are weaker the older we get."

Pops scowled. "Just say it outright, Doc."

Doc Avery drew in a breath and slowly released it. "Four to six months, but I can't be certain if that leg will ever hold you up again."

Betsy's heart began to race. "You mean he might not walk again?"

"It's a possibility." He turned back to Pops. "If you do get strong enough to walk, it'll mean using a crutch for the rest of your life. But I have to warn you: I don't like how weak your heart sounds. And if you don't breathe deeply enough, you're at risk for pneumonia. So make sure you try to take deep breaths several times a day—even when it hurts."

Betsy held her breath, waiting for Pops to throw a fit. Instead, he lay very still for so long she thought he might have gone to sleep or become unconscious again. When he finally spoke, he sounded weak and small. "I reckon I best learn to read, or I'll be getting mighty bored."

"George enjoys an occasional game of checkers," Mrs. Avery said. "I'll bring the board in here."

Pops nodded. "Thank you kindly."

The doctor stood. He gazed at Betsy. "I'll let the two of you visit for a few minutes. Then your grandpa needs his rest."

"Yes, sir."

Dr. and Mrs. Avery left the room, closing the door behind them. Betsy turned to Pops. But his eyes were closed. She sat back and kept quiet, watching him.

Finally, he opened his eyes again. "I heard what you said."

"Then you're hearing things. I haven't made a peep."

"I mean before."

Betsy realized he meant before Mrs. Avery came in with lunch. "Oh. Well, there's no point in talking about it now. There's nothing to be done about it."

"I'm sorry I didn't tell you before."

Betsy's eyebrows went up at his uncommon humility. "Save your strength, Pops."

He shook his head. "I heard you say Leo tried to take liberties."

With a sigh, she revealed the events at the cabin.

His free hand squeezed into a fist next to him on the bed. "I'll kill him."

"You're the one who said just two days ago I ought to have married him."

"I thought he'd keep you safe. But I wouldn't have let you sell yourself in marriage just to save the farm."

Love for her pops welled up in Betsy's chest. Pops might be the crankiest, strictest man alive, but he lost the land rather than see her marry a man she didn't choose. "He won't be bothering me again. And you don't have to worry. I'm working now, so everything's going to be okay."

His brow furrowed. "What do you mean you're working? Who's going to hire a little girl like you, and what kind of work?"

She told him about Miss Annie.

He shook his head. "You ain't working for that woman. She'll eat you alive. And I especially don't want you living by yourself in a little room over the restaurant. You won't be safe."

Did he really think Miss Annie could intimidate her after Joe Lowell had raised her? The very idea almost made her laugh, but she didn't want him to accuse her of sass when he was so sick, so she focused on the last part of his concern. "I have your pistol. And you know I can shoot straight."

As weak as he was, Pops still wasn't willing to let it go. "You heard me, gal. Now I mean what I say. You get the notion of Miss Annie this and Miss Annie that out of your mind."

"I heard you, Pops." She looked straight at him, knowing she couldn't back down. "But I have to have work to pay the doc and to get us a place once you're well again."

"No woman's going to take care of me."

Frustration nearly made her forget about his condition, but she forced herself to calm down. "I'd like to see you stop me. I won't be here much. Probably just on Sundays after church."

Pops scowled. "Church? Why you going to go there?"

"It's one of Miss Annie's rules."

"See? You can't work for that woman. She's going to ruin you."

"Well, I'm going to. It's the best position I can get right now. I'm also selling the wagon and two horses."

"Not Job!"

"No, sir. I wouldn't sell your favorite horse. But you don't have any objection about the wagon and other horses?"

Pops shook his head. "I reckon we won't need a wagon without a farm. And no need for the farm horses, neither. I reckon we can use the money to get us a little place in town, and you won't have to work like a man."

Betsy had started shaking her head even before he finished. "I intend to settle our bill at the general store and anywhere else we owe." She was tired of not being able to hold up her head in Tucker's Creek.

With a sigh, Pops closed his eyes and nodded. "Do what you want. You will anyway."

Standing, she bent down and pressed a kiss to his cheek. "I'll go now so you can rest. Remember I likely won't be back until Sunday."

With one last glance back at Pops, she slipped out of the room. Poor Pops. He seemed so small and frail. But he'd raised her to be strong, and she had enough strength for them both.

Chapter Six

Stuart offered Ma his arm as they stepped off the boardwalk and started to cross the street to Miss Annie's restaurant. "Honestly," Ma said, slipping her hand inside the crook of his arm. "I don't see why you insist on us paying good money for bad food."

It had been a week since the day he'd walked in the cabin to find Mr. Blakely threatening Betsy. He had seen her only once since then—three days ago when she'd come into the store to settle the bill. He and Ma had both tried to talk her out of it, but she was adamant. In the end, they agreed. He'd discovered later that day that she was working for Miss Annie. Since then, he'd been waiting for a night Ma was so exhausted that a meal at the restaurant might seem like a good idea. Today had been busier than any since the ice storm. Not only had they had a steady stream of customers, but they'd also begun their fall inventory.

He opened the door and hung back to let Ma precede him. As he joined her, she turned to him with a wry grin. "Now I see why you insisted on eating here."

Stuart's neck warmed as he followed her gaze to Betsy, who set plates down at a table with three men, her cheeks flushed.

As she turned away from the table, her gaze caught his. She smiled all the way to her eyes, and Stuart felt like a king. She walked to them. "Good evening, Mrs. Fields. Stuart. Would you like a table?"

"We certainly would," Ma said. "What on earth are you doing working for that woman?"

Betsy smiled. "It's not so bad." She led them to a table.

Ma reached out and took Betsy's hand. "That attitude just shows what an angel you are."

Angel? Betsy might look like one, but she was far from angelic. Although, Stuart had to admit, her sharp tongue and abrupt ways didn't seem nearly as common or annoying as they used to.

He tried not to watch her as she moved about the dining room. She brought them tea and moved quickly to the kitchen, coming out a minute later with two plates that she took to a young couple in the corner. "Betsy!" Miss Annie called from the kitchen, and Betsy quickly answered the call.

"I vow that woman is working our Betsy to death. Are we going to let that go on?"

Stuart scowled. "What are we supposed to do about it? You already know she's stubborn as that horse of Old Joe's. She's not going to accept anything she suspects is close to charity."

Ma lowered her voice as Betsy swung back through the kitchen door, carrying two more plates and headed straight for their table. "I'll just have to find a way to convince her she's the one being charitable."

As Betsy set their food on the table, Stuart noted the dark smudges beneath her eyes. Ma was right; they would have to find a way to get her out of this place. If she would let them. One thing he knew for sure: she would have to believe it was her idea.

He ate as slowly as he could, but an hour later, when the table next to them had changed customers three times while they sat there, his mother leaned over. "Stuart, I'm tired. You can't stay here all night."

He glanced around as they stood, looking for Betsy, who hadn't been in the dining room for the past fifteen minutes. To his disappointment and Ma's annoyance, Miss Annie had taken over at the tables. "You two leaving us?" Miss Annie hurried to them, smiling as though she had no idea how much Ma despised her. But was there any reason for her to know? Ma had a way of being sweet as pie, and only he could tell she was spitting mad all the while.

He nodded and reached into his jacket pocket for the price of their meal. "It was delicious, Miss Annie."

The older woman flushed with pleasure. "Why, thank you. And how did you find our new girl?"

Ma patted his back. "We found her simply delightful, didn't we, Son?"

"Yes, ma'am."

"And such prompt service. Why, we would have had a wonderful meal even if, say, the chicken had been a little dry, not that I'm saying it was, of course."

Miss Annie sniffed and lifted her chin. "I should say not."

As they left the restaurant and began the short walk home, Stuart smiled. "Did you really think the chicken was dry, or were you just trying to get under Miss Annie's skin?"

"I'd have been ashamed to serve it. I had to wash down every bite with a sip of tea."

They walked in silence, while Stuart replayed the evening in his mind. Betsy had moved around the dining room in a blur without making the customers feel her rushing. She'd remained pleasant and smiled, even when Miss Annie bellowed her name from the kitchen. Never once had she revealed the frustration she must certainly have felt, nor had she neglected the patrons' needs.

"She's something, isn't she?"

Ma gave a huff. "I know you're not talking about Annie."

He chuckled. "No, Ma. I mean Betsy."

"Don't pretend you've never noticed how special that girl is before now. I remember when you were a boy in school. . ."

"Yes, Ma. I was a little sweet on her."

"That's the first time you've ever told the truth about that. It's about time. That Betsy's a flower in a field of crabgrass."

"She's mighty quick tempered."

Ma gave a snort as they reached the edge of the wrought-iron fence surrounding their house. "She has a backbone."

"Which some people consider to be stubbornness."

"Nothing wrong with that. Why, your pa was the stubbornest man I ever knew, but that didn't stop me from loving him every day since I came to Tucker's Creek to teach school." She sighed. "And he was awfully good to you and your sister, as well."

Stuart helped her up the steps. Ma had been growing stiffer and complained about the steps being hard on her. It was a shame his sister, Ruth, had married a wanderer and moved out West after Pa died. She would have been a big help for Ma.

As he opened the door and let her walk in first, he hung back. "I believe I'll sit out here for a few minutes."

"Something on your mind?" He could tell by the lilt in her voice that Ma assumed she knew exactly what, or who, was on his mind, but he wasn't about to give her the satisfaction of confirming her suspicion.

"Just don't think we'll have too many more nights like this before winter sets in all the way."

She smiled and nodded. "All right, Son. Don't stay up too late. We have another full day of inventory tomorrow." She hesitated. "I suppose we should plan to eat at the restaurant the rest of this week. I'm afraid the extra work tires me out."

"Ma. . ."

"Fine. If you'd rather I wear myself to the bone, cooking your supper, I guess I can. Of course, we're also about out of bread, so that'll need to be done, too. I best stay up all night so it can rise properly."

"For mercy's sake, Ma. Of course I don't want you wearing yourself out. We'll eat Miss Annie's dry chicken, and you can keep an eye on Betsy." He grinned. "Feel better?"

"I don't know what you mean."

"Of course not." Leaning forward, he kissed her cheek. "Go to bed, Ma. You need your rest."

Ma's eyes softened, and she reached up and patted his cheek. "I'm glad you're finally seeing Betsy for the fine young woman she is. Will you be giving her back the watch?"

Annoyance tightened his chest. "No. I bought it. It's mine. I'm sorry, Ma. But you know I can't give it up. And you know why."

"Fine. Break that girl's heart when you have it within your means to give her a moment of happiness that she so richly deserves. A little kindness—"

"Good night, Ma."

Reaching forward, he grabbed the latch and pulled the door shut. He walked toward the rocking chair that sat on the porch just to the right of the door and sat, staring into the starry sky. Ma knew why he wanted that watch, and he'd bought it fair and square. Truth be told, he'd probably paid too much. And as much as he was beginning to admire Betsy Lowell, he had just as much a claim to it as she did. More so now, because he was the one who owned it.

Betsy's legs felt wooden as she trudged up the long steps to her small room above the restaurant. The weather had turned cold again in the past two weeks, but she barely felt it as she dropped onto the top step and lay back, staring at the sky. It had been three weeks since Pops' accident, three weeks since everything she thought she knew about her life had turned out to be a lie.

The work was hard but honest, and she was grateful and proud to hand over three dollars each week to Mrs. Avery for the doctor fees. Each week, Doc and his wife tried to give the money back, but she wouldn't think of it. Rather than argue, they eventually gave in.

Miss Annie was a harsh taskmaster, but Betsy admired a woman who had become a widow only five years after her marriage and had enough pluck to start a business and care for herself. She smiled through the criticism and did as she was told. After all, Miss Annie didn't ask any more of her than she did of herself. She was at the restaurant an hour before Betsy and left an hour after, every day.

Betsy was beginning to settle into her daily routine, and constant fatigue was becoming as familiar as washing her hands or eating dinner. But she couldn't think about how tired she felt or the years of drudgery ahead of her.

Pops was recovering slowly. On Sunday, the doctor had expressed concern that his lungs didn't sound good and pneumonia was a possibility. The thought terrified her, and she prayed more often and with more fervency than she'd ever prayed before. That was one good thing about being forced to attend services on Sunday. She was finding peace in silence and had learned that talking to God made her feel better about things in general. It was almost as though He was helping her get through each day.

With a deep sigh, Betsy closed her eyes, determined to stay there only another minute while she gathered the strength to pull her weary body from the porch and fall into bed.

Betsy awoke, shivering, and sat up, realizing she'd fallen sound asleep. Her dress was covered with snow and her hands felt like ice. She hurried into her room. The fire had long since gone out, but she was too cold and weary to start another. Stripping off the dress, she hung it up on her peg, hoping it would dry before she had to rise in a couple of hours. She crawled under two heavy quilts, closed her eyes, and drifted off again.

The next time she woke, it was to insistent thudding on the floor. She opened her eyes slowly, her brain messy and confused as she sat up and tried to make sense of the sound. *Thud-thud-thud.* Suddenly she realized where the sound was coming from. She flew from her bed and grabbed her still-damp dress from the peg. There was no time to iron it, but that couldn't be helped. Dread twisted her stomach as she hooked her boots and raced down the steps.

Miss Annie glared at her. "You're fifteen minutes late."

"Yes, ma'am. I'm sorry. I didn't wake up."

"I didn't hire you to be a lay-about. I hired you to work. If you can't be here on time…" Her frown deepened as she scanned Betsy's appearance. "Did you sleep in that dress?"

"No, ma'am." Well, not exactly. She'd intended to iron it crisp and tidy.

"Obviously you can't serve customers that way. Go upstairs, and don't come down until you're presentable. You'll have to come in early tomorrow to make up the time."

Relief flooded over Betsy that she wasn't being fired on the spot. "Yes, ma'am."

"And be quick. I can't do everything myself."

"Yes, ma'am." Breathless, Betsy took the steps two at a time. She built a fire in the stove and set the iron on top to get warm, then stripped off her dress. While she waited for the iron to heat up, she straightened her disheveled quilts and then sat on the edge of her bed. Overwhelming fatigue came over her, and if she sat there a second longer, she would lie back and risk falling asleep. She forced herself to stand.

By the time Miss Annie resumed her thudding on the ceiling, Betsy was already headed toward the door. She had washed her face, brushed out her thick, long hair and retwisted it into a neat chignon. Her gown looked as though it had just been laundered. All in all, she owed Miss Annie forty-five minutes, but the extra time today was worth it. Or so she thought.

Miss Annie's face was mottled with anger. "High time you got back here," she snapped.

"I'm sorry, ma'am. I had to build a fire to heat the iron."

"I don't want your excuses." She grabbed Betsy's arm, her fingers shoving into delicate skin. "Get over here and watch this bacon. If it burns, I'm taking it out of your wages."

Betsy couldn't imagine what had happened to anger the woman so much. She had never seen this side of Miss Annie and had certainly never been on the receiving end of a violent outburst. But she didn't dare speak up. She had to keep this position.

She worked harder that day than she'd ever worked before, trying desperately to make it up to Miss Annie. By the time the lunch customers were all gone and they closed down to clean up and prepare for supper, Betsy's stomach felt hollow. She hadn't eaten since lunch yesterday. Despite Miss Annie's promise of two meals a day—one for working at the restaurant and the other included in her rent for the room—Miss Annie often forgot to allow her to stop for lunch.

She waited for Miss Annie to tell her to get something to eat before they started to clean up, but the woman seemed preoccupied. After the rough start that morning, Betsy didn't have the nerve to request a meal. At five, Miss Annie opened the doors, and once more, the dining room filled with customers. Betsy fought a wave of dizziness as she took out her first plates. She'd never been a heavy eater, but she'd always had regular meals.

Her spirits lifted when Stuart and Mrs. Fields entered the restaurant an hour later. They hadn't been in for supper at all this week. She hurried to the door and led them to an empty table.

Mrs. Fields frowned a little. "Betsy, you're getting much too thin, honey. That dress is practically hanging from your bones. Are you eating?"

Averting her gaze, Betsy did the only thing she could. "Yes, ma'am. I'm just not used to working so much."

"I think I should have a talk with Annie. She certainly doesn't look like a woman who misses meals."

Alarm seized Betsy. If Mrs. Fields said anything on her behalf, the woman would think she'd been complaining. And that wasn't tolerated. "Please, no, ma'am. I eat plenty. I promise."

Stuart reached across the table and touched his ma's hand. "Ma. Leave Betsy alone." He glanced up, but Betsy noticed his somber scrutiny, as well. "Bring us the special and two glasses of tea."

"Yes, sir." Grateful to be away from their watchful eyes, Betsy hurried to the kitchen to place the order with Miss Annie. "Two plates of roast venison, fried potatoes, and green beans for Mrs. Fields and Stuart."

Annie turned from the stove. Her face glistened with sweat from the heat. "They've been coming in here a lot lately. Something special between you and the Fields boy?"

"Why, no. He's been kind about Pops, is all."

"Well, you just remember what I said about gentleman callers."

"Of course."

"Did. . .Mrs. Fields. . .say anything?" Miss Annie turned back to the stove and dished up the plates. She set them on the counter. Betsy couldn't help but eye them hungrily.

"I asked you a question, Betsy. Did she say anything?"

"I'm not sure what you mean."

"It's not a difficult question." Her voice was gaining an edge that sent Betsy's heart racing.

"Ma'am, the only thing she said was that I was getting too thin and I should eat more." A gasp from the older woman jerked Betsy's head up. "Are you okay, Miss Annie?"

The older woman's shoulders slumped, and her eyes softened. "Betsy, why didn't you remind me you didn't stop to eat today? Honey, go take that out and then get yourself back in here and eat. It's been a. . .difficult time today and I've been distracted. I'm sorry."

"What about the customers, ma'am?"

"Don't you worry yourself about them until you have a proper meal inside that little body." Her eyes moved over Betsy's form. "She's right.

You're growing too thin."

More confused than ever by Miss Annie's odd behavior, Betsy grabbed the two plates and set them in front of Stuart and his mother.

She noticed the glow in Mrs. Fields' eyes as she stared into a locket pinned to her dress. As the woman glanced up, Betsy realized that glow was the glisten of tears. "Is everything okay?"

Mrs. Fields closed the locket and placed her napkin on her lap. "Of course, dear. Everything is fine."

Betsy frowned, turning to Stuart.

"My pa died six years ago today. We've been to visit his grave."

Placing her hand on the woman's shoulder, Betsy gave a sympathetic squeeze. "Seems like today hasn't been too good for anyone."

Mrs. Fields reached up and covered Betsy's hand with her own. "Everything okay with your grandpa?"

"Oh, yes. I just overslept and made Miss Annie angry. But she is also having a difficult time today. I just feel awful that I caused it."

With a sigh, Mrs. Fields sought her gaze. "That woman's difficult day has nothing to do with you."

Betsy turned to Stuart as Mrs. Fields attacked her food, ending the conversation. Stuart frowned and shook his head, clearly just as confused as she was.

Trudging back to the kitchen, Betsy sat at Miss Annie's command and ate. How grateful she would be when this day ended and she could crawl into her bed and forget it had ever happened.

Chapter Seven

Stuart sang with gusto as the minister led the congregation in a rousing chorus of "Bringing in the Sheaves." He tried not to stare at Betsy as she stood next to Miss Annie, sharing a hymnal but not moving her lips. He had a feeling she wasn't crazy about the idea of being forced to keep the Sabbath, but it was widely known that one of Miss Annie's rules for her employees was propriety at all times and regular attendance on Sundays.

A nudge from Ma brought heat to his neck, and he forced his eyes to the front as the song ended and Reverend Beck told them to be seated.

Sitting on a hard bench, Stuart found it difficult to concentrate on anything coming from the man's lips, but after an hour, the service was dismissed. They greeted the reverend at the door, and Ma spent a few seconds extolling the man's speaking gifts. Stuart scanned the church-yard and found Betsy standing with Miss Annie. He wanted badly to go and speak to Betsy, but with practically the entire town standing around, he didn't want to give anyone a reason to gossip.

Ma took his arm as they walked—he with reluctance—toward home. The doctor and Mrs. Avery pulled up beside them in the buggy. "Hello, Nan, Stuart," Mrs. Avery said. "You left so fast I didn't have an opportunity to invite you to dinner this evening. Will you join us?"

"We'd love to." Ma smiled. "That's very kind. I'll bring a pie."

"Bring enough for Betsy." Mrs. Avery cast a sly glance toward Stuart and grinned. "She'll be there, too."

A little giggle left Ma as Doc and his wife drove away.

"What?"

"Seems as though I'm not the only one who knows you're sweet on that girl."

"Ma, please." He released a heavy sigh. "I don't need help with courting."

"Well, she's been in town for almost a month, and you haven't so much as taken her flowers."

"Flowers? Where am I going to find flowers in the winter?"

"Then I suppose you'll have to get creative until spring." She shrugged. "But I warn you, you are not the only young man in this town starting to notice that girl. There are more widowers and bachelors in the township than you can shake a stick at—at least two for every marriage-age young woman. If you're not careful, someone else is going to snatch her up and carry her off before you can find a flower. Not to mention courage."

"Ma, this is my own concern, not yours. And Betsy Lowell is certainly not looking to get herself hitched. The first thing she did was go and find a position to take care of Old Joe." Most other girls would have found a man, not a place to work.

Ma waved aside his objection. "Nonsense. She did what she had to do because there's no man to take care of her."

But Stuart wasn't so sure about that. As weary and thin as Betsy appeared lately, he had a feeling she enjoyed standing on her own two feet. Especially after losing the farm through no fault of her own. The day she'd paid off Old Joe's account at the store, he'd seen deep satisfaction in her eyes.

"You enjoy working at the store," he pointed out.

Ma nodded thoughtfully. "True, but I didn't work there when your pa was alive. I enjoyed taking care of the house and you and Ruth." She smiled at him as they reached the steps to the house. "Since he died, I find the store provides me with distraction from missing him so much."

Stuart held on to her hand as she slowly negotiated the stairs, and they entered the house together. "I'll call you when lunch is ready," she said.

"Ma, about Miss Annie. . ."

She turned and frowned. "Annie? What about that woman?"

"The other night at dinner you said something that I haven't been able to stop thinking about."

She gave a snort. "I wish you'd listen to what I say about Betsy Lowell with that kind of attention."

A smile tipped the corners of Stuart's lips. "Don't change the subject. What did you mean when you said Betsy's tardiness had nothing to do with the way Miss Annie was acting?"

Ma shrugged and walked toward the kitchen as though that was supposed to end the matter. Stuart followed her and leaned against the doorframe as she pulled out an iron skillet and stoked the fire. "Well?" he asked, folding his arms across his chest.

"She remembers what day that is, too."

"I don't understand." He frowned. "You don't mean about Pa's death."

"Just leave it be, Son."

Her jaw was set, so Stuart knew there was no point in pushing the issue. She pulled a bowl of potatoes off the shelf and began to peel them. Stuart stood for a minute longer, then walked back toward the sitting room. He glanced out at the gray day. He had a feeling more snow was on the way.

At six o'clock that evening, he stepped over the threshold of the Avery home, carrying a warm apple pie. Mrs. Avery smiled. "Stuart, so nice to see you." She looked over his shoulder. "And your ma?"

"Feeling a little poorly, I'm afraid." The coming weather was bothering her hip, and she'd decided to lie down with the hot-water bottle and a book. "She sent the pie and her regrets."

"We'll send her a plate home, and I'll have the doc stop by and see her tomorrow."

"If I can convince her to stay home." Ma hadn't missed a day at the store since Pa died. But Stuart knew that couldn't continue much longer. With all of her aches and pains, it was becoming increasingly clear she needed to let him take over.

Maybe he'd discuss Ma's condition with the doc, even though she'd be furious at him for doing so. He shed his coat and hat just inside the door, and Mrs. Avery hung them on the peg board. He glanced around, shifting his gaze first toward the kitchen, then toward the room he'd helped carry Old Joe into a few weeks earlier.

Mrs. Avery patted his arm. "She's in there with Old Joe. He's not perking up the way Doc wants him to."

Seeing no point in denying that he was looking for Betsy, he nodded and handed Mrs. Avery the pie.

"Smells wonderful," she said. "And still warm."

"Yes, ma'am." Stuart glanced at Old Joe's door again.

"Come on into the kitchen. I'll get you some coffee. Dinner will just be a few minutes." She winked as he held the door open for her. "Mrs. Vale had twins last week, so Mr. Vale paid the doctor a chicken for each of his new sons. Don't they smell delicious?"

Stuart laughed. "Yes, ma'am, they certainly do." She poured a cup of coffee and set it on the table.

"Can I set the table for you?" he asked.

"I should say not."

"Oh, now, I help my ma in the kitchen all the time."

"And that's good of you." She gave him a look that said not to argue and waved him toward the chair. "But you are my guest, and my guests do not work for their supper."

Which was all well and good, but Stuart felt ill-at-ease just sitting there, doing nothing while she fluttered about the kitchen, setting the table, pulling the chickens out of the oven. By the time Doc Avery joined them, everything was on the table.

"There you are." Mrs. Avery kissed her husband's cheek. "Where's Betsy?"

"She's finishing up Old Joe's shave. She asked us to go ahead and start."

"I should say not. We'll wait for her."

The doctor's eyes twinkled. "That's what I told her you'd say." He sipped the coffee his wife poured and turned to Stuart. "Your ma couldn't make it?"

"The weather makes her hip act up, so she went to bed with a hot-water bottle."

"I'll go see her tomorrow."

"That's what I told him." Mrs. Avery winked at Stuart.

Stuart looked from one to the other with a mix of emotions. Amusement at their banter, but a sense of longing also. What would it be like to grow old with someone? These two had an obvious affection for each other. But it went beyond the marriages he'd observed. The Averys were friends. That was the sort of marriage he hoped to have someday.

Unbidden, Betsy Lowell's face came to mind.

The kitchen door opened, drawing him from his reverie. He stood quickly, nearly upending his chair as Betsy came in. She carried a tray with a bowl and cup. Stuart walked to her and reached for the tray.

She gave him a weary smile and relinquished the burden. "Thank you, Mr. Fields."

He wished she'd stop going back and forth between calling him Stuart and Mr. Fields. He much preferred the former, and almost said so, but with the Averys looking on, thought better of it. He set the tray on the counter and resumed his place at the table.

They bowed their heads, and Doc Avery said a hasty blessing. As soon as he finished, Mrs. Avery placed her napkin in her lap and lifted her fork. "So, Betsy, tell us how things are going at the restaurant."

"We've been very busy."

"I suppose that's a good thing." She smiled kindly. "But you don't want to tire yourself out too much."

Betsy met her gaze with a smile. "A little hard work never hurt anyone."

"Is your room staying warm enough?"

"Too warm sometimes. It's over the kitchen."

"You know, we have the extra room. You're more than welcome to come back here."

"Thank you for your kindness, ma'am, but my room is fine."

Betsy cast a quick glance at Stuart, obviously not wanting to discuss this in front of him. He cleared his throat. "I hear the new teacher is already moving on," he said. He hated to repeat any of the gossip that filtered through the general store, but Betsy needed the focus taken off her.

His ploy worked. Mrs. Avery's eyes went big. "Already? Why, she's only been here for three months."

"Apparently, she's had an offer of marriage."

"For mercy's sake. The entire reason for hiring a spinster of her advanced years was to avoid this very thing. So many of the young, pretty ones come and get snatched up the second they get off the stage."

Stuart grinned. "That's what my ma did. She came to teach and was married to my pa in six months."

Doc Avery laughed. "Maybe we should start hiring men teachers instead of women, or the next generation of children are going to be complete imbeciles."

Laughter continued along with the meal, and the conversation stayed safely away from Betsy's fatigue, job, and living conditions.

When they had eaten the last of their dessert, Mrs. Avery stood and began clearing. Betsy rose to help, but she waved her back to her chair. "Not tonight, Betsy."

"Oh but, Mrs. Avery, I couldn't just let you do all the cooking and then the cleaning, too."

"Don't be silly. You're not to lift a finger."

Faced with Mrs. Avery's determination, Betsy sat back in her chair. She glanced at Stuart. "Please tell your ma I'm sorry she's feeling poorly."

"Thank you. She'll be pleased you said so."

Mrs. Avery set a covered plate on the table. "Be sure to give this to your ma. And I'm sending the rest of the pie back as well. Not that we left much."

By the time the table was cleared, Stuart began to feel as though he might be in danger of overstaying his welcome, but he hated leaving Betsy. They had barely spoken to each other during the entire meal. Reluctantly, he stood. "Thank you for the wonderful meal, Mrs. Avery."

The doctor stood and extended his hand. "It was good to see you. Now don't forget to tell your ma I'm dropping by tomorrow, and I'll expect to find her at home."

Stuart grinned and accepted the proffered hand. "Doctor's orders. I'll let her know. But she's not going to be pleased."

"Stuart, hon. If you're leaving now, would you mind walking Betsy back to her room?"

Betsy started and jerked her gaze to the other woman. "Why, there's no need for that, ma'am. I'm fine walking by myself." She gave a wry grin. "As a matter of fact, I do it every week."

"And it makes me very nervous. So do me a favor and set my mind at ease."

Stuart could have kissed the meddling woman. This was the opportunity he needed to spend some time alone with Betsy. And they'd be out in the open, so there was no impropriety. "It's no inconvenience, Miss Lowell. I have to walk right by Miss Annie's anyway."

Finally, she nodded. "Let me just peek in on Pops first; then I'll be ready to go."

When she disappeared through the kitchen door, Mrs. Avery gave him a nudge. "Don't waste the opportunity."

The doctor clicked his teeth. "Hon, meddling is unbecoming in someone as beautiful as you. Let the young people alone."

She gave a snort. "Mind your own affairs, Doctor. And leave me to mine. This boy needs all the help he can get."

Stuart felt his ears burn and knew he was likely red-faced. "I'll do my best, ma'am."

Betsy knew Mrs. Avery was doing her best to push Stuart to court her. But even if Miss Annie allowed gentleman callers, when would she ever have time to accept a man's attention? Her days were filled with work, and Sundays were for Pops. She wasn't like other young women her age—well, most young women her age were married with two or three children already. But she couldn't think about finding a husband. Pops needed her to continue working so that she could pay his doctor bills. Otherwise, how would he ever be able to hold up his head living in town?

She watched his breathing, hearing the rattle of each rise and fall. Doc Avery said he likely had pneumonia. The thought terrified her. How could Pops survive his awful injuries with pneumonia on top of it? As grateful as she was for the opportunity Miss Annie had given her, she felt guilty that she wasn't here every day, caring for Pops. If he died when she wasn't there, she'd never forgive herself.

He moaned softly and jerked away, his eyes opening.

"Hey, Pops."

He frowned. "What are you still doing here? Don't you got to be back?"

She nodded. "I have a few more minutes. We just finished supper."

"I ain't crazy about you walking home by yourself."

A smile touched her lips, and she pulled the quilt up around his shoulders. "Stuart Fields is walking me home, so you have nothing to worry about."

He snorted. "You have a better chance of keeping him safe than the other way around."

"Don't be mean. Remember he came just in time to stop Leo Blakely from taking advantage?"

He nodded and began a coughing fit that lasted a couple of minutes. The doctor opened the door, carrying a poultice. "This will help some." Betsy moved out of the way and watched as the doctor laid the warm wrap on her grandpa's chest, then put the quilt back in place.

He took a small amber bottle from his pocket and lifted it to his patient's lips.

"What's this?" Pops asked, a frown deepening the lines between his eyes.

"It's just some laudanum. It'll help with the pain and let you get some sleep."

With uncommon meekness, Pops allowed the doctor to pour some of the medicine down his throat. He closed his eyes and a minute later had fallen asleep.

Doc Avery placed a hand on her shoulder. "Go on back to your room, hon. He'll likely sleep until morning now."

With a sigh, she took another glance at her grandpa and followed the doctor from the room. Stuart stood waiting, his coat on and buttoned, hat between his hands. "All set?"

"In a second." Betsy turned to the doctor. "Do you think Pops is going to make it?"

The hesitation in his eyes told her everything she needed to know, but Betsy had to hear it from his lips. "I'm doing all I can to make sure he does."

"But are you on a fool's errand?"

A sudden smile tipped his lips. "Well now. We doctors like to believe we can perform miracles, and I wouldn't call this a fool's errand, as you say, but I do feel we have an uphill battle with Old Joe. His leg isn't healing like it should, and I'm beginning to worry that he's not going to land back on his feet, even with a crutch. We might need to look into ordering a rolling chair for when he's able to get out of bed."

"A rolling chair? I've never seen one." Were they expensive? How would she ever afford to purchase such a thing?

"Well, Old Joe's as stubborn as they come, so there's a chance he'll weather all this fine."

"Thank you, Doctor. If something changes with him, will you get a message to me?"

"Of course." He looked at Stuart. "Get her home safely."

"Yes, sir."

Cold air blasted the foyer as Stuart opened the door after Betsy had slipped on her coat and scarf. "Looks like we're in for a storm," he said, tucking his free hand into his pocket. He carried his ma's dinner plate in the other.

"I suppose so." They turned toward Miss Annie's, making tracks in the newly fallen snow. The night reminded her of the day Pops had fallen off Job and started this whole nightmare. "You know the doc was lying."

"How so?"

"He doesn't believe Pops' stubbornness will make him walk again. And honestly, I'm starting to think he's expecting the pneumonia to take him before his leg heals enough to think about a crutch or a rolling chair."

Silence filled the cold air between them. Betsy appreciated that Stuart didn't try to console her with more lies. Instead, he took her elbow and led her gently across the street. When they reached the front of Miss Annie's, she turned to him. "Thank you for walking me home."

"Don't you live around back?"

She nodded. "Yes, but Miss Annie forbids me to have gentleman callers. If you walk me around back and word gets back to her, she might misunderstand."

"Well, I don't like not walking around there with you. It's bound to be dark. Anyone could be waiting. . ."

Pressing her hand to his chest, she smiled. "Stuart, truly, I'll be fine. There's no one lying in wait to do me harm."

He glanced down at her hand, and she snatched it away as though he were on fire.

"Thank you, again." She backed away and turned, then walked around back. Once inside her room, she stoked up the fire in the woodstove, dressed for bed, and slid beneath the heavy quilts. She closed her eyes and dreaded the beginning of another week.

Chapter Eight

Stuart closed the shop at five o'clock and headed straight to Miss Annie's. He'd take a meal home to Ma and try to convince her to stay home another day. Though after she saw the receipts for today's business, she'd likely insist he needed her help. The store had been overrun for two hours, and even after it slowed down some, there was still such a steady stream, he'd been unable to take a lunch break.

Betsy greeted him with a smile when he walked into the restaurant. "Your ma still under the weather?" she asked.

"She is. I'll need to take her a plate when I leave."

"The store seemed busy today."

She'd been watching the store? Stuart's heart sped up at the thought. Did that mean she was trying to catch a glimpse of him? Truth be told, he'd found himself looking out the store window several times today, hoping to catch sight of her moving about the restaurant.

"Miss Annie bought some fresh steaks from Mr. Vale this morning. He butchered a couple of steers over the weekend. Otherwise, the special is chicken and dumplings."

His mouth watered at the thought of steak, so he ordered that. "And when I'm ready to go, Ma would most likely prefer the chicken and dumplings."

"I'll be back with your food, soon."

Stuart watched her as she disappeared inside the kitchen. He had to admit, she didn't seem quite as tired as she had last week. Maybe she was getting used to the hard work and long hours, although he had to admit he hoped he had a little to do with it. The thought drew a smile to his lips.

He tried not to let his eyes follow her as she went from table to table. She'd grown into a capable worker, and her smile worked on every customer in the place, including him.

He ate as slowly as possible but knew his ma would be getting hungry. Without thinking, he pulled out his watch, never knowing if it was going to be keeping the time he'd set the last time it started working again. Before he realized his mistake, he heard a gasp and looked up, dread tightening his stomach as he faced stormy eyes.

"Where did you get that?" Betsy asked, her voice rising.

"Betsy, I was going to tell you." When, when had he planned to tell her?

"Give it to me this instant." She reached for the watch, and instinctively he snatched it back. She lost her balance just as Miss Annie burst through the kitchen door. His water glass tipped and spilled into his lap. But Betsy didn't seem to notice as she lunged for the watch.

"Betsy Lowell!" Miss Annie's boots made quick clicks on the floor as she hurried across the room amid all of the curious stares. "Betsy Lowell!" But Betsy didn't seem to hear the older woman. She was too intent on the watch.

Stuart reached out and grabbed Betsy's arms. "Betsy, stop."

"What'd you do? Take it from the street when Pops fell that day? Are you a lousy thief?"

He scowled at her, anger building. "I bought it at the auction. The auction your pops is responsible for in the first place. So if you want to—"

"You went to the auction like all these other vultures?" She waved toward the patrons, and the room began to buzz at the implication. Tears sprang to her eyes, and Stuart recognized them as more than tears of anger. Her words and tone revealed how betrayed she felt by him.

"Miss Lowell," Miss Annie spoke low and through clenched teeth. "Did I not explain to you that I wouldn't tolerate rude behavior to the customers?"

Betsy gathered a deep breath and turned to face her. "Yes, ma'am, you did."

"Miss Annie," Stuart stepped forward. "This wasn't entirely Miss Lowell's fault."

"Please, Mr. Fields. While I'm sure Miss Lowell appreciates your chivalry, I assure you, it is beside the point."

"I don't appreciate it at all. And he isn't chivalrous. If anything, he's a low-down thief."

Outrage once more pierced his chest. "I am not a thief."

"Then give me back my watch."

"My watch. I paid for it fair and square." He set some bills on the table. "More than fair and square if you want the truth. You'll be pleased to know it doesn't even keep time."

Somewhere in the dining room, laughter began, then moved across the entire group of diners. Miss Annie glanced at Stuart. "Mr. Fields, I'm sorry for your treatment. Please come back."

Without looking at Betsy, he walked, wet and angry, into the cold, snowy night.

A moment later, someone called out to him. Dread hit him in the gut at the sound he recognized as Betsy's voice. He turned to face her. "Betsy, I'm not going to argue with you."

"I don't want to argue, either." She shoved a plate toward him. "You forgot your ma's dinner."

"Oh, I did, didn't I? Thank you."

"I'm not finished." She reached out and pulled him around. "You owe me a job."

Gaping, he shook his head. "How do you figure that?"

She stomped her foot. "You cost me this one. Miss Annie let me go."

"Over spilled water?"

"You know that was only part of it. But there's no changing her mind, and I need a position."

He hesitated. While he felt in no way responsible for her present circumstances, Stuart did need help in the store with Ma indisposed. Having Betsy there would ease Ma's mind considerably and might encourage her to stay home and rest her hip.

"Just until Ma feels well enough to come back."

"Fine. What time shall I be there?"

"We open at eight. Come at seven thirty so I can show you how to enter what people owe into the account book. I assume you know how to count back change?"

"Obviously," she said, sarcasm dripping from her lips.

"Good. Then you won't have that much to learn."

"I want my watch back, Stuart."

"It's not yours. How would you feel if I went around to everyone's homes after they bought items from the store and asked for the merchandise back? That's how things work. You pay for it. It's yours."

"Fine, then tell me how much you paid for it, and I'll buy it back. Pops left it home that day by accident."

Stuart knew he was on shaky ground with her. Maybe a true gentleman would just hand it over and let it go. One thing was certain: if he didn't return the watch—or sell it back to her—he'd never have a chance at winning her heart. But he had his reasons for wanting it in the first place, and they had nothing to do with the value of the watch or a desire to be stubborn. Unfortunately, he couldn't tell Betsy the reason. And even if he did, she'd never believe him.

"The watch isn't for sale."

"Exactly! It was never for sale. It was a mistake, and you need to sell it back."

He shook his head. "No. Do you still want that job or not?"

"And endure your presence every day? No thank you."

"That's up to you. The offer still stands."

As he walked away, he could almost feel her glare, and he imagined those blue eyes boring into the back of his head. He doubted seriously she would come to work, and part of him was relieved. He could do without hours of daily anger from her.

Now, how on earth was he going to tell Ma that Betsy had been fired and he was the inadvertent cause? She would be furious and insist he give the watch to Betsy.

With a sigh, he shook his head and turned toward home. One woman angry with him was enough. But once Ma joined forces with Betsy, he was in for a very uncomfortable few days.

───────◆───────

Betsy spent a restless night in her room, seething over Stuart's duplicity and her own stupidity. She had actually been sweet on him. Sort of. She had been every kind of fool believing that he cared for her, too. She wrestled with whether or not to go to the store in the morning. How could she look at him every day, knowing what a cad he was?

A knock on her door made her decision for her. She opened it to find Miss Annie standing on the step, frowning her disapproval, still clearly angry. She walked inside without being invited and started to speak without saying hello. "I have reconsidered your position."

Relief flooded over Betsy, nearly buckling her knees. "Thank you—"

Miss Annie cut her off with an upraised palm. "There are conditions, of course. For the next week, you will have no contact with patrons. Rather, you will work in the kitchen only, and I will serve. This means, of course, that you'll need to be at the restaurant thirty minutes earlier each day and will likely have to stay later."

"Yes, ma'am."

"I will also be cutting your pay by one dollar each week."

Betsy gasped. More work for less wages? She barely made ends meet as it was. "Miss Annie, that isn't fair. I know I broke a rule by getting so angry at Mr. Fields. But I assure you there were extenuating circumstances."

"Yes, everyone heard those extenuating circumstances. We all realize that Mr. Fields went to your grandpa's auction and purchased a keepsake that was dear to your heart. While I do have pity for you over that, the fact remains it was not Mr. Fields' fault Old Joe lost everything, nor was he in the wrong for purchasing anything at the auction. He was in the right and did not deserve the sharp edge of your tongue nor a lapful of water."

She narrowed her gaze. "Now, I need your word that you will never speak to a customer that way again. I have never given an employee a second chance like this, and I will expect you to conduct yourself with the gratitude that I most definitely deserve from you. You've done a remarkably good job for me until last night, and considering your circumstances, I find my conscience bothering me over letting you go. Now, make yourself presentable and join me in fifteen minutes to begin breakfast."

She strode across the room and left without another word. Betsy dropped onto her bed, listening to the irritating, persistent clacking of Miss Annie's boots on the steps as she descended.

Replaying the woman's words in her mind, she grew angrier. Miss Annie blamed Old Joe for Stuart's betrayal? Cut her wages by a whole dollar? And pity? And she expected gratitude? Suddenly the entire diatribe seemed so ridiculous, she started to laugh. Flinging herself back on the bed, she grabbed her pillow and pressed it to her face to muffle the sound of her giggles. Tears of mirth streamed from her eyes. What had she become that a bullying woman truly believed she could walk into her room and demand she be grateful for more work, less money, and more rules?

When the laughter finally abated, she sat up, stripped off her nightgown, and dressed for the day. Then she grabbed her bag and packed the few belongings she called her own. She tidied up the room, smoothed the quilts so there was not one wrinkle. She took the broom and swept out every speck of dirt. Below, she heard the thud of the broom handle being knocked against the ceiling to get her attention. She laughed again.

Poor Miss Annie was in for a hectic day.

Betsy glanced around the shining room with a sense of satisfaction. At least the woman couldn't say she left a mess. She slipped on her coat, grabbed her bag and reticule, and headed down the stairs. It was too early to go to the general store. And she hated the thought of explaining her change of heart to Stuart, but she knew he wouldn't turn her away.

The restaurant door flung open as she walked past. "Betsy Lowell, where do you think you're going?"

A pit formed in her stomach. She turned to face her former employer. "Miss Annie, I can't accept your new terms. A dollar less per week isn't acceptable. I have doctor bills to pay for Pops. And I can't be cooped up in that kitchen for that many hours every day. I am grateful that you reconsidered firing me, and I truly apologize for embarrassing you with my outburst last night, but I think it's best if I move on."

The woman's eyes grew wide as she stepped onto the boardwalk and straight to Betsy. For the first time, there was none of the haughty attitude from Miss Annie, only true worry. "Now, Betsy. Perhaps I was a bit hasty in my renegotiation of our arrangement. Come on inside, and we'll go right on like before. We can forget that unfortunate incident occurred last night."

This was certainly a surprising turn of events. For a split second, Betsy considered the offer. After all, there was no guarantee Stuart would hire her, and if he did, Mrs. Fields might be back in two days and then where would she be? Not to mention she now had no place to sleep. Although, Mrs. Avery would likely insist she take the room at their home. She liked the feeling she'd had the past few weeks. The feeling of making her own way, paying her bills, and taking care of Pops.

"Well?" Miss Annie said. "Are you coming?"

"Miss Annie, I'm sorry—"

"Now, Betsy, honey. I know we said we'd go back to how things were. But I can offer you another dollar a week. I think you've certainly proven you are worth a little more than I'd pay other girls, and we'll just call your room part of your wages rather than taking two dollars each week. How would that be?"

She'd be a fool not to take it. Betsy knew the woman was getting desperate. But she had another reason for wanting to have different hours. "I'm grateful."

Miss Annie's face brightened. "Then let's get inside and get to work."

"What I mean to say is that while I'm grateful—and I truly am—my pops isn't doing too well. He's got himself sick with pneumonia, and I need to see him more than a few hours each Sunday. The hours here don't allow me to visit him." And she was terrified he was going to die without her there to soothe him.

Sudden anger flashed in Miss Annie's eyes. "How are you going to find another position? After I tell every business owner in town how you berated a customer and walked out without so much as a day's notice, everyone will see that you're as unreliable as Old Joe."

She'd been about to offer her assistance until seven thirty when she had to be at the store, but no longer. "I've already procured another position. And a roomful of witnesses saw and heard you order me out and tell me never to come back. So I did not just walk out without notice."

"Betsy, I need your help. How will I get through the day alone?"

Compassion rose in Betsy, but after what she'd said about Pops? She wouldn't be stepping foot back inside the restaurant for the rest of her life. Besides, Miss Annie knew all she had to do was put a sign in the window and someone would ask for work. No less than two girls and one gentleman had come in looking for work while Betsy had been there. People were moving into the area all the time, and with winter coming, those who were new to the township would be needing funds to feed their families.

"Oh, never mind. Go, just go." Miss Annie's voice quaked with anger. "Go on. Get out of here." She spun around and hurried back to the restaurant.

Betsy tightened her scarf against the biting wind. Two-and-a-half hours remained before Stuart would be opening the store, but since she had nowhere else to go, she crossed the street and made her way to the boardwalk just outside the store. Wrapping her coat closer, she folded her arms to provide more warmth and sat on the bench by the door. Mercy, the temperature must be below zero. Her face had grown numb while she stood talking to Miss Annie. She couldn't feel her fingers or toes, even with her gloves and boots and thick stockings. Her body began to shiver, and her teeth chattered so hard she was afraid she might break one. She stood and stomped up and down the boardwalk for the next forty-five minutes. The minutes dragged on, and she finally dropped onto the bench again. How long before frostbite set in?

She began to feel more comfortable, warmer, though she knew without the sun, she shouldn't be. Her eyes began to close.

Chapter Nine

A t six o'clock, Stuart stepped up onto the boardwalk two stores down from the general store. He squinted. Horror slapped him as he recognized Betsy's coat. He broke out into a run. What on earth was she doing lying on the bench? Had Miss Annie forced her to leave her room last night? Oh, dear God, had she been on that bench all night?

He shoved his hands into his pocket, retrieved the key to the store, and quickly opened the door. He spun back to Betsy. Lifting her in his arms, he carried her to the bench next to the stove. To his utter relief, she began to stir as he built up the fire. He could only thank God for waking him up early and giving him the idea to come early because it might take awhile to warm the store with the temperature so cold.

"What happened?" Betsy's voice sounded thick and sleepy.

"You went to sleep outside. Don't you know better than that? If I hadn't come along when I did, you could've died out there on that bench."

"Lucky for me you came along then, I guess."

How could she be so obtuse? He wanted to reach out and grab her, pull her into his arms. He went to a shelf across the room and grabbed two blankets. Against her protests, he wrapped her up, then knelt down in front of her and began to unbutton her shoes.

"What do you think you're doing?"

"Getting these boots off before you lose your feet."

"Oh."

He pulled off one boot, then the other, then his face warmed when he realized she was wearing stockings. He turned on his knees and faced the other direction. "You'll need to. . .um."

"What?"

"The stockings."

"You want me to take them off? Why, that—"

"Not proper, I know. That's why my back is turned. I won't look at anything but your feet, but I need to rub the blood back into them." He paused, not hearing movement behind him.

"Betsy, I'm not trying to take any liberties. You have my word. But the temperature is ten degrees below zero, and you fell asleep out in it. You could've died."

"Okay, wait just a minute."

When she allowed him to turn back around, she was covered chin to toes with the blankets. He liked her modesty. Betsy might be stubborn and opinionated and have a quick temper, but she was virtuous. Slowly he reached out, almost afraid to touch her. But he had to get her feet warm—and fast. Taking a deep breath, he lifted one ice-cold foot and began to rub it. She drew in a sharp breath. He ventured a glance at her face. Her bottom lip was firmly between her teeth, and pain burned in her eyes. "I'm sorry this hurts," he said. "But the pain is an indication the blood is flowing. I'm pretty sure it means your feet will be fine. Why were you sitting on the bench? And how long were you out there?"

"Miss Annie fired me last night."

His heart nearly stopped. "You slept on the bench?"

"Of course not. I'm not a fool." She paused. "I'm sorry. I didn't mean to snap at you."

Surprised by the uncommon show of humility, Stuart kept his gaze focused on the task at hand.

"I slept in my room but figured I ought to leave since the room is Miss Annie's. She asked me to come back to the restaurant, but I need to work where I can see Pops more often. He's not doing so well." Her voice broke. "Anyway, I know you might not need me to work for very long, but I was hoping I can go ahead and work with you until your ma comes back."

"As a matter of fact," he said, gently placing her foot on the floor and lifting the other, "Ma isn't coming back." The sound of her pain as he began working on the second foot went straight to his heart.

"Is she all right? I mean, I hope nothing is seriously wrong."

Her concern touched him, and he looked up and smiled. "Doc saw her yesterday and said it's likely arthritis in her hip. He advised her to stop working here since she has to be on her feet for so many hours a day. She flatly refused until I told her last night that you were coming to work at the store."

Betsy's eyes went wide. "But I told you I wasn't going to."

"I hope you'll forgive my presumption, but I figured you'd rethink the idea and see it was for the best."

A slight smile tipped the corners of her lips. "You were right. And I thank you." Her face darkened as she frowned.

"What?"

"I'm still angry about Pops' watch. I mean, I don't understand how on earth you could just go and—" She stopped and gathered a deep, full breath, then exhaled. "I suppose there's no point in dwelling on what I've lost. I'll try not to let it affect how I work here. And. . .I'm grateful for what you're doing now." Her eyes dropped to his hands. "But I think you can stop."

He did so immediately. She reached for her stockings, but he shook his head and stood. "Don't put those back on. They're wet." Walking to another shelf, he picked out the warmest pair of wool stockings he could find and brought them back to her.

She glanced around. Then frowned and looked at him. "Where are my bags?"

Stuart gaped. "I don't know. . . . I carried you in."

"For Pete's sake, I have money in my bag." She stood abruptly, swayed. Stuart sprang forward and grabbed her before she hit the ground. He could feel her breath on his neck. Warmth filled him, and his chest seemed to swell to twice its size as he held her in his arms. Gently, he set her back on the bench.

"I'll go. You stay put."

He barely felt the cold as he stepped outside and retrieved the reticule he'd noted around her wrist before. He spied a larger bag he assumed carried the rest of her meager belongings. How could someone have so little? He wanted to shower her with gowns and ribbons—like the one she'd been eyeing the day of the accident. At the very least, she needed another dress. The one she wore was torn at the bottom, probably from losing so much weight. It dragged the ground when she walked. A girl that looked like Betsy ought to be wearing the best a town like this had to offer.

He walked back, noting the stove had begun to warm the store, and Betsy had shed one of the blankets. She still held on to the socks.

"You planning on holding those all day or putting them on your feet?"

Rolling her eyes, she reached for her reticule. "Thank you." She reached inside and retrieved a dime. He stared at her as she reached out to hand it to him.

"What's that for?"

"My new stockings."

"Take them."

Her gaze narrowed, and he recognized the fire back in her eyes. That was good. She was perking up. "I don't take charity. Remember?"

"Fine." There was just no point in arguing with her. He walked to the drawer with the cash box, unlocked it, and drew the box out. He dropped the dime inside and glanced back at her. "Happy now?"

"Yes." She grinned but kept her focus on him. Finally, she let out an exasperated breath. "Well?"

"Well, what?" Mercy, she could get so snippy.

"Are you going to turn around so I can put these on?"

"Um, yeah. I have some things to do in the back anyway." He escaped to the storage room, grateful to be away from her. How was he supposed to work with her every day, all day? He was going to be a blubbering fool by the end of the week.

Betsy found the work at Fields' General Store barely any work at all compared to the hours and hours of grueling, body-exhausting work at Miss Annie's. She and Stuart hadn't discussed salary, but she couldn't imagine it would be as much as she earned for the backbreaking work at the restaurant. As much as she wished she could make more, she knew she would work here for free if Mrs. Fields and Stuart asked her to. After all, Stuart had saved her life this morning.

When Stuart left to make a delivery, she waited until the store was empty, then pulled the catalog from beneath the counter. She flipped through the pages until she found the one she was looking for. Her stomach sank at the prices for the various styles of rolling chairs. The doctor had said Pops would likely need one, but she would have to save for six months to afford even the lowest-priced chair. Better six months from now than never. The bell clanged, and she left the catalog where it was to help the customer.

For the next hour, a steady stream of customers came in and out of the store. Around noon the bell clanged above the door. Betsy glanced up from filling an order for Maggie Fremont, the local seamstress, and waved at Mrs. Fields. Maggie Fremont had ordered the loveliest soft, light blue material, and lace to put at the collar. Betsy tried not to covet what she knew would be the most beautiful of gowns, but she was afraid she had failed miserably. She certainly couldn't be buying new gowns or material to make her own when Pops needed a rolling chair. Mrs. Fields' entrance into the store gave her something else to think about as the seamstress gathered her goods, instructed Betsy to add it to her account, and said hello to Mrs. Fields just before she left.

It was easy to see Mrs. Fields was moving slowly and favored her hip. Betsy hurried over to her and took the basket she carried. She offered the older woman her arm and led her to a chair by the fire. "Why are you out in this cold, ma'am? Stuart said the weather makes you hurt."

A gentle smile touched the older woman's lips, but she waved away the comment. "My son worries too much. The doc said I couldn't be on my feet all day. He did not say I couldn't be on them at all."

"Well, Stuart had to make a delivery to the doc's office, so he asked me to keep an eye on things."

"You must be a very fast learner for Stuart to trust you so quickly." She cocked her head to one side. "Why didn't he send you on the errand? You could have peeked in on Old Joe."

He had given her the option, but her feet still hurt from nearly freezing and her legs felt as though she'd walked through a thick, deep, muddy mire. All she wanted to do was lie down and sleep. She had tried not to think about where that was going to be. But she knew as a last resort she could bed down in Mr. Mahoney's livery. "It was more practical for him to go. I'll get to see Pops tonight after we close."

"I hope he gets back before the chicken gets cold."

The aroma coming from the basket made Betsy's mouth water. She hadn't thought about what she'd do for lunch. She hadn't eaten since this time yesterday, and her stomach felt hollow.

"What were you looking at in the catalog?" Mrs. Fields asked, glancing at the counter.

Forcing herself to look away from the food, Betsy walked over and closed the book. "Doc says my pops will likely need a rolling chair. I was looking at some."

"I see."

Betsy put the catalog back under the counter, wishing Stuart's lunch didn't smell so good.

"Well, are you going to eat?" Mrs. Fields lifted the towel from the basket she had set on the bench.

"Oh no, ma'am. I don't want to eat Stuart's lunch." Well, she did, but she knew it wouldn't be nice. Especially after he'd saved her this morning and rubbed her feet.

A chuckle came from his ma. "Honey, I made enough for you both. Just consider it part of your wages for working here. Lunch is included."

"H—how much will you be taking from my wages for lunch every day?" Maybe if she just had lunch a couple times a week. If what was in the basket was any indication of the sort of meals Mrs. Fields was going to cook, then she wouldn't have to pay for another meal on those days. This would keep her satisfied until tomorrow.

"Betsy." She lifted the basket and patted the bench next to her. "Come sit down."

"But shouldn't I keep working?"

"Doing what? There are no customers. We'll be slow for the next hour. Everyone is eating lunch right now."

Grateful to be off her feet, Betsy gave a little sigh and dropped down onto the bench. Mrs. Fields handed her a plate and fork and napkin from the basket. "Now, you get as much of that bread and chicken as you can eat. And don't you worry about us deducting pay for this."

Betsy dropped the chicken leg back into the basket. "Oh no, ma'am. I couldn't let you pay me and feed me both."

"You most certainly can. I own this store, and it's my decision what and how much my employees are paid. Speaking of which, has my son explained the terms of your employment?"

Sinking her teeth into the leg, Betsy shook her head and began to chew.

Mrs. Fields frowned. "Mercy. That boy. Well, your salary is eleven dollars a week. Room and board are included. Does that sound fair?"

Betsy was grateful she had swallowed the bite before Mrs. Fields finished, or she surely would have choked on it. "That's too much. I couldn't possibly accept such a high wage for the small amount of work I do. Plus room and board? Mrs. Fields, it sounds like you're feeling sorry for me."

"What? Not at all. We have an extra room and plenty of food, and the salary is fair. If you weren't making twice that working like a servant over at that restaurant, then you were being robbed. As far as food and shelter, if you would feel more comfortable helping out with some of the housework, I will accept it, but it is not necessary."

A sigh of relief worked its way through Betsy's lips. That was an arrangement she could accept. "Thank you, ma'am. Is my room back there?" She jerked her thumb toward the back of the store.

"I should say not. You'll walk home with Stuart and take his sister's room." She lifted her hand. "Now before you say that isn't proper, you should know Stuart stays downstairs. He converted his father's study to a bedroom after he died. He says he feels safer being closer to the front door. As though anyone is going to break in. Your room is upstairs and at the far end of the hall in the opposite direction. Plus, I am just next door to you. No one will think anything of it."

The thought of impropriety had never crossed her mind. She was more worried about what people would think of them walking home from work together. People would talk. At least until the next piece of gossip came along. And there was always something.

Mrs. Fields left a few minutes later after Betsy had finished her lunch. "I'm sorry he hasn't returned yet," Betsy said. "He said he'd be right back."

"It's not of consequence. Tell him to bring back the basket when he closes shop. And I'll see you at home tonight."

Luckily, the store remained mostly empty until Stuart finally returned twenty minutes later. "You missed your ma," Betsy said, nodding toward the basket she had placed on the counter. "She brought us lunch. Although she didn't need to bring me some, too."

"You know her well enough by now to know she enjoys doing things for people. Especially cooking, though she doesn't have nearly as much time since Pa died and she started working here. She'll be happy to start cooking again."

"She already is. The chicken is delicious." She noted he seemed a little tense. "Is everything okay at Doc Avery's?" Fear shoved at her gut. What if something had happened to Pops and Stuart was trying to help? "It's not Pops, is it?"

Stuart shook his head while he wolfed down his food. "That watch. It won't keep time for more than half a day. I thought it was running, but it wasn't. And I lost track of time drinking coffee with Doc and Mrs. Avery."

Betsy gave a snort. "Serves you right. Although Pops never had a problem with it. Maybe the watch just knows it doesn't belong to you."

He rolled his eyes, annoyance evident in his face.

Betsy grinned. Pops actually did occasionally have trouble with the watch. But he knew what to do to keep it running most of the time.

"Wait a minute."

She jerked her chin and stared at him as his sudden words startled her. "What?"

"You know how to fix it."

Betsy averted her gaze. Grabbing the feather duster from the shelf behind the counter, she moved to the shelves and began fluffing it over the already spotless items.

"Betsy Lowell. You do know how to fix my watch."

"It's not your watch."

"Are we going to start this again? I thought we agreed not to let the watch affect how we work together."

She shrugged. "Then perhaps we shouldn't discuss it."

"Are you telling me you won't show me how to keep it working?"

Betsy held the duster in both hands and turned. She looked him square in the eyes. "Not in a million years."

Chapter Ten

Stuart glared at Betsy over the dinner table that night. She was the most ungrateful girl. Here, they had given her a job, a roof over her head, food to eat, and she wouldn't show him how to get his watch running again?

The tension was so thick that finally Ma stopped eating, set her fork and knife down, and stared from one to the other. "All right, you two. What happened?"

"Ask her." He pointed his fork toward Betsy.

Betsy continued to eat, pretending she hadn't heard.

Ignoring his suggestion, Ma frowned at him. "I'm asking you. Did the two of you have words?"

"In a manner of speaking." Stuart slid another bite of roast venison into his mouth.

"What manner?"

Betsy drew a breath and released it as she set her utensils down and pushed back her half-eaten meal. "Mrs. Fields. My pops has a gold watch that everyone in town would recognize. I imagine you've even seen it."

"He *had* a gold watch," Stuart corrected.

"I have seen it, hundreds of times. Old Joe's had that watch as long as I can remember." She cast a sideways glance at Stuart. "Of course, I've seen it a lot more lately than I used to or ever thought I would."

Stuart felt his face warm, but more than embarrassed, he was angry. His mother's words felt like a betrayal, like she was taking someone else's side against his. "I bought it fair and square."

Betsy gave a very unpleasant snort. "I told you Pops never meant to leave that at the cabin. The watch is supposed to be mine on my wedding day. And that's that."

The very mention of Betsy someday getting married conjured up the image of her in a gown of lace, her dark hair piled atop her head. Her beautiful blue eyes staring up at. . .

He shook off the image. He wasn't about to marry the most selfish, unpleasant girl he'd ever met just because she was beautiful.

"Well, if he didn't want to sell it, he shouldn't have left it. It's not my fault I saw the watch and decided to bid on it."

"Oh," Ma's voice jolted Stuart back from his staredown with Betsy. "Oh what, Ma?"

"It's just I didn't realize you happened to see it there. I was under the impression you went to the auction specifically to purchase Old Joe's watch."

"Ha!" Betsy stood and glared down at him. "I knew it. You—coveter. You've been wanting that watch for years. Why, that practically makes you an idolater. In that watch alone you've broken at least two of the commandments—three if you count robbery."

Stuart stood as well. "I did not break any of the commandments over that watch. And if you cared about what the Bible has to say, you'd fix my watch."

Ma's laughter fueled his anger, but Betsy didn't seem to notice.

"Oh, is there a passage about blessed are those who fix a robber's watch?" Her voice rose. "Because I'd like to see it if there is." She turned to his ma, her voice still raised. "Thank you for dinner, ma'am. I'll just clean these dishes and go to bed."

Stuart tossed his napkin on the table. "Good night, Ma."

As he walked away, Betsy called after him. "You might want to check the sitting room clock in the morning. Wouldn't want to be late to the store like you were at lunch."

He slammed out of the house and onto the porch into the cold night.

———————◆———————

Early the next day, Mrs. Avery came to the store and invited Betsy to dinner. After a tension-filled day, Betsy was only too relieved to avoid another dinner with Stuart staring daggers at her. Mrs. Avery opened the door for her and greeted her warmly. "Just in time to see your grandpa awake for a while."

Betsy pulled on her scarf until it came free, and shrugged out of her coat. "How's he doing?"

"The doc says he's doing better. The fluid in his lungs seems to be breaking up."

Relief flooded over her. She tapped on his door and went in. For the first time since the accident more than a month ago, Pops was out of bed. He sat up in a rolling chair next to a table. Doc sat across from him, and they were playing checkers. Tears sprang to her eyes. Perhaps Pops truly was going to keep getting better.

"Well, look at you. Where'd that chair come from?"

Pops' face brightened like a candle. "Ain't you a sight for sore eyes."

"Thank heaven you came when you did," Doc said, his lips curved in a wry smile. "Your pops here has beaten me three out of five games and was just about to beat me again. If I don't leave soon, I may never have the confidence to play checkers again." He waved toward the chair. "As for that. Someone in town didn't need it anymore and showed up here with it. Said to give it to anyone who might need it."

"That was kind. If you'll tell me who left it, I'll just go by and pay them for it."

The doctor scowled as he made a move and Pops jumped the piece. He was still frowning when he looked up at Betsy as though she were the reason he was about to lose the game. "I said they wanted to donate it. And they did it anonymously, so I couldn't tell you if I wanted to."

Doc made another move, and Pops jumped his pieces four times. "And that makes it four out of six." He began collecting the pieces and slid them into a tin container. "You're a good player. That's for sure."

"It's all the practice he gets with Mr. Mahoney at the general store."

"Speaking of that," the doctor said, standing and offering her his chair. "Mrs. Avery says you are working at Fields' now. How do you like it?"

"Fine, thank you."

"Well, I'm sure you'll enjoy having more time to see your grandpa."

"Yes, sir." Which was the only reason she hadn't gone running straight back to Miss Annie after last night's blowup over dinner.

As soon as the doctor left the room, Pops narrowed his gaze, scrutinizing her with his sharp senses. He always knew when something was wrong. Even now. "Tell me everything."

She started with the way she discovered the watch and then got dismissed from the restaurant. Shamefaced, she told him about Stuart bringing her inside and rubbing the blood back into her feet.

Pops scowled. "You mean to tell me you let yourself get caught in the cold? I taught you better than that."

"I didn't know what else to do. Where was I supposed to go? I had to wait for Stuart to show up."

"You could've come here. The Averys are up at five every morning, and you know that."

"I was just so upset I didn't think."

"Well, can't help but admire a man who saves a girl's life and then her toes."

Betsy's cheeks heated up at the memory. He had been so gentle and so kind and generous with the stockings and blankets. But that didn't excuse his refusal to sell her back the watch.

"So the Fields boy got the watch." Pops scrubbed at the stubble on his chin.

"Yes, and there's no point in trying to buy it back from him. He's being a mule."

"Seems to me you're a little sweet on that mule." He shook his head. "Can't say I'm surprised."

"You think I'm sweet on Stuart Fields, the thief? Are you daft, Pops?"

"I might be daft, but I'm not blind. And even though you're spittin' mad at him, your eyes brightened up when you talked about the way he saved you. By the way, didn't he save your honor at the cabin one day?"

"Yes," Betsy mumbled. She was humiliated that she had suddenly turned into the sort of woman who needed rescuing. She'd always been able to take care of herself.

"Well, if you marry him, seems to me you'd have the watch anyhow. So why fuss about it?"

Betsy gasped. "What are you saying? That I should just forget that the watch was supposed to go to me? A watch that has been in our family for over one hundred years? That your pa gave you and you gave to my pa? Why, it's all I'm going to have left of my family once you're gone."

"Well, I ain't planning to go anywhere soon."

Betsy gave a short laugh and took his hand, covering it in both of hers. "You almost went to glory just a few weeks ago. So you never know the day God'll call you home."

Pops frowned. "When did you get religious?"

Betsy shrugged. "You know Miss Annie made me go to church. I guess I sort of like the feel of it. Of course, if they let people like Stuart in, maybe it's not such a nice place, after all."

"Girl, I think I best come clean about something." He shifted in the chair and cleared his throat, then turned his gaze on her. "It ain't going to be easy to hear."

"About what, Pops?" Surely it couldn't be worse than telling her they had lost the farm.

"That watch you're so upset about."

Upset about? Her anger went so far beyond upset. She felt betrayed, heartsick, enraged every time she saw Stuart pull the watch out of the cash drawer where he kept it during the day. Her only consolation was that each time he looked at it, he scowled, so she knew it still wasn't keeping the time. He might have the watch in his possession, but he certainly wasn't enjoying it.

"What about the watch?"

"I might have told a bit of a falsehood about how long it's been in the family."

Was that all? Relief flooded over her. Old Joe was known for his exaggerations. This was nothing new. "That's nothing, Pops. And it's beside the point now."

"But it wasn't so much a legacy piece. I sort of came by it on my own."

Betsy frowned. "What are you saying? You didn't get that when you married Grandma?"

"Well, I got it the night before I married her. But not from my pa." He gave a short laugh. "Only thing my pa gave me was a lickin' every other day and not enough to eat till I got tired of it and ran away from home at seventeen years old."

"But you said you lived in a big house back East next to the ocean and left without a penny because you wanted to make your own way in the world."

"That's a lot more interesting than what really happened, ain't it?"

"Pops!"

"Fact is, I was born and raised in Kentucky. Grew up in a little log cabin with six brothers—all crammed into the loft. We ate coon and possum and chewed tobacco by the time we was six."

Mercy. "Everything I know about you is a lie. Why not tell the truth?"

"What do you think I'm doing now?"

"Only because you think you're going belly up in the grave soon." Outrage flooded through her like one of those big waves he used to tell her about—but apparently had never seen.

"It don't matter why I'm owning up, just that I am. Besides, what I want to tell you about is the watch."

"You just did. It isn't a legacy."

"Turns out, it was a legacy."

"Good gracious, Pops, you're making my head hurt."

"So hush a minute and let me finish." He coughed deeply, holding on to his cracked ribs. "The watch. . .night before the wedding, Old Mr. Fields drank a bit much at the saloon."

"Tucker's Creek doesn't have a saloon."

"Not since all the womenfolk came to town." He shook his head. "Town went downhill mighty fast once Tuck brought his family here and got a preacher involved in building things. But back then the saloon was a tent sitting where the church is now." He peered closer at her. "They did that on purpose."

"Okay. So you were in the saloon tent, and Stuart's pa got drunk?"

Pops shook his head. "Not his pa, his pa's pa. Three of us came to town together. Tuck stepped foot on the land first, that's why we named the town for him. Then me, then Robert Fields. We all grew up together in Kentucky. Was heading to California but got tired of travel and decided to settle here. Besides, Fields was missing his wife something awful. They'd only been hitched a few weeks when he left to make his fortune out West."

"He did pretty well with the store."

Pops nodded. "That he did."

"What about the watch?"

"It were Fields' pa that came to Kentucky from the ocean. His folks came over from England not long after the War for Independence. They had more money than they knew what to do with. But Robert's pa didn't want that hoity-toity life, so he traveled as far as Kentucky and settled. His pa—Robert's grandpappy—give him the gold watch before he left. So it is a legacy, just not yours. That watch came from Stuart's great-grandpappy."

"How'd you get it?" Betsy gasped. "Pops! You didn't steal it?"

He shoved his finger toward her, anger flashing in his blue eyes. "I might be a liar, but I ain't no thief. And you know it good and well."

"But I didn't know you were a liar until ten minutes ago." A truth-stretcher, to be sure, but to flat-out lie about the only thing she'd really ever counted on? Her legacy? No, it was Stuart's. That must have been why he was so keen on buying the watch. "Just...tell me how you came by the watch."

"Obviously, I won it in a game of poker. Robert got so likkered up he wouldn't stop playing, even though he went through all his money. And he knew I'd always had my eye on that watch so he threw it in the pot. Thought he had a winning hand with three queens." Pops grinned. "Had me a full house. He was madder than a big fat wet hen. The next day he accused me of tricking him out of it. But enough folks had seen me win it fair and square to protect my honor, so I didn't have to shoot him. Course, if I had shot him, you'd still have the watch, 'cause Stuart wouldn't have been around to go buy it out from under us."

"That's an awful thing to say!" She couldn't imagine her life without Stuart. They'd known each other since they were small children. They'd never exactly liked each other, but he was a fixture in her life—like the general store and the church. And she'd been just awful to him about a watch that he deserved as much as she did—more, really. He'd obtained

101

it in a much more honorable way than Pops had gotten the watch from Stuart's grandpa. With a sigh, she sat back in the chair.

Stuart and Mrs. Fields would be gone the next couple of days. With Betsy at the store, Mrs. Fields believed it was a good time to go visit her sister in Topeka.

While they were gone, Betsy knew what she had to do.

Chapter Eleven

Stuart couldn't believe how much he'd missed Betsy over the past two days. They'd left things tense between them. As he rolled into town, he wanted to go straight to the store and see her, under pretense of checking on things of course, but he had to take Ma home and get her settled into bed with a hot-water bottle first. Her hip was hurting her something awful after the long drive.

"It was sure nice to see Ellie, but gracious I'm glad to be home," she said as they pulled up in front of the house. She glanced at him as he helped her from the buggy. "I guess you're pretty glad to be home, too."

Stuart knew exactly what she was getting at.

"You know, Betsy has every right to be angry about that watch."

"Ma..."

"I'm not saying you didn't buy it fair and square—although you know how I feel about your going to the auction in the first place." She winced as she put weight on her hip, and her movement was halting as they headed up the steps. Silently, she concentrated on getting up to the porch, but as soon as he opened the door, she resumed her conversation. "The fact is, Betsy was counting on getting that watch as a gift the day she got married. Old Joe gave it to her pa and promised it to her."

"So she said the other night."

"Yes, but I don't think you realize just how much something like that means to someone like Betsy. She lost her parents when she was still a child. Losing that watch was like losing the only thing she had left of her pa."

"I know, Ma." All he had thought about the past two days were Betsy's words about inheriting that watch. He warmed the water on the stove while Ma climbed the steps to her room, leaning heavily on the wooden rail. Once he had filled the hot-water bottle and made sure she was settled in, he headed toward the livery to leave the horse and buggy. By the time he reached the store, Betsy had closed up for the day.

That was almost better, he thought. This way, he could do what he planned to do without her looking on, glaring at him. He pulled out his key and opened the door, heading straight for the cash drawer. When he opened the drawer, he noted Betsy had locked up the cash box inside. He smiled that she'd remembered. Then he looked over the rest of the drawer, pulled it out farther, and ran his hand over the inside.

The watch was gone. Anger once more lit a fire inside of him. There could be only one explanation.

He slammed the drawer shut, left the store, and walked home, anger propelling him. Once inside, he stomped up the steps and past Ma's room.

"That you, Son?"

"Yes." He turned the doorknob and shoved open the door to Betsy's room.

"What are you doing?"

Without answering, he opened the top dresser drawer. Predictably, she had hidden the stolen watch there. He snatched it up and strode into his ma's room.

"What on earth were you doing in Betsy's room? She is entitled to her privacy."

"Is she entitled to our things as well?" He held out the watch.

"What are you saying?"

"It was in her room. Hidden away in her drawer."

Ma's face drained of color. "Oh, my. . .I never would have believed."

"Well, believe it. The proof is right here. There's no telling what else she's stolen. I'm going back to search her room."

Ma sat up straighter in bed. "You'll do nothing of the kind. There has to be an explanation, and we are going to give that girl the benefit of the doubt."

"Ma, there is no doubt. Betsy has bills to pay, so she helped herself to our things."

"Have you forgotten this is the same Betsy who sold her horses and came straight to the store to settle a two-year-old account? She has much more integrity than you are giving her credit for."

Stuart held the watch tight and paced the room, silently fuming.

His mother got out of bed and slowly walked toward him. "I'm assuming Betsy is at Doc's. Let's just calm down and eat a light meal while we wait for her to come home."

Ma fixed fried ham slices and eggs, and they ate fresh bread that Betsy must've baked while they were gone. It was better than Stuart wanted to admit. How could Betsy have stolen the watch from him? Disappointment drove his anger. He had truly believed she was better than that. He felt foolish for all the feelings he'd been having. The thoughts and plans. The dreams for his future that included Betsy Lowell. Somehow, without even realizing it, he had fallen in love with her. And she had done this?

"I think we ought to go see the sheriff," he said.

"Under no circumstances will you go to the sheriff about this. Even if Betsy did steal the watch, which I find difficult to believe, we will settle it between the three of us. Is that clear?"

"I bought it. It belongs to me. Now, I don't mean to be disrespectful. You know I love you, Ma. But if there's a thief in town, she needs to be dealt with through the legal system."

Ma glared at him. "Would you just listen to yourself? Do you even realize how ridiculous you're being? Now, you're right. The watch is your property, and she apparently took it for some reason. Did it occur to you that maybe she just wanted to have something familiar close to her and took it home while we were gone? You certainly didn't need it. You left it behind."

Stuart tried not to consider Ma's words. He wanted to hang on to his anger so that when she walked through the door his heart didn't cause him to lose all common sense. But Ma's idea did seem reasonable. More reasonable than his suspicion, the more he thought about it. He and Ma had just finished eating when Betsy strode inside.

She stopped short at the sight of them. "I didn't expect you back until tomorrow." She swallowed hard and glanced from one to the other nervously. "If you'll excuse me, I'll just go to my room."

"Wait." Stuart stood, ready to confront her right then and there. She wasn't acting like someone who was innocent.

But Ma spoke before he could pull the watch from his pocket and demand an explanation. "Of course we'll excuse you."

"Thank you, Mrs. Fields." Her face was flushed as she hurriedly walked to his ma, kissed her cheek. "Welcome back to you both." She barely glanced at Stuart.

As the sound of her steps faded away, Stuart turned to Ma. "You see? Guilty as the day she was born." He tossed his napkin on the table and went after her. He was getting to the bottom of this. And whether Ma liked it or not, thieves belonged in jail.

———————◆———————

It was gone! A thief must've broken into the house while she was at the store. Everyone knew Stuart had taken his mother away for a couple of days. Fear clutched at her throat. How on earth was she going to tell Stuart? The watch meant so much to him.

The door opened without a knock, and she spun around. Stuart stood at the threshold. He leaned against the doorframe and nodded toward the open drawer. "Looking for something?"

Betsy frowned. Why did his voice sound so strange? She shoved the drawer closed. "Yes, as a matter of fact, I am."

"Really? What are you looking for?"

She couldn't tell him that until she found it, could she? She needed to get away from him and go report this to the sheriff. "What are you doing in my room? This isn't proper."

"It's my house." He gave such a nonchalant shrug, she knew something was very wrong.

"Did something happen while you were gone? Is your ma okay?"

"Ma is fine." He shoved his hand into his pocket. "But something did happen. Only it happened here, not in Topeka."

Growing annoyed with his cryptic answers, Betsy walked toward him and took hold of the door. "You're acting odd. I have no idea what you're talking about, so either say what's on your mind or get out of my room before I call your mother."

Stuart gave an unpleasant laugh, and Betsy began to grow uneasy. Was he going to try to take liberties? After he had saved her from Leo Blakely and saved her from freezing, did he feel like she owed him something improper? She took a step back. "Stuart, I think you'd better go. Please."

His eyes widened. "For the love of. . . I'm not thinking. . . that, Betsy." He drew in a heavy breath and released it quickly. In a swift movement he pulled his hand out of his pocket, and suddenly it all became clear. He believed she had stolen his watch.

"Explain this." His voice was so gruff, so angry, she took another step back.

"I was going to put it back before you got home."

"Really? And what else have you taken that you intended to return? Or did you plan to sell the silver?"

Shock zipped through Betsy at his implication. "You're calling me a thief?"

The words were barely audible around the sudden lump in her throat.

"What else am I to believe?"

Spinning on her heels, Betsy went straight to the wardrobe, flung it open, and yanked out her bag. She opened the clasp, turned it upside down, and shook with all her might. "See? No silver." She walked to the dresser and yanked out every drawer, letting them land how they would on the floor. "Nothing there. Except. . ." Embarrassed, she snatched up her nightclothes and extra underthings and stuffed them in her empty bag.

"What are you doing?"

"What does it look like?" she snapped back. "I'm showing you there's nothing in here for you to accuse me of stealing."

"I meant why are you packing?"

"I should think that would be obvious. You certainly don't want someone under your roof you don't trust. And I wouldn't live under the same roof with a fool who would call me a thief." Her breaths came fast and heavy from the exertion and fast talking. She'd never been so angry in her life.

"You called me a thief!"

"Well, you are. . ." She scowled. "I'm sorry for that. You bought the watch. It's yours fair and square, like you said."

His eyebrows rose in apparent surprise. "Where do you think you're going to go?"

"Anywhere is better than here."

"Betsy Lowell." At the sound of Mrs. Fields' voice, Betsy stopped all movement, all speaking. The room spun from the sudden stop, and she dropped to the floor, exhausted.

"Mrs. Fields," she said, "I did not steal that watch. I was just—"

"You don't have to explain. Of course you haven't stolen anything."

"Ma," Stuart stepped into the room. "She hasn't stolen anything else, but she clearly did take the watch. I found it in her drawer."

"When you had no business being in her room in the first place. What sort of man are you?"

"A man looking for his watch," he said dryly. "And I found it. In her dresser. Would I have ever gotten it back if I hadn't come looking for it?" He addressed his question to Betsy.

Slowly, wearily, she stood up and snatched her bag and reticule from the bed. "Yes. I planned to give it to you tomorrow. But when I saw you had returned, I came upstairs to retrieve it."

She walked to the door and met him at the threshold. They stood so close, she could feel the warmth coming from him. Sorrow seeped from every ounce of her body. How could the man she had grown to love believe such terrible things of her?

"Betsy, where are you going?" Mrs. Fields asked.

"Mrs. Avery has said I can stay there. I'll do that tonight. Tomorrow I'll go back to Miss Annie, hat in hand. She hasn't found anyone yet."

"Oh, Betsy, don't go. Stuart is sorry."

Betsy looked up into Stuart's brown eyes. He did indeed look as though he regretted being so hasty. But it was too late.

"Good-bye. Thank you both for everything you've done for me."

Without another word, she squared her shoulders, trying to find an ounce of dignity. She descended the steps and found her coat and scarf where she'd left them hanging from the hook by the door.

"Betsy, wait."

"No."

She opened the door, unwilling to turn and show Stuart the tears streaming down her face. But he was unrelenting and followed her to the porch. He stepped quickly around her and took her by the arms. There was no point in fighting. She looked into his eyes. He sucked in a breath as he studied her face. "Betsy Lowell, I believe you. But I still don't know why you had the watch. I. . .was looking for it at the store tonight. I wanted to give it to you. When I didn't see it there, I thought. . ."

Tears flowed harder and she didn't even care. Let him know that he had hurt her. That she'd begun to care about him, had dreamed of becoming his wife. "That was kind of you. I guess we both had the same thought."

"What do you mean?"

Placing her hand flat against his chest, she offered a trembling smile. "Your watch is fixed."

While he was recovering from the surprise of her words, she quickly disengaged from his arms and descended the steps.

Chapter Twelve

Stuart stared out the window at Miss Annie's trying desperately to catch a glimpse of Betsy. She'd been back there for three weeks, and his mother refused to eat there and shamed him into staying away himself.

"That girl has made it clear that she wants nothing to do with you—not that I blame her. If you want any chance to get her back, you best respect her wishes."

He'd even tried to give her the wages she had earned in the few days she'd worked at the store, but she'd sent it back three times.

The winter dance was tonight, and he'd sent her a note asking her to attend with him. But he'd never received an answer. He supposed he deserved what he got, but he missed her dreadfully, and if there were any doubts in his mind about the way he felt, these past weeks had driven them from his heart. He was in love with Betsy and would remain a bachelor the rest of his life if she didn't relent and give him a second chance.

Miss Annie always closed the restaurant for the town dances. There was no need to stay open. Besides, she enjoyed dressing up and dancing, herself. So Stuart knew Betsy wouldn't have to work.

He pulled his watch out of his pocket. It had kept perfect time since Betsy fixed it. He'd accused her of stealing it, but every time he looked at it, he felt like he'd taken something that didn't belong to him. Betsy or no Betsy, he'd never have a moment's peace until he did the right thing.

"Ma, I'll be back in a few minutes."

From the chair next to the fire, she nodded. "I'll be fine."

Betsy peeked out the window. "Miss Annie, he's gone. I'm going to run across the street."

"That's fine. Don't be long. We need to hurry with these dishes so we can get ready for the dance."

"Yes, ma'am." The last three weeks had been like working in a completely different place from the first time Betsy worked at the restaurant. Miss Annie had been so happy to have her back she actually gave her the raise in wages she had proposed the day she tried to keep Betsy from leaving. The work was still backbreaking, but it was more bearable.

Mrs. Fields' face lit up when she saw Betsy walk through the door. "You just missed Stuart." She paused. "But I suppose you know that, don't you?"

"Yes."

Mrs. Fields struggled to get up, but Betsy waved her back to her seat. "I know how to get what I want and pay for it."

She walked straight to the ready-made dresses.

"Get the red velvet," Mrs. Fields said.

"You don't think it's too. . .much?"

"Oh, honey. It's a Christmas dance. There'll be a lot of red and green." She got up despite Betsy's protests. "And you must have the ribbon as well."

Betsy's face warmed. "I'm afraid I have only the price of the dress."

"You will not pay one dime for either. And go over and pick out new stockings and a pair of those ladies' boots."

"I'll do no such thing."

"Yes you will. We owe you for the days you worked here. I know you won't take our money, and I can't say I blame you after the way you were accused, but these things have been in the store for months, and I always meant for you to have this gown. Remember how I told you red is your color?"

Betsy smiled. "Yes, ma'am, I do."

"For me. Take these, and be the belle of this dance."

Betsy gave her a quick hug. "I'll tell you what. I will take these things if you will go back and sit down and let me get them all wrapped up."

Reaching out, Mrs. Fields pressed her palm to Betsy's cheek. "Consider giving my son a second chance. He's finally realized that he loves you."

Drawing in a breath, Betsy felt her eyes go wide. "He said that?"

"He doesn't have to. He's only had eyes for you since he was a little boy." She smiled and moved her hand. "And unless I miss my guess, you love him, too."

Betsy averted her gaze.

"It's okay, dear. No need to say it. But if he asks you to dance tonight, don't let your pride keep you from saying yes."

Stuart walked into Old Joe's room and promptly felt the anger coming from the old man. "What are you doing here?"

"I've come to talk to you."

He scowled. "Well, if you think you're getting my blessing to ask for Betsy's hand after what you accused her of, you're an ignoramus."

"That's not why I've come. Although I'd marry her tomorrow if she'd have me, I know I did the unforgivable. But if you'll allow me just a couple of minutes, I'd appreciate it."

"Fine. Two minutes. And don't sit down."

Stuart pulled the watch from his pocket and set it on the table next to the bed. "I want to give this back."

Old Joe's eyes narrowed. "What sort of game you playing, son? You think this'll get you my granddaughter? Because I won't even tell her."

He shook his head. "No. But Betsy told me you never meant to leave the watch behind."

"That's the truth. But since I did, and you bought it, it belongs to you."

"Technically, I know." He grinned. "But the fact is, you won it from my grandfather, and it should never have even been at the auction for me to buy."

A grin reached Old Joe's lips. "You know about that, eh?"

"My pa told me years ago. He wanted that old watch badly. I think that's why I wanted it so much. But it was promised to Betsy, and she's always counted on having it on her wedding day. I don't want to take that away from her."

The old man gave a short laugh. "So you think after this, Betsy'll forgive you and marry you and you'll have the watch anyway."

"Well, I can't say that's not a hope. But the truth is, I want her to have it on her wedding day, no matter who she marries."

Old Joe nodded. "Okay, boy. If you're sure that's the way you want it."

"It is. It's the right thing to do."

———————◆———————

Betsy entered the schoolroom-turned-dance-floor with Miss Annie. She tried not to look for Stuart but found it difficult to hide her disappointment when she didn't see him among the dancers or along the walls. "Don't worry. He'll be here," Miss Annie said. She nodded toward the refreshment table. "Look."

Betsy caught her breath at the sight of Stuart in a fresh black suit.

"He's as handsome as his father." Miss Annie's voice held such sadness, Betsy turned to her.

"In another life, Stuart might have been my son. His pa and I courted at one time, but he loved Nan from the day she stepped off the stage to teach school. I tried to win him back, but it was no use."

"Well, it won't be that way for Stuart and me."

"Don't be a fool. What he did was wrong, but he's apologized and tried to make it right. Don't let your pride keep you from love." She nudged Betsy's arm. "Someone wants to speak to you."

Following her gaze, Betsy noted Mrs. Fields waving her over to a group of chairs close to the refreshments. She hesitated only a moment, then headed her way as Miss Annie moved toward a group of older women.

Mrs. Fields looked lovely in deep brown velvet that brought out the color of her eyes. "You look lovely, ma'am."

"Why, thank you." She glanced over Betsy's shoulder. "Did I see you come in with that woman?"

Betsy turned and followed her gaze to Miss Annie. "It's too bad she never got married. She's a good person."

A snort left Mrs. Fields. "A man-hungry woman if I ever saw one."

Betsy leaned close and pressed a kiss to her cheek. Then spoke close to her ear. "Don't be too hard on her, ma'am. You had the life she thought she'd have. And let me tell you, she only says the kindest things about you and Stuart."

Her eyebrows rose. "Is that so?"

"Yes, ma'am. It is."

Mrs. Fields took Betsy's hand as she stood up. "You're as beautiful as I knew you'd be. And the ribbon woven through your hair is perfect."

Betsy reached up and touched the ribbon. "Thank you."

Behind her, she heard a man's voice: "Excuse me, miss."

Her belly fluttered as she turned, then her heart sank. "Good evening, Mr. Carter."

"May I have this dance, Miss Lowell?"

She couldn't think of a polite way to refuse, so she nodded. "I'm honored."

For the next two hours, she danced with one man after another. Young men, older men with graying temples looking for a young wife, even a few boys who she had a feeling asked her on a dare. Everyone, it seemed, except for Stuart. He hadn't so much as looked at her for the entire dance. She finally gathered the courage to refuse a request for the last dance, and as the violins began to play she went to the refreshment table and requested a glass of punch.

When she felt a warm hand at her elbow, she knew before she turned that it was Stuart. "Will you honor me with the last dance, Miss Lowell?"

She nodded, and he took the cup from her hand and set it on the table. Silently, he led her onto the dance floor. It seemed as though she melted into his arms, fitting perfectly as he began to move to the music. "You're the most beautiful woman here tonight."

"Thank you. And you're the most dashing man."

He smiled, she smiled in return, and the tension seemed to fall away as though they'd never argued.

"I went to see Pops tonight before I came here. He's never seen me dressed up."

"And did he tell you how lovely you look?"

Betsy laughed at the memory of her grandpa's scowl. "He told me I looked positively indecent and if he had the use of both his arms and both his legs he'd hog-tie me and keep me in."

Stuart threw back his head and laughed. "Somehow that doesn't surprise me."

"He told me you went to see him earlier."

Stuart's face darkened. "He said he wasn't going to say anything."

"You shouldn't have given him the watch."

"It was never meant to be mine."

"But that's not true, Stuart. It came from your family in the first place."

"If only my grandpa could've beaten a full house."

Betsy rolled her eyes. "If I know Pops, half those cards probably came from his sleeve."

Stuart chuckled and turned her on the floor. She wished the music would go on forever and ever. A man approached, tapping Stuart on the shoulder to cut in. Ever the gentleman, Stuart reluctantly stepped back, but Betsy had waited too long for this dance and she had no intention of cutting it short. She looked at Mr. Carter. "I'm sorry, but I want to dance with him."

Both men showed surprise on their faces, then Stuart stepped back up and took her in his arms. "Sorry, Jonathon. Lady's choice."

He turned to Betsy. "That was an unexpected honor."

Betsy drew a deep breath, determined that she would never again let her pride get the better of her where Stuart was concerned. "The truth is, I came here tonight only to dance with you. If you'd asked me first, I never would have accepted an invitation from another man."

Much to Betsy's disappointment, the music ended just then, and the room erupted in applause for the band. Annoyance showed on Stuart's face. He glanced around, then grabbed her hand. "Come on." Grabbing their coats, he took her outside into the schoolyard.

He placed a hand on either of her arms and looked down into her eyes with such intensity, she almost couldn't breathe. "Say it again."

Betsy refused to play coy. She knew exactly what he wanted to hear. "The truth is," she said, returning his gaze, "I came here tonight only to dance with you. If you'd asked me first—"

His face descended, and his lips pressed against hers, warm and firm. He slipped his arms around her waist and pulled her closer as her arms reached up, hands clasping behind his neck. She lost all sense of time, and they stayed that way until they heard the door open. Then slowly, they pulled apart.

"I'm taking you home."

"What about your ma? Besides, Miss Annie won't allow gentleman callers, remember?" It was one thing for her to allow a few dances. Another for her to change her entire set of rules.

"Hang on. Stay here." She watched him walk inside, and when he returned a moment later, he took her elbow, and they began to walk.

"What about Miss Annie?"

"She agreed to my walking you home. As a matter of fact, she said we can go into the restaurant for pie."

"I don't believe it!"

He held up a key. "She gave me this."

"Well, let's go." She stopped short.

"What?" Stuart asked.

"Your ma? We forgot about her."

He grinned, shaking his head. "Miss Annie is driving her home in my buggy. They were together when I went inside. It was my ma's idea. Must be a Christmas miracle."

Grinning, she slipped her hand into the crook of his arm and took a step forward, but he didn't budge. "Is something wrong?"

He nodded. "I don't want to wait."

"What are you talking about? Wait for what?"

"I was going to ask you to marry me when I took you home, but I can't wait that long to ask you."

Betsy's heart raced, and she stepped close to him. "Yes."

Leaning forward, he pressed his forehead to hers and pulled her closer. "Are you sure?"

"Well, we haven't actually courted yet, so I'm not sure it's all that proper."

"Oh, Betsy Lowell. I've been courting you since the first time I dipped your hair ribbon in ink."

"Is that what you were doing?"

"Of course. Couldn't you tell I was sweet on you?"

She smiled. "If I'd known, I wouldn't have given you a fat lip for your trouble."

"It was worth it. I'm just glad it's healed now."

Betsy allowed him to pull her even closer, and just before his head came down, she whispered, "Why's that?"

"Why do you think?"

Then his lips were on hers once more.

When he pulled away, they smiled at each other. Betsy widened hers into a teasing grin. "You know what this means, of course."

"What's that?"

"We'll be sharing the watch."

"As it should be."

Betsy's mind whirled with questions. Where would they live? What about Pops? Would she work at the store? Should she continue her position at Miss Annie's until the wedding? When would the wedding be? But she wanted to savor this moment.

"What are you thinking about?"

"It's not important right now."

"Are you sure?"

"I'm sure. I'd rather you kiss me again."

Lowering his head, he obliged.

All the things she had thought about fled her mind. They could discuss them later.

They had plenty of time.

Tracey Bateman is a prolific writer of more than forty novels. She has more than a million books in print and has won numerous awards, including the prestigious Christy Award for Excellence in 2010. Tracey makes her home in the beautiful Missouri Ozarks with her husband and four children.

Something New

Joanne Bischof

Chapter One

Blue Ridge Mountains, Virginia
Spring 1893

Wren knew this earth. It would always be here. Tucked in the hollow where the sugar maples grew and the breeze blew easy over the western ridge, this mountain ground had yet to fail her. If she planted, tended, and pulled, it would sustain and provide. Kneeling against the poky garden gate, she tugged a weed from the soil and set the spindly leaves in her willow basket, then searched for another.

Her hands were as quick as her hope of getting the garden weeded and the lettuce seeds planted before chores. With a day of laundry still ahead, Wren was glad no patrons had occupied the guest room this week. Though it meant fewer towels and sheets for her to wash, it also meant less income for her family. And that they dearly needed. Not nearly as thankful as she'd been a moment ago, she sat back on her heels and reached for the tattered seed packet.

Her grandmother had sent the seeds all the way from England along with a note of planting instructions almost a year ago. As had always been their little pastime. *Rouge d'hiver*, the packet read. A European variety that Wren had never seen before, which, of course, was all the fun about trading seeds with her grandmother.

Wren poked at the soil with her spade, suddenly fighting the melancholy of all those lost to her. First her beloved father. Then her spry grandmother; the woman she'd only been able to love from afar. And then there was Tate. Her. . .her. . .

Stomach just about flipping at the thought of *her best*—until the day he abandoned her—*friend*, Wren reminded herself of the many reasons she'd set that girlish fancy aside. Yet as she unearthed another weed, pulling out the old, moving on with the new, she whispered a prayer that he was still safe—wherever he was.

Wren tried to check a sigh, but it slipped out all the same. Her time here, where uneven pickets held the garden snug against the log cabin, was often the only moment of solitude she would have through the day. The cabin, no more than a humble *ordinary*—wasn't large enough to be an inn. It was simply a dwelling for travelers in need if they had mere coins to spare. And with its three little rooms and cramped loft, it had always been home.

Knowing her minutes in the garden were nearly spent, Wren savored the warmth of the sun on her shoulders. This place of refuge and quiet—especially with twin brothers to look after. And with the sound of footsteps drawing near, it was about to come to an end.

"Hello, Little Bird," said a deep, smooth voice.

Wren froze. A gasp caught the air in her chest, and she clamped her mouth shut. *That* was not one of her brothers. Stomach utterly flipping, heat rushed her cheeks. Then down to her toes. Eyes trained on the dark soil, she couldn't lift them. She knew that nickname. No one had called her that since she was a girl. Slowly she looked up.

Tate Kennedy peered down on her.

Short hair shoved back haphazardly, the faint shadow of a beard on his jaw, he smiled pensively. Not the lighthearted grin she'd always known.

She'd heard distant rumors of his coming—but like snatching leaves on the breeze, she hadn't been able to catch hold of much. No hope of heart, she'd written it all off.

For folk had speculated before.

Unable to pull her gaze from his face, she slid her hands from the dirt, wiping them absently on her apron as she rose. "Where have you been?" she asked weakly as if the phrase weren't common—what you asked when someone had been gone since breakfast.

It wasn't that simple, and they both knew it, for his expression seemed pained.

He cleared his throat. "I was in Norway."

She couldn't keep the shock from her voice. "Norway."

"And other various countries." Amusement flitted through his expression.

She drank in the sight of his face. The face she'd clung to in her memories. Her mouth opened, then closed. "For four years." She cursed the ache that lived in her voice.

He blinked slowly, then pulled off his glasses. She'd only known him to need them while reading, and now, having a clear view of his brown eyes, she couldn't look away.

"How did you end up there?" Her words slipped out sounding strange, emotionless. Though the question was anything but.

He glanced around the yard a moment, then back to her. He seemed to study her as she did him; soaking in the familiar, making sense of the new. "Do you remember. . ." His broad throat shifted, Adam's apple dipping toward a tanned hollow. "I worked the ice season at Shirley Plantation."

She nodded slowly. Just one county over, Shirley Plantation. Tools in hand, and as green as grass with but nineteen years to his name, Tate had gone with his brother to work as an ice cutter as he had in the past. By the strength of his back, and that of others, the wealthy had their ice for the following summer. Tate had always come home after a few weeks' time. Not that year. The memory of that final winter struck her afresh, for it was the last she'd seen or heard of him.

He shifted his pack on his shoulder. His skin was bronzed. Shirt a few washes shy of the rag bag. He was only a mite taller than she remembered, but broader, much so.

Heavens, she was staring.

"We worked awhile there at the plantation, Timothy and I. Not long, and we kept hearing talk about the trade routes overseas." Tate wrapped a hand around the pack strap that draped his shoulder. His other, he kept at his side. . .and seemed to be favoring it.

She brushed aside the thought before she could begin to worry.

"Ships that brought cargo—ice—to ports along the American East Coast and other places." His sculpted thumb brushed back and forth across the frayed threads, eyes dancing over her face. "A growing demand that required imports."

Money to be made, then. Off wealthy New Yorkers who liked their lemonade cold. Years that could have been with him. . .gone like that.

Lungs on fire, Wren had to remind herself to breathe.

"Both Timothy and I thought we could see more of the world. We thought maybe just one trip. But there was plenty of work on the trade routes, the ships."

So easy, then. No looking back. "And Timothy?" The words slipped out numb.

"He stayed. Not as interested in returning as I was. Sailing may be in his blood."

"But not yours."

He studied her without answering. What was he looking for? Some indication that she cared? She'd long since written Tate Kennedy out of her life. How she hoped he might know that.

She took her time wiping dirt from the sleeve of her striped dress. "If you haven't been home yet, you'll find things more crowded than you last saw."

Of the three sons the Kennedys had, it was the eldest and his wife who had taken over the humble cabin of Tate's childhood. They'd recently added twins to their growing brood. Six little ones it was now. Tate had to know. Surely not all people had been distanced from his life.

With the May sun bright on his shoulders, he nodded, neither confirming nor denying her tip. "I am headed there, next."

So he came here first. Not sure what to make of that, Wren focused on simply retracing his words. "You talk. . .you talk a little odd," she blurted, brushing soil from her palms. A tingle swept her cheeks at how silly that was to say. More so that he was even standing here before her. She dared not let her eyes trace the shape of him again. "More so than I remember."

"Do I now?" Even there, the hint of an accent. One side of his mouth lifted. Shifting his weight onto one leg, he leaned back casually and eyed her closely.

She nodded.

"And I don't remember you being this tense."

"I'm not tense." She pressed her hands into fists at her side and tipped up her chin.

His smile only filled out. A picture of the mischievous boy she'd known. Then all humor faded, and he kicked at a pebble, then another, finally pinning her with his gaze. *"Jeg har savnet deg."*

She squinted at him.

His hand moved to the gate latch as if to open it. She pressed her own to the rickety pickets, holding them firmly in place. He seemed to take in the silent exchange. His unwelcome. The act had them standing closer now. She peered up, only to see that he was studying her so intensely it nearly took her breath away.

"That means 'I've missed you,'" he said softly. "In Norwegian."

She wouldn't smile. She would not.

But he must have put a fissure in her stony expression, for the skin around his eyes crinkled. "See now. You're already less tense."

Tate. Always trying to make her laugh. Well, those days were gone. Stepping back from the gate—from him—she bent for another weed, then tossed the soiled root aside before straightening. "Go away." She wiped her hands on her apron. "That means 'you're wasting your time.' In English."

He made a short sound in his throat—not quite a chuckle. Sliding on his glasses, he placed the earpieces with suntanned hands. He glanced to the house where she'd once bandaged his misadventures, the roof where they'd sat beneath the stars, then back to her face. He looked down on her a moment, then nodded slowly. His regret so clear that her words tasted bitter.

"I understand." He tapped his thumb against a weathered picket. "Take care, Wren Cromwell."

He'd never called her that before. Only Wren, or Little Bird. Sometimes even Raven when he wanted to annoy her, an ode to her dark hair.

But nothing formal. Not ever.

She watched him go. Watched him walk down the path that would lead him the mile to home, his weather-worn canvas pack slung over his shoulder. One hand in a pocket. He seemed to survey the surrounding hills and sloping braes as if seeing them for the first time. A pang struck her, knocking deeper with each step he took into the distance.

They'd spent years by each other's side. Him reading her stories of faraway lands, her watching the clouds, listening on to the deepening cadence of his voice as the months turned into years. . .

Then just like that, he'd left her with no word. Not a single reason why she never saw him again.

Until now. Showing up at her garden gate, an adventurer through and through with the shoulders of his blue shirt bleached and faded. If she had drawn nearer, touched him, would she have felt the salt of the sea? Smelled its brine on his skin? Blinking quickly, she fought the sting of tears. Here he was, returned to her. The man who'd had her fifteen-year-old heart.

Yet it hadn't taken long into that first empty winter for her to realize the sentiment had been unrequited. Lifting her basket, Wren clutched it in front of her as he disappeared over the hill.

Chapter Two

Well, that could have gone better.

"I don't remember you being this tense." Really? He had to go and say that?

Forming a fist, Tate used it to bump himself in the jaw. He didn't need to glance back to know that Wren had long since faded from sight. Hitching his pack higher, he strode down the path that had carried him to her countless of times. But never had he felt so distant from her. Not ever.

"For four years." The way her voice had broken over the words. Heartache so clear in her eyes. If he could only make her see. Make her know that it was for her.

It was all for her.

His left arm hanging limp at his side, Tate flexed his hand. A burn in his forearm reminded him that he needed to look at the gash that was shooting pain into every nerve there. At least the bleeding hadn't gone through his shirtsleeve. He'd need to bandage the cut again and was pretty certain he was down to his last roll.

He tried to ignore the pain as he watched for his family's cabin to come into view, the first telltale signs appearing with the chicken coop and then the tree swing he'd hung with his brothers. Sandwiched between wise Jase and the baby, Timothy, Tate had always been the nondescript boy who became infamous for getting into scrapes and scuffles of one kind or another.

Why Wren had followed him along on all of his adventures he couldn't begin to guess, but she'd been by his side. Knobby-kneed and dark haired. His little guardian angel. A throb in his chest, Tate rubbed his hand there.

The cabin seemed to grow larger as he drew near. Little purple crocuses bloomed all around the steps, and wedged off to one side of the porch rested a stout rocking horse that had seen better days. On the stoop, Tate held his breath and knocked on the door. Footsteps sounded, and the door opened slowly, creaking until it thunked into the wall. Tate stood face-to-face with Jase.

The man squinted at him through pale blue eyes and tugged a napkin from his snug collar. "I thought you were dead."

Tate lifted his eyebrows, feigning regret. "Still kickin'."

"I expected you months ago."

"I got delayed." His arm throbbing, all Tate wanted to do was sit down and see to it, but he stood his ground, waiting his brother's next move. Even though the house wasn't entirely Jase's.

"Come in. We're having an early dinner." Tall and as broad-chested as a barrel of molasses, Jase stepped away.

Tate ducked under the low doorway as half-a-dozen blond heads turned his way.

Among them, Jase's wife rose with a smile. "Tate. You're home!"

"Abigail. Good to see you again."

With spunk in her smile, she hadn't changed a day. Her golden hair was wound in a thick braid at the base of her neck, and her coarsely woven skirt swished as she moved about the children with ease. She motioned him forward. "Come in!" She pulled a chair out for him at the table, then pushed aside a rolling pin and flour sifter to make room for the plate of brown bread she brought over a moment later.

Tate set his pack beside the empty chair and sat.

"How 'bout some stew?" she asked.

"Thank you."

Jase prompted the children to say hello to their uncle Tate, and a few mumbled greetings sounded around. Tate smiled back, took a few minutes to match faces with names, then wished he'd thought to bring them something. But he didn't have much to work with in his pack beyond holey socks, stale hardtack, and an old newspaper. Maybe he could tell them a story or two soon. They would probably enjoy a few of the tales he had to tell. Tate glanced around at the little faces scrutinizing him and smiled again, but it was short lived when the throbbing in his arm drew his attention back to the gash.

Tate shuffled in his canvas pack, then freed a half-empty whiskey bottle while Abigail slid a plate of steaming stew in front of him. Even as his stomach growled, he pulled back his shirtsleeve and used his teeth to uncork the bottle. With his arm held out, he poured the amber liquid over the swollen cut. He grunted, then clenched his teeth. Whiskey sloshed onto the floor, and it struck him that he shouldn't have done that. This was a home, not the belly of a ship.

He looked up at Abigail. "I'm so sorry—"

"Nonsense. It'll wipe up. 'Tweren't but an accident." She reached for a rag. "I s'pose you ain't too used to domesticity." She winked, her deep-hollow accent as muddy as ever.

He smiled. She went to sop up the mess, but he gently took the rag to tend to it. "You could say so."

When he straightened, his gaze traced along the loft where he'd once bunked as a boy only to see three little faces peering over the edge. He cleared his throat, feeling the crush of need in the crowded space. His own presence, no doubt a burden. If not in this moment then in those to come…if he lingered. Abigail bustled about and returned with a rolled bandage in hand. Tate thanked her.

From a rocking chair in the corner, Jase puffed his pipe, eyeing him. His plaid shirt was patched but looked freshly ironed, and while his hair was a little thinner around his ears, it was the same brown as Tate's own. As Tate wound the strip of cloth around his forearm, he counted six little heads, as he'd meant to. Though the possibility of one more arriving without his knowing wasn't lost to him. He glanced at Abigail, discreetly noting the mound beneath her apron. Going on seven…

Tate ran his thumb and forefinger over his eyes and tried to think.

"What happened?" his brother asked flatly.

"Walked across the deck at a poor choice of time." Tate slipped the cork back in the bottle, then tucked it all away. "Off the coast of Connecticut."

"Just…walked across the deck, huh?"

Tate nodded, really not wanting to look at his brother, but he did anyway, barely noticing how Abigail placed a spoon in front of him.

Jase slipped his pipe from his lips. "And the other half of that story would be?"

Tate picked up the utensil and took a bite of stew. The flavors were heavenly—fresh herbs and vegetables and the perfect amount of salt and pepper. He almost groaned and likened the feeling in his stomach to that of a hollow log. He spooned a second and then a third piece of meat, chewing and swallowing before giving his brother an answer. "Beware of crew members who drink too much and then decide to go fishing. Those tuna hooks. . .they hurt."

Abigail winced as she lowered a cup of coffee in front of him. Tate thanked her and took another bite of stew, chasing it with a sip of the strong brew. A reviving energy trickled all the way into his weary bones. Forcing himself to slow down, he took the chance to ask his brother of their parents. Tate knew they'd gone to Kentucky to see to Ma's ailing father. With their children all grown, they had been gone nigh unto a few years now, but Jase told of a visit they'd paid these parts less than a year ago. Sorry that he'd missed them, Tate nodded thoughtfully.

Tate polished off his stew in a few more bites, refusing Abigail's offer for seconds. The pot was nearly empty, and still little ones scraped spoons against tin plates. One of the older girls, who was maybe six, came to sit on the bench beside him. Remembering the newspaper, Tate pulled it from his pack and set it beside his plate. His other arm still aching, he cradled that hand in his lap.

"Who stitched that up?" Abigail cleared his dishes away.

"Some fella." Tate winked at the little girl beside him, and she flashed a toothy grin.

His brother rolled his eyes.

With one hand, Tate folded the paper in half, taking care with the creases. Grateful for the distraction from the pain, he flipped it and folded it the other way. When he needed help, the little girl assisted him. Within minutes, she was giggling at his creation, and as more children gathered around, Tate finished folding the little captain's hat. He shaped it open and set it atop her white-blond hair.

"Fit for the high seas." He saluted, and she giggled again.

The others cried out for hats of their own, and Tate promised to scrounge up some more newspapers soon. The children spent a few minutes peppering him with questions, and Tate answered as best he could. He was just assuring one of the littlest boys that he'd never been bitten by a sea turtle when Jase declared it was the chore hour. The man didn't take his time with shooing them outside before reaching for his own hat.

The throbbing still heavy in his arm, Tate used the palm of his hand to swipe the sweat beading along his hairline. He needed air. Could tell that Jase needed space. Standing, Tate reached for his pack. "Well, I'd better be off, myself. I thank you both for the meal."

"Where you goin'?" Jase's voice nearly passed as concerned. Nearly.

"Got a place to stay up the way," Tate said—not quite thinking that one through. "Just thought I'd stop and say hello." He glanced around the small space. "See the children." He apologized again to Abigail for the mess he'd made.

She assured him it was fine and made him promise to have a doctor look at his arm. He told her he would, then lifted his pack. Abigail glanced to her husband, and a flash of disappointment lit her eyes. Jase peeled his gaze away from her and began to dig around in the rolltop desk beneath the window. Knowing exactly what he hunted, Tate let himself out.

Striding down the steps, he heard his brother right behind. Tate turned to face the man. "It's done, right?"

Jase tapped the edge of an envelope on his palm. "It's done."

"Do I owe you anything?"

"Nope. You sent the perfect amount."

"Thanks for taking care of it."

Jase held out the envelope. "Weren't nothin'."

Tate took it, and his brother stepped back. Shifting his pack to his front, Tate tucked the envelope inside—the contents precious. He thought about saying something more. Some better way of thanking his brother for aiding the biggest purchase Tate had ever made. But Jase was looking at him in such a way that Tate simply said, "Be seeing you."

"Sure."

Starting away, Tate drew in a deep breath. The sun was about an hour past noon, which meant he still had some time to form a plan of where he'd be staying tonight. His arm throbbed, and sweat from the pain—and perhaps something more serious—made his shirt cling to his shoulder blades. A dizziness in his head had him craving a seat, a bed. Perhaps another splash of whiskey on that gash was in order. Even a lie down on the grass would suit him, as he'd done for the last week since leaving the coast. He might camp in his meadow that was now the closest thing to a home that he had, but if he was honest with himself, he longed for a mattress and some hot, soapy water.

It would be cold within a few hours. And dark. He cared not a lick for either, for he'd kept watch in gales darker than what this night could possibly hold. But he was tired. Oh so tired. And he *really* wanted a bath.

A bed. A bath.

Mrs. Cromwell's voice rushed his mind, for he'd heard Wren's mother say it to guests a hundred times. *"A half dollar for lodging, another for three meals. Baths are extra."*

And he had coins.

The idea sparked days ago, but after his conversation with Wren, the notion had been hard to kindle. Now, with his brother's home bursting at the seams and Tate's throbbing head aching for a pillow, he looked in the direction of the Cromwells. Decided. Then headed back the way he'd come.

Chapter Three

Tall grasses blew against her skirt as Wren sat in the middle of the meadow. Knees to chest, she plucked a wilted wildflower, turning the faded stem in her fingertips. She looked across the land, taking in the gentle dips and rises of this meadow that she and Tate had vanished to more afternoons than she could count. Now it was nothing more than a place where she could come and simply be. Breathe. Pray.

It had sold six months ago. Just like that. Out from under her. From him.

Their little dream.

Looking into the distance, Wren could nearly see him again. His shirt one size too big, as were all the clothes passed down from Jase. His bare feet running wild as he hunted the flowers she wove.

"Just you wait, L'il Bird," he'd said. "One day this'll be mine, and I'm gonna build you the finest house you ever saw. And there'll be a clutch of chickens here. And a garden there." He'd arced his hands overhead to mock out the shape of an arbor.

Then he lowered the flowers in front of her where she sat in the grass, same time of year as it was now. She'd poured herself an imaginary cup of tea as he hunted the hillocks for a stick, waving the one he found through the air like a sword.

"And what might that weapon be for, may I ask?"

"This," he'd said, holding it up to study it, "is to protect the fair maiden." His merry eyes danced to hers.

With a smile, she shook her head, knowing he'd forgotten his real sword back in his father's hay loft—that careless way of his. "You've been reading too much *Robin Hood.*"

He'd sat beside her, bumping her straw hat askew with his closeness. His skin smelling of sun and creek water. She'd straightened her hat and made a show of pouring him his own tea. Which he forgot to drink. She had also laid out invisible scones, which he'd have crushed had they been real when he stretched out on the warm grass beside her, opening the book to where they left off. Sitting beside him, legs folded under her skirt, she wove a necklace of the violets. Forming it with care even as she listened to the adventures he spoke of.

Her heart full of his promise.

That wherever he went, he would take her with him.

Now Wren's eyes slid closed, and she moistened her lips. A silly promise to make to a ten-year-old, but she'd believed him. As she always had. *Foolish, Wren.*

Blinking, she forced the memories away. Standing in the glow of a late-afternoon sun, she brushed at her blue skirt. She'd tarried here long enough. Really, she shouldn't have come at all. The land belonged to someone else now.

It was gone. As was the dream.

Though she longed to take her time walking home, she hurried down the faint path, for supper dearly needed to be started. At the log bridge over the creek, Wren swiped her skirt out of the way and her bare feet hurried easily across. A hop down on the other side and she tossed a wave to her brothers, who were in the far field, plucking weeds from Mr. Paddock's rows of ankle-high corn. The neighbor paid the boys weekly for their work and unloaded several sacks of corn on Mama's doorstep every harvest.

The twins had been in the fields since dawn, and Wren intended to fix them brown-sugared butter for their bread tonight. Their favorite. Though they rarely splurged, she was sure Mama wouldn't mind today.

At the house, her mother met her in the entry. "We've company. He's even paid for several nights."

"What can I do?"

"Supper's already on, if you'll just take him up some water."

"Up? In the loft?" Wren glanced into the front bedroom with its pretty quilt smoothed and folded, three windows boasting glorious light. "With the guest room empty?"

The room they sorely could have used, but they needed the coin even greater. Crammed in the back room, the four of them, no one complained, ever. As was the rule in the Cromwell house since Papa had passed and they'd taken on this new venture. Wren didn't mind so much since she had a narrow bed all her own, which was more than she could say for her brothers.

"Our guest wanted the loft." Her mother lifted her chin in that direction, amusement in her shining eyes.

Brows tugged together, Wren eyed the ladder that led to the loft, which was only for overflow. "Then I'll bring water up there." She checked the kettle, felt that it was hot, then used a knitted pad to carry it to the ladder. How she hated interrupting guests in the loft. It was rarely used, for with no door, checking in on them was a mite awkward. Having climbed the ladder countless times with a kettle in hand, Wren called a greeting when she reached the top. "Hot water. May I bring it up?"

"Certainly, m'lady."

Jaw hinging open, Wren popped her head above the opening. "Tate," she hissed in a whisper. "What are you doing here?"

Sitting on the edge of the low bed, his open pack beside him, he gave a lopsided grin. "Nesting?"

She would not smile at that.

He was pulling things from his pack with one arm. The other lay cradled against his stomach. Wren frowned for more reasons than one. He tugged off his glasses and set them on the nightstand before rubbing his eyes.

After nudging the kettle aside, she climbed to her feet. "I'm sorry," she blurted, realizing her mother would have heard her rude remark. And to a guest, no less. Even if it *was* Tate Kennedy. "I brought you hot water."

"Thank you." He asked if he could help her and went to rise.

"Just sit," she said flatly. "I can do this."

She filled the porcelain pitcher below the window and, from a little cupboard nearby, grabbed a pair of small clean towels. Hanging one on the rack, she draped the other over the edge of the bowl, then checked that there was a small cube of soap in the glass dish. Wren adjusted the curtains on the tiny window to give him more light. Sun warmed where she stood. "Supper's at six." She felt him watching her every move.

"I know."

Of course. "Do you need anything else?"

Slowly he set his pack aside and for a moment didn't move. Finally, he stood. "Actually, yes." He ducked under the low eaves and straightened only when he stood before her in the center of the roof pitch.

Tate shoved his hand in his pocket, then pulled out one of his folded bills, which he held out to her. "May I take a bath, please?"

Had her eyes always been that green? Speckled around the Virgin Islands, the sea took on an emerald hue so vivid, he could watch it for hours. He was staring at that very color now. Her eyes so very wide. And wondering.

"This is too much—"

"Then maybe I'll take one tomorrow." Though he planned on forgetting.

She stared at him, uncertainty clear in every blink. He wondered if it had something to do with how her family had scraped to make ends meet since the doctor's death. Her sculpted cheeks had always been nothing but pretty to him, even now. But there was something in her face that made Tate fear she was hungry. His chest constricted.

Releasing only when she closed her hand around his money. "I'll draw the water."

"Thank you." He slowly lowered his arm, then wished he'd reached out with his other when she watched him closely. The way he was favoring it.

"You're hurt," she said.

"I'm what?"

"Hurt." Her eyebrows lifted with the word, a trace of worry just beneath.

"I. . ."

Stepping closer, Wren pressed her hand to his forehead, taking him by surprise. Her touch was so gentle, he had to fight to keep his eyes open.

"You have a fever." She moved her hand so the back of it brushed his cheek. "How long have you been this way?"

Her skin was so cool. So soft. Nearly losing the battle, his eyelids fluttered, and he shifted his feet, relieved when she pulled away. "Just a few days."

"What is it?"

"It's a cut. I'm fine."

"No, you're not. You have a cut and a fever, which means you have an infection."

"You, Little Bird, are very—"The endearment stopped him up short. He hadn't meant to say that. Or perhaps he had.

Either way, she was frowning.

"Wren. I'll let you look at it, all right? You can tell me what you want me to do, and I promise to listen. But can I take that bath first? I haven't had one in a while. And we both know an hour won't make any difference at this point. If I'm to die. . .at least I'll die clean."

When she rolled her eyes, he grinned. Some things never changed.

"It will take a bit for the water to heat." She snatched up the kettle. "I'll have it ready in a half hour. In the lean-to."

He dipped a nod. *"Takk."*

Her eyebrows furrowed.

"Sorry. I meant 'thank you.'" A hard habit to break, that language.

Her mouth set in a straight line. Did she hate the whole country of Norway? Or just him?

Probably better that she couldn't answer that.

"You're welcome." She turned away.

With her gone, he waited his half hour, trying not to listen to the low murmurs of her and her mother below. A peek out the window showed the twins weeding the neighboring field. Wren's brothers were mere tots when their father died. Wren had been twelve, four years shy of his own sixteen. He did the math in his head. That was seven years ago, which meant the twins were close to eleven if not twelve. How time flew.

Feeling a tremble, Tate thought of that bath and moved to his pack, but no matter how much he shuffled through it, there wasn't a clean thing left. He cursed the idea of putting the same shirt and pants on, but that's what he was going to have to do. Tomorrow he would ask Mrs. Cromwell if there was somewhere he could do his wash. Maybe he'd even take it down to the creek to be out of their way.

With his arm paining him, going down the ladder was harder than climbing up, and Tate was glad when his feet landed on the bottom floor. He shot an exhale against the pain and stepped into the yard. His shirt clung to his skin, and he remembered Wren's worry that he had a fever.

The lean-to was on the back of the house, the little door propped open. The faint scent of soap hung in the air. He stepped in just as Wren was pouring another steaming kettle into the sloped metal tub. He hated the thought of her doing this work for him, but he'd paid her—and handsomely—and if he knew one thing about Wren, it was that she had a system to everything. He would no doubt be in her way if he started fumbling around.

"You can put your things here on the chair." She eyed him. "Where are your things?"

"I'm wearing them."

"Hmm." She glanced from his threadbare shirt to his face, then moved to the tub and checked the water. Her dark hair, loosely tucked and pinned off her shoulders, caught the light. "Soap here. A washrag. Towels in the cupboard along with a shaving kit should you want it." She pulled a towel out and draped it over the chair, and turning to leave, she hesitated. "Will you. . ." She didn't quite look at him. "Will you wait just a moment?"

"Uh. . .sure."

She slipped away, and Tate watched the water steam from the tub, craving everything about getting out of his clothes and climbing in. But he stood as she'd asked him to. She returned not two minutes later with a bundle in her grasp.

"Take these." She held out the little pile. "These were Papa's."

He thought of the doctor's jovial smile. His goodness. All they'd lost. "Please, I can't..."

"Take them. If you want, you can give them back." Her eyes finally found his. "But you don't have to." When Tate didn't move, she held the offering closer.

Slowly, he took the stack of clothing, and with a weak smile and a twirl of her skirts, she left.

Chapter Four

The room smelled thick of meat and spices. Cooling bread.
Fresh from his bath, Tate ducked into the cabin and fought a wince as he closed the door behind him.

"Have a seat." Standing at the stove, Wren motioned him to the bench along the wall.

His hair still damp, Tate dropped his bundled clothes on the bench and cursed the fact that he was shivering. In passing, Mrs. Cromwell pressed her hand to his forehead as Wren had done. He feared what Wren might have told her mother when he was gone. They practically asked him where the cut was in unison. If he had any energy left, he would have smiled at that.

Wren was nearest as he rolled back the right sleeve of the shirt she'd given him. He unwound the bandage, then rested his forearm on the table and set his palm up so she could see the stitching that could hide the infection no longer.

Behind him, Mrs. Cromwell cleared her throat. He really didn't want to see her expression.

"Tate," Wren breathed out his name. Eyes round and wide lifted to his. "What did you do?"

He relayed the story in a better fashion than he had at his brother's. Of how his ship had been off the coast of New England—nearly home. How his mates had mixed tuna fishing with too much rum. A poor cast. . .the rip of the hook across his arm.

Though the sun was still up, Mrs. Cromwell lit a lantern and set it near.

"We need to open those stitches," Mrs. Cromwell said.

Tate released a thin laugh. "Can't we just pour more whiskey on it?

I have some in my pack." He tugged the bottle out and set it between them when she traded places with Wren.

"I'm afraid not. Who stitched this?"

"Um. . ."

Wren watched the exchange. A lie flitted through his mind, but he left it where it fell. "A friend."

"You needed a doctor."

"I didn't have a doctor."

"Wren, if you'll boil some water, I'll fetch my sewing basket."

Tate sat there as the women bustled about. The door opened and the twins burst inside, followed by the *clackity-clack* of a dog's paws. Seconds later, a brown mutt crashed into Tate's leg.

"No, Destry," Mrs. Cromwell cried.

One part furry, panting mess, one part curiously guarded, the dog backed up, tail wagging furiously against the ground. Wren bent to rustle his ears. The twins spotted Tate and looked about to rush him as well, but Mrs. Cromwell halted them with a promise of supper and time with Tate within the half hour. Clearly disappointed, they obeyed and took in what Wren was making.

"Sugar!" one of them cried. "We haven't had real sugar since—"

Wren shushed the freckled-faced boy. A few whispered words for her brothers and she shooed them out. The dog, she shooed out as well, but he turned and lay in the open doorway. Panting tongue hanging down, watchful eyes on Tate. Shaking her head, Wren smiled a little. She quietly sprinkled the spoonful of sugar into a cornmeal batter, and Tate prayed they ate this well without company on hand, but by the way she eased the jar onto a high shelf, he feared they didn't. He hoped she wasn't going to any trouble for him. He'd eat boiled potatoes a lifetime over if he could just sit across the table from Wren Cromwell.

Her mother disappeared into the bedroom, poured a trickle of water, and returned wiping her damp hands with a towel. "All right, let's see." The woman sat across from him again. Having been married to a naturalist who was renowned for his knowledge of homegrown remedies and the body's ability to heal itself, she turned Tate's arm slightly and studied the stitches. "How have you cared for it?"

He told her of trying to keep it clean and dry. Changing the bandage every day. And how once he realized something wasn't right, he'd flushed it with soap and water as hot as he could stand it. When that failed, he'd moved on to the whiskey.

"You did very well, considering." Mrs. Cromwell slid the bottle back to him and must have sensed his regret when she gave him a kind smile. "These things just happen sometimes." Lifting the lid on her sewing basket, she pulled out a sharp tool, which he really hoped was just for the stitches. Still, his arm was so tender that the slightest touch shot fire into the tips of his fingers, up to his shoulder.

She motioned with her head toward the glass bottle.

Blowing out a slow breath, Tate uncorked it with his free hand and took a swig, feeling Wren's nearness as he swallowed the bitter liquor. It warmed him from shoulder to shoulder. Not wanting any more, he set the bottle aside.

Mrs. Cromwell fetched a bowl and filled it with hot water and rags. "Wren, please go to the garden and see if there are any fresh plantain leaves. If not, I have some dried in the pantry. Then start a poultice." She pressed her finger near the swollen gash, and Tate winced.

With her brow furrowed in clear confusion, Wren stepped out.

Mrs. Cromwell looked at him. "I'm going to need to clean this well. And there is no plantain in the garden right now."

Tate glanced in the direction Wren had left, realizing what Mrs. Cromwell had just orchestrated. "You'll do this before she gets back?"

Her response came in the way she lifted her thread cutter and wrapped her other hand around his elbow. Without speaking, she set to work. The first thread snapped, and she had to tug it free. Tate couldn't even fight the grunt that ground from his throat. He clenched his jaw.

Another snap of the thread and she pulled that slip free, giving it a gentle yank when it was as wedged in as the last. Tate hissed in a sharp breath. Mrs. Cromwell peeked up at him.

"Keep going," he blurted.

And she did, making quick work with her thread cutter. Pulling the string loose, the gash in his arm burning as if he were being singed by hot coals. Then with water so hot it made his head light, she flushed the cut and cleaned it with her rag. Tate crushed the heel of his boot against the floor. He could do this. He could do this. He could—

"Finished." Mrs. Cromwell leaned back and gave him a wry smile. "And here I thought you would have sworn like a sailor."

He chuckled weakly, his stomach feeling like it was upside down. "Complete myth." He drudged up a faint smile, glad he hadn't spoken the choice Norwegian words that had rushed his mind. Sweat slicked his brow, and he used the clean rag she offered him.

Mrs. Cromwell smiled as she poured another splash of hot water on the wound. Tate winced, relieved that Wren was just returning.

"This is infected. Which is why it's so tender." She worked with quick, practiced hands. A testimony to all the years she'd spent assisting her husband. "And why you're feverish."

He nodded and realized just how hot his skin was when she pressed her cool hand to his forehead. From a cupboard, Wren pulled out a mortar and pestle. Next, she fetched a jar from the pantry and set to scooping out dried leaves.

"I'll put the poultice on it tonight, and that should help." Mrs. Cromwell adjusted the strap of her apron when it slipped down her shoulder. "Tomorrow I'll replace it fresh. We will do that until it's better."

"Thank you." The words felt so inadequate.

She pressed a warm strip of fabric to it. "This will keep for now until the poultice is ready. Just sit back and take it easy. Dinner will be ready soon." Mrs. Cromwell set about putting her sewing things away and wiped down the table with a steaming cloth. When the wood was dry, Wren draped and smoothed out a fresh tablecloth. Set a loaf of bread on the center, then disappeared outside. She returned with the twins bounding in after her. They barreled into Tate.

As if on cue, the dog hopped up from his lounging position and sniffed Tate's boot. His wagging tale thumped the leg of the bench.

"Easy!" Mrs. Cromwell called.

Tate brushed the dog's head, then gripped the boys' shoulders one at a time. "Look at you two." He poured as much strength into the words as he could muster. "As tall as church steeples."

They flashed him identical smiles and, barely drawing breaths, pelted him with questions.

"Wait." Tate held up a hand before letting it fall back to his lap. "Which one is which?"

"Odin," the twin on the left said. "Ansel." He thumbed to his brother.

Behind them, Mrs. Cromwell made a little motion to hint that they'd switched identities.

Tate chuckled, enjoying the sight of their shining faces, realizing how much they looked like their father, who had been one of the finest men he'd ever known. "I've got something for the two of you. It's upstairs. The pack is by the bed, if one of you can grab it."

"Really?" they cried in unison.

Tate made a motion of crossing his heart. "And I have something for your ma." Though already he knew it was so inadequate.

Mrs. Cromwell smiled at him over her shoulder.

"What about Wren?" Odin asked when Ansel beat him to the ladder. He watched his twin climb up.

Stirring a pot at the stove, Wren slowly looked at him. A little lock of dark hair draped one side of her forehead. The setting sun that lay golden against it traced along her cheek, the hollow of her throat.

"I have something for her, too," Tate said, unable to look away. A bead of sweat slid down his temple, and he swiped it with his arm. Ansel scampered back down the ladder with Tate's pack slung over his shoulder. Tate took it and, using his left arm, dug down to the secured bundle at the bottom. He finally fished it out and, with Ansel's help, had the twine-bound canvas undone.

From there, he pulled out a paper-wrapped parcel, which he handed to Ansel for Mrs. Cromwell. With awe in her eyes, she opened it to reveal a white apron. Bold, lacy embroidery in an X pattern ran the length of the hem. She gasped and smoothed her fingers along the airy shapes. "Tate, this is stunning. However did you?"

The side of his mouth quirked up. "I'm glad you like it. It was from a village near Kristiansand."

"It's beautiful." She clutched it and gave him a smile so kind, he only wished he had more to offer. "Thank you."

"Now us!" Odin cried, and Mrs. Cromwell scolded him gently.

Tate pulled out two whistles. "For the able seamen."

With grins, they took them and began tooting away, which sent all hands over ears. Laughing, Mrs. Cromwell waved them outdoors. "What on earth are those?" she cried when the noise was mostly out in the yard.

"They're brass whistles. The same we use at sea. If they get a taste for adventure, I'm so sorry." But he knew his smile probably said otherwise.

Mrs. Cromwell laughed again. Beneath the bench, the dog whimpered, then rubbed his ears against the side of Tate's pant leg.

Tate ducked his head to speak to the poor pup. "Sorry about that, boy."

Wren was yet to say a word, but she was watching it all with wide eyes, giving Tate just enough strength as he slipped a small parcel free, followed by another, which was bound up in a thin cloth. He beckoned her closer, then his fingers nearly touched hers as he handed the bundles over. In a whisper of skirts, she sank on the bench beside his pack and stared at what she held.

"For me?" She looked over at him.

"It's not much. . . ."

The newspaper crinkled in her grip, but she barely moved.

"Well, let's see, Wren," her mother said kindly.

A gentle tug on the string and Wren opened the first bundle, pulling out a pair of dark blue mittens that were embroidered in vibrant colors. Her bottom lip fell a little, awe showing in her green eyes before she blinked the emotion back some.

Tate spoke softly. "Those were made by an eighty-year-old *Sami Duodji*."

With a fingertip, Wren touched the wrists, which were decorated in colorful knots of red and gold. A glorious, curving pattern detailed the backs of the hands. Tiny stitched flowers sprung off the twists, formed with such detail she couldn't begin to count the hours the woman must have sat with needle in hand.

"What does that mean?" Ansel asked, rushing through the open doorway with his brother.

"A Sami Duodji? It's an artisan from way up north in Lapland." When Ansel looked just as confused, Tate chuckled and promised him a geography lesson soon. It would have to be when he was feeling better, because right now, his head was spinning. And with Wren suddenly looking at him with wet eyes, his heart pounding.

"Oh, Tate," she murmured. "I can't take these."

"They're a gift." He drudged up a wink. "You have to."

"Thank you."

She said it softly. Just enough to give him hope that she might one day forgive him. Tate swallowed hard, willing his heart back in its place. He had a bad habit of getting ahead of himself.

"Those, as you might guess, are from Norway. And this one"—he touched the package she was yet to open, then fought a wince when he used the wrong arm—"this one is from England."

"England?" She turned the package—wrapped in a lace handkerchief—over. "You were in England?"

He smiled a little, wondering if he would one day get to tell her the tale. "For just a short while."

The embroidery on the handkerchief bore her initials, yet it looked aged, as if it had borne them for a life much longer than her own. "What for?" she whispered, clearly overcome.

"Just open the package, Wren." His gentle tone matched hers.

Wren pinched the knot and unraveled it. The handkerchief fell opened in a whisper. Inside were thin paper packets. Seeds. Wren turned them over to reveal that each one was laced with a faint, delicate script. She squinted at the writing. *Forget-me-nots*. Then turned to another. *Hollyhocks*. Another said *Pansies*. With an unsteady finger, Wren traced the curlicue on the *P*.

Then she seemed to realize that beneath the seed packets was a small book. Tate's vision felt unsteady, but he was pretty sure her hands were trembling as she opened it. She glanced over to her mother, who was watching with shining eyes. Wren gazed down to the pages that fell still when her fingers did. The same airy script filled every available spot. Closing it again, her thumb grazed little dips on the leather cover, and Wren turned it to see *W.C.* in worn gold lettering.

Her grandmother Willow.

"How did you. . ." She blinked quickly as if to ward off tears.

"I used a map." He smiled, though the rest of him felt unsteady. "England's actually quite easy to find once you walk in the right direction."

"You walked to England?"

"I was somewhat close. It took a bit of asking around to find her, but the folks there were friendly. She was surprised to see me standing on her stoop, but. . ." Despite himself, he smiled again. "I think she knew who I was—"

"Tate?" Wren's voice seemed distant.

He realized he was still trembling. Mrs. Cromwell must have noticed, for suddenly she was pulling the boys away with an order to wash up.

The twins did as they were told, though they pushed and shoved the whole way, reminding Tate of his brothers. Jase had always been the biggest, but Tate and Timothy had been scrappy enough to take him if they teamed up. Tate thought of Timothy, who was still at sea. How many days and weeks had they spent by each other's side? Through gales that tugged at their fur-lined hoods to seas so calm they could see their reflection over the bow of the ship as the sun darkened their backs.

The crunch of ice beneath their two-man saw. The sea's freezing spray in their faces.

"Would you like a blanket?" Wren whispered.

Standing over him, she lowered herself to a crouch.

"I'm all right." But he was so cold.

In her hands she held a bowl. He could only guess it was the poultice. She motioned for his arm, then replaced the cooled rag with a smear of warm herbs. He watched her face—some reaction. A wince or even outright disgust at the inflamed cut, but she worked quietly, a thoughtful look in her eyes. A trace of worry. When she finished, she rinsed her hands, then carefully wrapped a thick bandage around his forearm. Sealing in the steaming herbs that already soothed.

She looked up at him. "Just. . ." Lifting her hand a little, she hesitated. "I'm sorry, I just need to check you." She touched his jaw, then the side of his neck. Her skin so, so cool.

The fight long since dead in him, he closed his eyes. She said something to her mother, which he didn't hear. Then a bowl of soup was in front of him. Followed by a slice of crusty bread and butter. He waited for grace and ate slowly, struggling with only his left hand as he'd done for days now. Exhaustion tugged at him. The air in the room hot and heavy.

Though the soup was rich and filling, he couldn't seem to reach the bottom of his bowl. Or was he no longer eating? Again, a hand to his forehead, fingers grazing gently into his hair. He heard Wren speak to him.

"You should go lie down."

Yes. But he wasn't sure how.

Her arm slid behind his back, and she gripped his side. "Come on," she urged, rising. "Up you go. You can lie down in the guest room."

"No, I'm fine." He shook his head to force the room into focus and spotted the ladder. "I can get up there." He was slow up the rungs but managed. In the loft, he spotted the bed, and casting not a care to pants or boots, laid down and let the world go black.

Chapter Five

Wren slid her bare feet from the sheets. She rose, grabbed her robe, and wrapped it snug around her nightgown. A glance at the clock on the mantel showed half-past midnight. Thinking of Tate above and the fever he'd gone to bed with, she debated as to whether or not she should check on him. From his spot in front of the door, Destry tipped a floppy ear and lifted his brown head. The dog looked at her—quiet and still. Wanting to reassure him that nothing was wrong, Wren scratched the top of his head.

Straightening, she nibbled her bottom lip. Dropped her hands to her sides.

There was a time in her life when she and Tate hadn't been friends. Though they went to the same schoolhouse with a dozen other children, she hadn't spoken to him until a few days after her ninth birthday.

Each student in school was to bring something from home. An object that was dear to them, then tell the class about it. Wren had toted in a teapot that her father had brought from England as a young man. With his body growing weaker with an ailment he couldn't seem to cure, she had prepared a little speech about his childhood, including his mother, Willow Cromwell. An Englishwoman who, by the tales, had a grand heritage.

Wren had shown the teapot and told of how her father had left the small manor where he was raised to study naturalism in these American woods. A pair of school chums had later teased her for the rest of the day. Curtseying and calling her Lady Wren. Wren had tucked the teapot out of sight, wishing she could disappear as well.

She was sitting on the side of the schoolhouse at day's end, still swiping tears, when a tall boy came around and spotted her. He'd knelt, his eyes as golden-brown as the acorns beside her fingers. She'd known before he even introduced himself that he was Tate Kennedy. A new student at school. He hadn't attended before, as his parents kept him and his brothers home to work.

For the show-and-tell, he'd brought in a Civil War canteen—describing the different aspects of soldier life. The strap was broken, and the children had snickered. Though Wren knew from her parents' quiet conversations that the Kennedys were much poorer than her own family, Tate had talked on as if he hadn't a care in the world, proudly displaying what he'd brought. A few years older than her, they hadn't spoken yet, but he took her hand that afternoon, pulled her to her feet, and said he would take tea with her any day.

She'd smiled at that.

As they had walked toward her home, he'd asked more about her grandmother, her family, and her father's knowledge of plants and animals. He told her how nice her name was and that wrens were considered small and inconspicuous but that their songs were complex. How they were even known to sing in duets.

Wondering how he knew all that, she asked as much, and he confessed that he read a lot of books. Something about not having been to school before. Learning at home when he could carve out the time. She'd asked about that as well, and he told her how he worked the fields—potatoes, corn, and wheat, depending on the time of year. Then she'd told him that she'd never seen a war relic quite like his. He'd grinned over at her. Her cheeks had long since dried by the time he'd escorted her to her door.

"Thank you for the walk, Little Bird," he'd said, smiling.

The following day, he was waiting for her after school and picked up their conversation right where they left off. He walked her the rest of the week.

And the next. For two years, until necessity forced him back to the fields. And though he never set foot in a school again, he was rarely found without a book in hand.

Now Wren glanced up at the ceiling. She was fooling herself if she didn't confess that she was desperate to check on him. Never liking to be far from her, Destry wined when she climbed the ladder. Wren took care to listen that Tate was asleep before lifting her head above the opening in the loft floor.

The bed creaked when Tate shifted. Wren climbed quietly to a stand. She stepped across the floor, certain the rickety boards would alert her mother to her presence here, which was just as well, for she really didn't want to be up here alone.

She felt his neck, and a brush of her hand against his shirt only sealed the damp fabric to his skin. Wren hurried back to the loft opening. "Mama," she called down. "I need you."

At the sound of stirring, Wren knew her mother wouldn't be but a moment. Wren moved back to Tate's bedside. Even in the dim moonlight, she could see that he still wore his boots. She unlaced the first and was starting on the second when her mother appeared.

After sliding a candle to the nightstand, Mama felt his skin. Next, she moved to the window and opened it. A cool breeze trickled in. "I'll brew a tea for his fever. He needs it to fight that infection, but we oughtn't let it rise any more. That damp shirt needs to come off. Better wake him." She moved back down the ladder.

Wren patted his hand. "Tate, wake up."

He didn't stir.

"Tate. I need you to wake up." She patted more firmly, then moved her hands to the sides of his face to try and wake him that way. He was burning up. And not stirring. Quickly she listened to his breathing. It came out ragged. Rushed. Before she could change her mind, she started on the top button of his shirt. And then the next.

Nothing to it. But it felt like a lie, especially as she moved to the one below it, the tips of her fingers grazing the smooth dip in the center of his chest. She was relieved that he was asleep. Then again, if he were awake, she wouldn't be doing this. Her nervous hands stilled.

"Tate!" She called to him louder. "Wake up."

He groaned and moved to roll over.

"No, no, no." It took all her strength to hold him fast.

Suddenly he grasped her wrist. She bit back a yelp at both the jolt and fierceness of it.

Eyes clamped shut, he mumbled something about what had happened to the last man who'd tried to rob him. His grip burned on her arm.

By the size and strength of him, fear twisted her stomach, and knowing of nothing else to do, she spoke her name to him. His hand gentled. Air lodged in her throat; she waited, realizing that though his touch was tender, he wasn't letting go. Eyes still closed, his voice was husky as he whispered words in a language she didn't know. Gentle words. His thumb traced across her fingers. Sweat dripped down his temple. He finished with her name on his lips.

Her eyes smarted. "Shhh," she said softly. "It's going to be all right." She dared not move until he laid back. Her hand cooled as his own fell away.

Chest rising and falling slowly, he seemed asleep.

Best just to hurry and get it over with. She worked her way down the buttons of the shirt, and when the last was freed, she knelt with a knee on the edge of the bed. Leaning over him, she slid her thumbs beneath the collar, pulling it away from his neck and down, baring his shoulders.

Her cheeks flushed.

Don't think. Don't think. Don't think.

This wasn't Tate. Not her Tate.

Oh, but it was.

Wren! Don't think!

She slid the shirtsleeve past his bandage ever so carefully. Moving around the other side of the bed, she lifted his shoulder and tried to coerce the rest of the shirt from beneath his back. The damp fabric clung to his skin, lodged beneath his weight. He stirred, muttering something about blueberry pie and half a deck of cards before falling quiet.

Hovering over him like this, Wren didn't realize how loud she was breathing until she clamped her mouth closed. Just another tug, perhaps.

"Wren Cromwell!" Her mother blurted.

Suddenly pulling too hard, Wren fell back against the end of the bed with an *oof!*—the shirt victoriously in her grasp.

"What on earth are you doing?"

"I did it!" Wren uttered in triumph.

Humor warmed her mother's face as she carried another flickering candle over. "I can see that."

"I'll wash this tomorrow." Wren set the shirt aside and moved to the washstand, where she rinsed and wrung a rag.

"Why don't you head on to bed, then. I can sit with him."

"No. I don't mind." Wren slid the cloth from his forehead to his neck.

"Wren." Gray eyes looked at her knowingly. "You don't have to. If it's easier, I—"

"I don't mind." Wren said again. She held out the rag when her mother motioned for it.

"He's restless." Mama dabbed at his collarbone.

"Yes."

Maybe Wren should enjoy his suffering. Some tiny twinge of satisfaction that he was uncomfortable. She watched him as her mother smoothed the cloth over his forehead before returning the rag to the bowl.

The sight did nothing to Wren but put a sting behind her ribs.

"Call me if you should need anything." Mama squeezed her hand. A knowing look lit her eyes as she took the second candle. "He's always been so safe with you."

Wren smiled, determined to keep her heart from showing. Her mother moved down the ladder and was gone.

Wren looked at Tate, then around the room. She wasn't tired, but Tate seemed restless. An idea tiptoed through her mind, so she moved to the corner beneath the opposite window where a narrow cushioned bench was built into the gable. Lifting the seat, she dug past an old plaid blanket, then a wooden sword where her hand lingered a moment. A twinge in her throat, and she swallowed against it. Wren searched deeper and finally found what she was looking for. She quietly closed the lid and returned to the bed, wishing for a chair even as she nestled on the edge of the mattress.

The footboard was her backrest, and pulling her feet in took up hardly any space on the bed at all. Braid slung over her shoulder, she shoved her robe sleeves away from her hands and opened the book, then let it rest against her knees.

She glanced at Tate before beginning.

"So. . ." She moistened her lips and peered down to the pages. "'Turning their backs upon the stream, they plunged into the forest once more, through which they traced their steps. . . . Till they reached the spot where they dwelled in the depths of the woodland.'"

A broad hand resting just there, Tate's chest slowly rose and fell. The dips and rises that caught both light and shadow from the lone candle bespoke years of wielding a saw. Bracing a rope, taut with load. Despite the fever, he looked almost peaceful, and she hoped it meant he was cooling a touch.

The curtains ruffled in the breeze, stirring her hair as Wren looked back to the book. "'There they had built huts of bark and branches of trees, and made couches of sweet rushes spread over with skins of fallow deer—'"

He coughed a little, and she lowered the story. Reaching out, she leaned forward and touched his hand, felt his heat. She slid from the bed and used her finger as a placeholder to clutch the closed book against her chest. Snagging the cool rag, she pressed it to the side of his neck, then drew it up along his jaw. He turned his face into her hand, and her whole body stilled—save the pulsing of her heart. Which had her folding the rag with her thumb and fingers to lay it across his brow. . .and pull away. Wren returned to her perch at the edge of his bed. Her bare feet nestled warm against the blankets.

She opened his book again.

"'Here stood a great oak tree with branches spreading broadly around, beneath which was a seat of green moss where Robin Hood was wont to sit at feast and at merrymaking with his stout men about him. . . .'"

Chapter Six

The ship wasn't rocking, no timbers creaking, which meant only one thing: no wind. And no wind meant being stuck in the heat for who knew how long. Reef sharks circling the hull off the coast of Tortuga. Shady palms teasing in the distance on Barbados. Norway but a memory at their backs.

Tate's eyes opened.

He stared at the ceiling for several seconds. Judging by the light slanting across the beams overhead, it had to be past noon. He wasn't swaying, which meant this wasn't a hammock. Sitting up, he regretted the jolt to both his arm and head. He groaned from the pain and sank back to the pillow.

He wasn't on a ship. He was at the Cromwells'.

Wren. Tate opened his eyes again and searched through a mind as parched as sand until he pulled together the pieces of what had happened. Albeit slowly.

He looked around and, remembering his wound, forced himself to rise against the pillows and iron headboard. With a grunt from needing the use of that arm to slide himself up, he pulled his hand into his lap and studied the bandage that wrapped midway to his elbow. It was fresh, and he remembered how Wren and Mrs. Cromwell had changed it.

Needing his glasses, he found them on a little bedside table and struggled to slide them on with only a few fumbling fingers. A candle was there, burnt down to a stub. He didn't recall having a candle, but then again, he didn't recall much over the last few hours. A rustling sounded below. His gaze shot to the opening in the loft floor just as Wren's dark hair appeared, then her glittering eyes.

She spotted him and stilled. "You've woken."

A few responses came to mind, but his mouth was so dry, he didn't speak. Just watched her draw herself up and come toward him, both bowl and basket in hand. She set each on the bed and touched his forehead. Tate tried not to stare but was pretty sure he failed. Through his years at sea, he'd heard countless tales of mermaids. Always of their beauty. Though never any more than myths to him, it had always been Wren's face that rushed to his mind when the seamen's tales whittled away the night hours below deck.

Still mute, Tate kept his gaze on her face. Too weary to even smile, he wished he had the words to tell her how grateful he was for all she and her mother had done. This bed. The bandage. The clothing. Even as he thought of her father's shirt, he pressed a hand to his chest, only to find it bare.

He looked down slowly, lest his head whirl again. Wait. He wore no shirt. Simply a covering of mismatched quilts about his waist and— *Lord help him*, he braved a glance—his pants. He felt his shoulders sink a touch in relief.

That mouth of hers curved up. "Don't worry. We didn't compromise your innocence for the sake of a fever."

"My innocence," he whispered almost soundlessly. His amusement at her choice of words fell lost on the rasp of his voice.

She moved about and asked for his arm in the way she gently turned his wrist so the smooth side faced up. With tender fingers, she loosened the knotted bandage. He watched her work, words still failing him. Even a request for water seemed beyond him. But then she was offering him some.

A nod was all he could muster.

"I'll be right back. This can wait a moment."

She was gone in a breath and returned near as quick, her rustling skirts as blue as the pattern on the china cup she brought him.

He sipped the tepid water and was glad it was neither cold nor hot, for he feared his throat would tolerate neither.

"Thank you," he said, his voice husky.

"You're welcome." She bowed her head to unravel the last pass of bandage around his forearm, and he noticed her hair—the rich brown of wet planks—was done just as the day before. Neither down and free, nor coiled tightly, it was simply pinned loose, draping in soft curves at the base of her neck. As if she'd done it with no thought or care. But that was never her way. All the more reason it surprised him. He studied the twists that looked likely to tumble free any moment, if but a pin were pulled free.

He brushed his thumb and forefinger together, minding his hand to stay where it lay.

Suddenly her eyes were on him. His first instinct was to look down. For her to not know all that passed through him with her so near. With her anywhere. It struck him hard that he loved her no more in this moment than he had at sea. He simply had let his feelings lie unkindled. Out of necessity and nothing more, and even at that he'd failed miserably. But now, with her beside him. . .for him to speak words instead of wishes.

Yet he couldn't draw anything sensible to his tongue. He simply sat there, mute—and frankly, dumb—as she laid towels out beside the bowl. She poured a trickle of warm water, flushing his wound and the spent herbs. She worked as quiet as he was, and though he was a man who had always filled the space with talk, it didn't seem to unnerve her. Her touch was feather-soft, and he had to remind himself that he wasn't dreaming. Time and time again.

"You're what?"

He looked to her face. "Sorry?"

"You said you were dreaming."

"No." He shook his head fiercely. Regretted it. "Ow."

"No?"

In his mind, he tracked an excuse for his slip, but the best he came upon was "Uh. . ."

She smiled. "That's not the first odd thing you've said."

Oh, Lord, help him, what had he said? His eyes beseeched hers, and her smile only deepened. He took another sip of water, intent on finding his voice.

"Don't worry. It wasn't anything worth regretting."

He cleared his throat. "I'll be the judge of that, if you'd be so good as to tell me what it was I'd said."

She was nearly laughing. How he'd forgotten the sight.

His chest aching, he pressed a hand there, only to be reminded that he was bare from the waist up. "My shirt?"

"Drying on the line with some of your other things." She smiled sweetly—the sight of her mouth suddenly making him think of plum sauce, whether the taste or simply the craving for it, he didn't know. He realized it was the latter—for he'd never kissed her.

He'd remember if he had.

And why he was likening her to food was surely due to his empty stomach. But truth be told, he wasn't thinking of food. He rubbed his free hand back and forth through his hair, wishing his mind wasn't scrambled so. He tried to remember what they'd been talking about. "What did I say?"

Voice still light, she relayed his midnight request for pie and how he'd said something about playing cards.

Tate felt his brow dig in and shook his head. "I suppose I didn't eat enough supper." Relieved, he reached for his cup again. "Is that all I said? You'd tell me if there was anything else?" Though what could he take back now? A smarter man would have kept his mouth closed.

She cleared her throat.

God in heaven, please help him if he said something foolish. Heat crawled up the back of his neck. "If I—"

"You were confused. I think you thought I was someone else."

He racked his brain for whom that might have been, but there was no one else. How he hoped she knew that. His distress must have shown, for she was smiling again.

"I believe you thought me a robber."

He let that sink in. Wondered what he might have said. . .or done. "Did I. . .?" He searched her face that was tilted down. "Did I hurt you?"

"No." She said it too quickly as her eyes flicked to his, then away. "Though you seemed bent on it for a moment."

"I'm so sorry."

"Don't be." She dabbed the last of the warm herbs onto his cut. "I won in the end."

Relief shoving away his tension, he looked around a moment, making a show of studying his person to make sure all was well. "Did you hurt me, then?"

She laughed. It was small, then in a motion that caught him by surprise, she gave the top of his ear a gentle tug as she used to do. "I didn't use strength." Humor fled her face, eyes round but trusting. "I'd not have won."

It was a wonder he'd known to draw in air, for he surely couldn't now. "And what. . ." He swallowed hard. "What did you use?"

She set about gathering up the mess, dropping the soiled bandage in the bowl, followed by a stray rag.

"You're not gonna answer that, I take it."

"Are you hungry?" She looked at him, her face smooth and innocent as if she hadn't just made a heat stretch across his back. "I'll bring you up some breakfast. You just rest. You've had quite a time of it. And I'll see about your shirt. It's likely to be dry within the hour, but it'll need mending. You've slept half the day away."

"Have I?" He suddenly thought of burdening them. Overstaying this welcome. "Do you need this room? For another guest? If you do, just tell me, and I'll—"

"The room's yours so long as you need it." She discreetly slid a straw hat down from a peg and held it beside the folds of her skirt. "We've the front bedroom should more company come." A kind answer, though indifferent.

He forced himself to keep from trying to read into her matter-of-fact tone. It changed nothing, as he hadn't a place to be other than here, at least not for a few days and, truth be told, a bit longer. His head spinning for more reasons than one, he watched her cross the loft and lower herself out of sight.

Chapter Seven

Bringing Tate meals would have been easier if he didn't keep falling asleep. After setting yet another tray on his bedside table to cool the hour away, Wren nudged the quilt higher up his shoulder, wondering if he hadn't slept in a month and marveling at how far he must have traveled. And in his condition. One more night his fever returned, and with her mother's help, they tended to him. Which had Wren wanting him to rest as she tiptoed off to her next chore.

The task drew her out to the garden bench that was little more than a few rotting boards spread across its base. Wren settled several pots in the center and rolled up her shirtsleeves. She and her mother had forced nearly two-dozen daffodils near the end of winter just to have the cheery blooms all around the house. Now tired and spent, the bulbs were ready to be planted outdoors with the rest of their narcissus companions.

Tipping one of the pots over, Wren let the earth crumble free, and a trio of bulbs rolled into her palm. She set them aside and tossed the dirt into the garden. The pot she stacked off to the side, only to add several more within minutes.

Nearby, her mother sat in the sunshine, mending basket—and a snoozing dog—at her feet. "Oh, for pity's sake." She held up Tate's sun-bleached shirt to the light. "Did he wear these clothes or scrub the decks with them?"

Wren laughed softly. "With Tate anything is possible." She peeked up to the loft to make certain the window was shut. Not that it mattered; he was likely still sound asleep.

Mama unraveled a length of white thread before searching for what must have been a needle. Wren unearthed several more daffodil bulbs and piled them in one of the pots. At the sound of running feet, she knew the twins were about to barrel into the yard. They did, even as they held up their haul from checking traps. A rabbit and two squirrels. The twins were old enough to use a gun and had done so from time to time, but for the most part, Mama preferred that they stick to trapping small game until they were older.

It meant that meals were humble, but no one minded. It wasn't delicate food they all missed. It was the man who had once sat at the head of the table. The man who had walked these woods and this garden. How Wren missed her father. She missed his deep laugh, his Londoner accent, and the way the whole world felt safe because he was in it.

Her hands stilling in their work, Wren clutched the edge of the workbench when she was hit afresh with the memory of gathering bulbs with her father. A naturalist from the first day he'd toddled through his mother's English garden, he always loved working with the soil and what grew from it. He had cultivated everything from remedies to vegetables. For that which grew wild, he set out, walking stick in hand. Wren would trail along, swinging an empty burlap sack even as they chattered about what they might discover. One of his favorites— American ginseng.

It had been his specialty and the very reason he'd landed in the Appalachians where they cut through eastern Virginia. To carve out a humble life far from the grandeur he was raised with. Straying from the expectations of his prestigious upbringing, he'd married Mama, a barefoot mountain woman. And never went back. Years later, Wren had knelt beside him, learning all she could even as Mama did the same.

Some seeds and roots he collected himself. Others he had brought with him from the south of England or purchased through other botanists. Never would Wren forget the time he'd planted hundreds of heirloom pansy seeds all over the front yard, right up to the door, in honor of Mama's birthday. One of his most prized varieties, he'd saved them for years, and though Wren had only been a wee thing, she'd known no gift could hold more value as he slipped them into the earth a few weeks prior to the special day. Wren had been his ally in the secret scheme. For days, she crouched in the yard, watching the earth—awaiting the little shoots that would one day blossom into Mama's surprise.

The shoots took a week or two, and the buds didn't bloom on her birthday as Papa had hoped. No. They began to open two days before. His wife just stood there, making a fuss over the blossoms, pretending to be stunned. White, purple, yellow, and burgundy glinted everywhere one looked—like magic. With mischief in her eyes, Mama confessed she hadn't noticed them growing. Papa had laughed and swung Wren up in her arms. They'd done a little dance among the pansies, and with his arms outstretched and Mama's belly blooming with two babies at once, they'd turned in a slow circle. It was the best birthday party Wren had ever known.

Tears pricked her eyes from the memory as she toted the pot of bulbs around to the front of the house and crouched in the shadow of her favorite dogwood. With some effort, she buried all the bulbs, then patted each little mound of soil with her spade. She was just wiping her fingers on her apron when something dipping in the sky drew her attention. Wren sat back on her heals, realizing it was a hawk. The great bird swooped along the sky that was tinting the softest shade of pink—like a baby's blush. With her hair pulled back loosely, several wisps tickled her cheek in the rising breeze. Wren brushed them away.

Mama toted her sewing basket up to the house and slipped inside, no doubt to start supper. Tate would be awake soon, if he wasn't already. Knowing his dressing would need to be changed, Wren nearly took a step in that direction. But she paused, thinking perhaps it would be best—easier—if Mama tended to him from here on out. Though her heart pulled her toward him more strongly than she wanted to admit, Wren made herself linger in the yard. She stood fast and still, watching the mountains with their smoky grays and purples promising sunset. Then she lowered her gaze to the garden and wished the state of her heart could be labeled as easily as the thin sticks she'd plucked from each pot of soil.

Though chilled without the sun's warmth, she stood fast because she feared it would be better to shiver in this spot than to sit beside Tate just now. His nearness, the very thing she'd yearned for all those years. *Still* yearned for. She'd been reckless with her heart the first time. And though it pained her, she was determined to be wiser.

When three knocks sounded on the wood below, Tate lowered the boot he was oiling and peered over to the opening in the loft. "Uh. . . come in?"

Mrs. Cromwell appeared. Her hair was done up just like Wren's, except wisps of gray tinted what she had swept back and pinned.

"Hello, Mrs. Cromwell." Finished with his second boot, Tate set it on the floor beside the other, then the rag as well.

"I have your things. Freshly mended."

He shifted his hips farther back on the bed. She made quick work of unfolding the shirt, which she handed to him. Gaze falling, she cleared her throat a little and fiddled with the odds and ends in her basket.

Tate slid into the shirt and buttoned it up. "Thank you."

When she looked at him, her smile was warm. "My pleasure. I'm sorry you woke to find it missing." She slipped him a kind wink. "I've come to check your bandage again. It should only take a few minutes." Stepping away, she nudged the curtains farther apart, letting in more light.

Tate squinted.

"How did you sleep?"

"Good. But I'm kinda tired of lying here."

"Well, you'll just have to be tired of it for a while yet. Wait. What are you doing?"

Having risen, Tate steadied himself on the edge of the bed when his head went light. Fortunately, his legs felt less like jelly than he'd expected. "Oh, I thought I'd go fetch some water from the well. Then maybe chop a cord or two of wood."

Alarm filled her voice. "Truly?"

He chuckled as he went to go sit on the windowsill. She tossed a hand at him, but laughed herself.

Settling down on the cushioned seat felt good. The bed was awfully comfortable, but after spending a handful of days in it, he was more than a little stiff in the joints. Kicking one leg out, Tate leaned against the wall and savored the coolness of the wood and the way it filtered through his shirt. Part of him wanted to close his eyes because he was still that tired. But with Mrs. Cromwell here, he was glad for a reason to stay awake. If he slept too much, he'd grow soft altogether.

She brought over her basket and removed a fresh bandage roll. Next, she took advantage of his unbuttoned cuff by rolling it back to his elbow. Tate did everything he could to hold still for her.

Her face was gently lit by the pink sky glowing through the window. A pensive slant to her brow made him wonder if she hadn't come up for something more pressing than herbs and strips of torn linen.

"It's healing nicely." She tipped her head to the side and studied the cut as she unwound the bandage. "The infection is all but gone."

He could see how pleased she was by that.

"All thanks to you and Wren. I could have used your help a great many times over the last few years."

"Are you saying this wasn't your first run-in with a fish hook?"

He chuckled. "No. That was the only fish hook. But there were other accidents, and most of them were the same kind of lousy timing." He showed her the thin scar on the side of his neck and relayed the story of how a piece of rigging had come loose while he was hoisting sails. He'd walked away fine enough, but her eyes were still wide when he finished the story.

"And what of this one?" Using her littlest finger, she pointed to the small scar living on his palm, just at the base of his thumb.

Spreading his hand, Tate studied the thin line a moment. "This one..." Other memories swelled to the front of his mind. "This one was on purpose."

"On *purpose*?"

"It's quite a tale." Probably a fool-headed one.

Still beside him, she drew a bowl of water near and began to flush his wound, rinsing away the herbs. Finally, she peered over at him as if waiting to hear the story. When Tate hesitated, she lowered her head, urging him on.

"I promise not to interrupt," she said.

"That's Wren's job, isn't it?"

Mrs. Cromwell's eyes crinkled, for they both knew that one couldn't tell Wren a story without her interjecting something at least a dozen times.

"All right, then." But uncertain of how to explain the scar, Tate searched for where to begin. "Are you familiar with Norse mythology?"

She scrunched her nose. "Not entirely."

"It's sort of their legends. Or folklore." Stories he had learned at sea when spoken words were the only thing to chase away the bleakness of black, frost-covered nights. "As the tales go, there was supposedly a great battle between two enemies. Warriors. A Norwegian and a Swede." He peered over at her to see if she was following that.

"Two warriors—two different lands."

He dipped his head in a nod. "So as the story goes, this Norwegian by the name of Örvar-Oddr had fewer ships than his Swedish rival, Hjalmar." Tate scratched the back of his head, wondering if Wren's mother really wanted to hear all this. "But Hjalmar, too proud to have the upper hand that way, well, he sent some of his ships away, equaling the balance. I don't know, maybe he didn't feel like a man if he had an unfair advantage."

She smeared a pale green salve onto his skin, then unraveled a length of bandage, her gray eyes fixed on his face.

"So as it's told, the two warriors fought for days. It must have been quite a fray. Lots of blood-spilling, which I'll spare you." His arm growing tired, he was relieved when she lowered it to his lap. "But the moral of the story is that finally, realizing that they were equals, the two men took an oath. Formed a bond. They became not only friends but blood brothers." As if holding an invisible blade, Tate made a small swipe across that side of his palm. He looked down at his scar when Mrs. Cromwell did.

"Blood brothers?" Slowly, she added, "So this is a true story as well."

He nodded.

She eased the tip of her finger against this skin where the blade had pierced by his own will. "And you and the other man. . .were enemies?"

He nodded again. "A Norwegian fella who was born in the States. Not too far from here, actually. Maybe we had too much in common. I don't know. But I wanted to wring his neck. He probably felt the same."

"What made you dislike him so?"

Tate fell quiet a moment, not sure how much he should relay. While he was certain Wren's mother knew more about the ways of men than her daughter, it still felt improper to color in any kind of picture. "Let's just say that he wasn't the most moral person."

"And you hated him for that."

Tate tipped his head to the side. "I wouldn't say that I hated him. I was angered by him. The way he treated others in his past. Then hid from it. Not all men go to sea because they are brave." He glanced sideways at her. "Some are there because they're cowards."

She set her mouth, eyes searching the ground beside her small black boots. "Yet you befriended him?"

"Strangely, yes. I saved his life once." Brow furrowed, he shifted himself so she could more easily knot the bandage. "Awhile later, I suppose you could say that he saved mine. It was then that we knew it was time to call a truce."

Her smile was soft. "And you became friends."

Tate nodded. "There's more to it than that." In all honesty, he didn't really care to burden her with any of this, but it was an easy way for her to know where he'd been the last four years since he'd left them with no word of his whereabouts. "It came to the point that it was time for us to stop wanting to kill each other and realize that who we were both angry with was ourselves. That there were things that we both needed to turn around and face." Tate glanced over at Wren's mother. "It seems trite to use a ship analogy—but we were each like a vessel without a sail. Because of that, I think we spurred each other on. First in the wrong ways and then in the right ways."

Feeling the pain of the scar afresh, Tate smeared his hands together. He missed the sea. Missed Timothy. And now he missed his Norwegian brother.

But he remembered the promises they'd made when sealing their brotherhood. The one that sent his friend back home and Tate back across an ocean to return to the place where he'd left his heart. "Mrs. Cromwell?"

"Yes." Glassy eyes searched his own.

"I missed her. I missed Wren terribly."

She slipped her bottom lip between her teeth and slid her gaze away. He watched her swallow once and then again. He wondered how much heartache he'd put upon them with his leaving the way he had.

Finally, she looked back at him. "Have you told her?"

"I don't know that I've done the best job of it. I think she may be unhappy with me."

Mrs. Cromwell glanced toward the window where the last traces of day were nearly gone. The collar of her white blouse was tinted gray—as was her skin in the failing light. Someone ought to light a candle, but neither of them moved.

"Sometimes we're separated—even from those we love. At times, it's not by choice." Her voice was heavy with sorrow, and he could only imagine that she was thinking of the doctor. "Other times, it is by choice." Her eyes found his. "Each one brings a different kind of pain."

Getting his mouth to move proved difficult, so he simply nodded.

She patted his hand, then slipped her own into her lap. "But I know why you left. At least, I believe I do."

"May I ask what that might be?"

"That you made a vow to someone." The saddest smile he'd ever seen passed over her lips. "And—while I think there may have been other ways to go about it—I think you went about it the way you felt was right at the time." She rose quietly and dug around in a nearby drawer. A few seconds later, Tate heard the strike of a match, and she had lit a fresh candle. Mrs. Cromwell shook out the match and set it aside. "But you were gone a long time." Slowly drawing her basket onto the crook of her arm, she rose and crossed the floor. At the top of the ladder she paused and glanced back. "I think Wren has convinced herself that a bond like you two had couldn't last forever."

He tried to think of what to say to that. Some way to blow Wren's worries into oblivion—where they belonged. But as he'd said. . .

Not all men who went to sea were brave.

It was time to make sense of all the reasons he'd left. There were three of them. At least, three that he'd learned to see. The first was that just a few days before Jase's wedding to Abigail, the oldest Kennedy had told his younger brothers to either straighten up or get out. Wanting to heed his warning, Tate and Timothy, who was two years his junior, had passed the winter in the barn. When a second winter rolled around, they couldn't take that kind of living anymore. Poor as dirt, they had nothing to their names except strength, comradery, and a taste for adventure. All of which served them well.

Which led him to his second reason—wanting to be able to provide for Wren.

She'd have married him while he had nothing to his name because she loved him that much. And he loved her the same. Which was why he'd toted himself off before he was reckless enough to ask her to make a life with him when he hadn't a thing to offer her save the left side of a hayloft.

And the third. Well. . .

He knew now that Mrs. Cromwell already knew that one. So he simply spoke her name when she set down her basket at the ladder opening. At her pause, he asked if he could stay on a little longer. "Maybe a couple of weeks? I'll pay my way, of course. But if I could just have some more time, there's something I'd like to ask Wren. With your blessing. . ." He moved to his pack and dug around in the bottom, finding what he was looking for quickly. He withdrew a small leather satchel and handed it to Mrs. Cromwell. "Wren's grandmother. . .she gave that to me, for her."

With a tug of the strings, Mrs. Cromwell peeked inside, and her eyes brightened. "Oh my." Then she looked at him—joy flooding her face. "Tate," she whispered excitedly.

He grinned, but it fell just as quick. "It's awfully pretty, so I suppose she'd like it, but I don't know that she'd want it from me. And rightly so."

"This pleases me to no end." She squeezed his arm, holding it. "But to your worries—you just follow your heart. I know she'll follow hers." Mrs. Cromwell clutched both sides of his head, pulled him lower, and pressed a kind kiss to his forehead. "Nothing would make me happier."

Still smiling, she stepped down, and when she was gone, Tate looked at his palm, flexed his hand—the scar as much a part of his flesh and future as he prayed Wren might one day be. He remembered afresh the vow he'd made—not to the great sea, the salty air, or the brilliant sky, and not even to the friend who would always be one of his brothers. But to Mr. Cromwell. The man who wanted the best for his daughter. The vow Tate had made before he left. The final reason why he'd left.

Chapter Eight

With afternoon light spilling through the window, Wren buttoned up a clean blouse. She'd just finished dumping a jar of pickled watermelon rinds down the front of her bodice, and with the stain now soaking in the washstand and the spoiled rinds thrown to the chickens, she smoothed the waist of the fresh blouse into the hem of her dark blue skirt.

Footsteps overhead declared that Tate was up—and restless. Quickly, she buttoned the front of her waistband and was just straightening it back to rights when a loud crash made her jump. It was followed by a groan and a scuffle. Lying in the bedroom doorway, Destry tipped his head to the side and quirked an ear. Wren stepped out in bare feet to see what all the commotion was.

"Tate Kennedy, what on earth are you doing up there?" she called out.

"Ow," Tate groaned again. "Just a moment..."

Hands to hips, she stared up at the loft opening until he appeared and started down.

"What was that noise?"

"I might have broken a chair that I shouldn't have been standing on." He lowered himself the last rungs.

"What were you doing on a chair?"

"I was trying to see out of that upper window."

"What for?"

"To see how far I could see."

"Are you insane?"

"No. Just not used to being bedridden." He rubbed his shoulder even as he apologized for the chair. "I promise to fix it."

She rolled her eyes and motioned him to the table, where the twins were waiting. "Like the time you nearly sank us in that boat you were supposed to have fixed?"

"I fixed the boat. Afterward."

"How about the time you got us lost on your hunt for the James River?"

The twins' large eyes moved from Wren to Tate in rapt curiosity.

"We weren't lost. We were just taking our time getting home." Winking at the boys, he sat.

Wren fought a smile as she followed suit. Mama said grace and, when she finished, served Tate two pieces of fried fish. Wren scooped him a mound of creamy turnips, followed by two hot biscuits. Then she dished up plates for the twins and noticed their empty cups.

"Oh, the milk." Wren plunked the serving spoon back into the turnips. "I'll be right back." She stepped out and down the lane to the springhouse, where she ducked inside the hut. Built into the hillside over a spring, the structure held air, cool and still. The floor was uneven stone with a trough down the center that filled from the earth. Round cheeses and winter vegetables lined small shelves. Pale butter was packed into stout crocks.

Wren lifted the lid off a large crock that sat half submerged in the water. Dipping a ladle into the milk stored there, she poured several servings into a quart jar. The glass chilled instantly. Slipping from the small stone hut, she started for the house and was just steps from the door when she heard Mama and Tate talking in easy tones.

"And when will you head off?" her mother asked.

"Probably sometime in the next couple months. Hopefully sooner." Wren's feet slowed.

"It will be a good time of year to travel."

Then Tate's voice. "It will be."

Drawing in a shaky breath, Wren retraced his words, but they only hit her heart harder. Fearing her chin might set to trembling, she slowed altogether. And there it was—the realization that she may very well lose him all over again. She'd tried not to hope for anything other than the emptiness that she had been facing. Had tried to press her heart from him, but when it came to Tate Kennedy, it was as impossible as holding on to the tides.

With one last shaky breath, Wren stepped into the kitchen and filled her brothers' cups without a word. Tate gently moved his closer, asking if he might have some.

"There's coffee on the stove," Mama offered.

Wren's face must have been troubled, for Tate seemed reluctant to pull his gaze back to her mother.

Finally, he did. "I haven't had a cup of milk in over a year. Coffee. Always black and boiled to death. One of the few things safe enough to drink at sea. Nothing"—he turned the cup in his hand and looked back to Wren—"nothing like this."

Without a word, Wren set the jar down beside him.

Mama cast her a curious glance. Smoothing her skirts, Wren sat. She ate without looking up and was glad when the boys and Tate fell into easy conversation about their work for Mr. Paddock. It wasn't until her mother stood and mentioned spotting a stranger coming this way that Wren realized how quickly the dinner hour had gone.

Mama went out to meet the prospective guest, and the twins darted into the bright yard, scaring a cluster of crows, making as much noise as possible as they went back to the fields. The breeze swept in through the open door, and Tate gently said her name.

"Is everything all right?" That same breeze stirred his short brown hair.

Several responses came to mind, so she made herself speak the one that was most true. "You're leaving, aren't you?" She stacked two cups, her voice feeling small. "Please be honest with me this time."

Broad shoulders pressed to the bench behind him, he lowered his head. "Yes." He peered down at the table. "But not for a little while, and to be honest. . ." He glanced over at her. "I was—I was hoping. . . That you might. . ." His brow scrunched.

Puzzled, Wren stood and had just tugged her skirt free of the bench when he spoke again.

"This is all in the wrong order." He blew out a slow breath. Then to her surprise, he rose. His boots sounded strong and solid against the floorboards. "Wren, there's something that I need to tell you. I mean, ask you." He gulped, forehead creasing under a visible uncertainty. "You see, I spoke with your grandmother—while I was in England—and she had something else for me to give you. It's up there." He motioned to the loft, then smeared unsteady hands together. "I wasn't going to do this now. . .like this. . .but maybe it's best." After a moment's hesitation, he stepped closer.

"Stop." Her own hands were trembling. She said it softer. "*Please*, stop."

His eyes went wide.

"I don't want gifts. I don't want chivalry. I—I don't want anything from you." Because the only thing she longed for was the one thing he wouldn't part with.

Her hopes drowning in the realization that the winds would bear him away again, she stepped into her bedroom, snatched up the bundle he'd brought her, and carried it back out. "I'm sorry, I can't accept this. It would be better that way." A cleaner break. Not like last time when he'd packed her heart in that satchel of his and toted it across the world.

Tate nudged his glasses up and stared at what she had. Wren tried to read his expression, but he turned his face and looked out the window to where her mother was closing the coop door. A muscle tripped through his jaw. He wet his lips, then pressed his eyes closed. Perhaps she'd spoken too harshly. Her words digging into her peace, Wren hoped that he realized she meant to make this easier on him. To let him know that he need not try and make up for any lost time. She was letting go. Setting him free.

Oh, if he would but let her.

Finally taking what she held for him, Tate worked at the bundle with suntanned hands—separating the seeds and journal from the mittens he'd brought her. "Well, keep these," he said softly, laying the packets and stout book on the table. "They're not from me."

Golden-brown eyes peered down at her.

Wren nodded, willing a sudden twinge of tears away. She didn't want to hurt him. Truly she didn't. But this had to be done. He took up the mittens and gripped them in one hand. Tate glanced back to the window, then up to the loft.

He started up the ladder, and the wood creaked with his footsteps. The whole house breathed silence. Wren looked at the packets and book sitting lonely on the table. Saw in her mind his fallen smile. A clatter had her glancing over to where her mother was propping the door open. "The man was looking for the road, but he seemed so weary, I have a hunch he may be back."

Wren nodded and, not knowing what to do, wiped the table with a rag much too slowly.

"What's the matter?" her mother asked.

Folding the rag over on itself, Wren whispered that Tate was leaving again.

Mama spoke so softly, she nearly mouthed the words. "Did he tell you this?"

Wren nodded and, after a moment's hesitation, pulled her mother into the open doorway where she might whisper and not be heard. "I can't stand by and simply watch this time."

"He said something to me about it, too," Mama said in a low voice. "But I thought he was just going to visit his folks. I'm certain that's what he said." She gripped Wren's hands in her own. "Did he tell you differently?"

Wren's mouth fell. "His parents?"

"In Kentucky. He said it was time."

The ground surely dipped beneath her feet—shoving everything on its side—including the staggering dose of wonder that she didn't deserve to feel. "K–Kentucky?" Wren repeated. Hope and regret collided within her, churning her stomach. The breeze tugged at their skirts, pushing and pulling in the cooling air.

Mama smiled sadly. "He also said something about trying to be responsible. Poor fella. I think he's a bit overwhelmed."

Wren pressed a hand to her forehead.

Her mother slid a comforting hand to Wren's lower back. "Is everything all right?"

Eyes closed, Wren made herself nod. No words would come. Probably because she'd already said enough. Regret souring inside her, she breathed in slowly through her nose.

Burning inside her was the need for her mother's wisdom, but before she could find the words, Tate climbed down the ladder. He didn't look at Wren. Just tipped a nod to her mother, moved around them and out the door. The sight of his knapsack slung over his shoulder slammed all words from Wren's lips.

Her mother said something that Wren didn't hear.

"I need to follow him." Not wanting him to get far, Wren started off.

Destry beat his paws against the path ahead of her.

With his long strides, Tate was already out of the yard and into the pasture. Clutching up her skirts, Wren started at a run. Away from the house, she called his name. But it had just fallen from her lips when Destry hobbled and let out a sharp whimper. Wren nearly stumbled over the dog. Her heart still tumbling onward, she sank to her knees on the path. Destry kicked his hind leg, whimpering fiercely. He licked at his front paw.

She spoke softly, lifting it onto her lap, but he only whined harder. He tried to pull his trembling leg from her grasp, and suddenly Tate was there. Kneeling. His hand warm and strong as he took Destry's paw.

"Easy, boy." Brow knit in concentration, Tate turned the foot up to study the pad, and Wren spotted a sliver wedged deep. Wren smoothed Destry's fur. With quick, steady fingers, Tate worked the shard free. The dog's cries turned to a pant, and he licked at Tate's arm. Rising, Tate gave him a solid pat and ruffled his ears.

Tall and steady, he plucked up his pack.

"You're not going to Kentucky, are you?"

His brow pinched. "Right now?"

"I—I thought maybe you were."

"This late in the afternoon?" He said it dryly, then hefted what she now realized wasn't but a half-empty pack.

At a loss for words, she asked where he was going. Tate just eyed her curiously, took her hand to help her up from the dirt, then started off the way he'd been heading.

Destry circled her, whining. As if torn.

Wren watched Tate walk out over the low hill. It was there that he slowed as a stranger drew near to him. They shared a few words, and nodding, Tate pointed back to the house. The stranger—who she assumed was the same man from earlier—limped toward Wren. After watching the man for several steps, Tate turned and vanished over the hill. By the look of the strange man's small, worn satchel, he was a traveler. Wren greeted him and, after leading the silver-haired man toward the house, brought him to her mother, and they swapped familiar introductions. Destry sniffed at the man's shoes.

The dog had an uncanny way of greeting guests, and with his coat smooth and settled, tail wagging, he gave every indication that the guest—who she learned had hailed from Virginia Beach—was about to pass the test.

Which meant they would have company for the night.

Knowing she couldn't stand in the yard all evening, Wren led the way to the house. Mama showed their guest—a Mr. Parkinson—to the front bedroom as Wren fetched the packages Tate had left on the table.

"Have you an idea where Tate is heading?" she whispered to her mother.

Stirring a pot of stew on the back of the stove, Mama just shook her head. Puzzled, Wren toted the bundle to the back bedroom.

Promising their guest water as soon as it was hot, Wren reached for the stack of plates. A little *thunk* had her glance over to see Mr. Parkinson hanging an old coat on the rack behind the door. She offered him soap and a rag, then filled his basin from the steaming kettle.

His quiet thanks clipped to an end when the twins elbowed their way toward the house. With slicked-back hair and shining faces from the pump, they entered with a scuffle. Odin reached out a hand of greeting to the stranger, and as if not wanting to be outdone, Ansel did the same. Wren smiled at the way they suddenly acted like little men. She bid Mr. Parkinson to take a seat. He thanked her heartily for the stew she placed beside him, then slipped her his charge. Wren tucked the coins in the tin can beneath the wardrobe in the bedroom.

As was always the way with company, supper passed in a flurry of conversation.

Yet still, Tate didn't show.

When the road-weary guest was fed and settled in his room, which he requested for several nights, Wren sat on her narrow bed. A frog croaked beneath the open window as she splayed Tate's small brown envelopes out. Seven packets in all. She gave each a rattle, smiling at the bright jangle of the tiniest seeds, the *clickity-clack* of the larger ones. She thought of her grandmother, who had shared a love of gardening with her. Though they'd never met, letters had journeyed back and forth since Wren was old enough to hold a pen. Recipes, stories, even a few drawings. . .and Wren had felt a little less lonely in the world.

She turned her attention to the book and studied each page slowly. Her grandmother's writing was so small and fine, it would take some time to read through the many entries with care. She spotted *self-seeding* in reference to hollyhocks and *Mrs. Thompson's favourite* beside a drawing of English lavender. And on another page, *Do not place Queen Anne's lace on the table when Beatrice is coming to call. It put her into a sneezing frenzy.*

Wren let out an airy laugh, struck afresh by how much her father and grandmother had shared the same pluck. The twins were no different, and she loved them all for it because she herself had always been too sensible. Too orderly and practical. Which had the daring Tate Kennedy winning a lot more than smiles the day they'd met.

A fresh ache in her chest, Wren closed the book and tucked it in her lap. She blinked out the small window.

Running fingertips over her forehead, she closed her eyes. Why, oh why had she told Tate she couldn't take them? This was a gift indeed. Desperate for sight of him, Wren rose and strode to the front door. Opening it she saw the last bits of daylight fading on the horizon. She glanced out the dimming window. There was no sign of him.

It wasn't until any trace of the day was but a memory, everyone quietly in bed, save her and her mother, that Wren heard the door open again.

Tate ducked out of the night and looked at her.

Mama glanced up from her sewing. "We missed you at supper." She went to stand, but Wren motioned her down.

"I'll put something together," Wren said.

"You don't have to do that." Tate looked at her.

"I don't mind." She gave him a smile, knowing he deserved much more.

His brow furrowed, but he sat. She poured him cider, then sliced bread, cheese, and pickles. She added a hefty dollop of apple butter to the bread and carried the full plate to Tate. He thanked her and ate quietly. Mama went out to the porch rocker. The silence wore on, and after breaking off another piece of bread, Tate glanced around the small room, and Wren was struck by how alone he looked.

"Thank you for the gifts," she whispered.

He lifted his head.

She stepped closer and, still trying to make sense of this afternoon, placed her hand on his shoulder. Knowing only what lived in her heart, she kissed his cheek softly. A thrill shot through her at the warmth of his skin. She nearly regretted the action when she saw how taken aback he was by it. In little ways, she could see the boy she remembered, but it was a man that was wearing those stunned eyes that peered up at her and in the deep-timbred voice that whispered, "You're welcome."

His gaze fell to his shoulder where her hand had just been.

"I'm so sorry for earlier. Might you accept my apology?"

Slowly, Tate nodded.

"I'll plant the new seeds tomorrow. I'm looking forward to it. I'll keep those lovely mittens as well, if you'd let me."

"Might you wait a little while?"

"For the mittens?"

A light hit his eyes. "To plant the seeds." Setting his fork down, he unfolded his napkin, thumb fiddling with a frayed thread. "Could you wait a month, perhaps?"

A month? With spring here, it was the perfect time.

He must have sensed her hesitation. "Two weeks, then?" Which was followed by a wince of regret. But he pressed on. "There's something. . .there's something I want to do first. If you could just maybe. . ."

He searched her face. "Trust me."

The very thing he'd lost. The very thing she wanted to give him the time to rebuild.

"Will you trust me?"

She wished she could give him the answer he wanted, so she gave the best she had. "I'll wait."

Chapter Nine

While Wren had mentioned the incident about getting lost in the boat with a sparkle in her eye, once she had been genuinely in danger. More than once he'd led Wren on an adventure that had gone asunder. More than once he'd put her safety at risk by his own fool-headedness.

God help him, he wouldn't do it again.

Surveying the land he'd spent four years working toward, Tate prayed that he wouldn't do it again. He'd spent countless hours thinking about the land. Deciding where the house should go, a barn, and a well. All the things needed to support a family. Tate crouched, picked a blade of spring grass, and tore it in two. He looked out across the meadow, a thousand thoughts whirling in his mind. Wren didn't need a ring from him. She didn't need promises. She needed so much more.

And with this blasted gash on his arm, he knew he was going to need help. Because he'd just sealed himself into a tiny window of time—two weeks.

Two weeks? To build Wren a whole house.

There was timber to be had nearby, but he couldn't swing an ax just yet, which meant he'd needed to find someone who could. He hadn't been about to ask his brother, which left few options. So he'd spoken to Mrs. Cromwell, and she'd agreed that the boys were old enough. He'd promised to pay them as Mr. Paddock did. He knew what the extra money would mean to Wren's family, and he could play a role in teaching the boys carpentry, a skill that would surely come in handy down the road.

Which was why Ansel and Odin had walked with him to the meadow this morning, axes slung over their thin shoulders. And why they were standing behind him now, one of them clearing his throat.

Rising, Tate nodded for them to follow him across the meadow and toward the woods that bordered his—and hopefully Wren's—land.

Tate had spent the time before breakfast watching the twins sharpen the ax blades, and now with a hefty prayer that he'd bring them back home in one piece, he led them to the creek bottoms where they set to work. The twins had assured him that they'd been chopping firewood for years, and Tate tried to rest in that as he showed the eleven-year-olds which trees he wanted to come down.

Swinging the ax with one arm, Tate made a gash in a tall, slender oak. "You can start here, Odin."

"Yes, sir," the lad replied solemnly.

"Keep your feet squared and a good grip on that handle."

Odin nodded.

Tate explained how the tree would fall where they'd direct it, and after Odin chipped away at the trunk, Tate helped him form the wedge for a precise fall.

"You yell 'timber' when it starts to give."

Odin nodded again.

Tate stepped back and watched him work. The twins were good listeners and caught on quickly.

At Odin's shout of "Timber!" the first oak snapped, and after a few long seconds of leaning, it crashed to the forest floor. Never had Tate seen such a moment of pride on a young man's face.

Letting Odin rest, Tate set Ansel up for his turn, and by the time he had promised to have them back for dinner, seven thin trees were felled. Tomorrow Tate would have to brave a visit to his brother to see about borrowing a wagon, but for now, he left the logs where they lay and, with a pat on Ansel's back, led the twins toward home. As promised, the boys ate quietly, saying not a word to Wren as to what they were up to.

Tate watched her sweep beside the hearth, her broom making a soft *swish-swish* sound. That brow of hers folded in confusion at their evasiveness.

"Will you be back for supper?" she asked her brothers, who

exchanged glances before looking to Tate for direction. Having advised them on absolute silence, they were proving to be excellent students.

"Absolutely." Tate gave her a smile, which only seemed to confuse her more.

The three of them walked back to the meadow side by side, and while Tate had mused over the idea of felling a few more trees, he knew the boys would be sore enough in the morning as it was, so they spent the rest of the afternoon staking the corners for the house. Tate had spent the last year envisioning the layout, but now, standing in the very meadow he'd promised to Wren years ago, he suddenly felt overwhelmed.

"What do you think?" he asked the twins. Using his hands as a frame, Tate held them up. "A kitchen window here? It faces west, which would catch the sunset."

The boys looked at him as if they'd rather be catching frogs than sunsets. Tate chuckled, then set them to work breaking up the sod to lay the footings, which left him to worry about windows and doors and nineteen-year-old females. Tate twisted his mouth to the side. He had just enough money to spare for six windows. If he hewed the floor, doors, and furniture himself, that would leave enough to live on a little while and buy seed corn and potatoes for planting.

Seeds. Planting. Farming. The very existence he'd once tried to run from. How much of his life had he spent in the fields? How many years had he toiled under the sun amid the whisper of the wind through shoulder-high wheat? Counting off the days of his life amid rows upon rows of something steady and sure and common. It clashed in his mind mightily with the memory of a seagull's cry. The creak and moan of a great ship and the shouts of a hundred sailors at the sight of dry land. A clearing storm. Whales cresting beside the bow.

As a yearning for the latter life rose, it was tempered with the memory of missing her.

Of missing her so fiercely he was willing to trade the wonder of the sea and of distant lands for the chance to simply see her face again. The determination had turned to a prayer, and that prayer had led him back here. A prayer that he could build her something strong and safe. A steady place to call their own.

Clipping the blade of his ax against the nearest log, Tate stripped away branches. He worked until his arm burned, then let Odin take over. It was a simple task really. Something a boy would learn from his pa at a young age. When Odin got off to an unsteady start, Tate directed him with each splice of the ax, and Odin's instincts soon kicked in. Tate smiled at that and the way the young man's concentration hinted at memories of Mr. Cromwell with the very same expression. The way the man had befriended Tate when he was that same young, green age.

Wren had been twelve when her father passed away. Dr. Cromwell had once described his ailment in terms Tate hadn't quite understood, but it had whittled the man's body away until there was little left to bury. It was only weeks prior that Tate had requested a few minutes at Mr. Cromwell's bedside. Knowing the man was fading fast, Tate had asked him a question—if he might marry his daughter. She was still a girl really, but Tate had wanted to give Mr. Cromwell the chance to answer him and for the doctor to hear his vow that he would cherish her always.

A wet sheen in his eyes for reasons Tate couldn't even begin to imagine, Mr. Cromwell had consented, asking only two things in return.

The first was that Tate not dabble around with her affections. A bit embarrassed, Tate had scratched his head, and with a sparkle in his fading eyes, her father had simply told him to make sure she was of age and better yet that there was a wedding on the horizon before he even so much as thought about kissing her. Tate vowed that he would hold to that.

The doctor's second request was that Tate never make her a promise unless he kept it.

For Mr. Cromwell declared that he himself was letting her down in leaving this life sooner than any father should. They'd both witnessed it crushing Wren. Flooded with emotions, Tate had agreed.

He looked at the twins now. Realized they were staring at him. Tate straightened and motioned the boys to follow him. His thoughts still on Wren and her pa, he said, "Did you know that your father was one of the smartest men I ever knew?"

Their brows lifted in unison, a hunger shining in their eyes.

"He was," Tate said, letting both solemnity and awe fill his voice, for it was true. "He could read any book and figure anything out. He even made me believe that I could, too. So the same goes for you boys."

"Really?" Odin asked.

"Oh yes. And when he wasn't doing that, he was discovering things or helping people."

"He was a naturalist," Odin said proudly.

"And a doctor!" Ansel added.

"He sure was. I can't tell you how many times he helped me. Once"—Tate held out his arm—"I broke this wrist. It was winter, and I'd crashed my sled right into the side of our barn. Smashed the thing to bits, and my arm right along with it. It wasn't much of a sled, I confess, but it was all I had. And your pa"—he swallowed hard, taking in the sight of their faces watching him, no doubt thinking of the man they'd barely had a chance to know—"he needed to set the bone. And I was crying. I'm sad to say that I was twelve."

Tate made a play of being sober at such a revelation and knew he had the twins' rapt attention.

"He told me not to cry and that everything would be all right. But I was so scared. And then he started telling me a story about a sled he'd been building. He said it could hold three boys, easy. And that if the blades were waxed just right, it would fly."

Tate used his hand to motion how that sled could slip right down a slope. The twins watched him in awe.

"I was sitting there on the kitchen table, and he was feeling my wrist. He told me all about that sled and promised to let me give it a whirl, and before I knew it, I looked down and he was done. My arm wrapped and everything."

"And did he?" Odin asked. "Did he let you try it?"

Tate grinned and gave a little nod. "He made me wait until my arm healed. And made me promise not to crash into anything. But my, how that sled flew."

The twins exchanged glances.

"I bet it's still there in your barn. Have you seen it?"

"We've never checked."

"I'll help you," Tate said. "We'll look together."

They smiled at him.

They passed another hour stripping branches from the logs, and after seeing the lads safely home for their chores, Tate headed off for his brother's cabin to see about borrowing some horsepower.

Jase met him on the steps, and Tate stated his request.

While seeming intrigued about the notion of his little brother building a house, Jase simply stuck up his bottom lip and pointed Tate toward the barn where the team was. Thanking him, Tate hitched up. Before the sun went down, he had just enough time to haul the first load of logs up to the meadow. The twins joined him on his trek home, them scarcely able to walk and Tate's arm bleeding a little.

With supper bubbling on the stove, Wren sat Tate down at the table and gently scolded him as she changed his bandage. "What on earth have you been doing?"

"Honestly, I'm not entirely sure." He smiled up at her. "But as soon as I figure it out, you'll be the first to know."

Chapter Ten

Curled up beside the windowsill in the corner of the main room, Wren savored the sound of chirping crickets. A cup of tea sat beside her, and with Grandmother Willow's notebook in her lap, she tried to focus on the words on the page, even lighting an extra candle to make out the airy print. But with the laughter coming from the kitchen table as Tate and Mr. Parkinson swapped stories of the sea, she was having a difficult time indeed. Tate's own book had long since been abandoned. From her rocking chair, Mama watched the scene with laughing eyes and rosy cheeks.

"So wait." Holding up a hand, Mr. Parkinson leaned toward Tate, a chortle shaking his shoulders and the threadbare shirt there. "You jumped into the Atlantic Ocean, off a brigantine in the middle of the night, and were surrounded by whales."

"Not exactly surrounded, but they were close. You could see their dorsal fins in the moonlight." Tate raised an eyebrow. "If I wasn't trying to get to my friend, I'da been screaming like a little girl. As it was, he was doing it enough for the both of us. Have you ever seen an orca up close?"

Mr. Parkinson laughed. At the opposite end of the table, Odin and Ansel's eyes were round as saucers. Pretending not to listen, Wren glanced back at the notebook, only to lift her gaze again when Tate continued.

"For one, it was freezing." He leaned back against the wall, folding his arms over his chest. "And two, I'm deathly afraid of whales. Especially orcas. They're hunters, you know. You should see what they do to a pod of seals."

"Which is why your mate was screaming like a girl," Mr. Parkinson pitched in.

Tate pointed at him. "Exactly."

Wren covered her face with her hand and didn't know if she should laugh or cry.

"How did they get you two out?" Odin asked, still looking stunned.

Hiding the side of her face with her fingers, Wren peeked over. Tate caught her watching him, so she gave up on being discreet. He smiled a little as he pulled his gaze from her. He eyed her brothers, then Mr. Parkinson, who was as amiable a guest as they'd ever had.

"They threw down a rope, and we got it knotted around him. Then I held on for dear life."

"Was he still screaming?" Ansel asked.

"I do believe I joined him at that point."

The twins laughed, and Mr. Parkinson slapped Tate on the back. Tate winced good-naturedly, and Wren remembered his arm. She'd need to check it before he went to bed.

His book on the table beside him, Tate turned it over, fiddling with the tattered cover. "Honestly, though? He was pretty quiet at that point. He was half frozen. Had been in the water longer than me, and he was tired. The cold water, it slows your blood. Even his breathing was quiet. I'll never forget those sounds." Tate glanced toward the dark window. "The sound of the water lapping against the hull. The creak of the rope, our weight, and the rumble of a dozen Norwegian sailors working to pull us up." He swallowed and pulled his gaze back. "It was very orderly. Very calm. And even though you're scared, you know that everything is gonna be all right because they're gonna do everything they can to get you back."

A sting pricked Wren's eyes.

"Which is what you did for your mate."

Tate looked over at Mr. Parkinson after he spoke. "He was my friend, and when he went under, I think I jumped before I thought." His brow knotted. Looking down at his hand, he rubbed at a small scar there.

Wren didn't dare move. She simply stared at Tate, realizing how lost he could have been to her. And then it gently hit her. With his eyes shining like that at the memories—his fondness for them ever so clear—he was lost to her in a different way.

"It sounds like you were born to be a sailor," Mr. Parkinson said.

Tate looked up.

"The sea. It's hard to get out of a man."

Tate nodded soberly. His brown eyes lifted to Wren, and she didn't look away.

"So tell us more stories," Odin chipped in. "Where do you sleep? What do you eat? Do they make you swab the decks when you misbehave, or is that just for pirates?"

"Oh!" Ansel joined in. "Did you see any pirates?"

Tate chuckled and seemed grateful for the shift. "We slept in hammocks. They're actually quite comfortable." He tipped his head from side to side. "Most of the time—"

"Do they sway during storms?" Ansel reached for a cookie. The plate of them a splurge Mama had allowed on account of the two guests.

Tate took a sip of his milk. "Like you wouldn't believe." He seemed to think a moment as if needing to recall all the questions. "Oh. Food. We ate fairly ordinary things. Stew and potatoes and any fare the cook had on hand, which didn't vary much. Lots of hardtack." He made a face. "I wish I'd brought you some. It would put you off sailing for life."

Wren hid her smile with a bow of her head. The book still in her lap, she folded it and set it aside.

"What was the name of the ship you sailed on?" Ansel asked.

"There were a few different ones. The first"—Tate scratched his head—"was the *Styrke*. It means strength. That was another brigantine. Before that"—he scratched his head again, further mussing his short hair—"Oh, after that was *The Favorite II*. It was fashioned after the first ice ship ever built."

"And what were your duties?" Wren hadn't realized she'd spoken until everyone looked her way. She gave Tate a shy smile. "When you weren't rescuing people from the sea."

"Um…" He rubbed the side of his jaw, and she could see how something in her words had jarred him. "When we weren't cutting, I helped load the ships. We packed the ice with sawdust. It helps insulate everything, and shipments can be made as far as India or the Caribbean that way. I did a lot of different things. I picked up on the languages quickly, which was helpful to the captains." He glanced over at Mr. Parkinson as if uncertain how to say all this to her. "Dutch and a bit of French, which were both useful in the tropics, and Norwegian the rest of the time. They used me for trade and different positions, which allowed me to stay inland at times as a cutter to build up those relations. Other times I went to the tropics." He looked back at Wren. "They used me however they could really."

"Basically you were a great asset to them," Mr. Parkinson said.

"Uh, you could say that."

Wren could see in the humbleness of his expression that he was trying to phrase it modestly. Never had there been a thing that Tate Kennedy couldn't learn when he set his mind to it.

He talked on, and the notion of those different places flitted through her imagination. She could scarcely picture them even as he described the clear blue oceans. White sands. She said as much, and Mr. Parkinson asked her if she had ever seen the sea.

"No," Wren said with a soft smile. "I've never been. I haven't been much beyond these four walls." She realized Tate was watching her, and she forced herself not to look at him until Odin spoke.

"Did you do anything else?" he asked Tate.

Tate turned his cup in his hand and seemed reluctant to talk about it anymore. More so, Wren knew, when he looked at her again. A hint of apology in his expression as if he feared talking of his adventures would hurt her. Yes, there was a time that she was a part of that. But those days were gone. And if he were pressed to choose, she had a feeling it would mean him leaving over those hills again. His spirit was too wild. Too free.

She wasn't the adventurer he'd made it seem she could be. She wasn't much more than an anchor. Tethering him. He'd cut the cord long ago, and she was thankful. She couldn't bear to simply be what held a man into place. Not when the current was pulling him. Wren clutched her hands in her lap and leaned her shoulder against the cool glass of the window. She'd long since known it was time to try and let him go. She didn't know how, but she wanted to be brave enough, for his sake.

That was the sensible side of her. The other side of her thrashed against the very thought.

Clearing his throat, Tate turned his attention to the twins when they threw more questions his way.

His voice was mellow as he answered. "Ice begins to melt during shipment, and though we do all we can to prevent that, it does happen, and the ice can slip. One storm and a cargo of shifting ice could bring down the ship. So there was the work for keeping it stabilized. Then of course there was deck-swabbing." He threw Odin a playful scowl. "Only when pirates weren't attacking."

Odin and Ansel grinned in unison, and knowing it was well past their bedtime, Wren said as much. Tate tousled their hair as they rose with complaints. But she could see how tired they were after their day with him. Mr. Parkinson belted a thanks for both the stories and the fine meal and toted himself to the front room, where he closed the door. Already, Mama had quietly slipped off to bed, for she was always the first to wake.

Pulling her legs in, Wren looked over at Tate. He eyed her a moment, then his chest lifted in a slow sigh. He propped the side of his face against his fist and turned back to his book. He read awhile, and not knowing what else to say, Wren remembered his arm.

"Were you careful, today?" she asked. "With what it was you were doing?"

He lifted his head and seemed to take a moment to register her words. "Very careful. Do you think. . ." He felt his arm just below the cut. "Do you think I could be a little less careful tomorrow?" His eyes held a hint of humor.

"If I say no, will you listen?"

The side of his mouth lifted.

She rose and moved toward him to peek beneath the bandage. Her mother had changed it before supper, so it was clean and fresh, and the wound seemed to be healing nicely. When his eyes lifted to hers again, they were so vulnerable that she spoke to break the spell.

"It sounds like you had quite an adventure." She swiped at a few crumbs, then rested her hand on the table. When he nodded gently, she added that she was glad he was home safe.

"Me, too."

Hand resting beside hers, he shifted it and brushed his thumb along her fingertips, his expression focused. The touch tingled into her hand, her arm, and she pulled away. He clasped his fingers and rested his fists on the table. Ducking his head, he seemed to stare down at nothing.

"How long will you be staying here?" The words would barely slip out.

"It won't be too long," he said softly.

She swallowed hard against the sting.

"I owe you for a few more days. Would you rather if I paid you or your mother?"

"My mother, please." When his expression conceded her request, she added, "Where will you go? After Kentucky?"

He ran his hand over his mouth. His hair was askew. A little cowlick tempting her fingers.

"Um...honestly?" He pressed his glasses against his face. "I don't know what will happen after this." He looked up at her. "But I'm hopeful."

She drew in a breath. Held it. Then let it out slowly. "I wish you the best, my friend."

Eyes falling closed, he rose and pressed his hands to the table. Tate lowered his head between his arms. He seemed to be fighting something, and when he slowly shook his head, she wondered which part of him lost. "I don't want to be your friend, Wren." The words—softer than his touch had been. "I mean. . ." He peered over at her. "I want to be your friend. I just thought maybe. . ." His shoulders rose. Then he set his mouth. "Do you still have those seeds saved? The new ones?"

"I haven't planted them yet." How she wished she could know what he wasn't saying.

More so when he straightened, collected the book, and touched it to his heart. "Thank you."

Chapter Eleven

For the next three days, Tate worked on the beginnings of the house with the twins, and each afternoon they pestered him as to whether or not he was going to marry Wren. He'd evaded their questions for the first two days, but by the third, as they hounded him during their lunch break, he gave up.

"I'd like to," he finally said. "That's my hope." Tate finished the last bite of his sandwich and licked the tip of his thumb clean.

"I thought that's what you were up to, seein' as you tried to get her to go for a walk with you yesterday," Odin said.

"How did you know about that?" He was glad Odin didn't mention the way Wren had politely declined. *Really* glad the kid didn't bring up how she'd declined the day before and the day before that. Wren's first excuse had been sheets awaiting a hot iron, and her second involved a pail and a scrub brush, while yesterday she'd simply mumbled something about grubby windows—a sparkle in her eyes giving him a mind to keep trying until she ran out of things to clean.

Odin eyed him. "You do realize what trouble she is?"

"I've got an idea." Tate smiled.

"And she's awful bossy."

Tate tipped his head at that, his smile growing.

"And she'll want you to wash behind your neck, and you'll never be able to leave your shoes in front of the door."

"Oh." Ansel hit his brother's arm and spoke around his mouthful of rhubarb pie. "Don't forget to mention the snoring." He gulped a swallow. "She hates snoring. She's always throwin' her pillow at me." Never had an eleven-year-old's warning been more somber as he scrutinized Tate. "Are you sure you've thought this through?"

Tate gave into a chuckle. He certainly had. Wren could throw her pillow at him any day of the week. He said as much, and the twins made faces that reminded him of himself at that age; when Wren had been by his side and he hadn't quite known what to do with her. She'd been his friend, yes, but not anything more.

Time changed that awfully quick.

His chest tight over thoughts of her, Tate knew he needed to get back to work. He wiped his hands clean on his pants. The hot sun overhead had faded any trace of the cool morning air. Not wanting to make more laundry for Mrs. Cromwell, he peeled off his shirt and tossed it aside. Within a minute, he glanced over to see the twins doing the same. Their thin chests and shoulders reminding him of his boyhood spent in this very meadow. They watched him, then looked to each other and tried to stand a bit taller and broader. Reaching for his ax, Tate bit his bottom lip to keep a smile from inching up.

By no means had he been small growing up, but without enough food on the table and the hours spent in Pa's fields, his strength had been lean. Maybe it was hefting 120-pound blocks of ice for seasons on end, but the years away had changed him. Though he wasn't the only one. Tate thought back to the sight of Wren in the garden but a week ago. Which gave him a mind to carry her—blushing and all—over this threshold.

If he could just finish the threshold. And if she would let him.

Feet stationed on each side of the nearest log, he squared his grip on the ax handle and cut at the notch. While still sore, his arm was holding up all right. Thanks to the Cromwell women, the infection was all but gone, even if he wasn't exactly following their orders to take it easy. Tate pulled the ax back and sliced it into the soft spruce. Pale woodchips flew, and he did it again.

After years with ice saw and gaff in hand or climbing masts and binding sails, labor calmed him. His body hungered for it. Arms, back, shoulders. With a tool in hand, his muscles began to relax, and sweat formed along his spine. Despite the muted throb in his forearm, he swung and chipped, grateful for this work.

He'd cut so many over the last few days, he could do it in his sleep, but he kept his gaze on the task and carefully scored the end of the log so it would fit against another. Layer by layer, log by log, the walls would grow. It would be a home.

Tate glanced over to see Odin pausing for a break. The boys were working hard. Harder than plenty of the seamen he'd met over the years. He told the lads as much, and they beamed.

Every night that week, he and the twins had collapsed into their seats at the supper table, and more than once, Tate was awoken by Mrs. Cromwell's gentle nudging. Last night he'd startled awake to mashed potatoes on his elbow and Wren gently shaking his shoulder. He'd blinked up only to see her smiling down at him with a rag in hand. The twins were nowhere in sight, and she admitted to having nudged them off to bed. Starving and more than a mite embarrassed for falling asleep again, Tate downed his supper and thanked her for the fine meal. A smile in her eyes, she'd helped him stand.

He'd liked that. Her closeness. Her thoughtfulness when he climbed up to the loft only to see that she'd turned down his bed for him. She had even left a lit candle so he could make his way in the dark. He'd blown the flame and, missing her company terribly, knew it was time to bring her to the meadow before the week was out. Even if the house wasn't finished, he'd at least show her what he had.

He felt no fear over that. Only hope.

Panting and lowering his ax, Tate eyed the shape of the foundation the twins had helped him lay. He ran a hand over his mouth. The shape was just as he'd planned it. A quaint front room with a place to dine and a spot for a kitchen. Off that, a bedroom, and above the living space, a loft. It wouldn't be very large, but it would be cozy. He liked cozy—and had a hunch Wren did, too.

"There he goes again," Odin muttered. "That silly grin on his face."

Feeling his neck warm, Tate told the kid to hush up and get back to work. Tate nudged the nearest log with his boot. Already, the house was two logs high, and once it was tall enough to begin thinking about a ceiling, the loft beams could go up. The going was slow, thanks to his arm, but at least it was going. Tate tugged at his hair, counting up the days.

With his request for two weeks, he had five days left.

Which meant he had an ax to swing. Tate gripped the wooden handle and got back to work. He had both ends of the log notched and ready to roll into place by the time the twins had finished off a jar of sweet tea. He'd been working them hard, and with their tasks in the fields, perhaps too hard.

Tate took a few chugs of the tea, remembering what he'd learned of the men who worked under him—how to motivate and reward. "What do you say we get this house three logs high and then go swimming?"

The boys heartily agreed and spent the afternoon making good on the deal. With sweat making a mess of his hair, Tate worked between the boys as they notched, then lifted yet another log. And then another.

When they reached their stopping point, the twins whooped, and Tate went over to his toolbox. He pulled out a squat bag of money that he'd stashed under some nails. Tate counted the bills as the twins watched on with wide eyes.

Freckled cheeks bookending their open mouths, they each took their payment.

"I'll have the same amount for you again when we're done."

"Are you serious?" Odin finally breathed.

Tate made a point to shake each of their hands. "More than serious. You two are working hard."

Still visibly awed, they stashed the bills in their pockets.

"Do you think. . ." Ansel began, pulling the bills back out. He peeked at his twin a moment in that silent exchange Tate was getting used to. Then Ansel took Odin's money, and his own, and handed it back to Tate. "Maybe you'd better hold on to it until we get home. Just so nothing happens to it."

"I'll keep it safe," Tate said, tucking it in his toolbox.

The boys scampered away for their tools, laughing and musing over the things they'd buy if they could. At the top of Ansel's list was a gun. Odin said something about putting it in the bank. Tate watched them gather their tools and knew they'd give it to their mother when they got home. That she'd tuck it in that hiding spot of hers, and it would put food on the table.

When Tate was their age, he would have had to do the same thing. He would never gripe or complain, because Jase never did. Tate would just stand beside his older brother as they lowered earnings from any side jobs into the can and heard the coins clink at the empty bottom.

He could still remember the autumn when the work never ended. He could never seem to find the end of it. For the good side of a month, all he saw of Wren was on Sunday mornings, and even then they'd only been allowed to greet each other quietly before taking their seats.

For weeks he'd been trying to carve out time to spend with her. It wasn't until the day the last of the wheat was finally shocked, leaving him with a few unexpected hours of time. And just like that, he'd gone off looking for his little Wren. They'd gone on a walk, some direction never gone before by the two of them. And thanks to him and his ill planning, had ended up getting lost. They hadn't come home until well after dark.

Jase hadn't seemed too pleased by that when Tate finally wandered in to find his brother sitting up, smoking a pipe. "Where were you?"

"Got lost in the woods. Why?" Tate had stepped in and closed the door.

"Was that Cromwell girl with you?"

"What of it?"

Blowing a puff of smoke, Jase had eyed him. "Sure you were lost?"

Lowering his hand and his tone, Tate had stepped closer. "Do you have something you want to ask me?"

"Jase, give it a rest," Timothy had added from up in the loft, his voice just reaching young manhood.

Still eyeing Jase—and aware of his implications—Tate had gone off to bed. It wasn't until the winter winds had blown in and he and Timothy were elbow deep in snow and ice that they spoke of it again.

"It's the way you two are always together," Timothy had said. "I think people have begun to wonder."

"Begun to wonder what?"

"Why you two spend so much time together. Why don't you just up and marry her?"

Wondering why people couldn't just mind their own business and leave him and Wren well enough alone, Tate reminded Timothy that, at fifteen, she was rather young.

"Well, she follows you everywhere you go. It just sets people to talkin'. You might as well just keep your distance for a time. It'll all blow over."

Keep his distance? From the best friend he had in the world. And the only thing he wanted when it came to all and forever.

But he'd heeded Timothy's advice and, after working their time at Shirley Plantation, had kept on down the road. Walking with his younger brother until he saw that glittering gray and blue. Because he'd realized something in the hours before that moment. The moment when his boots first touched the deck of that great ship. That his time with Wren was only making folk talk, and one way or another, that would end up hurting her. Which meant he needed to keep his distance for a spell. Give her the time she needed to grow up. That's what he told himself anyway, while the crew first lowered the sails, the ship blew from the harbor, and his heart tore in two.

Tate asked her not to plant the seeds. He didn't say she couldn't at least ready the soil. And with their guest, Mr. Parkinson, a few days gone, Wren had the time to spare. With a gloved hand, she furrowed her spade through the garden earth and pondered what might go well there. It was nearest to the house, so the hollyhocks would be fitting as those grew tall and spindly. "Then here," she said to herself, poking at the soil beside the gate. "Can be the lavender. Easy to reach down and pluck a few sprigs when need be." She'd read in her grandmother's journal that one of lavender's many benefits was to slow bleeding. Wren smiled to herself. With Tate around, she would need plenty.

Then she sobered.

What was she thinking? It wasn't likely he'd be here much longer.

"Tate Kennedy." Resting back on her tucked legs, she pointed her spade to a fence post as if it were the man himself. "Always making me hope for things I can't have." The soil around her shadowed.

"I said no such thing."

Wren's head shot up.

Tate grinned down at her, hair damp, an amused expression on his face.

"I was—I was just. . ."

"Scolding me?" His enjoyment was clear. "Next time you do that, at least let me be around to defend myself." He leaned on the fence post and peered down at her. "Now what is it that I've done to you, fair lady?"

She exhaled. "That's just it! That's the very thing. Always calling me the fair lady or some such nonsense, and you and your swords and stories of distant lands." She stood and flung a hand at him, which only sent bits of dirt flying. "But you're always marching around like we should all believe them. It's time you grew up, Tate Kennedy. It's time you grew up and looked around you."

He sobered. She was near enough to the gate now to touch him. Not that she would have wanted to, and before that notion even faded, he was sliding his hand to the back of her neck, cupping it gently. Her next breath had him pressing a kiss to her cheek. The scruff of his jaw brushed her skin, his mouth soft and warm as he moved the kiss to her forehead, lingering. He whispered something in French that she couldn't even begin to understand.

As if he did that kind of thing every day, he pulled back and peered down at her.

"What was that?" she demanded, the words slipping out too thin to hold any threat.

"Just doin' what you said. You told me to grow up and look around. And you're standing there not an inch away, prettiest thing I ever saw." He moistened his lips, a sparkle in his eyes. "There wasn't anything make-believe in that."

She clamped her mouth shut.

"Now you go on ahead and scold that fence post all you want." He winked and strode off.

She stood speechless. Tate let out a sharp whistle, and with a wave of his arm, the twins barreled across the yard toward him. Their pants were dark and damp as if they'd just taken a swim in the creek. Shoulder to shoulder, the three of them strode to the barn. Wren tried to ignore their banging about and the butterflies flitting through her stomach as she went back to her furrows and dirt. But she couldn't recall what it was she'd been doing.

Well, this would never do. Pressing her palms to her thighs, Wren squinted her eyes closed, determined to get her bearings. But in the darkness, all she saw was Tate's face, so she groped in her pocket for her grandmother's notebook.

Discarding her gloves, she slipped the book out, turned to nowhere in particular, and decided to become very studious.

More thunking came from the barn.

Wren pushed the book up higher in front of her face, forced every bit of her focus onto the sketches that filled the open pages. Her grandmother had had a knack for drawing, and one of Wren's favorite parts of the book was the tiny pictures that filled the margins. Pencil-drawn herbs and flowers, birds, even a quaint, bubbling spring just below handy uses for yarrow.

She turned the next page and admired the sketch of a toddling baby. More than admired, for this was the very page she'd found her mother studying the day before. Unshed tears in Mama's eyes. With delicate pencil strokes, her grandmother had captured chubby legs and a little jumper, large eyes and ears that were the tiniest bit lopsided. Papa.

Wren tried to imagine her father sitting in the garden back in England—just a baby. The scene was easy to conjure with the open book in her lap. How she wished her father were here. Her grandmother, too.

For she was so very lonely. She knew she shouldn't feel that way, not with the twins and Mama around and guests from all over the country. But she was lonely all the same. Wren flipped forward a few more pages, wondering if there was a remedy for that. She knew there was, but it couldn't be grown in any garden. Sighing, she traced her finger along another page, absorbing the words of a woman she'd only had the chance to know through these snippets.

Forget-me-nots meant both true love and hope. That was a nice thought. Wren shook the seed packet, deciding to plant them nearest her reading bench. *Bindweed* symbolized persistence. Wren gave a little laugh. Tate probably ate that for breakfast.

The clattering in the barn stopped and was replaced by her brothers' whooping and hollering. Ansel and Odin bounded out of the barn, trailed by Tate. An upside-down sled burdened one of Tate's shoulders. He gripped the metal runners with one hand and carried it out into the yard, where he directed the twins to take the other side. Then they marched onward—going who knew where—with an old sled and grins as big as half moons on the first of June.

The sight of Tate striding tall and steady, her spindly brothers and Destry running beside him, did something tight to her chest. And she realized she'd never seen such a thing. Her brothers following in the shadow of a man with trust. Admiration. The boys were hollering out some kind of cheer. Tate glanced her way and gave a salute. Wren gave a small wave. Then simply stood there, trowel in hand, quite certain she was failing in fighting the smile—and the hope—that bubbled up inside her.

Chapter Twelve

With a few more days of work behind him and no luck at a walk with Wren, Tate sat on the edge of his bed and pulled off his glasses. He set them on the nightstand to rub a hand over his eyes. His hair was still damp for when he'd come to the Cromwells' that evening; between sweat and wood shavings, all he'd wanted to do was take a bath. Now in clean pants and shirt, he was so tired, he didn't know how he was going to make it down for supper.

He'd already told Mrs. Cromwell that he would be leaving. For one, they were treating him much too nicely and he feared being a burden. He also wanted to free this room up. He had a sense by a shawl hanging behind a cupboard door and a folded nightgown on a high shelf that Wren slept up here when it was empty. It was just a hunch, but either way, he had his own place to sleep. Sort of.

He'd still need meals and wanted to be able to pay them for something. Though it surely wasn't much, he hoped it helped each time he saw Mrs. Cromwell tuck the coins out of sight.

The last of his things crammed into his pack, Tate latched it snug, and the room was as if he'd never been there. He went to stand when he heard Wren call out.

"I have hot water. . .may I bring it up?"

"Uh. . .sure."

She appeared at the top of the ladder and gingerly slid a kettle aside. Tate rose to help her, wincing even as he walked across the planks. He took the kettle and gave her a hand up.

"I'll just fill the pitcher," she said weakly. "I'll bring up some fresh towels, too."

"This one's fine." Tate refolded the small towel she'd left for him the day before.

"If you're sure."

Uncertain, Tate scrubbed a hand across his forehead, then spoke before he could change his mind. "Will you sit with me a minute?" He winced at the words, since they weren't remotely how he'd planned on beginning this conversation.

But she adjusted the hem of her apron, gave him a kind smile, and glanced around. She moved to the bed, tucked her skirts beneath her, and sat quietly on the edge.

Now he was really nervous.

Tate followed and sat beside her. Hands clasped between his knees, he fought the urge to bounce his foot. Not wanting the silence to linger, he searched for the words he'd rehearsed, but then Wren was speaking.

"I have something for you." In a rustle of skirts, she moved to the window seat and lifted the lid. It was but a moment of digging before she returned, and he realized what she had. "They're not mine to keep, and I'm sorry I didn't give them to you sooner." She handed him a wooden sword and an old book.

He knew right away what the book was, and mercy. . .he hadn't seen these things in ages. He turned the sword in his hand. Felt the rough blade that he'd hewn from an old fence picket. A twist of his wrist and he twirled the sword forward once as he had always imagined a knight would. Then he settled the weight in his hand and, without a word, set it on the bed between them. Next, he eyed the book. "I was wondering what had happened to this."

"You left it here one day. I think you were too old for it by then. Or you thought you were."

Her words jarred him. She didn't say it unkindly, only honestly. And she was right. He had thought he'd been too old for these things. It was the winter he'd turned sixteen. As much as he'd wanted to hold on to his adolescence, his pa had made it clear that it was time for him to grow up. Tate had already spent his childhood in the fields, and his father was asking him to let go of the one thing that had kept him afloat.

Tate creaked the binding of the book open and looked over at Wren.

"Your pa gave me this."

That pretty mouth of hers parted. "He did?"

Tate nodded. "He gave me books now and again. He was a good man." Knowing how much she missed the doctor, he gave her a muted smile. "Your pa knew how much I liked to read, and my folks, they couldn't...we couldn't..." Tate fought the words back. "There weren't a lot of books to be had. I read the same three over and over. One on history and another on animals and then the Bible. The one about animals was my favorite." He dipped his head. "Which was why I gave you that dumb line about wrens the day we met."

"I thought it was charming."

He elbowed her gently. "You did not."

She brushed her hand against his, so subtly, he'd have missed it had he not been watching. "Then maybe you didn't know me as well as you thought you did."

Which had him looking at her. Taking in the soft plait of her dark hair. Her green eyes peering up at him. Even the smattering of freckles across her cheeks. She smelled of earth and sun and all things good. The hem of her dark blue skirt was soiled and perfect, and the shirt she had rolled past her elbows was a few sizes too big—no doubt having been cut and sewn for her father. Only making her sweeter to him. She was sitting so close. A hard pulsing in his chest, Tate stared at his hands. Gripped the book tighter, the tendons in his forearms shifting.

"I should give this to the boys. There's no sense in me keeping it. I'm not a little kid anymore. It's like you said...." He smoothed his thumb across the binding. "I need to grow up and look around me. And this ...this doesn't matter anymore." He set the book aside.

He felt her gaze on him as the breeze blew at the curtains in the open window. Then Wren pressed her hand into the mattress between them and leaned the tiniest bit closer. With her other hand, she reached around him for the book. She straightened and bowed her head, studying the faded title of *Robin Hood*.

"If you don't keep it," she whispered, "can I?" Her fingers flipped through the pages as she smiled at dog-eared pages and blackberry fingerprints. "These were some of the best days of my life."

His chest rose and fell. More so, when she reached for his hand. He let her take it, wishing his own was steadier.

"Not because of any book. . .or anything else, really. But because of you." She laced her fingers through his. "This"—she gave a little squeeze—"is all I ever wanted." When her eyes brimmed with tears, she wiped at them and looked at his face. "All I'll ever want."

Tate had to force himself to swallow.

Lowering her head, she brushed the side of her face against his shoulder. "But if you're leaving," she whispered, more tears on her voice. Gripping the book tight to her chest with her other hand, she shrugged and seemed unable to speak. When she finally did, her voice was so very faint. "I have to confess, this is so insufficient." She pressed her forehead to his shoulder, then lifted her face just enough to kiss his jaw.

Heat shot across his back. Down to his toes.

"I'm sorry for not telling you that sooner. I was afraid. But. . ."

At a loss for words, he slowly shook his head.

"I love you, Tate Kennedy. I hope you know that."

Tate lowered his head. Pinched his eyes closed. Everything he'd ever wanted in his life sitting right beside him, he hadn't a single word to give her. Except the truth. "You beat me to it, Little Bird."

She'd pressed her cheek to his arm, and he felt her smile. They sat that way for a little while. Her leaning so sweetly against him, her hand still tucked inside his. Finally, he cleared his throat and said what he'd been needing to confess.

"I'm sorry that I didn't write to you. I was thinking a cleaner break was best, but I see now—and really, I feared it then—that I was wrong. I regret it." He ran his thumb over hers, liking the feel of it. Everything about this moment. "I thought I was protecting you. But I was wrong. Maybe I was just protecting myself. My pride. I loved you so much, and I didn't know what to do with that. I should have stayed and figured it out." At the very least, told her what his hopes were for the future. "I'm so sorry I didn't."

She gave his palm a squeeze, setting the book in her lap so she could grip his forearm—her touch as tender as her words. "I forgive you."

He wanted to look over at her but couldn't shake the thought of kissing her, so he forced his eyes to stay on the floorboards.

"I'm glad you got to have your adventure," she whispered.

His words came just as sure. "I hope you know you're all I thought about."

Mrs. Cromwell's voice sounded from below—calling her daughter. Wren's grip on his hand tightened a bit, and his did the same.

"Coming," Wren called back. She rose and glanced around. Seemed to spot his fastened knapsack for the first time. "You're leaving." Her eyes rounded, worry slipping forward.

And he loved her all the more for it. "I am leaving. But not far." He cleared his throat when the words came out weak. He needed to pull himself together. "I've got a place to stay around here now, and should you need this room, I want you to have it." Bending, he pushed the pack aside so it wouldn't be in her way. "But I'll still be looking for meals. I promise I'll pay."

He could see that she was saddened.

"Will you do me one thing?" he asked.

Wren nodded.

"There's something. . ." He glanced around the loft, his nerves rising. "There's something I'd like to ask. . .er. . .show you." Though really, it was both.

She clasped her hands in front of her skirt, the breeze from the window stirring the loose bits of hair that were slipping out of her braid.

"Will you come to the meadow? Tomorrow? Maybe about four."

Her mother called for her again, and he watched as Wren stepped toward the ladder. But she looked over at him, smiled, and promised she would come.

Chapter Thirteen

With her brothers groaning about sore arms and backs before they even climbed out of bed, Wren offered to do the morning milking. She toted a pail out to the barn for the chore, but with her mind on anything but the task, it took her longer than usual to get settled and fill the pail.

Destry trailed her to and fro, and when she was finally back in the kitchen, Wren set the milk aside for the cream to settle. With Mama at the stove, spooning out pancakes, Wren went to the cupboard and pulled down a stack of plates. She clanked them into place, then went back to the cupboard for a handful of forks. Thinking the table might look cheery with some flowers, Wren slipped into her garden, snipped a few early roses, and prepared a jar of the deep red blooms.

"Oh, one too many," her mother said, toting the platter of golden-brown griddle cakes to the table. Wren went back for the butter and slipped it into place as her mother dipped her head toward the place settings. "Just you, me, and the boys."

"No Tate?"

Her mother shook her head, half distracted by the eggs she'd set to sizzling in her skillet. A lift of the towel showed that half-a-dozen pancakes were gone.

"He's paid for a week of meals, so it was no surprise to see him."

"He was here?"

"Just a few minutes ago. I asked him to join us, but he said he had to get back to work, so I sent him off with breakfast." Mama's smile was easy as she glanced over at Wren. "Never known that boy to turn down a meal."

"No, he never has." Her gaze drifting to the path, Wren plucked up the plate and silverware she'd set out for him and returned it the cupboard.

Mama called the twins to table, and Wren took her seat, then reached for her mother's hand and Odin's. She looked to the empty edge of the bench where her father had once sat. Where Tate had sat. He wasn't the first guest to sit there, for her mother always offered it. Wren had always wondered why, and now she knew. Because it made this room—their lives—feel a little less empty.

Closing her eyes, Wren listened to her mother's prayer and fought the urge to peek at the bench again. Which was why when the prayer ended, Wren told her mother that she would need to slip away for a spell tomorrow.

"Where could you possibly have to be?" Odin asked.

Cutting into her breakfast, Wren wasn't sure how to answer.

"Oh, I know!" Ansel blurted, and Odin kicked him under the table. "Ow, that hurt!" Ansel gave his twin a pinched look.

"But it's not done," Odin whispered.

Mama tried to hide her smile behind her cup.

Wren glanced at them all. "Does everyone know what's going on except me?"

When her mother simply fiddled with a loose petal on one of the roses, Wren sensed an answer wasn't coming. "Lovely that these flowers are in bloom. Thank you for cutting them and bringing them in."

Wren sat silent.

Her mother turned the jar. Much too slowly. "Such a pretty bouquet."

"Thank you," Wren said hesitantly, still eyeing her mother. "Grandmother Willow had a list of blooms for her favorite June bouquet. I just looked for the few we had around here and—why are you looking at me like that?"

Mama pressed her lips together and demurely evaded Wren's gaze.

Wren stood and took her plate. "That's it, then. I'm eating on the porch." She strode out, unable to ignore her brothers' snickers as she did. "You are a meddlesome family. I hope you know that." Fighting a smile, she glanced over her shoulder and saw the three of them exchanging grins over Grandmother's bouquet.

She sat on the porch, looked out across the farm, and set her plate aside. The tiny garden book still in her apron pocket, Wren pulled it out. She slipped the ribbon that had been marking the page for a June bouquet, and just before she closed the book again, she turned back several thin sheets to where her father's very own sketch toddled across it. Wren let her fingertip graze the pencil drawing. Her mother joined her then. Sitting quietly.

"I'm going to miss you."

Surprised, Wren looked over at her mother. "I don't know that I'm going anywhere." Which was met by a look that said differently. Wren dropped her gaze. "Did he. . .say anything to you?"

Mama deflected the question by leaning closer, admiring the open pages in the little book Wren held. "How I love this picture."

Wren looked down at it. "Me, too." She handed it to her mother and folded her hands tight in her lap. "I used to wish that I could be just like him. Papa. I realized, though, years later, that I think I'm more like you."

Mama smiled. "In ways. . ." She nodded gently. "But there's a spirit in you that I saw in him. The way he used to wander these hills, his heart for those herbs he hunted. That ginseng that brought him halfway across the world. He was a dreamer. An adventurer."

"I wouldn't say that I'm an adventurer." Wren rolled her eyes so theatrically that her mother laughed.

"Oh, I don't know about that." Her mother slid a finger between the pages of the book to hold it open as she leaned forward, resting her arms on her knees. She stared off toward the rising sun. "From the moment you met him—that boy—I do believe you up and slipped your heart inside his pocket."

Feeling her cheeks warm and that very heart swell, Wren looked down at her shoes.

"And since that moment, you've been just like your father. Off on some adventure." She tapped Wren's chest. "There's a dream in there that just won't die, isn't there?"

Wren smiled softly.

Mama leaned toward her again, cupped the side of Wren's head, and kissed her hair. "And that boy's heart has been in that pocket of yours since that very same day."

———————◆———————

With a few hours until Wren would arrive, Tate decided to put in as much work on the little house as he could. The twins were at their own tasks, so he'd set to work alone to notch another log or two. He was just beginning the second notch on the first log when he looked over to see Jase—of all people—walking across the meadow. The man led a calf by a rope. Tate's ax hung limp in his hand where he stood.

"Call that a day's worth of work?" Jase said in clear jest.

Tate smiled and turned the handle in his hand. He looked back up as he spoke. "Just wasn't expecting company."

Jase slowly nodded, and it was enough. He lifted the end of the rope in his hand. "This is for you. Abigail and I thought you could use it."

Tate felt his brows shoot up. "For me?"

The side of Jase's mouth quirked, and he glanced from Tate's expression to the meadow that would one day be called a farm. "I think you'll need a barn first."

"I think I will, too."

Jase nodded slowly again. "Well, I can lend you a hand. Between the two of us, we could have it up in no time."

Tate dipped his head in gratitude. "I appreciate that."

"I'll keep her until you can claim her." The cuffs of Jase's plaid shirt were undone, as if he himself had called it a day.

Kneeling, Tate held out his hand, and the calf stepped closer. Her long, knobby legs a light brown just like the rest of her. When she drew near enough to touch, Tate smoothed his hand along her soft hide. Large brown eyes blinked at him. She'd make a good little dairy cow one day.

When Jase took a step back, the calf lingered. Jase climbed up the first log and turned to sit on the top of the low wall. Tate staked the yearling's line into the soft turf, then left her to graze. He joined his brother and settled just a few inches beside him on the log wall.

They sat awhile without talking. There were so many fragments—so many unspoken words between them—that Tate didn't know how to put any of them back together again. Broken things had a way of doing that.

But Jase spoke into the silence first. "What's it like?"

"What's what like?" Tate asked, intentionally mirroring his brother's drawl. The very accent he himself once had.

Jase smirked. "That place." He rolled a meaty hand forward as if to help words along. "That place you went off to."

"Norway."

"You and Timothy."

There was something in the way Jase said those three words that had Tate looking over at him. Realizing that they'd left Jase behind. Tate had never once imagined that his older brother would have been anything but glad to see them go, but with the way he spoke and the look in his eyes, Tate realized there might be much more to his brother than he'd ever taken the time to see.

Not knowing how to make up for all the years they spent angry with each other, Tate simply told his brother of the Norwegian snow—how high and white it was. Of villages with peaked roofs lining icy fjords. Dark green mountains so tall, one could barely see the tops of them.

He told Jase of the Caribbean, too. Of Tortuga and Barbados. Palms and hot white sands. Waters so clear he could see fish of more colors than he knew existed. And turtles with their clumsy fins and shells. Smiling, Tate told his brother of the first time he and Timothy had ever shared a coconut. Of how they'd both decided that they would have gotten into it a lot faster had Jase been around.

Jase chuckled. "I'da like to have seen that kid's face." His eyes shone.

"It was worth the effort." Tate rubbed his hands together and realized that he wasn't the only one missing Timothy. It struck him then, what else that implied.

Tate thumped his fist on his knee, wishing he were better at words with this man.

He looked over at his brother, and knowing Jase's life was no less vibrant, Tate asked about the children and Abigail. Jase took a little while to warm up to the subject—he'd never been much of a talker. But within a few minutes, Tate saw in his brother's eyes just how much Abigail and those children were loved. It was in the little things. The fields his brother planted. The way he took his oldest boys out to check traps and teach them the land. How he and Abigail picnicked with them all last Sunday near the creek.

Jase finished by saying, "Ain't no grand tale like yours."

"Yeah, well I don't know about that. Sounds pretty nice to me."

Jase bumped his heel against one of the logs and looked across the land.

"And you've got something I don't have." Tate thought of Abigail and how there hadn't been a thing standing in the way of her and Jase getting married.

"That's true. But you're thinkin' of one-uppin' me, ain't ya?"

Now it was Tate's turn to chuckle. "I've a mind to, now that you mention it."

Jase nodded slowly. "Well, the Cromwell girl. . ." He tugged at his light brown beard. "She'll be looked after. There's no mistake about that."

Dipping his head, Tate nodded a quiet thanks—the words so simple, yet nonetheless meaningful coming from the brother whose shadow had always been impossible to catch. Maybe the feeling was mutual.

Perhaps it was the evening sun beating down on them. Or perhaps it was the cool breeze coming in from the north. Maybe it was the call of birdsong or the fact that for the first time in a long, long time, Tate felt a fresh sense of peace. Whatever the reason, he lowered his head and closed his eyes. Thankful.

After a few moments, Jase cleared his throat, and Tate looked over just as the man motioned toward the east. "You ever think of headin' off again?"

Slowly, Tate shook his head. "Nope. Right here's the place for me."

Nodding, Jase leaned forward and clasped his thick hands together. "I'm glad you came back. And I hope the kid comes back one day, too."

Adopting his brother's position, Tate looked toward the very direction he himself had walked from. And thought of their little brother. "He'll be back," Tate answered, remembering Timothy's promise to do just that. "He'll be back."

Chapter Fourteen

Wren smoothed her skirt. The blue-and-white-striped cotton was nearly threadbare in places, so she'd tied her mother's new apron around her waist. The walk to the meadow was short but laced with so many memories the minutes seemed much longer. As Wren ran her hand along the tall grasses, she thought of how many times Tate had chased her over these very hillocks. How many times he'd led them on some quest. And she knew.

It wasn't this place. It was that man.

She didn't need anything else. If she could just have him, she would be happy all her days, and life—even though it wouldn't always be easy—would be beautiful with Tate Kennedy holding her hand throughout it.

Desperate to find him, she glanced around. The meadow was empty—all save a house in the distance. Well, the beginnings of a house. Wren looked at it. Swallowed hard. It shouldn't take her aback. She knew the land had sold all those months ago. Dipping her chin, she looked to the grass, then back to the small building. And wished the new owner the best.

And heavens. Whoever was building it was sure working fast, for it hadn't been there the last time she'd come this way. She didn't blame the tenant for being eager. She would be, too.

Wren glanced all around her again. Tate had told her four o'clock, and it was a few minutes after, for it had taken her as long to walk here. Eager to spot him, Wren turned in a slow circle. Then she froze. Hanging on one of the logs of the house was Tate's pack. Wren drew in a chestful of air. Let it out.

So this was what he'd been doing. Had. . .had someone hired him?

Perhaps he had been working to save his money. But remembering his words from the day before, something else was rising up inside her. The realization that he had wanted to meet her. Here.

The jolt that had her pressing her hand to her stomach.

He hadn't. . .

No. Not possible. She drew closer and, with a final glance around, hiked up her skirt and climbed over the low wall. Even before she landed in the grass that would someday be a floor, she saw the lunch pail Odin had forgotten the day before. Her pulse beat faster, rushing hot through her when she spotted a pallet in the far corner. A few blankets and a pillow. All askew, but all very clearly. . .

Tate's.

Wren's chest lifted as she forced herself to draw in air. She released it in a rush, suddenly dizzy. It was well past four now. Where was he? Overwhelmed, Wren turned. She looked around at the rough-hewn logs and sank down on unsteady legs. She didn't know how long she sat there, but at the sound of cheery whistling, she rose and looked to the west. Tate was walking through the grass, ax slung over his shoulder. The logs rising no higher than her chest, she had a clear view of him. She knew he spotted her when he slowed. He glanced around, then back to her.

"Wren," he breathed when he drew near. "What are you doing here?" Sweat laced his brow and the breeze ruffled his slit-top shirt. The very one he'd been wearing when the winds had blown him back to her.

"You told me to come. Four. . ." She gulped, struggling for words. "I believe it's past four now."

"No, it's not." He glanced up at the sky and studied it a moment, then he lowered his head and thunked himself in the forehead with his fist. "The sun is in the wrong spot in this country."

Wren didn't mean to laugh, but a giggle bubbled up.

He squinted over at her—his expression equal parts flustered and amused. "I can't believe I did this."

"Tate, what have you done?" She must have said it too soberly, for he smiled.

"Well, as you can see, nothing's *done*. But this is what I wanted to show you." He seemed nervous. It was just as well, for she was shaking. "Would you like me to give you the grand tour?" He gripped the top log of the low wall and climbed over, landing on the other side where she stood. He turned to her, that light in his eyes. "I promise we won't get lost."

She smiled.

"This"—he motioned around them—"is a house, as you can see." Then his hand was on hers, warm and strong and perfect. "Here will be the kitchen—I think. And here." He pulled free to shape a frame with his hands. "Will be a window. But that could be changed. And here"— he pointed up—"will be a loft. There's still some things to do before I start it. But I thought that would be a good place to put little people." His eyes widened as if he hadn't meant to blurt that out.

Biting her lip, Wren took his hand again, missing the feel of it.

He pulled away a moment later only to help her over the side of the house again. He hopped back over himself before leading her around the outside corner of logs. A small picket fence edged this side of the house, and a knobby arbor cast lacy shadows on freshly tilled soil. The warm-springy scent of it rose up, greeting her.

He motioned with his arm toward the back meadow. "There'll be crops, of course. But this would be just for flowers, herbs. Whatever you like." He hesitated on *you*. As if just realizing he was making an assumption.

Wren was ever so glad he was. She touched the gate—her eyes taking it all in at once.

He stood silent as if to give her time, then he spoke softly. "Those seeds your grandmother sent with me. . .there's a story there that I've been meaning to tell you."

Turning, Wren gazed up at him.

"I just need you to know something." He tossed his hand back and forth through his hair. "There were other things your grandmother thought to send that day. She showed me all around the different rooms of her house. Where your father used to play." He smiled softly as if aware of the bittersweet way that knowledge washed over her.

"She sat me down in the kitchen. Turns out she makes really good gingerbread." He winked. "We talked, and she asked all about me and you and the boys. Everything. We talked for hours. I think she kind of adopted me."

Her heart bursting, Wren smiled.

"We also sat in the garden for a spell. You'd have loved it. She showed me her potting shed and all around the grounds." He lifted his gaze to the horizon, then back to Wren. "You might like to know that she had eyes like yours. And laughed just like your father used to."

Her throat tight, Wren pressed her palms together and leaned against the logs. Felt their strength. Took in his words.

His brow furrowed. "There were other things she thought you might like, but nothing I could fit in my sack." He flashed her a hint of regret. "Then as we were talking, I realized that she was preparing those little packets. I always knew the two of you swapped seeds, so I didn't think much of it. But when she finished, she slid them in my hand and said they were for you. For a new beginning." He tilted his face to the ground and kicked at a clump of dirt with his worn boot. Finally, he looked back at her. "Something about making a home." His broad throat dipped. "With me."

A slow draw of air didn't seem enough time to take in those precious words, so Wren did it twice.

Such vulnerability lived in his eyes. "I was just chatting away about you and all the things I loved about you, all the times we had together . . .and there she was, planning a garden." His sleeve brushed hers as he stepped nearer and leaned against the wall beside her. "And. . ." He opened his mouth. Closed it. Skimmed his fingers down the side of his temple.

Wren sensed there was more he wanted to say, but he looked a few moments shy of needing to sit down.

Not wanting him to feel rushed with what he might have to say or, as he'd phrased it earlier, ask, she peeked over her shoulder. "What goes in there?" she asked to try and ease him. Wren looked over the low wall that would surely rise much higher than her head before long. "I mean"—she leaned on the edge and pointed to where the loft would go—"If that's to be for little people. . ." Her heart soared at the thought of a family—with Tate.

"Oh. . ." He followed her gaze to the wide space beside them. "This is for the big people." He grinned impishly. "I was thinking you and me." He leaned on the edge of the wall beside her, his shoulder pressing strong against hers.

"I like that idea," she whispered.

Head bowed between them, his words were soft. "Do you?"

She nodded, which seemed to do something for his nerves, for he smiled again. His eyes were the warmest brown as he bent to kiss her hair. "There's something I need to ask you."

She held her breath, having waited for this for so long.

Straightening, he squared his stance. Hope in those eyes of his. "Wren Cromwell. If I promise to never forget to wash behind my neck and to leave my shoes in front of the door only occasionally and to. . .to never, ever leave you again until the good Lord takes me home, would you do me the honor of being my wife?" Then he quickly added that he would do everything in his power not to snore.

Every hope she'd clung to unfurled. Joy bursting forward. Wren opened her mouth to speak, then closed it.

He made a face as if that had come out all wrong. He wet his lips and seemed to struggle before blurting, "Can I try that again?"

But every word had been perfect.

Squinting down at her, he clearly disagreed. "Have you ever heard of the Northern Lights?"

As desperate as she was to answer him, she wanted to let him finish. "No."

"They're colors in the sky. Brilliant colors. It would take your breath away." When he tilted his head to the blue sky, she did the same as if a hint of them might appear. "I watched them shine more nights than I could count, and every time I did, I wished you were there to see them. I know I didn't write you any letters, but I was writing you in my heart. As I watched those lights color the sky, I sat and talked to you. I probably sounded like an idiot." He gave her a half grin. "And I wondered what you were doing and if I might have lost you. And it only made me want to work harder and quicker and be stronger so I could hurry up and come home to you and have something to give you."

Tate watched the sky, and she watched him.

"There was something about those lights. Maybe it was the way they moved or the way they changed. Or the sheer impossibility of it all. Color up in the sky." His eyes found hers. "And that's what kept me holding on. That if God could make a miracle like that, then surely He could get me back to you."

Tears rising, Wren pinched the bridge of her nose. She thought of the way he'd walked up to her that day in her mother's garden. Having come so far. . .

"You're already my best friend." His fingers grazed her sleeve, reaching around her back, holding her gently in a way he'd never done before. "And life just isn't right without you."

Needing him more than she'd ever confessed to him, Wren clutched his sun-faded shirt, then slid her hand to the top of his chest before gripping the back of his neck. She rose up onto her toes. But then he was backing away, only to bump against the side of the arbor he'd built for her. The knobby branches trembled, and he sidestepped, almost stumbling again.

"You're about to break my promise to your father." An ardent look in his eyes made her realize how strong his struggle was.

She wondered if so simple a word could ever be sufficient. "Yes." She stepped closer, and he didn't back away. "Yes. If you'll have me."

He stared at her, then ducked his head, closed his eyes, and seemed to collect himself. As if he hadn't been certain that would be her answer. Her throat tight, she remembered every moment of their years together. Even the ones spent apart. The ones readying his heart for hers. Or perhaps it was the other way around.

Rising back onto her toes, she slipped her arms around his neck again.

A muscle in his jaw shifting, he looked at her—uncertainty on his voice—a readiness in his eyes. "Now, I've never done this before, mind you."

"Me, neither." She gently tugged his ear, suddenly unsteady for so many reasons.

The boy who had always had her heart grazed his fingers against the waistband of her apron, pulling her closer. There was a warmth to Tate Kennedy. Maybe it was the life in him, his jovial ways. Maybe it was his years beneath the sun. Or the goodness that beat beneath her palm when she pressed it to his chest. . .the way he had always kept her safe and how he was the only good thing she could remember about the year her father died. Wren laced her fingers into his hair, holding on. The last thing she saw as his faced brushed hers was his smile. And then he kissed her, as if they never had another place to be but there.

"So where are you taking me first?"

Tate looked over at Wren when she spoke. With her hand in his, they walked across the meadow—the sun sinking in the sky just behind them. "*First?*" He squinted playfully. "Who's going anywhere?"

"Well, you've got to take me somewhere."

"Is that so?"

She smiled up at him.

"How about Virginia Beach? I think you'd like it there."

Tipping her head to the side, she nodded thoughtfully.

"I'll take you, then. First chance we get. Rent you a cottage, and you can collect seashells."

She all-out grinned now.

"And then one day, we'll go a little farther. What would you say to that?"

She squeezed his hand as they walked on. "I'd like that. I'd like that a whole lot."

Joanne Bischof has a deep passion for Appalachian culture and writing stories that shine light on God's grace and goodness. She lives in the mountains of Southern California with her husband and their three children. When she's not weaving Appalachian romance, she's blogging about faith, folk music, and the adventures of country living that bring her stories to life. She is a Christy Award finalist and author of *Be Still My Soul*, *Though My Heart Is Torn*, and *My Hope Is Found* (WaterBrook Multnomah). www.joannebischof.com.

Something Borrowed

Kim Vogel Sawyer

Dedication

For Kamryn,
who rescues creatures in distress;
and for Mom,
who still calls Minnesota home.

*Jesus said unto him, Thou shalt love the Lord thy God with all thy heart,
and with all thy soul, and with all thy mind. This is the first and great
commandment. And the second is like unto it,
Thou shalt love thy neighbour as thyself.*
MATTHEW 22:37–39

Chapter One

Wilhelmina, Minnesota
Spring 1881

Clara Frazier fastened her father's faded dungarees to the thin wire running from the house to the barn. The late morning breeze flapped the freshly laundered clothes, filling her nose with the scent of lye soap. She stepped away from the line and turned her face to the north, drinking in the crisp spring air until the sharp tang of lye abandoned the back of her throat. How different the country smelled from the city. She closed her eyes for a moment and savored the unique prairie perfume.

Her senses filled, she scooped up the empty basket and made her way across the hard-packed ground toward the small wood-sided house that had been her home for less than a month. The solid, rhythmic whacks of an ax against wood echoed from behind the house, and Clara paused to listen. Papa had been so happy this morning to awaken to sunshine after days of gray clouds and drizzle. He'd proclaimed, "Ah, what a gift the Lord has given! A perfect day for clearing our field, Clara Rose."

Clara hadn't argued—she never argued when Papa spoke of the Lord—but she couldn't help worrying. Clearing a field for planting was a job for a young man. Papa was fifty already. And until the purchase of this property, he'd labored behind a desk rather than behind a plow. Even so, the steady *whack! whack! whack!* continued. Papa's determination outweighed his aging back. Hadn't his determination convinced her purchasing this farmstead and seeds for a corn crop would give them a fresh start? If he intended to work hard and bring this abandoned property to life again, she'd do her part. For as long as he needed her.

She placed the basket on the porch and reached for the door latch.

But a series of shrill, panicked yelps pulled her off the porch and across the yard in the direction of the sound. The yips became more frightened and pain filled, spurring her to hurry. Her full skirt tangled around her ankles, hindering her progress, so she grabbed the rose calico in her fists, lifted her skirt to her knees, and took off at a run.

In a grassy patch on the opposite side of the road, a hawk wrestled with a small, furry creature. The little thing continued to release short, sharp yips of panic. Clara's heart rolled over in compassion and fear. She could not let that bird eat a puppy for dinner! She dropped her skirt and waved both hands over her head, hollering as she dashed directly at the feathered predator.

"Git! You there, you foul fowl! Git, I say!"

The hawk flapped its wings at her, its steely eyes daring her to stay away.

Clara snatched up a handful of long, dry grass stems and slapped at the bird. "I said *git!*"

The bird screeched in protest, but to Clara's relief, it hopped a few feet away and then took flight, leaving the little ball of fur still yelping on a patch of matted weeds. Clara threw the grass at the retreating hawk and then dropped to her knees. The poor little sandy-haired pup continued to cry in pathetic yelps even when Clara scooped it up and cradled it to her chest.

She stroked its head, murmuring, "Shhh-shhh," and it finally quieted, although it trembled within her grasp. She lifted it and pressed its soft ear to her cheek. "There, there, little one. You're safe."

Now that the puppy had calmed, she laid it in her lap and examined it. Such a tiny thing, not much bigger than the palm of her hand, with scraggly fur, little rounded ears, and deep blue eyes. Two spots of blood stained its coat where the hawk's talons or pecking beak had broken the skin. Clara used the handkerchief from her pocket to wipe the wounds, clicking her tongue on her teeth in sympathy. "Poor baby. Look what that mean old bird did to you."

It curled into a ball on her rumpled skirt and peered up at her with apprehensive eyes.

Clara continued to stroke the pup with the wadded handkerchief and scanned the landscape. "Where's your mama, huh? You're not big enough to be out here all by yourself." While she searched for a sign of a mama dog, a prickle of awareness crept across her scalp. She held her breath, listening, wondering what seemed amiss, and then recognition dawned.

Papa's ax was silent.

Her breath whooshed out. He must be at the house, looking for his lunch, and here she sat worrying over a lost puppy. Clumsily, she pushed to her feet with the puppy clutched in the bend of her arm and jogged toward the house. As she neared it, another sound—this one soft, quavering, but as chilling as the puppy's frantic yelps had been—reached her ears.

"Help me... Clara Rose... Help..."

Clara gasped. She placed the puppy in the woven laundry basket and broke into a run for the second time that morning, now to the field behind the barn. The tree Papa had claimed would be kindling by the end of the day lay on its side. But where was Papa? She slowed to a stop, scanning the area for a glimpse of her father. "Papa?"

"Help me."

Her pulse pounding in trepidation, Clara inched forward, hand shielding her eyes from the bright sun. "Papa, where are you?" Her heart leaped in fright when she spotted his plaid shirt beneath the snarl of the fallen tree's thick branches.

She darted forward and clawed at the branches, tearing her hands and her dress in the process. "Papa! Papa!" Her breath heaved in frightened puffs. She tugged, grunting, inwardly begging God for the strength to free her father from beneath the tree's weight. "I'll get you out, Papa!" If only she had his determination, she'd have him out in the space of one heartbeat.

"Clara Rose, stop." Papa extended his hand through the snarl of small branches and newly unfurled leaves. His flesh was scratched and bleeding, his shirtsleeve torn. "Listen to me, child."

Clara gripped his hand, biting her lip to hold back her sobs.

"You can't...lift the tree. We need many hands. Or mules...and a chain." He closed his eyes. His white face contorted. He licked his lips

233

and squinted at Clara. "Go to town. Get help."

A sob broke free. "But I can't leave you alone like this! I—"

"Go." Although a mere, raspy whisper, Papa's voice held strength. "I'm not alone. The Lord is with me." His lips twisted into the most pitiful smile Clara had ever seen—even more pitiful than the one he'd worn all through Mama's burial. "He'll be with you, too, as you bring help. Now. . .go, Clara Rose."

Clara wadded her skirt in her hands and took off as fast as her shaky legs would carry her. Despite her fiercely trembling hands, she secured their trusty mare, Penelope, in the wagon traces, then climbed into the seat and took up the reins, all the while praying for God to preserve her father's life. She'd already lost Mama and Brant and Clifford. She couldn't lose Papa. Especially since it was all her fault he'd been clearing that field in the first place.

Chapter Two

To Clara's great relief, her prayers were rewarded. Dr. Biehler quickly rounded up a half-dozen men, who filled the back of a wagon and followed Clara to the farm. There, they lifted the fallen tree from Papa's form and carried him to the house. After a thorough examination, the doctor—who admitted he was only an animal doctor but all the small town could offer—set Papa's leg, poured a spoonful of reddish-brown liquid into Papa's mouth to help with the pain, and then escorted Clara from the room even though she wanted to stay by her father's bed and watch his chest rise and fall.

"He'll likely sleep the rest of the day," Dr. Biehler said, his voice low and soothing, "so don't be concerned when he doesn't rouse. His body took a terrible shock, and sleep is the best medicine I know for shock."

Clara tucked the strands of hair that had escaped her braid behind her ears. "What of his leg? How long will it take to heal?"

The older man pursed his lips, making his thick gray mustache hairs stick straight out. "I have to be honest with you, Miss Frazier. It's a clean break, but the bone snapped in two."

Nausea threatened. She clutched her stomach and willed herself to remain strong.

"It will take time before he can put weight on it again. At least six weeks. Maybe more."

Her mind whirled. Papa said for the corn to be knee-high by the Fourth of July, he needed the seeds in the ground by the end of May. If he was off his feet for six weeks, he wouldn't be able to return to the fields until early June. Or later, if healing took longer.

"Oh." She swallowed the bile filling her throat. "Oh my. . ."

The doctor gave her shoulder a few comforting pats. "Now, Miss Frazier, let's think positively, hm? A broken leg is easier to mend than a broken back. He suffered no internal injuries. All things considered, your father is a very lucky man."

Clara couldn't bring herself to apply the word *lucky* to Papa's situation, but she nodded and forced her lips into a weak smile. "Yes. Thank you, Doctor."

He gave her directions on caring for her father, promised to come by each day, and then stepped out on the porch. Clara, hugging herself, followed him. He moved past the laundry basket, and the little pup began yipping in short, panicked yelps.

"Oh!" Clara scooped up the distraught animal and nestled it against her bodice. "I completely forgot about you, you poor little thing." She turned a hopeful look on the doctor. "Sir, a hawk attacked this puppy and pierced its side. Would you look at the wounds and see if they need tending?" She held the puppy toward him.

The doctor pinched the pup's scruff. The little animal hung limp from the man's grasp. "Where did you get this?"

She pointed. "I found it in the field across the road, all by itself."

Dr. Biehler frowned. "Miss Frazier, this isn't a puppy. It's a kit."

Clara frowned, too, confused. A veterinarian mistook a baby dog for a baby cat?

"Well. . ." He scratched his head, squinting at the dangling pup. "I cannot say for sure it's a fox kit. It could be a coyote pup. They look a lot alike when they are small. But I can tell you this is a wild animal." He gave it a quick, disinterested examination and then put it in the basket, where it immediately set up a series of complaining yelps and whines. He shook his head. "You had better take him back to where you found him."

Sympathy for the helpless creature twined through Clara. "But isn't it—he—too young to fend for himself?"

Dr. Biehler nodded. "Certainly. He is probably no more than three weeks old. Big enough to venture from the den, but not big enough to find his way back. The mother will hunt for him, though, so put him in the field and leave him there."

Clara crouched and stroked the pup's ruff. He ceased his whimpering and nuzzled her hand. Having been raised in the city, she knew little about foxes or coyotes. "You're sure the mother will come get him?"

Dr. Biehler shrugged and stepped from the porch. "If the mother is alive. And if the human scent you have transferred to him doesn't cause her to reject him."

Clara jerked her hand back.

"But you cannot take care of him."

"You can't take care of him, Clara." The voice from her past swooped in and jolted her to her feet. "Why not?"

The doctor's eyebrows pinched low. "He is a wild creature."

"He's a grown man." She pushed aside the remembrance and plunked her fists on her hips. "But he's helpless." As she spoke to the doctor, she argued against the voice in her head: *He can't even boil water—how would he see to his own needs?* "How can I leave him in that field all alone, knowing he might starve to death? Or be attacked by a hawk or some other predator?"

"It is the nature of things, Miss Frazier."

"It's natural for a girl to leave her home." Clara shook her head hard. "No. I won't accept that. Families take care of each other. He has no other family. I will take care of him." Her thoughts jumbled. Was she speaking of the little lost creature or her father? Either way, her adamancy applied. "I won't leave him to fend for himself." Not even if it cost her yet another beau.

"I think you'll regret it."

She raised her chin. "No, sir, I will not."

He shrugged. "All right, then. Suit yourself. I'll come out each morning over the next week or two to check on your father. If you have concerns, send a message, and I'll make a special visit." The doctor strode across the hard ground to the waiting wagon.

Clara waved good-bye to the wagon of men, then plucked the pup from the basket and held it to her thumping heart. A warm, soft tongue swiped the underside of her chin, and she smiled. She wouldn't regret the decision she'd made in Minneapolis, and she wouldn't regret the decision she was making right now. Maybe she'd inherited some of her father's determination after all.

Over the next week, Clara's determination to keep the pup—as he grew, his tail lent evidence he was a coyote pup and not a fox kit—flagged. He required around-the-clock feedings, and when he wasn't sleeping, he wanted attention. Between caring for Papa and caring for the little coyote, she'd never been so exhausted. Yet she wouldn't wish away either responsibility. Papa had dedicated his whole life to her, even leaving his good job and their fine home in Minneapolis for this run-down farmstead and an uncertain outcome. There was nothing she wouldn't do for her father.

As for the demanding little ball of fur, he provided what was certainly her only chance to share the maternal love pining for expression. So no matter how many times she warmed milk to drip into his greedy mouth with a bit of cloth or scrubbed up the messes he left on the pine floorboards, she wouldn't complain. He made her laugh by scampering behind her, batting at her shoelaces or biting at her hem, and he made her sigh when he curled in her lap and gazed up at her adoringly. The joy he gave her far exceeded the weight of responsibility.

But other responsibilities weren't so easily balanced. Milking the cow, bringing in water from the well, feeding their livestock, and cleaning the barn stalls—all things Papa had done before his accident—taxed her. Papa fretted over her working so hard, and he didn't believe her when she assured him she could handle the tasks. She supposed her drooping shoulders and dark-smudged eyes told the truth. But not until the day she carried Papa's ax to the field and tried to hack apart the felled tree did he become stern and demand she give up trying to do his work.

She sat on the edge of his bed and took his hand. "Papa, the field has to be cleared if we're to put in a corn crop this year."

He scowled at her. "And do you intend to plow the ground and plant the seeds, too? Clara Rose, I appreciate your willingness, but it's too much for you."

She laughed softly. "I suppose my classes at the Fenwick Finishing School for Girls didn't prepare me for plowing and planting, but haven't you always told me I could do anything I set my mind to if I relied on God's strength?"

Papa leaned against the pillows and sighed. He looked so old and tired. Tears pricked Clara's eyes. He squeezed her hand. "God can do anything, and we can do all things through Him, it's true, but you don't have the muscles of a man, my daughter." He turned her hand over and used his fingers to trace the blisters forming a line across her palm. "Your mother would roll over in her grave if she saw this."

Clara gently extracted her hand and hid it in the folds of her skirt. "I think you forget Mama's last words, Papa. She bade me to be a loyal daughter and take good care of you. And that's what I intend to do."

"But at what expense, Clara Rose?" Papa's question hung in the room.

Clara bit her lower lip, trying to forget what her loyalty to Papa had already cost her. As if sensing his mistress's need for distraction, the little coyote pup made a clumsy dash for Clara and attacked the toe of her shoe. Laughing, Clara picked him up and put him on the bed. He bounced across Papa's chest, releasing little yips with each ungainly leap.

Papa laughed. "What a scamp he is." He twiddled his fingers, encouraging the pup to bat and snap at him. "Have you chosen a name for him yet?"

Clara sucked in a breath. "If I name him, I know I'll keep him. I wasn't sure if you. . ."

Her father arched an eyebrow. "Would let you keep him?"

She nodded.

"You're twenty-four years old now. I think you've gained enough wisdom to know if you can handle the responsibility of a pet coyote."

The reminder of her age pained her, but she smiled. "Then I guess I better choose a name, because I don't want to give him up." She tilted her head and watched the coyote pup jump and bat at Papa's hand. "How about Russet? Or Beau—short for Beauregard?"

Papa chuckled. "Those names are too refined for a rowdy little fellow like him."

Clara clapped her palms together. "Rowdy! That's the perfect name, Papa."

Papa caught the pup in both hands and held him in front of his face. "What do you think? Would you like the name Rowdy?"

The pup yipped, wriggling.

Both Clara and Papa laughed.

"All right, Rowdy it is." Papa plopped Rowdy in Clara's lap and then placed his hand on her knee. "With that decision made, we can turn our attention to the next important decision."

Clara put the wiggly pup on the floor. "What's that?"

"Who will clear the field."

She sighed. "There really isn't any choice, Papa. Only this morning the doctor told me your leg is healing well, but when I asked, he assured me you won't be up and working before June. So it's up to me to clear the field."

Papa shook his head. "I talked to the doctor this morning, too, about the field work. He recommended hiring a local man to do the labor."

Clara cringed. "Oh, Papa, no."

He frowned. "Now, hear me out. We have money in the bank. We can afford to hire a hand."

Hadn't they sold their house in the big city and moved to this remote town to be away from others? How could Papa suggest they bring someone to the farm? "I'd rather do the work myself."

"You have enough to do with the cleaning, cooking, laundry, gardening. . ." Rowdy jumped and clamped his jaw on the corner of the blanket. The pup growled and spun a slow circle. Papa chuckled deep in his throat. "And keeping up with Rowdy. It only makes sense to hire someone to do the heavy labor until I'm on my feet again and can take care of the chores myself."

"But, Papa—"

"No arguing, Clara Rose." Papa sent her a firm look that stilled her tongue. "Tomorrow is Saturday. First thing after breakfast, you're to hitch Penelope to the wagon and drive to the neighboring farms. Doc Biehler said at least two of our neighbors have fine, strapping sons who are accustomed to farmwork. You'll ask to hire one of them. And that's final."

Chapter Three

A wagon rolled up the long lane leading to the Klaassen farmstead. Titus Klaassen lifted his attention from the trio of bawling *Kose* at his feet. He shielded his eyes with his hand, ignoring the largest baby goat's attempt to eat the cuff on his pant leg, and watched the wagon approach. Saturday was chore day in his small farming community, so visitors were usually traveling salesmen. But this was no sales wagon, the driver no salesman. In all his twenty-five years, he'd never seen a salesman wear a ruffled bonnet and flower-sprigged frock the same color as the lilac blossoms budding on the bushes around the front porch. He released a short chuckle. Salesmen might be more successful if they all dressed as pretty as the *Me'jal* perched on that wagon seat.

He crouched and freed his cuff from the kid's mouth, then held the milk-filled bottle toward the greedy little goat. While the kid tugged at the bottle nipple, Titus observed the young lady bring the wagon to a halt on the cleared ground beside the barn, set the brake, and climb down from the high seat. Slender and as graceful as willow branches swaying in a breeze, her appearance pulled at him with the same force as the hungry kid on the bottle.

The young woman paused for a moment and shook the dust from her skirt. Then she reached up and released the strings on her bonnet. She lifted the bonnet from her head, revealing a braided coil as richly brown as the maple syrup Pa boiled every spring. Recognition dawned—the Frazier daughter. Titus rose, the empty bottle in his hand and a bleating *Kos* bumping against his shin, and watched the girl climb the porch risers and knock on the screened door. Moments later, the door opened, and the girl disappeared into the house.

Worry nibbled at him, as persistent as the Kos demanding a second feeding. Just last Sunday his minister had led the congregation in praying for the elder Frazier, who'd suffered an accident on their land. Even though the Fraziers weren't part of the local Mennonite fellowship, Titus had prayed for the newcomers every day. He hoped no other calamities had befallen the family.

Curiosity about his new neighbors trickled through him. The Fraziers kept to themselves. Not once had either of them ventured to the Klaassen farm even though Ma had delivered a loaf of her blue-ribbon pumpkin bread to welcome them to Wilhelmina. The other two of the rejected goat triplets needed to be fed, but he couldn't resist leaving the small pen and trotting across the yard to the house to find out why Miss Frazier had come calling.

He wiped the bottoms of his boots clean on the scraper at the base of the porch—Ma always mopped first thing on Saturday, and she'd scold if he brought even a speck of dirt in—and followed the sound of women's voices to the kitchen. Ma, ever the gracious hostess, had seated the visitor at the scarred worktable and was serving her a cup of *Koffe* as Titus stepped into the kitchen doorway.

Ma barely glanced at Titus, but he witnessed a knowing smirk crease her face as she sank onto the opposite chair and folded her hands on the table's edge. "Now, then, Miss Frazier, what brings you out on this fine spring *Morje?*"

The girl crinkled her nose. "More-yah?"

Ma chuckled. "Forgive me. The English words so close to my old language always seem to get swallowed by our Low German. What brings you out this fine morning?"

Miss Frazier took a sip of her coffee before answering. "I wish I could say I was making a social call, because I know we—my father and I—haven't properly thanked you for the delicious bread you brought to us last month." Pink filled her cheeks, her expression as sheepish as a child who'd been caught with her fingers in the sugar bowl.

Ma shook her head and clicked her tongue on the roof of her mouth. "You need not worry over a delayed thank-you. I know how much work needs done at the farmstead you and your *Foda* purchased. It sat empty for two years! I am sure you have both been very busy. And even more so now with your dear father injured." A worried frown pursed Ma's face. "How is your father, Miss Frazier?"

"He is healing well, Dr. Biehler says."

"Such a blessing," Ma said, and Titus nodded in agreement.

Miss Frazier ducked her head. "But he is unable to work. In our fields." She took another little sip of the coffee, the cup quivering in her grasp. She set the cup down and sent Ma a helpless look. "He sent me out today to inquire about hiring a farmhand. I already went to the Rempels, but they said they couldn't spare either of their sons. Mrs. Rempel told me you have six sons. So I came here, hoping, maybe. . ." She bit the corner of her lip.

Ma drew back in surprise. "Miss Frazier, are you asking to hire one of my boys to work at your place?"

Her lip still caught in her teeth, Miss Frazier nodded.

Ma grimaced. "Oh, I am sorry, but—"

Titus held out his hand. "Ma, couldn't—"

Miss Frazier sat up straight and began a rapid flow of words. "Mrs. Klaassen, please. Papa already bought seed corn, and the seeds need to go in the ground before long if we're to have a money crop this year, but the field hadn't been completely cleared before we bought the farm. Papa got hurt felling the largest of the trees, and now he's unable to finish clearing. The doctor said Papa won't be able to work for many weeks yet, and I"—she gulped—"am unable to chop up trees or break the ground. We must hire someone."

Ma patted Miss Frazier's hand and flicked a frown at Titus. "Please, let me finish."

Titus bit back his own objection out of respect for his mother.

With Miss Frazier quiet, Ma offered a warm smile. "It is true the Lord blessed us with six sons. Our oldest, Jonah, is married and lives on a farm near Mountain Lake with his wife and our *Grootsän*, Little Ben. Our two youngest, Mark and Paul, have not yet finished school. But our middle boys, Titus, John, and Andrew, live here at home and help their father with our fields and livestock.

"Since they have completed their schooling, and since all of them are familiar with every part of farming, any of them could certainly see to what needs doing at your farm."

Hope glimmered in Miss Frazier's expression.

Titus found himself holding his breath, his heart thudding in anticipation.

"But I am so sorry, Miss Frazier. I cannot possibly hire out one of my boys."

Miss Frazier's chin began to tremble and plump tears winked in her eyes.

Her reaction pained Titus. He gritted his teeth and inwardly protested. How could Ma, the kindest and most giving person he'd ever known, be so callous to this neighbor in need?

"*Nä*, nä," Ma went on, seemingly oblivious to Miss Frazier's distress, "my Ben would say the same thing. No hiring out of our boys. But"—she held up one finger—"we could *lieen* you one of our *Säns*." She made a face. "Lend you one of our sons."

Titus sucked in his breath and held it.

Miss Frazier gasped. "L–lend?"

Ma nodded, her eyes sparkling. "What kind of neighbors would we be if we made you pay for such badly needed help? The Lord would frown on us, for sure. But to lend you a pair of hands until your father is able to work again? That would be our pleasure."

Titus let out his breath in a loud *whoosh*. Both women looked at him. His face flamed, but he stepped forward—one wide stride that brought him within arm's reach of the table. "I will help Mr. Frazier, Ma. That is. . ." He locked his gaze on Miss Frazier's wide, unblinking brown eyes. "If you approve, miss."

"I tried, Papa, honestly I did." Clara petted Rowdy, who napped in her lap while Papa ate lunch. "But Mrs. Klaassen was very stubborn—or *stoakoppijch*, as she put it. She said the only way she would let one of her sons come help is if we 'borrowed' him rather than 'bought' him. I didn't know what else to do except agree. Especially since Mrs. Rempel said they couldn't spare one of their boys to work for us."

Papa sighed and toyed with his fork instead of eating. "It hurts my pride to have someone labor on my property without pay, but I was told that the Mennonite farmers around Wilhelmina were staunch in faith and work ethic. I imagine you're correct in calling them stubborn. I don't doubt you did your best."

Clara chewed her lower lip. If she'd had her way, she would have borrowed the younger of the two Klaassen sons who entered the kitchen during her visit. Both possessed wide shoulders and thick hands clearly capable of hard work, but the younger one, Andrew, just out of school and caught in the gawky stage between youth and manhood, was much less intimidating than the one who promised to come early Monday morning and get started hacking the fallen tree into firewood.

An image of Titus Klaassen—tall, with a thickly muscled neck and a firm, square jaw that spoke of strength, and sky-blue eyes, full pink lips, and wavy blond hair that spoke of something soft and gentle—filled her mind. Not a trace of youthful awkwardness lingered in this one. More handsome than either of the beaus she'd left behind in Minneapolis and so sweetly eager to ease her burdens, he might prove to be a greater distraction than even Rowdy.

"Did you convince the Klaassens to allow the son to take his meals with us, at least?" Papa's query pulled Clara from her musing.

She nodded so emphatically, Rowdy stirred. She scratched his silky ears, and he returned to snoozing. "I told Mrs. Klaassen we would serve him breakfast, lunch, and dinner, too, if he stays past five o'clock."

Papa finally carried a forkful of peas to his mouth, chewed, and swallowed. "And snacks both morning and afternoon?"

Would Papa deliver the snacks to Titus and spare her the discomfort? Of course not. Clara cringed. "Um. . ."

"A man working hard all day needs snacks, too."

Something pinched her chest, making it hard to breathe, but she forced a reply. "All right, Papa. Snacks, too."

Finally, her father smiled. "Good. And we might find some other ways to repay him for his kindness." He closed his eyes and sighed, his plate of food seemingly forgotten. "What a blessing to have such good-hearted neighbors. The Lord is taking care of us, Clara Rose." He drifted off to sleep.

Clara settled Rowdy on the bed next to her father and carried the plate out of the room. At the dry sink, she scraped the leftover food into a little bowl for Rowdy and set it aside. Then she stood staring at the small stack of dirty dishes, imagining adding one more plate, bowl, cup, and set of cutlery to the pile. The additional items didn't trouble her. If she'd accepted Brant's or Clifford's proposal for marriage, she would have washed more dishes every day. She'd so looked forward to tending to a husband—mending his clothes, cooking his meals, keeping his house neat and tidy, raising his children. . . .

But after losing not one but two beaus because of her dedication to her father, she'd packaged her dreams for marriage in a box and hid it away in the farthest corner of her mind. She didn't dare hope that another man would find her pleasing, because a third rejection would surely shatter her. Titus Klaassen's rugged, handsome appearance and kind nature appealed to her. He seemed exactly the kind of man any woman would want to claim as a beau.

She set her hands to work cleaning the dishes, and as she worked, a prayer formed and winged its way heavenward. *Lord, having our young, handsome neighbor in close proximity for weeks on end will surely wreak havoc on my old-maid heart. Please heal Papa quickly so we can send our borrowed hand back to his own work.*

Chapter Four

Early Monday morning, when the sun was only a sliver of red on the horizon, Titus saddled the oldest of his family's horses and set off for the Frazier farm. Unlike Andrew and Mark, who had to be coaxed out of bed each morning with the promise of bacon and eggs, Titus enjoyed rising when the moon still hung heavy and a few stars bravely winked from a gray sky. The world was peaceful, and a man could think without any other distraction than birdsong or a whispering breeze—if one could consider such beautiful sounds distracting.

He breathed in the cool morning air and hummed one of the hymns from yesterday's worship service, inspired by the rhythm of Petunia's steady *clop-clop* of hooves against the road. Quickly the tune gave way to boisterous words in his parents' native tongue. *"Lobe den Herren, den mächtigen König der Ehren!"*

Petunia snorted and shook her head, making her thick mane flop.

Titus laughed. He gave the horse's tawny neck a pat. "Oh, please excuse me, old girl, I forget you are an American horse." He sang the line in English. *"'Praise to the Lord, the Almighty, the King of creation!'"* He glanced at the sky, its blooming pink hue chasing away the remaining stars but bringing into view purplish streaks of clouds. "And such a creation He made, Petunia. Loveliness everywhere."

Including on the face of Miss Frazier.

Titus chuckled self-consciously. Ma was getting older, gray winding its way through her hair and lines creasing her face, but she was just as wise as she'd always been. She'd listened to his reasons why he should be the one to work at the Frazier place—as the oldest of the boys still at home he had the most experience, he was the earliest riser, so he could be to the neighboring farm by breakfast time, and he was the reigning fall festival log-splitting contest winner, so he possessed the know-how and strength to clear that field in short order.

When he finished his list, she nodded and added another reason. "And Miss Frazier's heart-shaped face and eyes as brown as a pecan shell are more pleasant to look upon than your brothers' square jaws and Klaassen blue eyes, yes?"

Sheepishly, Titus agreed. Then Ma had given him a caution, which he took to heart. "She is a comely young woman, my son, and you are at an age to take a wife. But before you allow yourself to be drawn to her, make sure she is a woman of faith. It would not bide well for you to be yoked unequally."

Titus pondered anew Ma's serious words as he guided Petunia up the short, rocky lane to the neglected little house where Miss Frazier and her father lived. He'd prayed for years for God to lead him to the woman meant to be his helpmeet. None of the young women of Wilhelmina or any he'd encountered from nearby communities had stirred his heart the way Miss Frazier had when she looked beseechingly across the table at Ma and asked to hire one of the Klaassen sons. But despite the strange yet intriguing pull inside of him, he would heed his mother's wise advice.

He reined Petunia to a stop at the edge of the unpainted porch railing and braced himself to swing down. As he did, the door opened and golden light spilled across the dingy boards. Standing in the flow of gold, Miss Frazier gave the appearance of an angel. Titus sank back into the squeaky saddle seat. His heart caught.

If she wasn't already a woman of faith, he'd do more than chores on her farmstead. He would introduce her to the Savior. Because as sure as his ma made the best pumpkin bread in Cottonwood County, Miss Frazier was destined to become Mrs. Titus Klaassen.

Clara opened her mouth to offer a greeting to her hired hand, but the words refused to form. How could the Klaassen son be so alert and spry this early in the morning? Papa never spoke a coherent sentence until he'd enjoyed his second cup of coffee, and her thoughts were cloudy until the breakfast dishes were clean and put away on the shelf. But this man sitting erect in the saddle with spine straight, eyes shining, and cheek dimpling with a cheerful grin appeared to pulsate with energy. Maybe he'd already had breakfast and coffee.

He swung down from the saddle, looped the horse's reins over the sagging porch rail, then stepped onto the porch in one lithe leap. "Good morning, Miss Frazier."

Clara willed her stubborn tongue to function. "G–good morning, Mr. Klaassen. You're bright-eyed and bushy-tailed this morning." Heat seared her cheeks. Had she really just called him bushy-tailed? Perhaps she'd be wise to not speak at all.

He laughed, the sound so spontaneous and natural, an answering smile toyed at the corners of her lips. He pulled in a deep breath, his nostrils flaring, then blew it out slowly. "Early morning is my favorite part of the day. The air smells so clean and fresh. Slugabeds don't know what they miss by lazing beneath the covers until midmorning."

Clara had never lazed until midmorning unless she was ailing. She locked her hands behind her back and searched for a proper way of inviting him in.

His blue eyes narrowed, and he sniffed the air the way Rowdy did when he played in the grass behind the small chicken coop. "Miss Frazier, I think something is. . .scorched."

With a frantic intake of breath, Clara whirled and darted inside. Thin spirals of smoke rose from the frying pan on the iron stove. The three hotcakes she'd poured just before opening the door were now blackened and shriveled. Using her apron to protect her hand, she grabbed the handle and shifted the pan to the cooler side of the stove. The awful smell of burnt batter made her wrinkle her nose. She gazed in disgust at the ruined cakes.

"Clara Rose?" Papa called from his bedroom. "Is everything all right out there? I smell smoke."

"All's well, Papa." All was not well. She'd just ruined breakfast, and their hired hand had witnessed it.

"Then why do I smell smoke?"

Clara sighed. She scurried to Papa's doorway. "I burned the hotcakes."

"Well, make some more."

She resisted emitting a huff of annoyance and turned toward the stove. Mr. Klaassen stood on the little throw rug just inside the door, glancing around at the room that served as sitting room, dining room, and kitchen. Embarrassment smote her again. Images of his family's decorated parlor and neat kitchen paraded through her memory. Although she'd done her best to make this little house feel like home by grouping the fine belongings they'd brought from Minneapolis in comfortable settings and keeping everything clean, how dismal the room must appear in comparison to his home.

He shifted his gaze and caught her watching him. Another smile formed. "Would your father mind if I . . ." He gestured toward Papa's open door.

Papa's voice blared from the bedroom. "Please, come in. We can become acquainted while Clara Rose fries a new batch of hotcakes."

He dipped his head in a slight nod as he passed Clara, and she hurried to mix more batter. While she worked, Rowdy awakened and toddled from his little basket behind the stove. He pawed at her foot, whimpering.

Clara frowned. "I suppose you need to be let out, hm?"

He swished his tail like a whirligig and bounced on his front feet.

His antics usually brought a smile, but the humiliation of her first few minutes with a hired hand on the property was too raw. She scooped him up and clomped to the door. "Hurry, now. I need to get breakfast finished before the morning gets away from us."

She left the door standing ajar and returned to the stove, trusting the coyote pup to come back in when he'd finished his morning exploration. He would want his breakfast. She'd recently begun serving him their leftovers, and he always waited under the table while they ate, bumping his nose against her leg as if encouraging her to hurry up and feed him. She supposed she was spoiling him, but Papa didn't seem to mind, and no one else was there to complain. She frowned, shooting a glance at Papa's open doorway. Would Mr. Klaassen find Rowdy's presence distasteful? And why should she care if he did? Giving herself a little shake, she set her attention on the hotcakes.

With Papa's and Mr. Klaassen's voices and occasional bursts of laughter—Papa had never been so merry before breakfast—spurring her to action, she fried several batches of nicely browned cakes. They didn't rise as much as usual, but she blamed the breeze whisking through the kitchen. With the hotcakes tucked in the warming hob, she scrambled a half-dozen eggs and fried slices of ham. She'd already set the table for her and Mr. Klaassen, but it seemed as though both men were enjoying their chat, so she filled two plates and carried them to the bedroom.

"Ah!" Papa aimed a beaming smile at her and pushed himself higher against the tall walnut headboard. "Here's our breakfast now. Just wait, Titus, until you taste Clara Rose's hotcakes. So tasty you don't need syrup or sorghum, and so light they melt in your mouth."

Clara scowled at her father, her cheeks flaming as hot as the grease in the frying pan. "Papa, really. It isn't becoming to brag."

Mr. Klaassen had leaped from the straight-backed chair beside the bed when she entered, but he sank back onto the seat as he took the plate Clara offered. "You can't fault a father's pride in his daughter. If half of what he told me about you is true, he has good reason to brag." His eyes crinkled with his grin.

Clara sent an uneasy look from the hired hand to her father. "And what have you been telling Mr. Klaassen, Papa?"

Papa held up his hand as if making a vow. "No exaggerations, Clara Rose, I assure you." He curled his fingers around hers and gave a gentle squeeze. "Even if you can't split logs or plow a field, you're still the best daughter any man could ask for."

If her face got any hotter, she'd scorch this batch of hotcakes. She gently extracted her hand and gestured at her father's plate. "Eat now."

"Stay with us while I ask the blessing," Papa said, and Clara obediently bowed her head. Papa's deep voice addressing God with familiarity borne of a longtime relationship chased away the uneasy feelings she'd battled since Mr. Klaassen's arrival. When Papa thanked the Lord for sending them a pair of willing, able hands to get their farm up and running, she almost sneaked a peek to see Mr. Klaassen's reaction. "And, our dear Lord, I thank Thee for this food and for my dear Clara Rose who lovingly prepared it. May it nourish and strengthen our bodies so we may do Thy will. Amen," Papa finished.

"Amen," Mr. Klaassen echoed.

Clara opened her eyes and found Mr. Klaassen looking at Papa with an odd expression on his face. If she wasn't mistaken, he appeared triumphant. Puzzled, she inched toward the door. "I'll be right back with coffee. Do you take cream or sugar, Mr. Klaassen?"

He glanced up from cutting his hotcakes into bite-size pieces. "No, thank you. I prefer it black."

"You sound like me," Papa said with a chuckle. "I need it strong and black to wake me up." He rolled one of the hotcakes into a tube and took a bite.

At the same time, Mr. Klaassen carried a forkful of hotcakes to his mouth. Both men stopped chewing, their brows descended in matching looks of confusion, and then they grimaced and bobbed their heads in forced swallows.

Clara fiddled with her apron skirt, her pulse thudding. "What's wrong?"

Papa swiped his lips with his napkin. "I'm not sure. Here. Taste." He held the rolled hotcake to her.

She returned to his side and took the hotcake. She frowned. What was wrong with this hotcake? It should be tender, not dense. She broke off a tiny piece and put it in her mouth. At once, she spat the chunk into her palm. "Oh, Papa, I'm so sorry. I got in a hurry to make the second batch after the first one burned, and I must have forgotten the sugar." And after he'd told Mr. Klaassen her hotcakes would melt in his mouth. What a shock the flavor must have been. She battled the childish desire to hide under Papa's bed.

Papa patted her arm. "Now, now, anyone can make a mistake. Especially when we're rushing." He offered a sheepish look. "That's how I ended up with this broken leg. I didn't take the time to back-cut the tree trunk the way the books I read advised, and it fell the wrong direction. I'd say your mistake, Clara Rose, is much less hazardous."

Mr. Klaassen had nearly finished the ham and eggs. He paused and aimed a grin at her. "You didn't make any mistakes with the rest of this breakfast. Everything else is just fine."

She appreciated his kindness, but she couldn't deny a deep sense of shame. What kind of incompetent dolt left out sugar in hotcake batter? She reached for his plate.

He held it away from her. "No, ma'am. My mother taught me not to waste food."

Clara gawked at him. "You can't eat those things. They taste like wallpaper paste."

Papa snorted. "Now who's exaggerating?"

Mr. Klaassen laughed. "They just need a little sweetening."

No, they needed disposal.

"Do you have some fruit preserves? Peach? Or maybe strawberry?"

Papa's face lit. "A fine idea, Titus! Clara Rose, bring out a jar of preserves."

Clara sent an uncertain glance across the pair. "Are you sure you wouldn't rather throw them away?"

"Waste not, want not," Mr. Klaassen said. "That's what my pa always says."

"An excellent dictum by which to live." Papa waved his hand. "The preserves, Clara Rose."

Clara scurried to obey. She would bring them strawberry preserves. They were the most sugary preserves in the cupboard. Those hotcakes needed all the sweetening they could get.

Chapter Five

Monday was usually wash day, but Clara decided to bake instead. After the morning's disaster, she wanted to prove to Mr. Klaassen she wasn't completely inept in the kitchen. After all, they weren't paying the man in dollars but in food. The least she could do was feed him well.

Papa was particularly fond of muffins sweetened with apple cider and made hearty with chunks of dried apples and black walnuts, so while the ring of an ax carried through the open window, she baked a batch of the rich muffins and wrapped two of them, still warm, in a cloth napkin. When she headed for the door, Rowdy rolled out of his basket and scampered after her, releasing little yelps.

She laughed. "All right, you can come, too. But you have to behave yourself and stay out from under Mr. Klaassen's feet."

Rowdy bounced along at her heels as she made her way across the hard, uneven ground, but her focus was on the man holding the ax. He employed a steady swing, bringing the blade behind and over in a perfect arc that reminded her of a windmill's paddles. How could he work so tirelessly? A bare trunk and piles of branches in various sizes proved his industriousness over the morning hours. If he continued at this rate, he'd have the tree turned into firewood by evening.

With his back to her, he couldn't see her approach, and she had no desire to be whacked by that swinging ax. So when she was within a few yards, she called his name.

He set the ax blade deep in the wood, released the handle, and turned. His face lit, sending a rush of heat through her frame in spite of the cool breeze. She lowered her gaze from his welcoming smile and found herself mesmerized by his exposed forearms—firm, muscular, with the veins standing out like ropes—below his rolled shirtsleeves. While she stared, he pushed the sleeves down to his wrists and yanked a bandanna from his pocket to mop his face. She followed the path of the bandanna and realized a red flush stained his cheeks. She jerked her gaze away from him. She hoped the color was from exertion rather than recognition of her blatant admiration.

Clearing her throat, she forced her feet to close the gap between them, and she held out the lumpy napkin. "A snack."

"Thank you, Miss Frazier." He took it and sat on the log, peeling back the layers.

Clara marveled at the eagerness with which he carried the first muffin to his mouth. Had he already forgotten the bland hotcakes, or was he just so hungry he didn't care how they tasted?

With the bite still in his mouth, he looked up at her with his eyebrows high in an expression of pleased surprise. "Mm, 'ese are rea'y good."

She frowned, unsure what he'd said.

He swallowed, wiped his mouth with his sleeve, and gave her a sheepish grin. "Please, forgive me. My ma would scold if she knew I talked with my mouth full. But these are really good." He took another hearty bite, and a piece of walnut rolled down his front. Rowdy leaped out from behind Clara and dove on it. Mr. Klaassen jerked back so sharply he almost fell off the log. "Whoa, there! Where did you come from?"

Clara reached in and caught Rowdy. The pup yipped in protest, but she held tight. "Didn't I tell you to behave, Rowdy?"

Mr. Klaassen gaped at the wriggling coyote. "He—he's yours?"

She nodded. "I rescued him from a hawk. He was too little to fend for himself, so I kept him." Rowdy's warm tongue swept her chin, and she shifted him a little lower. He began chewing on her dress sleeve. She shook her head, chuckling. "He's something of a rapscallion."

"Well, I'll be. . ."

He seemed more astonished than disapproving, so she added, "He's good company for me."

For a moment, Mr. Klaassen seemed to study her, his brow pinched and his lips sucked in, the muffins apparently forgotten. Then he gave a little jerk and stood. "I better finish my snack and get back to work. I'd like to have this spot clear of branches by the end of the day. I'll need to borrow your wagon, though, to haul everything to the woodshed."

Puzzled by his sudden change in topic, Clara nodded mutely.

"I'll only haul the branches large enough to be used in your stove. If you and your pa don't mind, I'll burn the smallest ones."

Rowdy fought her restraining hands, so she set him on the ground before answering Mr. Klaassen. "Whatever you think is best."

His gaze seemed to fix on Rowdy, who batted at a clump of dirt. One corner of his mouth twitched in a lopsided grin. She expected him to say something about the coyote, but he surprised her. "I'll bring your napkin back when I come in for lunch. Thanks again for the muffins, Miss Frazier. As I said, they're really good."

She knew when she'd been dismissed. Battling an irrational thread of annoyance with the man, she patted her leg and spoke tartly. "Come along, Rowdy."

The ornery pup leaped over the clump of dirt, lost his balance and landed on his chin, then scrambled upright, shaking his head so hard his little ears flapped.

Clara laughed and looked at Mr. Klaassen, wanting to share her amusement with someone. To her discomfiture, he stood staring at her with an expression of puzzlement creasing his sweat-dampened face. She grabbed up Rowdy and, ignoring the pup's whining complaints, scurried to the house.

Titus groaned as he slid down from Petunia's back. He caught the trailing reins and shuffled toward the open stall.

His youngest brother, Paul, glanced over from forking hay into the horses' feeding troughs and snickered. "You're moving as slow as Old Man Zemke."

Titus frowned. The eldest member of Wilhelmina had celebrated his ninety-fourth birthday last month and deserved to move at a snail's pace after a lifetime of toil. "Don't be disrespectful."

"To you or to Mr. Zemke?"

"Both." Titus unbuckled the saddle and pulled it free. His aching arms resisted bearing its weight, and he suppressed another groan when he tossed the saddle over the stall wall.

Paul ambled over, the pitchfork braced on his shoulder. "Phew, Titus, you smell worse than John, and he spent the day in the pigpen."

Titus gave Petunia's nose a rub. "Did the sow farrow today?"

"Uh-huh. Fourteen piglets. Took almost seven hours for them all to be born. Pa says we'll keep four to butcher and sell the others. He was real happy about the big litter." Paul chortled. "But John said that old sow nearly took his leg off when he started clipping the piglets' teeth. I said maybe he should've left their teeth alone. The sow would learn a lesson when she got bit good and hard."

Titus shook his head. "And then get infection and maybe stop nursing? Not a good idea, Paul." He aimed a light smack on his brother's shoulder as he limped past him on the way out of the barn. "Would you mind checking on the goats for me? I need to clean up, and it might take awhile." His whole body itched from the tiny bits of wood that had worked their way under his clothes and stuck to his sweaty flesh.

"Andrew fed them their evening bottles after supper and put them in their pen." Paul called after him in a teasing tone, "You missed a good supper."

"No I didn't." Titus licked his lips in remembrance. "Miss Frazier fed me fried chicken, boiled butter beans, and honey-glazed carrots." They'd sat at the table together for the meal, but she'd kept her head low and ate in silence, stealing a bit of the pleasure of the delicious meal.

"Well, Ma made *Verenike* with sausage gravy."

And the Klaassens probably enjoyed lots of talking and laughing, too. Titus paused and tossed a grin over his shoulder. "Sounds like we both got fed well. Finish up out there now instead of trying to stir me to envy."

Paul laughed and returned to his work.

Titus continued on through the early evening shadows toward the pump at back of the house. When he felt fresh, he'd go eat a plate of his favorite cheese-filled dumplings in gravy. If Titus knew Ma, she'd set aside a helping of his favorite meal. He hoped his brothers had all left the kitchen by now, because while he ate he wanted to talk to Ma about some troublesome thoughts rolling in the far corners of his mind.

He shucked off his shirt, boots, and socks and let his suspenders dangle beside his knees. His shoulder complained as he worked the pump, but by the time he'd dumped the third bucket of cold water over his head, his soreness had eased some. He shivered, though, when the breeze touched him. To make sure he'd chased away all the wood bits, he emptied one more bucket over his head, then hung it on the pump's spout, used his shirt to give himself a cursory drying, and trotted for the house on bare feet.

On the enclosed back porch he found a pair of longjohns, britches, and a shirt folded and waiting. He smiled. Bless Ma's heart. He ducked behind the changing screen in the corner and emerged in the dry, clean clothes. He entered the kitchen with his dirty items wadded in his hands.

Ma turned from the dry sink and snatched the clothes from him. "There's a plate of Verenike on the back of the stove, if you're hungry."

He wasn't, but he never turned down Ma's Verenike. "Thanks." He carried the plate to the table, where a napkin and fork waited for his use. He bowed his head to offer thanks for the food, but his prayer meandered in a different direction. *God, did You bring Miss Frazier to our farm so we could give more than help on her father's land?*

Ma poured herself a cup of coffee and sat across from him, curiosity lighting her features. "How did the day go?"

Between bites, Titus shared what he'd accomplished during the day. He told her about the unusual pet named Rowdy, laughing at her astonishment, and listed all the good things Miss Frazier had fed him, including the strawberry preserves–laden hotcakes although he kept secret the absence of sugar in the round brown cakes. While he talked, his brothers and father wandered in and out, and by the time his plate was empty and his stomach achingly full, he and Ma were the only ones remaining in the cozy, lantern-lit kitchen.

"So it went well, then," Ma said with a smile.

"Yes. But, Ma?" Titus pushed the plate aside and rested his joined hands on the table. "There's something not quite right."

Ma's forehead pinched into a series of furrows. "What do you mean?"

How could he put his misgivings into words? There was nothing concrete on which to base his uneasiness, yet something nibbled at him. "Well, I spent my first hour over there sitting beside Mr. Frazier's bed, just talking with him. He was so friendly, so open. He told me about his old job in Minneapolis—he was a bank accountant—and about his wife passing on when their daughter was barely out of girlhood. He talked and talked and talked." Mostly about his Clara Rose, but for some reason he didn't want to mention that part.

Ma shook her head, laughing softly. "What's wrong with talking? He's probably lonely since he has been laid up in that bed for two weeks."

"But think about all the weeks before his accident." Titus leaned in slightly, angling his head. "If he's so friendly, why hasn't he come in to town, become part of the community?"

Ma shrugged. "Maybe he's been too busy. Heaven knows that farmstead needed a lot of work." She rose, picked up his plate, and took it to the dry sink.

Titus followed her. "Not even stopping on Sunday to attend a service in town? He's a believer, Ma. I'm sure of it after listening to him pray over his breakfast. I'm surprised he hasn't tried to settle in with one of our churches."

Ma scrubbed his plate clean and set it aside. "Maybe you can invite him to service—when he is on his feet again, of course." A sly smile curved her lips, and she bumped his arm with her elbow. "You have talked on and on about the father. What about the daughter?"

Titus grimaced. "Ma. . ."

"What?" Her innocent expression made her look as young as a schoolgirl. "I gather she is a decent cook and a lover of creatures. What else?"

Realization struck with such force, Titus jerked. "That's it!"

Ma drew back.

Titus slapped his thigh and repeated. "That's it—that's what has bothered me all day."

His mother's lips formed a frustrated line. "Son, you are not making an ounce of sense."

He led her to the table and pressed her into a chair, then went down on one knee beside her. "Ma, Mr. Frazier is friendly as friendly can be, but his daughter. . . She isn't rude to me, but she keeps her distance. She said her coyote pup is her company. A coyote pup! What kind of company is that for a young woman?"

"Well, I—"

Titus hurried on, speaking to himself as much as to Ma. "Mr. Frazier moved from Minneapolis, where he'd lived for Miss Frazier's whole life, to a farm on the outskirts of a small town even though he doesn't know the first thing about farming. And I think he did it for his daughter. But why?"

Ma cupped her hand over Titus's shoulder. "Do you think he's trying to protect her from something. . .or someone?"

He sighed. "I don't know. Maybe. But I can't imagine a friendly fellow like Mr. Frazier hiding out there away from people, and I can't imagine a young woman like Miss Frazier spending her whole life with only a coyote as a friend."

"You know, Titus," Ma said slowly, her tone thoughtful, "when folks hide away, it's usually because of a hurt. We've been praying for Mr. Frazier's leg to heal. Maybe we need to pray for God to heal whatever hurts our neighbors carry on their souls."

Titus gave his mother a hopeful look. "Will you pray with me now?"

Ma smiled. She bowed her head and began. "Dear Father in heaven. . ."

Chapter Six

By the end of his first week at the Frazier farm, Titus had felled every remaining tree on the modest six-acre plot where Mr. Frazier intended to plant corn. He couldn't deny a sense of satisfaction as he gazed across the patch of prairie. Piles of limbs at the edges of the field awaited burning when the wind died down, and the stumps of the scraggly bur oaks still needed to be pulled, but he'd require the use of a good team and a sturdy chain for that task. And maybe another pair of hands—he'd ask Pa about borrowing Andrew for a day. Or two.

He headed for the woodshed, where he'd dragged the limbs and trunks large enough to be turned into firewood. He still had a few good hours remaining in the afternoon, and he wanted to get as much of that wood chopped and stacked as possible before he left for the weekend. Mice and other small creatures would quickly take up residence in the tumble of logs if they sat too long unattended. Miss Frazier wouldn't welcome such pests in her yard and house. Even if they provided entertainment for her pet coyote.

The smell of baking bread drifted past his nose, and his mouth watered in response. He'd intended to leave early this afternoon and enjoy a boisterous supper with his family, but the aroma tempted him to join Miss Frazier at her quiet table instead. For breakfast and lunch, he sat in the chair in Mr. Frazier's room and ate with him, but each time he'd come in for supper, the man was snoozing, so he sat with Miss Frazier instead.

He frowned, recalling his many failed attempts to engage the young woman in conversation. Miss Clara Rose Frazier puzzled him. He'd encountered snooty girls and shy girls, and he wouldn't classify Miss Frazier as either, but neither was she openly friendly like her father. The tug he'd experienced on their first encounter remained, which led him to believe he shouldn't give up, but she didn't make things easy for him.

She was talkative enough to her father, and several times he'd caught her talking to that mischievous coyote pup the way a mother spoke to her young child. But with Titus, she remained tense and distant. He squinted at the blue sky. "God, is it that she doesn't like people, or does she only dislike me?"

He came to a halt as an idea struck for finding out whether her dislike extended beyond him to others. The answer was more important than chopping his way through that pile of branches behind the wood-shed. He changed direction and charged up to the back door, which stood open to invite in the early May breeze.

Titus tapped on the unpainted doorjamb. "Miss Frazier?"

She bustled over, wiping her hands on her apron. "Yes? Do you need a drink of water?"

Damp squiggles of hair clung to her temples, and one loose molasses-colored coil trailed along her neck. Even dressed in a simple calico frock and stained full apron, with her hair a mess, she was pretty enough to set his pulse into a gallop. *Please let it not be a dislike of only me. . . .* "I'd take a drink, yes, but I also—"

"Do I hear Titus out there?" Mr. Frazier's voice boomed from the bedroom.

She whisked her face in the direction of the doorway, giving Titus a view of her sweet profile. "Yes, Papa. Did you want to talk to him?"

"Yes."

She turned a hesitant look on Titus. "Go see Papa. I'll bring you a cup of cool water." She brushed past him and hurried toward their well.

Titus sighed. He tapped his boots against the small stone stoop at the back door, then tromped to the farm owner's bedroom. His aggravation faded beneath the genuine smile on Mr. Frazier's face. "Yes, sir?"

"I've been watching out the window. You've nearly got that field ready for seeds."

Titus stifled a chuckle. The man had a thing or two to learn about readying a field. Those stumps had to go, the dried weeds and old stubble burned away, and the ground turned under. Maybe twice. He'd be busy for a while yet. He shrugged. "I've made some progress, that's true."

"Not only a good worker, but modest, too."

Titus scuffed the floor with the toe of his boot.

Miss Frazier entered the room. She offered Titus a large Mason jar. Moisture dotted its sides.

He gripped the jar between both hands. Partly because the wetness made it slick, but mostly because the cool glass felt good against his sweaty palms. He gave the young woman a wide smile. "Thank you."

She bobbed her head in a quick acknowledgment and hurried around the corner.

Titus, frowning, gazed after her.

"Titus?"

He turned to the father. A knowing smirk curled the man's lips. Titus braced himself for an inquiry about his feelings toward Clara Rose.

"You seem very handy wielding that ax. Are you as competent with other woodworking tools?"

Titus raised his eyebrows. "Woodworking tools?"

Mr. Frazier nodded. He released a heavy sigh. "I'm weary of being in this bed. Clara Rose helps me to the chair and back once or twice a day, and of course to the. . .er, commode the doctor loaned us. But she doesn't have the strength to support my weight for longer treks. Dr. Biehler said he could order crutches from a catalog, but they would take so long to arrive, I might not have need of them by the time they reached me."

Titus took slow sips of the water, thinking. Plotting.

Mr. Frazier went on. "I would enjoy sitting on the porch or coming out to the table for meals. So I wondered if you might be able to craft a pair of crutches from some of the smaller, sturdy limbs on the brush pile."

Thank goodness he hadn't burned those piles yet. He was sure there were some straight limbs with enough thickness to support Mr. Frazier's weight. He shrugged. "I have to be honest. I've never tried making crutches, but I don't think it would be hard. As long as you aren't expecting something of beauty."

"Simple is fine." The man laughed, shaking his head. "I spent more than thirty years working behind a desk and never found sitting all day tiresome, but sitting for two weeks in this bed has nearly driven me to distraction. It will be nice to be up and on my feet again. Thank you, Titus."

Titus held up one hand. "Don't thank me yet. I haven't made them."

"Oh, but you will. I have confidence in you."

Titus drained the jar to wash down his embarrassment. Having been raised to practice humility, he wasn't sure how to respond to such blatant praise. So he blurted a question. "If the crutches serve you well, would you consider going farther than your front porch?"

Mr. Frazier's eyes twinkled. "Are you wanting me to come out and help with those stumps?"

Titus laughed. "No, sir." He'd intended to broach this subject with the daughter, but the father might be a better choice. He settled in the chair beside the bed and rested his elbows on his knees with the Mason jar gripped between his palms. "If you're able to get around, it would please my family to have you and your daughter join us for church Sunday morning and then come to our place for *Faspa*."

"What is 'faws-puh'?"

"A cold lunch. It is traditional in our denomination so the women needn't work preparing a big meal on the Lord's day." He hadn't checked with Ma about inviting the Fraziers, but she wouldn't fuss at him. They often had Sunday after-service visitors, and she was always prepared for extras.

For a moment, Mr. Frazier closed his eyes and pursed his lips as if something pained him. Then he looked at Titus. He sighed. "I would like to attend a church service. Clara Rose and I read and study a lengthy passage from the Bible together each Sunday, but that isn't the same as worshipping with a body of fellow believers."

Titus leaned close, eagerness thrumming through him. "Then come. I don't know what denomination you attended in Minneapolis, but you would be welcome at our Mennonite Brethren church."

"If your entire congregation is as affable as you, young man, I'm certain Clara Rose and I would be welcomed with open arms. But. . ."

Titus waited. When Mr. Frazier didn't finish his sentence, he said, "All are welcome in the house of God. Can. . .can I tell Ma to expect you?"

Mr. Frazier's lips parted, but before a reply emerged, Miss Frazier darted into the room and moved between the two men. She gave Titus a glowering look and took her father's hand. "Even if you produced crutches by this evening, Papa wouldn't have the ability to climb into a wagon or make the long walk to town. Please don't put unrealistic expectations on him."

Titus bolted upright. So she'd been listening. Maybe that was good. He looked directly into her scowling face. "I don't think the expectation is unrealistic at all, Miss Frazier. Your wagon has a removable back gate, and with just a little help, he could slide in. My pa is fond of saying, 'Where there's a will, there's a way.' If your father wants to come to church, we can find a means of getting him there."

Fury snapped in her brown eyes. "Papa needs to rest now, Mr. Klaassen."

The good smell of fresh-baked bread, which usually evoked feelings of contentment and hominess, seemed out of place in the tense room. Titus gulped. "I didn't mean to offend you."

"I'm not offended." Her stiff pose and unsmiling face told a different story. "But until Papa is able to walk on two good legs, he shouldn't try to do too much. Going all the way into town would surely be too much."

Oddly, Titus found comfort in her reply. She wanted to avoid the town. She wanted to stay away from the church. That meant she didn't dislike him, personally, but something made her disinclined to be around people. He couldn't stop a smile from growing.

Her frown deepened. "Do you find something amusing, Mr. Klaassen?"

He took a step toward the door, shaking his head. "No, ma'am." He gave her the empty Mason jar. "But as soon as your father is able to walk, I'll be inviting you again." He headed outside and made his way to the burn pile, his lips twitching with another smile. He had a month to change her mind about hiding out in this little farmhouse. That was plenty of time.

———————————————

As soon as Papa awakened from his evening nap, Clara sat on the edge of his bed and took his hand. "I'm sorry."

He puckered his forehead. "For what are you apologizing?"

Guilt and embarrassment warred within her. "I heard what you told Mr. Klaassen about wanting to attend church services. I'm sorry I prevented you from going."

Papa patted her hand. "Now, Clara Rose. . ."

Tears clouded her vision. "I guess I didn't stop to think how being out here on our own was for you. I'm happy, so I—"

"Are you happy, my daughter?"

She paused for a moment. Although living in the country was very different from her former life in the city—quieter, fewer opportunities for entertainment, and more work—she liked the peacefulness of their little farmstead. True, the house was much smaller and lacked the refinement of their house in Minneapolis, but she had plans to paint the woodwork and put up cheerful wall coverings on the plain plaster walls. When she finished decorating, it would feel more like home. She nodded. "Yes. I think I am."

"And you never grow lonely?"

Clara hung her head. She was lonely in Minneapolis. All of her friends were married. Most of them already had a child or two. She didn't fit with them anymore. And she never would, because who would try to court a woman who'd already been cast aside by two beaus? She blinked several times and gave her father a wobbly smile. "I'm less alone here than I was in the city. You don't go away to work every day. And I have Rowdy." She squeezed his hand. "But if you're lonely, Papa, you should accept Mr. Klaassen's invitation to attend church services. I'll be fine here by myself on Sunday."

Papa yanked his hand free and shook his finger at her. "Oh no, young lady. If I go, you will go with me."

Clara made a face.

"None of that. You aren't the only one who made a promise to your dear mother before she stepped from this life into glory."

The seriousness in her father's tone held Clara's attention.

"Her most fervent prayer was for you to know and serve the Lord Jesus Christ. I know you've accepted Him as your Savior, Clara Rose, but to grow in Him requires teaching."

"But you've—"

He shook his head, stilling her protest. "More than reading verses and talking with me. You need real teaching from a preacher. Doesn't the Bible instruct us to gather with fellow believers?"

She looked away, unwilling to let her father witness the rebellion stirring in her heart.

Papa sighed. "It's unlikely I'll be attending any service until my leg is out of this splint and I can walk again. So you have a little time to adjust, to think and pray. But, Clara Rose, when I'm on my feet, I want us to become part of a church family in Wilhelmina."

She chewed her lip, her gaze aimed to the side.

He tugged her hand. "Clara Rose?"

Finally, she faced him. The pleading in his eyes stung, but she couldn't agree with him. Not when it meant witnessing young, happy husbands and wives. It would hurt too much. When she was much older—old enough to be considered an honorary auntie like the old maids from her church in Minneapolis—she would go to church again. But she would explain all that to Papa when he wasn't laid up in bed like an invalid.

She forced a smile. "I'll pray about it, Papa." Papa leaned back with a satisfied smile, and Clara left his room. She'd do as she'd promised—she would pray—but she held little confidence that her feelings would change. Not even God could change her from a young "old maid" to an old one in the space of four weeks.

Chapter Seven

F riday's stout breezes brought in a gentle, overnight shower that lulled Clara into deep, restful sleep, and Saturday dawned clear and sunny. She spent the morning giving their little house a thorough scrubbing. Rowdy helped by chasing the mop head across the floor and battling the small rag rug in front of the door into submission. Both Clara and Papa laughed at the growing pup's antics, and the morning passed quickly.

After a simple lunch of bread, cheese, and dried apples, Clara carried a pair of dining-room chairs to the porch. With Papa leaning heavily on her for support, she escorted him outside. She might not be able to accompany him to church as he wanted, but she could at least help him enjoy a bit of the pleasant spring weather.

He sat in one chair and propped up his legs on the other. He pulled in a deep breath and released it on a sigh. "Ahhh, this is perfect."

Clara lifted Rowdy onto his lap, and the coyote curled into a ball with his tail covering his nose. She smiled at the contented pup and her contented father. "Will you be all right for a little while? I have some more cleaning to do."

"I'm as right as rain." Papa shifted a bit, leaning the back of his head on the chair's high ladder back and linked his hands around the snoozing coyote. "Leave the door open. If I need something, I'll holler."

She deposited a kiss on his cheek, then hurried inside. She stripped her father's bed and remade it with clean sheets, dusted the furniture, and swept the floor. She also gave the commode Dr. Biehler had lent them a good washing. A distasteful task, but necessary. As grateful as she was for the wooden box equipped with a removable chamber pot so she didn't have to transport Papa all the way to the outhouse, she wouldn't be unhappy to see the spare piece of furniture go. Having a commode lurking in the corner of one's bedroom was indecorous in her opinion. She'd much rather tuck the pot under the bed, out of sight.

With Papa's room clean and smelling fresh, she gave her own bedroom a cleaning. As she worked, she mentally composed a shopping list. She hadn't been to town for supplies for more than two weeks, and many basic items were running low. As much as she hated the idea of depending even more on Titus Klaassen, she hoped she might prevail upon him to visit the local general-goods store and pick up some things for her. Papa already had established an account, so at least she wouldn't have to worry about him paying for her supplies.

She carried the rug that lay beside her bed to the backyard and tossed it over the clothesline. As she returned to the house for the rug beater, the rattle of wagon wheels caught her attention. Dr. Biehler must have decided to check on Papa today since he hadn't made it out on Friday. She rounded the house, ready to greet the helpful veterinarian, but to her surprise, Titus Klaassen and his mother shared the seat on the approaching wagon.

Mr. Klaassen drew the horses to a stop near the porch. He braced one hand on the wagon's edge and leaped to the ground. He gave each horse a quick rub on the nose as he hurried around the wagon, and then he helped Mrs. Klaassen down. They both turned toward the house with bright smiles. Mr. Klaassen lifted his hand in a wave. "Good afternoon, Mr. Frazier. It's good to see you out enjoying this fine spring day. I hope you don't mind some visitors arriving uninvited."

"Not at all." Papa spoke with such joviality, Clara experienced an unexpected stab of guilt. Rowdy awoke, so Papa put him on the porch. He lifted his chin and bellowed, "Clara Rose!"

Clara stepped from the corner of the house. "I'm right here, Papa."

He gestured her forward, his face alight. "We have visitors. Put on the teakettle."

"Oh, no." Mrs. Klaassen caught hold of Clara's arm. "We don't want to trouble you. Titus finished the pair of crutches last night and wanted to deliver them. And I thought, as long as we're bringing those crutches, why not bring a few more things you likely need?"

Clara frowned, confused.

Mrs. Klaassen laughed. The ease with which her levity flowed reminded Clara of her son. "Come with me, young lady, and I'll show you what I mean. Titus, lower the gate, please."

Clara trailed her to the rear of the wagon. Mr. Klaassen released the pins holding the gate in place and brought it downward. Three wooden crates waited in the wagon bed, along with the most ungainly set of crutches Clara had ever seen. Mr. Klaassen grabbed the crutches and took off toward the porch, and Mrs. Klaassen slid one of the crates to the edge of the bed.

"Now, Miss Frazier, I know you have been too busy caring for your father to make the trip to town for groceries and such. With Titus eating here every day, I presumed you might be running low on a few things. So when I did my shopping yesterday, I filled a few boxes for you, too."

Clara stared at the woman with her mouth hanging open. Had Mrs. Klaassen somehow read her thoughts?

"I asked Ira—Ira Voth is the grocer—to check his records for what you purchased in the past. I hope we brought what you need. If anything does not suit, no worries. Mr. Voth said we could return it, and he would credit it back on your account."

Clara managed to close her mouth. She shook her head slowly, touching the various items in the closest box. "It looks as if you've brought exactly what I would have chosen. Thank you, ma'am."

Her warm smile crinkled her eyes. She put her arm around Clara and gave a little squeeze. "You're very welcome, Miss Frazier."

A burst of laughter interrupted them. Both women peeked around the wagon, and Clara clapped her hand over her mouth at the sight. She darted toward the porch.

"Papa, be careful!"

Papa grinned at her even as he swayed on the crutches crafted from crooked twigs lashed together at the base and topped by a short, smooth piece of lumber. "Don't fret, Clara Rose. Oh my, it's dandy to be upright on my own!" He took two wobbly steps while Rowdy bounced along beside him and Clara held her breath. He stopped and sent a beaming smile to Mr. Klaassen. "You did a fine job, Titus. Just fine." He winced. "Of course, I might have to ask Clara Rose to put some padding on these pieces under my arms. That oak you carved for the support brace is pretty hard. But they hold me up just fine. Yes, sir, these are a real blessing."

Mrs. Klaassen folded her arms and chuckled. "When Titus showed those things to me this morning, I thought of the rhyme about the old man who walked a crooked mile. These crooked crutches would be a good fit for that fellow, I believe."

"I'd say not." Papa's eyes twinkled with teasing. "These are mine. That old crooked man will have to find his own set."

Both Mrs. Klaassen and her son laughed. Clara couldn't resist smiling. Papa looked so proud of himself, standing on those ridiculous crutches. She touched Mr. Klaassen's elbow. "Thank you for making them so quickly."

The look he turned on her—appreciation, admiration, and something deeper—sent her skittering to the rear of the wagon again. She grabbed the box waiting at the bed's end.

Mrs. Klaassen hurried over, tsk-tsking. "Now, let me help you. Those boxes are heavy." She took one side, Clara took the other, and they carried the box inside. As they placed it on the table, Mr. Klaassen entered with a second box. She marveled at the ease with which he carried the heavy crate. Clara had shared the task, and her muscles complained.

"I'll get the last one, Ma. And then"—his blue-eyed gaze fell on Clara—"if you have some cotton batting or some old toweling, I'll pad the crutch braces for your father."

He'd already done enough. "I can do that for him."

He grinned. "He wants to take a little walk right now—try them out. It might be better if we pad them before he goes very far so he doesn't hurt his underarms."

"All right, then." Clara eased toward her bedroom. Anything to separate herself from Titus Klaassen. His penetrating, attentive gaze was making her stomach dance, and she couldn't decide if she was flattered or frightened. "I'm sure I have something."

By the time she found scraps of soft worsted large enough to cover the arm braces, Mr. Klaassen had carried in the third crate and Mrs. Klaassen had the contents of the first two crates organized on the table. Clara handed Mr. Klaassen the fabric without quite meeting the young man's gaze—why did such a nice man intimidate her so?—and turned her attention to putting away the supplies.

"I appreciate you thinking to bring canned goods." Clara stacked the cans of tomatoes, corn, beans, and peas on a shelf above the dry sink. "I'll be canning my own vegetables after I put in a garden, but that's a few months away yet."

"I prefer home-canned, but I'm grateful for these factory-canned vegetables when we're between seasons." Mrs. Klaassen slowly emptied the bag of flour into its drawer in the possum-belly cabinet. Despite her care, fine dust rose in the air. Clara would need to sweep again. The woman sent Clara a speculative look. "Have you raised vegetables before, Miss Frazier?"

"Please call me Clara." Now why had she made such a request? Besides Papa, only her closest friends called her by her given name.

The woman smiled, clearly touched. "Why, thank you. If you like, you may call me Maria. And"—impishness twinkled in her eyes—"Titus wouldn't mind if you followed your father's example and called him by his Christian name. He said hearing you call him Mr. Klaassen makes him feel old and feeble."

Heat filled Clara's face. How disconcerting to know their hired helper spoke of them to his family. And she couldn't imagine calling the son or his mother by their first names. "My mother taught me to be courteous and address people by their surnames. Especially gentlemen or my elders."

"It sounds as though your mother was a very well-mannered woman."

Clara sighed. "Mama was a saint. I miss her terribly, just as Papa does. But we know we'll see her again someday. She waits in heaven for us."

The woman's eyebrows rose. "You are a sinner saved by grace, Clara?"

There were many uncertainties in life, but when it came to her salvation, she held no hesitation. "Yes, ma'am."

"That is good. That is very, very good." Mrs. Klaassen rolled up the empty flour sack and placed it in the bottom of one of the crates. She took the broom from the corner and began sweeping up the powdery white dust dotting the floor. "I think you'll discover in time, Clara, that we are less formal here in Wilhelmina than in the larger cities. The familiarity comes from knowing one another well. I wouldn't consider it discourteous for you to call me Maria, but if you are more comfortable with Mrs. Klaassen, I respect your choice."

Clara returned to the table for another armful of cans. "Mama taught me more than etiquette and to trust in Jesus. Even though we could purchase fresh vegetables at the market, Mama always kept a small garden behind our house. She especially enjoyed growing tomatoes and strawberries. I loved helping her."

Loneliness for her reserved, gentle mother pinched her chest. Would she ever stop missing her, wondering how life would be different if Mama hadn't succumbed to scarlet fever? "I hope to keep a large garden and grow all kinds of vegetables. If I can convince Papa to clear enough ground, I'll put in a patch of strawberries. Papa says there are mulberry, apple, and pear trees growing near the creek at the edge of our property. I hope to make use of those fruits, as well."

Mrs. Klaassen smiled. "You're very ambitious for someone who has never lived on a farm before." She returned the broom to its corner and then moved slowly around the room, seeming to examine the furnishings and the pictures on the walls. "I have no doubt you will do well with your garden. You've already turned this little house into a cozy home."

Clara swallowed a snort. "It's not nearly as nice as your house."

"Oh, my dear girl, I know what this place looked like before your father bought it." Mrs. Klaassen shook her head, pursing her face. "You've accomplished a great deal in the short time you've lived here. You should be proud of yourself."

Warmed by the woman's kind words, Clara found herself admitting, "I hope to put pretty paper on all the walls and paint the bedroom window and door casings white. Our house in Minneapolis had lovely floral wall coverings, and Papa gave our woodwork a fresh coat of paint every spring. The house always seemed so cheery. I want this house to be cheery, too."

Mrs. Klaassen hurried to Clara and took her hands. "Clara, this house is already cheery. Do you know why?"

Clara shook her head.

The woman smiled. "Because there is so much love between these walls. Titus has mentioned the special devotion you and your father share, and now I've seen it myself." She squeezed Clara's hands and released them. "Wherever love resides, dear child, there is joy. That is the best kind of cheeriness, do you not agree?"

Unexpectedly, tears pricked Clara's eyes. She sniffed and nodded. "I agree. Thank you."

"You're very welcome. Now..." She marched to the table and picked up a paper-wrapped lump. "Point me to your cellar and I'll put this salt pork away." Her eyebrows rose high. "Oh! I just thought of something. Our sow has a new litter of piglets. My *Maun*—" She made a face. "My husband plans to sell most of them. Would you and your father be interested in raising a pig or two for butchering?"

Clara bit the corner of her lip, uncertainty smiting her. "Um...isn't there a butcher shop in Wilhelmina?"

The woman laughed. "Nä, my dear, the farmers all butcher their own chickens, pigs, and cows. The townfolk buy their meat from area farmers." Her face crinkled in puzzlement. "What have you done for meat so far?"

"We brought several cured hams and sides of bacon with us when we moved here, and Papa sets snares for prairie chickens."

"I noticed you have a chicken house. You don't butcher your chickens?"

Eat her feathered friends? "No, ma'am. I use the chickens for eggs."

Mrs. Klaassen's lips twitched as if she fought a smile. "Well, eventually the chickens will stop laying. So you need to find a rooster and then plan to separate one hen as a brooder to hatch new chicks. Then you'll have more hens for laying and also roosters to butcher."

Clara's stomach rolled. She'd never be able to butcher any of the chickens who pecked in their pen. She'd given them names! One couldn't eat a creature who bore a name like Sally or Rosie. Had she and Papa gotten themselves into a situation beyond their ability?

"I'll have Titus talk to your father about the need to raise livestock. Titus can answer any questions your father has. We raise pigs, cattle, chickens, ducks, and goats on our farm."

Clara drew back. "Goats? Do you. . .eat them?" She hoped she wouldn't be expected to eat goat meat.

"Well, I suppose we could, but I use the milk. Goat milk makes the best cheese."

They even made their own cheese? Clara gawked at the woman.

Mrs. Klaassen must have sensed Clara's dismay, because she gave her cheek a soft pat. "Now, don't start worrying. You don't have to learn everything at once. That is the best part of living in a small community. There is always someone close by who is willing to help. Right now you think about getting your garden in. If need be, you can buy meat from your neighbors for a year or two. I assure you, Clara, we won't let you and your father starve."

Clara believed her. She'd already proven it by bringing out three crates of groceries.

"Let's take this salt pork and the potatoes to your cellar, hm?" She looped elbows with Clara and moved toward the back door. "While we're outside, show me where you want to put your garden. I have seeds saved from last year's garden. Once I know how large your garden will be, I will know how many seeds to share with you."

This family was too giving! "Oh, but—"

"Kindly do not argue with me, Clara Frazier." Mrs. Klaassen hugged Clara's arm, her smile wide. "We are neighbors, and neighbors help one another. I refuse to take no for an answer."

Chapter Eight

Titus flicked the reins, encouraging the horses to pick up their pace. Joy filled him, and he couldn't hold back a smile that grew into a soft roll of laughter.

Ma turned a curious look on him, her face framed by her plain blue bonnet. "What has amused you?" She glanced at the landscape, holding her hands out in silent query.

"Nothing out there, Ma. Something in here." He patted his chest with his palm. "Did you see Ezra on those crutches? To be honest, I wasn't sure they would hold him up. I've never built crutches before. But he walked across the porch and even got himself down the steps into the yard. If their yard wasn't so rough, he probably would have made it all the way to the barn." He pulled in a deep breath and then let it out in a hearty *whoosh*. "It did my heart good to see him so happy."

Ma squeezed his knee. "It did my heart good to see you being so helpful to the Fraziers. As the Bible teaches, whatsoever you do for the least of these you also do for Jesus. Your Savior is surely pleased with you, Titus."

Ma's words pleased him even more than Mr. Frazier's excitement over the crutches. He shot her a brief grin of thanks before turning his attention to the road.

"I enjoyed my talk with Clara." Ma shook her head, clicking her tongue on her teeth. "For someone raised in the city, she has certainly learned the meaning of hard work. But I worry she is getting in over her head. When I spoke of butchering animals for meat, her face became so white, I feared she might faint. She wants a large garden, but she's only grown tomatoes and strawberries in the past. How will she know when to put out the seed onions and potatoes or how far apart to set the cabbages? Will she know to grow the corn on the south side of the garden so it doesn't shade on the other plants? How will she ready the ground?" A weary sigh left Ma's throat. "If only she were part of our church. The women of our congregation take seriously the admonitions found in the book of Titus about older women teaching the younger ones. They would offer advice and counsel to Clara."

Titus crunched his brow. "You keep calling Miss Frazier 'Clara.'"

A smug look crossed Ma's face. "Yes, I do. She invited me to call her Clara instead of Miss Frazier." She bumped Titus's arm. "I like her, Titus. I think she likes me. And. . ." She winked, her lips twitching. "I think she likes you, too."

Heat attacked Titus's cheek, and it wasn't from the bright sun. "Ma. . ."

"No, it's true. I watched her when you were near. She tries not to look at you too much, but her eyes deceive her and she casts glances your way. Each time she does, admiration glows in her eyes. Whether she likes you because of the things you do for her father, or if she likes you for you, I can't say for sure yet. But I can say with certainty—she has a high regard for you." Her expression sobered. "That gives you a great responsibility, my son, to set a good example at all times. But I need not worry. Your father and I raised you to be honorable and trustworthy. Clara's esteem will not be misplaced."

Titus transferred the reins to one hand and put his free arm around his mother. "Thank you, Ma."

She pasted on a mock frown and wagged her finger at him. "Just remember to keep your mind on your work while you're at the Frazier place. I also noticed how you look at Clara. She is a very pretty girl, and she could steal your focus if you aren't cautious."

"I'll be cautious, Ma. I promise."

Her grin returned. "You know, I think on Monday I'll send Andrew with you. While you work in the field, he can start clearing a piece of ground for Clara's garden. Don't we have a roll or two of the fine mesh wire left over from protecting the apple rings as they dry in the sun?

After the ground is ready for seeds, you boys can use the wire and put a fence around the garden. It wouldn't do for rabbits to eat up her tender plants before they have a chance to produce."

Titus laughed. "You think any rabbits will come around with Rowdy there?"

Ma laughed, too. "Oh, that coyote of hers, such a cunning little thing! His belly is so round, I can't imagine him needing to catch a rabbit for his supper. I think Clara feeds him plenty well." Worry crinkled her brow. "Son, that is something else about which someone should give her warning. The other farmers might not take kindly to her raising a coyote for a pet. And to be honest, I can't say it is a wise idea. Although he seems tame now, he's still young. As he grows to an adult, his wild ways might overtake him. He could be a danger to Clara or their livestock."

Titus's chest went tight. Clara—now that Ma called her Clara he couldn't think of her as Miss Frazier—loved Rowdy. He couldn't crush her by giving her a warning even if it was for her good.

"Maybe you should say something to her father."

Titus sighed. Yes, he'd talk to Mr. Frazier. Then Clara's father could find the best way to let Clara know the dangers of keeping a wild animal. The joy of the early afternoon faded a bit when he thought of Clara's wistful admission, *"He's good company for me."* She depended on Rowdy for companionship. But maybe if she came to see him and Ma and some others in town as friends, her need for Rowdy would lessen and it would be easier for her to let the creature return to the wild. It wouldn't bother him at all to see her gaze at him with the affection she bestowed on Rowdy.

He flicked the reins again. "Come on now, Buck and Topper. Hurry on home." Maybe the rattling wagon would shake loose some of his concerns for Miss Clara Rose Frazier. No amount of rattling would make him lose his attraction for her, though. Only God could remove those feelings.

───────◆───────

Monday morning, with Andrew yawning behind him and a drawstring sack of sandwiches bouncing from the saddle horn, Titus hurried Petunia up the road to the Fraziers' place. He hated to push the poor old horse—she wasn't used to carrying two riders—but Andrew's slow start put them behind his usual leaving time of six thirty. Clara served breakfast promptly at seven, and he didn't want to make her wait. Besides, he needed to get there before Joshua Gosen and Floyd Korfe, who'd promised to arrive by half-past seven to help him burn off the field and the stumps. Their knock at the door would be a shock if he couldn't forewarn the Fraziers.

He had a lot of forewarnings to give Mr. Frazier and Clara. Yesterday at the close of the church service, Ma stood up and shared the many needs of their new neighbors—a coat of paint applied to the house's exterior, grass and flowers planted in the front yard, the roof patched on the barn's lean-to, ground for a vegetable garden readied, and a pen for a piglet or two built behind the barn. It was too much for one person, but Ma reminded the congregation, *Arbeit macht das Leben süz*—work sweetens life. So many folks approached her in the yard afterward with offers to help, she had to turn some away.

Andrew yawned again, ending with a short yelp.

Titus chuckled. "Aren't you awake yet? Be careful you don't fall off back there. I don't have time to wait for you to climb up again. You'll have to walk the rest of the way. But then, if you had to walk, maybe you'd be good and awake by the time you got there."

Andrew bopped Titus's shoulder with his fist. "Don't tease. You know I stayed out late last night at the Friesens' place with the other young people. You are like an old man already, going to bed with the chickens. Why didn't you come to the Friesens' with John and me?"

Titus grimaced. The unmarried young people of the congregation often gathered to socialize on Saturday or Sunday evenings. He'd given up attending their get-togethers more than a year ago. He was at least two years older than all the others, and he'd grown impatient with the young women's open flirtation. Now if Clara Frazier were to attend, then maybe—

"Next week we're meeting at the Rempels'." Andrew's voice carried a thread of excitement. "Luke and Lyle built matching pony carts, and we're going to take turns racing them with the *Mäakjes* as drivers. It ought to be great fun. You should come. I bet you would win some of the races."

Years ago when he was eighteen like Andrew or even twenty-one like John, he would have considered pulling a pony cart with a girl directing him a fine time. But now it only seemed silly. Still, he wouldn't hurt his brother's feelings by saying so. "I will think about it, Andrew, all right?"

They reached the Frazier yard, and Titus let Andrew use his arm as a support to swing down. He handed his brother the sack of sandwiches. "Wait here, and watch for Joshua and Floyd while I put Petunia in the corral. Wave them over if they come. Miss Frazier doesn't know anyone besides me is coming, and I don't want her to be startled if she sees strangers at her door."

Andrew grinned. "You are getting kind of protective of Miss Frazier, aren't you?"

Usually Titus didn't mind his brothers' teasing and he joined right in. But not where Clara was concerned. He scowled. "Just do as I say, Andrew."

"All right, all right." Andrew swung the sandwich bag. "But hurry, huh? There's a good smell coming from the house. I'm ready for breakfast."

Titus bumped his heels against Petunia's sides and aimed her for the barn. Andrew didn't know it yet, but his breakfast would be a sandwich. He'd have a sandwich for lunch and supper, too. Ma didn't want the extra workers she'd sent eating up all of the Fraziers' food, so she'd made enough sandwiches for Andrew, Joshua, and Floyd. He released Petunia into an open stall and trotted out to join Andrew. Maybe he'd be nice and eat some of the sandwiches, too. Then he got a whiff of what Andrew was smelling—sausage and biscuits.

Maybe he wouldn't be nice, after all.

Titus knocked on the door, and he let out a little huff of laughter when Mr. Frazier, leaning on his crutches, opened it and Rowdy leaped over the threshold to attack Titus's boot strings. He scooped up the pup while smiling at the man. "Look at you! No breakfast in bed today?"

Mr. Frazier blasted a hearty guffaw. "Oh no, I'm avoiding my bed as much as possible, thanks to my crutches. Come in, come in." His gaze landed on Andrew, and his eyebrows rose in surprise. "And who have we here?"

Andrew whipped of his hat, tucked it under his arm, and held out his hand. "Good morning, sir. I'm Andrew Klaassen."

Titus added, "Ma suggested I bring Andrew today to begin clearing the area for Cl—Miss Frazier's garden." Clara was at the stove, her back to them, busily stirring something in a frying pan. He gestured to the bag Andrew held. "But you don't have to worry about feeding him. Ma sent plenty of sandwiches to carry him through the day."

Mr. Frazier chuckled. "Your mother thinks of everything, doesn't she?" He eased back a few inches, balancing himself on the crutches. "Come in and have a seat at the table. Clara Rose will set out an extra plate for you, Andrew. You can save those sandwiches for later."

Andrew aimed a triumphant grin at Titus and hurried to the table. He sat in the chair Titus had always used. Swallowing a growl of aggravation, Titus set Rowdy on the floor and chose a different chair. Mr. Frazier stumped across the room and dropped into the seat across from Titus. He laid the crutches on the floor beside him, chuckling when Rowdy crouched and growled at the lengths of wood, and turned to Clara. "Daughter, we'll need another plate."

She flashed a weak smile over her shoulder. "Certainly, Papa."

Titus rose. "You're busy, Miss Frazier. Let me get it." He crossed to the shelf near the stove where stacks of plates, bowls, and cups were neatly arranged. Clara kept house with as much care as she kept herself, always in a clean dress with her hair swept into a braided coil. He forced himself to glance past her enticing appearance to the pan on the stove. Thick, creamy gravy bubbled, releasing the rich aroma of sausage with each pop. He licked his lips. "That looks wonderful."

While continuing to stir, she sent a brief sidelong look in his direction, a hint of a smile tipping up the corners of her lips. "Thank you.

If you'd like to take the biscuits to the table, they're on a plate in the warming hob. I'll bring the gravy in just a minute or two."

If she asked for his help, she must be starting to relax with him. The thought sent a tremble through his belly. He smiled. "Of course, Miss Frazier." He removed the filled plate from the hob, his mouth watering at the sight of the light, fluffy, perfectly browned biscuits. He retrieved a plate from the shelf and a fork from a little basket on the possum-belly cupboard, then settled himself at the table.

Clara scurried over, carrying a rose-painted bowl filled with the gravy. Pepper flakes dotted the creamy expanse, and chunks of sausage formed dozens of little islands. Titus couldn't wait to pour that gravy over biscuits and dive in. Clara slid gracefully into the remaining chair at Titus's right. At every other meal, he'd sat across from her. Having her near enough to reach out and clasp her hand made his pulse gallop.

"Titus, would you ask the blessing?"

Mr. Frazier expected him to form a sensible prayer when his senses thrummed like a bee caught in a jelly jar? Titus swallowed the knot in his throat. "Y–yes. Sure." *Lord, help me out here, huh?* He bowed his head and hoped everyone else did, too. "Dear Lord, we thank Thee for Thy care. We thank Thee for the food before us, and for the h–hands that prepared it." *Don't stammer!* "Bless it—the food—to our nourishment. Amen."

"Amen," Mr. Frazier echoed. He offered the biscuits to Andrew.

Andrew took three biscuits and passed the plate to Titus. Titus only took two, even though he wanted three. While they passed the food, he reined in his nervousness enough to speak coherently. The clock on the wall showed five minutes past seven, so he needed to let the Fraziers know about those who would arrive soon.

"Mr. Frazier, some men from town are coming out today to help burn your field. My pa suggested burning those stumps down, too, then hacking them out rather than trying to pull out the roots and leaving a big hole in the field." He aimed an apologetic look at Clara. "I know you usually do wash on Monday, but I advise you to wait until tomorrow, or maybe even Wednesday, so your clothes don't pick up the smoke smell."

She frowned. "How many men are coming out?"

"Don't worry about feeding them." Titus hoped his words would remove the look of concern creasing her pretty, heart-shaped face. "My mother sent sandwiches for them."

She shook her head. "I'm not thinking about the meal. Who will be here?"

Her consternation raised Titus's nervousness. "Two men from our church, Joshua Gosen and Floyd Korfe." He faced Mr. Frazier, hoping his explanation would put the daughter at ease. "Burning a field is never a one-man job. You want several people watching the fire. An out-of-control fire is not a good thing on the prairie. I'm sorry I didn't ask beforehand, but. . ."

Clara's uncertain expression remained intact.

Titus cleared his throat. "I suppose I should also tell you, next week—on Saturday—a group of men and women are coming out to paint your house."

Mr. Frazier drew back, his eyes wide and jaw dropping. "They are?"

Clara rose so quickly, her chair legs screeched against the floor. Rowdy let out a yelp and darted through an open bedroom doorway. Clara pinned Titus with a glower. "Please tell them thank you, but that Papa and I are capable of taking care of our house on our own. Tell them. . ."

She closed her eyes, grimacing as if a pain stabbed her. She looked at him again, and to his chagrin, tears swam in her brown eyes. She gulped. "Tell them not to bother." She hurried through the same doorway Rowdy had exited and shut the door behind her.

Titus turned to Mr. Frazier. "I apologize, sir, for offending you."

Andrew scowled at the closed door. "It was Ma's idea. She thought it would help."

Mr. Frazier sighed. "Andrew, your mother is very kind for arranging a house-painting. And, Titus, we aren't offended. I appreciate you being concerned for safety and asking for help with burning the field. My daughter is—Clara Rose only—" He picked up his crutches and struggled to his feet. "Please, excuse me." He made his way to the bedroom door, knocked, and then entered the room.

Andrew blew out a little breath. "She sure is a strange one." He jammed the last bite of his gravy-covered biscuit into his mouth.

"Don't be unkind, Andrew." Titus, his hunger gone, pushed his nearly full plate aside and stood. "Come on. Time to work."

Chapter Nine

Clara stroked Rowdy's ears and pretended Papa wasn't standing at the door, scowling at her. Why, just when she was beginning to appreciate Titus Klaassen, did he have to do something so unsettling?

"Clara Rose, you didn't eat your breakfast."

The concern in Papa's voice stirred Clara's guilt. She peeked at him through her eyelashes. "I'm not hungry. Not anymore."

Papa sighed and thumped across the floor. He eased himself onto the edge of the bed next to her and buried his fingers in Rowdy's thick ruff. "The promise of a kind act robs you of your appetite?"

Wasn't she being a ninny? She wished she could explain why the thought of people she didn't know swarming her home bothered her, but she couldn't find the words. "Oh, Papa..." She leaned sideways and rested her head on his shoulder.

Papa tipped his temple against her forehead. "Clara Rose, when I bought this farmstead, it was with the intention of giving us a fresh start. I know it was hurtful and difficult for you to be the girl from the Washburn District who'd lost two beaus."

Clara swallowed painfully.

"But no one in this town knows your past. You have no reason to hold yourself away from the people of Wilhelmina."

She found her words. She sat up and shifted to face her father. "You're wrong. Look at me, Papa. I'm twenty-four, not a girl anymore. Every other twenty-four-year-old woman I know is married with a family. I'm...different." Oh, it hurt to say it out loud.

"Because you turned down proposals from two beaus?"

She nodded.

A slow smile curved Papa's cheek. "Some would call you wise beyond your years. It takes strength to wait for the right person when everyone around you is half of a pair."

Clara nibbled her lip. "You think I made the right choice, saying no to both Brant and Clifford?"

Papa made a face as if he smelled something rancid. "Oh my, yes. Brant was too stuffy for you, walking around with his nose in the air. And Clifford's hands were always sweaty. I've never trusted a man with sweaty palms. It makes me think he's nervous because he has something to hide."

Clara raised her eyebrows and gazed at him. "You never acted as if you didn't care for them."

"Well, I didn't want to be rude, my dear daughter, if you were fond of them. But truthfully, I wasn't unhappy to see you part ways with either one of those men." Papa squeezed her hand. "They weren't special enough for you, Clara Rose."

She hung her head. It would take a very special man to understand she couldn't move far away and leave her father alone. He nearly mourned himself to death after Mama died. He needed Clara. And she needed him. No man would take a wife who insisted her aging father must be part of their family, too. She muttered, "Even if they don't know about Brant and Clifford, I'll still be different. I'll still be the only woman in her midtwenties without a husband or children."

"And that's why you want people to stay away? So they won't know you're different?"

Stated that way, it seemed rather petty and childish, but she nodded.

Papa cupped her head and drew her to his shoulder again. "Do you remember what I told you when you asked about keeping Rowdy?"

"You said I was old enough to make my own decision."

"That's right. And I'm going to let you make your own decision concerning involving yourself with the people of this town."

She sat up again. "You'll tell Mr. Klaassen not to bring all those people to our house next week?"

Papa offered a sad smile. "No, Clara Rose. I won't repay their kindness with rejection. Besides"—he chuckled softly—"the house needs a coat of paint, and I won't be able to get to it for months. Their willingness is a true gift." He pushed upright and settled the crutches into position. "But if you want to stay inside on that day rather than coming out and mingling with those who work, I will respect your decision."

Mrs. Klaassen had said something similar about Clara's choice to call her Mrs. Klaassen or Maria. She should be glad no one would force her to do something against her will, but at the same time, sadness pinched her. She wished she understood why.

Papa awkwardly leaned forward and brushed a kiss on her forehead. His warm breath eased past her cheek, reminding her of the nighttime kisses he used to bestow when she was a little girl. He'd always been the best, most attentive and loving father any child could want. Whatever decision she made, it would be for him. And then it would be right. An uneasy feeling tiptoed up her spine. Or would it?

Clara spent Monday morning holed up in the house with the doors and windows closed against the smoke rolling over the field. Papa watched the burning from the window in his bedroom, seemingly fascinated by the creeping line of fire that snaked its way across the acreage. Rowdy was afraid of the fire and smoke and refused to leave her side, and even after he had an accident on the floor, she didn't make him go out.

Since she couldn't do laundry, she pulled out her basket of mending and settled on the camelback sofa with a needle and thread. The closed-up house felt stifling after enjoying so many days with a breeze coursing through. Even while sitting on the sofa, only her fingers pushing the needle in and out—hardly a laborious task—sweat formed on her brow and moistened her flesh beneath her dress.

Midmorning she set the mending aside and made sandwiches using the leftover biscuits, cheese, and sweet pickles. None of the workers left their duties to partake of the snack, however, so she covered the plate with a cloth napkin and left it on the table in case they came in later. But they didn't even come to the house at noon. Instead, they gathered in the shade of the wind block of cottonwoods on the far side of the field and ate sandwiches from the sack Titus Klaassen's brother had carried in that morning.

Observing them from the window, Clara balled her fists on her hips and released a mighty huff.

Papa clomped up beside her. "What's the matter?"

She flapped her hand in the direction of the men. "Look at them out there eating sandwiches. I heated up the house by starting the stove and cooking a pot of beans with ham and baking corn bread—far more than you and I can eat. But now it will go to waste because they aren't coming in."

Papa's forehead pinched. "Maybe they didn't want to bring the smoky smell into the house."

She snorted. "The smoky smell is already in the house. Even with the windows closed, it came in. Maybe I should open them anyway and let some air blow through. I feel as if I've spent my whole morning sitting in an oven."

To her continued irritation, Papa chuckled. He patted her arm. "I believe the heat of the room has you in a dither. Let's sit down and have some of your beans and corn bread. A good meal might take the edge off your temper."

But the savory beans and moist corn bread did nothing to ease Clara's irritability. At the end of the day, when everyone left without a word of good-bye, she gritted her teeth and battled the urge to chase after them and berate them for their thoughtlessness. That evening, before the sun disappeared over the horizon, she and Papa wandered into the yard and examined the charred field and the fresh-turned ground behind the house, evidences of the men's industriousness.

Papa released a satisfied sigh. "Ah, Clara, how good to have neighbors who so willingly give of their time and talents. We owe a great debt of gratitude to the Klaassens and their friends."

Guilt pricked. Why did resentment rather than gratitude fill her? Papa was right—people had been so giving and helpful. Would she harbor a grudge because they didn't eat her food today? How childish and self-centered. She'd been taught better by both Mama and Papa. God must certainly be displeased with her peevish thoughts and actions.

She swallowed a lump of regret and forced her dry throat to form a question. "Will all the men who came today be back tomorrow?"

"I'm not sure, Clara Rose. It doesn't seem as if the garden plot is ready for seeds, and those stumps still need removal. Maybe they'll all come tomorrow to finish the jobs."

She slipped her hand through Papa's elbow. "Well, just in case, I'll bake something extra special for breakfast tomorrow to say thank you. Maybe an applesauce cake?" Mr. Klaassen had particularly enjoyed her apple-walnut muffins, and the cake was even more moist and flavorful with lots of cinnamon, cloves, and nutmeg stirred into the batter.

Papa smiled. "That's a fine idea." He turned her toward the house. "Even though the smoke smell is still heavy, let's crack a few windows, hang moist towels over the openings, and let the night breeze in, hm?"

Papa's suggestion of moist towels blocked some of the smoky scent from plaguing Clara's nose, and the cool air allowed her to sleep deep and restfully. Tuesday morning she rose early and mixed up the promised applesauce cake. Her heart lurched when the men praised her for her thoughtfulness, but then plummeted when Mr. Klaassen instructed them to pick up the large wedges and eat them on their way to the field.

Clara wilted in dismay. "You aren't going to sit at the table and visit"—she swallowed—"with Papa while you eat?"

A hint of apology showed in his eyes, but he shook his head. "We'll eat outside. Then we won't be tempted to dawdle. Joshua, Floyd, and I plan to have those stumps out by the end of the day, and Andrew wants to finish your garden plot so he can work at our place tomorrow." He bobbed the piece of cake. "Thank you again, Miss Frazier. This is a pleasant way to start the day."

A pleasant way to start the day was conversation around the breakfast table. But she held the protest inside and served Papa instead.

The Tuesday morning change in routine became the regular procedure for the rest of the week. No matter what she prepared for breakfast—pancakes, bacon and eggs with biscuits, crumbly dried apricot coffee cake—Mr. Klaassen found a way to transport it to the field. She considered making a pot of oatmeal. He wouldn't be able to carry oatmeal out the door in his hands! But neither she nor Papa cared for oatmeal, so it would only go to waste.

Mr. Klaassen instructed her not to worry about midmorning or midafternoon snacks. Instead, he brought jerky or nuts in his pocket to snack on between meals. He also stopped taking supper with them, claiming he needed to see to chores at his house and wanted to get back earlier. The only meal for which he sat at the table was lunch, and those fleeting minutes proved dissatisfying. She warred between irritation with him for being distant and irritation with herself for being so bothered by it.

Friday after a morning of baking that left the house smelling wonderful, she hitched Penelope to the wagon and made a trip to town. She hadn't gone into Wilhelmina by herself before, and her stomach churned with anxiety. While she drove beneath the sunny sky with a warm breeze touching her face and flapping the ruffle of her bonnet's brim, she sent up prayers for strength and courage.

She stopped at the bank first and withdrew money from their savings account. The teller's smile smoothed the frayed edges of her nervousness, and she entered Voth's Grocery and General Goods Store with less trepidation. The owner of the store, Ira Voth, cheerfully marked her account paid-in-full and waved a friendly good-bye as she departed. She retrieved their few pieces of mail from the post office, responding to the postmaster's hello with a timorous smile. Basking in the warmth of everyone's friendliness, she drove to the Feed and Seed. Thanks to Andrew Klaassen's diligent work, her garden plot was ready to receive seeds. Mrs. Klaassen had offered to share, but after everything else the family had done, Clara decided taking seeds would be one kindness too many.

To her delight, little flats of vegetable starts filled tables in the large lean-to beside the store. She leisurely browsed, touching the unfurling leaves and breathing in the musky aroma of moist soil. When she came upon flats of tiny tomato plants, such an intense longing for her mother welled up, the good feelings conjured from her previous encounters swept away. Tears pricked, and she sniffed hard.

She turned from the tomato seedlings, and her gaze fell on a display of flats marked *Bloomen*. She needn't understand German to know it meant "flowers." Only tiny sprigs of green poked up from the soil, but identifying tags hung by strings from each flat. She crossed to the display and examined the tags. She frowned. What were *Schwaulmauchkjes* or *Re'jiene*? *Bottabloom* she determined were marigolds. Their telltale pungent aroma rose from the green leaves and teased her nose. At least she understood the numbers indicating the price per flat.

"May I help you?" The woman's voice, laden heavily with a German accent, came from behind Clara's shoulder and startled her.

She whirled around, her face flaming. "I—I was just looking."

The woman smiled, her full cheeks dimpling. "You are Miss Frazier, *jo*? Who lives east of town beyond the Klaassen *Foarm*?"

Clara nodded.

The woman offered her hand. "*Mein name ist* Naomi Zemke. My *Ehemaun*, Ike, and I own the Wilhelmina Feed and Seed. Nice it is to make your acquaintance, Miss Frazier."

Clara accepted the handshake and then locked her hands behind her back. The friendliness glowing on Mrs. Zemke's face reminded her of Mrs. Klaassen. Despite their vast age difference—Mrs. Zemke was surely already in her late forties or early fifties—Clara suspected they could be friends. If she wanted to make friends. She cleared her throat. "You have a nice selection of vegetables and flowers. I want to put in a large garden so my father and I will have food for the winter months. You're familiar with the growing season here. Could you help me decide what to buy for planting now and what should wait?"

Over the next half hour, Mrs. Zemke proved her knowledge by instructing Clara on the best time to plant, which vegetables were best to grow from seed and which from seedlings, how to thin carrots and radishes for the best result, and which plants preferred wet soil to dry soil. By the time they'd finished loading her wagon with flats of little plants, Clara's mind whirled with the various instructions. She hoped she would be able to remember everything long enough to write it all down.

As Clara placed brown paper bags of seed potatoes and onions next to a flat of strawberry seedlings, Mrs. Zemke tapped her lips with her finger and surveyed the wagon's contents.

"*Ach*, Miss Frazier, your vegetable garden will be well filled with the choices you have made. But when I find you, you were admiring the flowers. Do you not wish to take home Bloomen for your garden, too?"

Clara closed the hatch. After paying off her balance at the grocer and paying for the items in her wagon, she only had a few dollars left from the money she'd withdrawn. If they bought a piglet, which Mrs. Klaassen had suggested, she would need the remaining funds. She offered a sad smile. "I would like to plant flowers in the yard." The sad little house needed some color. "But I have to wait."

The woman nodded in understanding. "Nä-jo, well, the flowers do not sell fast as the vegetables." She smiled broadly and put her hand on Clara's shoulder. "No worrying you do, Miss Frazier. Some flowers will be here for you when ready you are."

Mrs. Zemke's odd way of phrasing made Clara want to giggle, but she reined in her humor and thanked the helpful woman instead. Back on the farm, she laid the flats along the foundation of the barn where they wouldn't receive too much sun, as Mrs. Zemke had advised, then headed for the house. As she crossed the yard, she glanced toward the field, then came to a halt. Where was Mr. Klaassen?

Chapter Ten

Titus banged through the back door. "Ma!"

She appeared like magic in the kitchen doorway, her face alight. "Are you ready for tomorrow?"

He grinned, envisioning the paint cans, brushes, pickets, and chicken-wire rolls in the barn. "Yes. How about you?"

She gestured to the table. Plates of *Zweibach*, cookies, and cakes covered the entire surface. "People have been delivering things all day."

"We won't go hungry tomorrow, that's for sure." Titus reached for one of the double-decker rolls served at every Mennonite gathering.

Ma smacked his hand. "We will go hungry if you eat everything before tomorrow." She laughed, proving she wasn't really angry. "Come look here, too." She led him to the pantry. Three towel-covered platters rested on a low shelf. She lifted the corner of the towel draped over the closest platter. "Ham sandwiches here. That one over there has egg salad, and the last one cheese. Enough to feed half the town."

Titus couldn't hold back a laugh of delight. "Maybe half the town plans to come. That would be something, wouldn't it? Then the Fraziers would know they are truly welcomed to Wilhelmina."

For a moment, Ma's face clouded. "Titus, do you think we might be rushing things? They haven't yet attended a church service, and Clara is like a skittish colt, ready to bolt at a sudden noise. Are you sure we won't overwhelm her with so much activity at once?"

He'd observed Clara over the past days, standing on the porch or at the window and gazing out with an expression of loneliness. She needed company. And she wanted it, whether she realized it yet or not. "She might be overwhelmed at first, but I think she'll appreciate it once she understands we're all there out of kindness."

Ma closed the pantry door and crossed to the table. She fingered the chipped edge on one of the cookie plates. "I have done much praying about how to help her feel at ease in our community. She reminds me of a lost lamb."

Titus chuckled. "A skittish colt, a lost lamb. . . What animal will you use to describe her next?"

Ma pursed her lips. "Certainly not a lioness. I don't think she has so much as a tiny growl in her." She touched Titus's arm, her expression softening. "She is a lovely, kindhearted girl. Most important, she knows Jesus as her Savior. If you decide to court her, your father and I will not interfere."

Titus raised one eyebrow. "She isn't Mennonite, Ma."

An ornery gleam entered his mother's eyes. "Yet."

Titus laughed. Before he could reply, someone knocked on the door and called a hello.

Ma bustled through the back porch and threw the door open. "Naomi! Come in."

"Nä, you come out." The Feed and Seed owner's wife peeked past Ma at Titus. She crooked her finger at him. "You, too. You can help."

Both Titus and his mother stepped into the yard. Ma said, "What is wrong, Naomi?"

"*Nuscht*, nothing." She led them to her wagon and gestured to the bed. "I have some things here for the Frazier family. Neither Ike nor I can go out there tomorrow, but you take them with you, jo?"

Ma rose up on tiptoe and peered over the side. "Naomi!"

The woman beamed at them. "By the Feed and Seed she came today. She bought vegetables for her garden, but she said she must wait on buying flowers. I thought, why wait? So here you are. Pansies, petunias, cornflower, marigolds, zinnias. . ." She turned her smile on Titus. "You put some of the ladies to work making a colorful garden for her, will you? I have seen that house. A flower garden will do it much good."

Ma embraced Mrs. Zemke. "This is very kind of you, Naomi."

Mrs. Zemke waved her hands as if shooing away flies. "Nä, nä, I could not help myself. I see her pining over those flowers, and I say to myself, this girl is timid like a rabbit. She will not ask, but I can give."

Titus and Ma burst into laughter.

Mrs. Zemke frowned at them. "What is so funny?"

"Nuscht." Ma hugged the other woman again. "We are just happy."

"Nä-jo, well, get this wagon unloaded so I can get back to the store before closing time. Then my Ike will be happy, too."

After breakfast Saturday morning, Clara took the broom and headed for the front porch. Dirt and tiny bits of blackened grass littered the entire expanse, and she and Papa had carried the sooty mess into the house on their feet each day. It was time to get rid of it for good. Rowdy trotted along beside her as she propped the door open and stepped outside. The coyote darted to the edge of the porch, pointed his nose in the air, and released a series of shrill barks.

Clara recognized the sound as his warning barks. She marveled that even living with humans, away from a pack of creatures like himself, he still knew how to behave like a coyote. She reached down and gave his neck a little scratch. "It's all right, boy. We're safe."

Rowdy growled low in his throat and slunk back inside.

Puzzled, Clara scanned the surrounding area for anything that might speak danger to the pup. A cloud of dust far up the road caught her attention. She frowned for a moment, and then understanding dawned. Hadn't Titus Klaassen warned them a group would come paint the house today? When he'd departed early yesterday, she presumed he'd finished his work and had no need to return. Apparently, she'd been wrong.

She angled a glance over her shoulder through the open doorway. "Papa?" She turned her attention back to the cloud, which drew nearer with each passing second.

The *clomp-clomp* of crutches against the floor let her know her father was coming. He stopped beside her. "It must be the painters Titus promised us."

She couldn't determine from his even tone whether he was pleased or resigned. She flicked a look at him and noted the slight upturn of his lips.

The small smile disappeared when he turned and met her gaze.

"Would you bring out a chair, please, so I can greet everyone when they arrive and visit with them as they work?" He didn't ask if she intended to stay inside or come out and visit with the workers, but she glimpsed the question in his eyes.

"Of course, Papa. I'll be right back." She hurried inside, grabbed one of the chairs from the table, and carried it to the porch.

A trio of wagons approached, each with two people on the seat and several more in the beds. Both men and women, judging by their headwear. Clara paused with the chair in her hands, a spiral of longing finding its way through her center. Yesterday being greeted by towns-folk had been so pleasant. Should she stay out here with Papa?

Rowdy crept behind her, his fur ruffled and his lip curled back to show his teeth. She'd never seen the pup behave so fiercely. She couldn't leave him out here with Papa.

She put the chair down and scooped up Rowdy. "Papa, we're going inside."

He nodded, and although not a hint of disappointment colored his expression, regret stung her. He raised his hand in a wave, and several people in the wagons waved back. Many of them called greetings. Before they could approach the house and address her directly, she hurried inside with the growling coyote in her arms.

Clara spent the morning comforting Rowdy, who alternately growled, whined, and yip-yipped in protest at the intrusion of humans in his territory. Shortly before noon, the little creature crawled under her bed, curled into a ball with his tail over his face, and fell asleep. With him quiet, she could have gone outside, but fear Rowdy would awaken and be frightened kept her indoors.

She couldn't stay away from the windows, however. She moved from room to room, awed by the busyness she witnessed in every direction. In the cleared area behind the house, a half-dozen women swarmed her vegetable garden, planting the seedlings in neat rows with sticks and string separating the plants. Two men clambered on the barn's roof, hammering wood shingles into place. Two more men carried posts and railings behind the barn. She couldn't see what they were doing, but she could guess. They'd have a pen for their piglet by sundown.

Several times she stepped up to a window only to have someone look in, paintbrush in his hand and a smile on his face. Although she always gave a little start of surprise, she managed to offer a smile and little wave before turning and scurrying to a different window. Until she looked out from Papa's window and discovered Titus Klaassen on the other side of the glass. Then she froze as stiff as if she'd been caught in a blizzard and stared, wide eyed and unblinking, into his sky-blue eyes while he stood equally still and stared back.

She had no idea how many minutes passed with the two of them gazing at each other, not smiling yet not frowning, their lips parted as if words were trying to escape, her pulse pounding with as much force as the hammers coming down on nails. Then someone must have called his name, because he jerked his face to the left, appeared to listen, nodded, and started to turn back.

In those brief seconds of separation, her limbs thawed enough to move. She darted away from the window and around the corner. Ridiculous though it was, she pressed herself to the wall and leaned into the doorway just enough to peek with one eye at the window. There he was, hands cupped beside his face, peering in.

Heat exploded through her face and all the way into her chest. She bolted out of sight, then she dashed around, whisking the curtains closed at every window except the one where she'd exchanged the lengthy, nonverbal staring match with Titus Klaassen. Instead, her head low, breath caught in her lungs, and gaze aimed at the floor, she stepped into Papa's doorway, grabbed the door handle, and gave his door a quick yank that sealed the room away.

She sagged against the sturdy door and released her breath in a long, slow exhale that calmed her thundering pulse. The patter of feet and mumble of voices on the porch caught her attention. She inched to the front window, lifted the corner of the curtain, and peeked outside. Two women were spreading blankets on the ground in front of the house. Other women arranged platters and plates and jugs on the edge of the porch floor. Mrs. Klaassen and Papa engaged in what appeared to be a lighthearted exchange. Desire to join them nearly twisted her heart into a knot.

Mr. Klaassen ambled near. Clara felt like a voyeur as she watched him move beside his mother, plant a kiss on her cheek, then snatch up one of the odd rolls that looked something like a snowman and carry it to his mouth. He handed one of the rolls to Papa, and his face shifted in her direction. She ducked out of sight, then scurried to the table. She clung to the back of one of the chairs, a wild battle raging inside of her.

Go out. The voice inside her head was more demanding than any she'd heard before. Should she heed it? If she went out, she'd please Papa. She could talk to Mrs. Klaassen, which would please her. She could tell Mr. Klaassen thank you for bringing these workers to their place. Even if their presence frightened Rowdy and intimidated her, she was still grateful for their thoughtfulness.

One of the scriptures she and Papa studied last week tiptoed through her memory. *"In every thing give thanks: for this is the will of God in Christ Jesus concerning you."* When Papa shared the verse from 1 Thessalonians, he'd indicated it instructed believers to thank God for everything they encountered, whether good or bad, because all things served a purpose. But she knew God wanted His followers to treat others the way they wanted to be treated. If she worked hard for someone else, she'd appreciate being thanked. Thanking them would please her Father.

She straightened her shoulders and turned toward the door. They were all gathering to eat their lunch. She could tell everyone thank you at once. She lifted her foot to take a step.

Whines erupted from beneath her bed—Rowdy awake, fearful, and probably hungry.

Clara hurried to tend to her pet.

Chapter Eleven

The last wagon, driven by Titus Klaassen, rolled from the yard. Clara watched from the window until it disappeared over the gentle rise in the road, then she stuck her head out the door and addressed her father, who stood at the edge of the porch. "Are you ready to come in now? Supper is waiting."

Papa eased to the porch stairs and aimed a grin over his shoulder. "Supper can wait. Come with me."

Clara held her breath as Papa descended the two steps to the yard, wavering on the crutches. When he reached the bottom, she emptied her lungs in one *whoosh* and scurried after him.

"Don't look at the house until I tell you," Papa warned.

Temptation to sneak peeks tormented her as she moved alongside him to the middle of the yard, but she kept her gaze forward until Papa stopped.

"All right. You may look."

Clara turned slowly, and when she got a view of the house, she clapped her hands to her cheeks and gasped. "Oh, Papa! It looks. . . It looks. . ." She couldn't find appropriate words.

The old gray weathered siding bore a coat of crisp white paint. The shutters, which once hung crooked and bore stains from mud dauber nests, lay square against the house and glistened in a vibrant, deep green. The porch railings and posts were white like the house, but someone had taken the care to add green bands on the carved turnings on the posts.

At the base of the porch, freshly turned ground held dozens of flower seedlings. Within weeks, the whole patch would be ablaze with color and laden with scent.

Papa chuckled. "Did you know our little house could be so pretty?" Clara shook her head, marveling. "It's grand, Papa. So very grand." Papa set the crutches in motion. "Come with me."

She followed him to the backyard, where he pointed out the white paint on the sides of the chicken coop and the outhouse as proudly as if he had wielded the paintbrush himself. Then he led her to the garden. A short fence built from unpainted pickets and mesh wire circled the large plot of rich soil dotted with tiny green sprouts.

Papa tapped the fence with the tip of one crutch. "There's no gate, so you'll have to step over the fence. Mind you lift your skirt when you do so it doesn't catch on the wire. As Titus told me, the fence isn't the best, but it should keep rabbits at bay."

"That is what matters," Clara said, and she meant it. This fence looked nothing at all like the delicate fence constructed of lattice that housed Mama's garden in Minneapolis, but she liked it even better than the fence from Minneapolis. It wasn't as pretty, but it had been constructed by people with giving hearts.

"I won't take you to the pigpen." Papa grinned. "Before long, you'll be able to follow your nose and find it. I requested two pigs from the Klaassens' litter."

"Two?" Clara couldn't imagine them needing the meat from two hogs.

"Yes. There are some folks in town who don't raise animals. They buy meat from area farmers. So if we butcher—"

Clara clutched her bodice. We? Did Papa expect her to help?

"—two hogs, then we can sell some of the meat. Or maybe, if there's a family in need, we can share with them."

Her heart melted. "Papa, that's a wonderful idea. Everyone has been so kind to us. We should do something kind for someone in return."

"I think so, too."

Rowdy had followed Clara out of the house, and he darted around the yard, nose to the ground, fur bristling. Clara smiled at the pup. "Poor Rowdy. . . He didn't like having so much company today. Do you think he'll bother the piglets when they come?"

Papa didn't answer, and she looked at him. He was watching Rowdy, and lines of worry marred his forehead.

Concern rose in her chest. "What's wrong?"

Papa shook his head, as if dislodging a troubling thought. "My leg is tired. Let's go back inside. Come, Rowdy." Without a moment's pause, Rowdy gave up his sniffing and trotted to Papa's side. To her relief, her father's expression cleared. He began making his way to the back door. "We'll enjoy our supper, and then—" He stopped and turned a questioning look on Clara. "When we moved from Minneapolis, did we bring the wicker chair and rocker that sat in the screened-in porch?"

Clara nodded. "Yes. They're in the barn loft, remember? You put the chairs up there and wrapped them in burlap in the hopes no mice would chew on them."

"Ah, that's right. On Monday, remind me to ask Titus to climb up and bring those down. We'll put them on our grand front porch. Then you needn't carry out a dining chair for me when I want to sit outside."

"Will he come again on Monday?"

"Yes. The ground field still requires tilling, and then he'll plant the corn."

Clara lightly gripped Papa's elbow and escorted him across the yard. "Well, I will remind you on Monday if you forget to tell him tomorrow."

Papa stopped again. "Tomorrow?"

Clara put her hands on her hips. "If you can make it all the way across the yard and up and down steps on your crutches, I imagine you can get yourself into the back of the wagon for a ride to church."

Papa angled his head, peering at her from the corner of his eyes. "Church?"

She nodded, swallowing a smirk. "And I hope you won't mind if I accompany you."

Papa let out a whoop, and Rowdy plopped down on his behind, lifted his nose, and howled.

Titus lay in bed, hands locked behind his back, and stared at the ceiling. Every muscle in his body ached. Tiredness plagued him. But sleep refused to come. In place of the shadowy ceiling, he saw Clara Rose Frazier's wide-eyed gaze, but try as he might, he couldn't discern what thoughts trailed through her mind while she stared at him from the other side of that window.

Why hadn't she come outside during the day? Her father had never gone in. What word had Ezra Frazier used to describe Titus? *Affable.* That was it. Affable. Friendly. Clara's father was that—friendly. But Clara? *Unaffable,* if such a word existed, described her. He revisited the frustration he'd experienced when she closed the door to her father's room, closing him away from her sight. The frustration faded, and a deep hurt replaced it.

Why doesn't she like people, Lord? At least he knew for sure he wasn't the only one she disliked. Her refusal to come out and greet any of the workers made it clear her unaffability extended beyond him to the entire community. But knowing didn't ease his discomfort the way he'd expected.

The burden drove him from the mattress to the floor. He knelt, bowed his head, and closed his eyes. "God, I'm an affable man. You made me that way, and I do not wish to change it. You also opened my heart to Clara Frazier. When I saw her the first time, sitting at the table in our kitchen with Ma, I knew she was the one I've prayed for and waited for all these years. But, Lord, can an affable man and an unaffable woman comfortably join as one?"

He remained on his knees, listening for an answer. None came.

He sighed. "Well, Lord, You turned water into wine and parted the Red Sea. You can do anything. So I'm going to trust You to work in my life and Clara's life and bring us together if it is Your will. Amen."

Placing the situation in God's hands eased Titus's mind. He slid back into bed, closed his eyes, and before he even realized he'd fallen asleep, fingers of sunlight sneaked through his bedroom window and poked him awake.

The smell of bacon, eggs, and toasted zweibach propelled him out from beneath the covers, and he dressed in his best suit, then hurried downstairs. The ride to town with his parents and brothers proved pleasant. Titus liked Minnesota in mid-May better than any other time of the year. In June the humidity—and the influx of mosquitoes—would start. But for now, the cool-but-not-cold temperatures, the good scents rising from the earth, and the expanse of blue sky overhead lifted his spirits. Mid-May was a time for rejoicing, and Titus anticipated joining his heart with his fellow believers in praise for God's many blessings during the worship hour at church.

The churchyard was already crowded with wagons by the time Pa pulled their wagon up beside the church. Titus glanced across the horses drowsing within the traces of the various wagons. If any familiar horses were missing, the preacher would probably share news of an illness or a calamity, so Titus always hoped to see every area family's horse and wagon in the yard. He inwardly identified the Friesens' mare, then the geldings belonging to the Kerfes' and the Rempels'. Next was the Fraziers' mare, Penelope. And then—

Realization struck like a lightning bolt. Penelope—the Fraziers' mare? He leaped from the back of the wagon and pounded across the ground.

Ma's voice called after him, "Titus, slow down, Son. Wait for your brothers, father, and me."

But Titus couldn't slow down. Had Ezra Frazier somehow driven himself to church today, all alone, or had Clara brought him? He had to know. *Please, Lord. Please, Lord.* He leaped up the stairs, taking the six of them in only two bounds, crossed the narrow porch with one wide stride, and entered the church door reserved for the men's use with his heart thudding like a bass drum in a county fair marching band.

He looked to the left side of the church, where a sea of women's flowered hats greeted him. His breath coming in tiny puffs of anticipation, he bounced his gaze across each hat, and there she was, third bench from the back, her molasses hair covered by a pert straw bonnet trimmed in orange poppies. A smile broke across his face. *Thank You, my Father!*

Titus made his way to his usual bench, feeling as if he floated inches above the wide-planked floor. His father and brothers joined him just as the music leader stepped onto the dais and invited the congregation to rise for an opening hymn. Titus risked a glance over his shoulder as the gathered worshippers opened the *Gesanbuchs* and raised their voices in song. Ma had slipped in next to Clara instead of going to the bench across from Pa, and she shared a hymnbook with Clara.

Seeing the two women he loved side by side in his place of worship filled Titus so thoroughly, he lost the ability to speak. So he stood between Pa and John and listened as those around him sang, "*Ach bleib mit deiner Gnade. . .*"—"*Abide among us with Thy grace. . .*"

The service passed more slowly than Titus could ever remember. He tried to pay attention to Reverend Fast, but his thoughts continually carried him to the bench on the women's side. Clara had come. She had come to service. He couldn't wait for worship to end so he could approach her, thank her for coming, ask her if she liked the way her house now looked in its fresh covering of white.

At last they sang their closing hymn, and Reverend Fast released them to fellowship with one another. Titus pushed past Pa and strode directly to Ma and Clara. Women had already surrounded Clara, and he shifted impatiently from foot to foot, waiting his turn.

Ma caught his eye, and a knowing smile curved her lips. She took Clara's elbow and nodded to the women. "*Dankscheen*, everyone, for your kind welcome to Miss Frazier. If any would like to visit more with her, please come to our place for Faspa."

Titus almost socked the air in delight. Ma had invited the Fraziers to eat with them. He'd have lots of time to talk to Clara. He thanked Ma with a wink, then hurried out to the Frazier wagon. He'd be waiting to help Ezra into the back and Clara onto the seat. And maybe, if he was very lucky, Clara would allow him to drive her and her father to his farm. He couldn't imagine a better end to this fine Sunday morning than accompanying Miss Clara Rose Frazier to Faspa.

Chapter Twelve

Clara, still reeling from the enthusiastic welcome from members of the Mennonite Brethren congregation, held Papa's elbow and matched his slow, hitching stride as they left the church building. She'd been nervous at first when she realized she and Papa wouldn't be able to sit together, but Mrs. Klaassen on her right and the grocer's wife, Helena Voth, on her left—both so friendly and warm—bolstered her and sent the nervousness out the window.

What a pleasure to personally thank those who had come yesterday and worked magic on their property. Even if she and Papa chose not to join this congregation, she would always think kindly of them and ask God's blessing on them.

They reached their wagon, and Clara started to release the hatch. Another pair of hands crowded in, and she turned her startled gaze on Titus Klaassen. "Why, hello."

His smile sent a tremor of reaction from her scalp to her toes. "Hello, Miss Frazier. May I help your father?"

His strength was greater than hers. She'd nearly tipped Papa on his nose while assisting him before church. She took a step back. "Please."

Papa braced his palms on the edge of the bed. Mr. Klaassen bent down, gripped Papa by the good leg behind his knee, and gave a push. Papa was sitting in the bed almost before Clara realized he was moving. She shook her head, laughing softly as Mr. Klaassen straightened.

He grinned at her. "What?"

"You make everything look so effortless."

"Everything?"

Heat filled her face. Why had she made such a blatant statement? Now he would think she watched him perform every task. . .and

311

admired him. But didn't she owe him words of praise? She forced her embarrassment aside and looked directly into his eyes. "Yes. Papa and I both appreciate the work you've done. All the work."

He sucked in his lips for a moment, seeming to study her. He said in a near whisper, "All the work?"

How she knew he referenced yesterday's accomplishments she couldn't guess, but she knew. So she nodded. "Yes."

A smile lit his handsome face. "Thank you." They stood on opposite sides of Papa's extended feet much the way they'd stood on either side of the window gazing at each other. But this time they both smiled. Clara much preferred being able to smile with ease at this man. She could have remained there forever beneath his blue-eyed gaze, but Papa cleared his throat.

"Can we go now, Clara Rose? The churchyard has emptied."

She glanced around, and a second wave of heat attacked her face. How could she have been so oblivious? She gasped. "Oh! Your family has gone on without you, Mr. Klaassen."

His smile didn't fade. "I know. I told them to go since Ma wanted to get things set out for our lunch." He shrugged. "I guess I'll have to ride with you and your father."

Papa scooted back several inches, bringing his feet all the way into the bed. "Put up that hatch, then, and let's go. The next time I decide to ride in this wagon bed, I'm throwing a feather mattress in first. I'll probably be black and blue by the time we're home."

Mr. Klaassen closed the hatch and offered Clara his arm. With a self-conscious giggle, she allowed him to escort her to the front of the wagon and assist her onto the seat. His strong hands on her ribs should have frightened or perhaps offended her, but instead it seemed right for him to lift her. She settled on the seat, but he didn't climb up beside her. She glanced at him, confused.

"Would you prefer I rode in the back with your father?"

His solicitousness touched her. She should probably send him to the back. If people saw them sharing the tight seat, they might get ideas. But how often would she be able to enjoy the company of a handsome man on a Sunday afternoon? Surely God would understand

and not condemn her for her answer. "Please, take the reins, Mr. Klaassen. You're more familiar with the road to your home."

He hooked his toe on the hub of the wheel and pulled himself up in one smooth motion. The bench bounced on its springs when his weight descended, tipping her in his direction. She grabbed the far side of the seat, and he sent her a brief, apologetic look. She smiled to assure him no harm had been done, and he lifted the reins. Before bringing them down on Penelope's back, however, he pinned her with a serious look.

"Miss Frazier, when we reach my house, you will be in the company of six Klaassen men. You can't call all of us 'Mr. Klaassen.' It would be too muddling. So would you consider reserving that title for my pa and calling us boys by our given names?"

He was hardly a boy. Sitting so close, gazing into his square, honed face, she realized more than ever how fully masculine he was. His suggestion made sense, but she hesitated. What would Mama tell her to do?

From the back of the wagon came Papa's droll voice. "For mercy's sake, Clara Rose, agree with the man so we can get going. My backside is falling asleep."

Clara covered her mouth with her fingers and giggled. If Papa could be unconventional enough to mention his backside, she could call Mr. Klaassen by his given name. She lowered her hand and grinned at the driver. "All right. Titus it is."

No simple declaration had ever pleased him as much as her willingness to call him by his name. Titus arched one brow, inwardly praying. "And I may call you. . .Clara?"

Her cheeks bloomed a delicate pink, but she nodded.

"Thank you, Clara," he said.

"You're welcome, Titus," she replied.

"Let's go," Mr. Frazier groused.

Titus laughed and flicked the reins. As the wagon rattled out of the churchyard, he couldn't resist asking, "Were you satisfied with the color of your house, Clara?"

Her face lit, making his pulse stammer. "Oh yes! It's lovely. Especially the porch posts. What a wonderful touch, the bands of green at top and bottom."

His chest puffed. Painstaking work, painting those bands, but well worth it to please her.

"Thank you for organizing the work party. Papa and I both appreciate all you and your friends accomplished."

Relief flooded him. "I'm glad. But. . ." Should he ask? He might offend her, but he had to know. "Why didn't you come out at all when we were there? Everyone wanted to meet you."

Her slender shoulders rose and fell in a feminine shrug. "I wanted to. I meant to. But Rowdy was very upset by all the commotion. I didn't want to take him out with me, and I didn't want to leave him alone."

Her tenderness toward that furry scamp never ceased to amaze him. "I suppose that makes sense." It didn't explain why she'd scurried away from him, though, when he found her at the window. He searched for a way to ask the reason for her strange reaction.

"Until the house was painted, I had a hard time envisioning it truly being Papa's and my home. But now it's easy to imagine living there with him." She sent a smile over her shoulder. "Right, Papa?"

No answer came from the back.

Clara giggled and whispered, "He's fallen asleep."

Titus jolted. How could anyone sleep on that hard surface while bouncing along the road? But the man's silence offered him the chance to ask a more probing question—one her father might consider too personal. He blurted it out before he could change his mind. "But couldn't you at least have talked to me? You could have opened the window and talked to me."

She bit down on her lower lip and stared outward. The seat rocked with each bounce of the wagon wheels, occasionally bringing her shoulder against his. He kept his gaze forward, too, waiting for her answer.

"I can't talk to you, Titus. Not the way you. . .you want. You see, I sense you like me. And while it's flattering, I cannot encourage it."

He cringed. He wished he hadn't asked. His traitorous tongue formed another question. "Why?"

She glanced into the back again, blinking rapidly. "Because of Papa." She lowered her head and gripped her hands together in her lap, the hold so tight her knuckles turned white. "I'm all he has. He needs me. If I let myself fall in love, the man will take me away from Papa, and I can't leave him." She finally looked at him. Tears shone in her brown eyes, proving how deeply she loved her father—enough to sacrifice her happiness for his. "So, please, don't like me, Titus. It will only lead to hurt."

Titus gritted his teeth. Her advice had come too late. He already liked her. He more than liked her. Oddly, her strong dedication to her father endeared her to him even more. A woman so devoted to her father knew how to love deeply. If only she could love him with such depth.

He tugged the reins, guiding Penelope to turn into the lane leading to his family's farmhouse. He drew up beside the house and set the brake. Before getting down, he shifted to look at her sweet, sad, pleading face. "You're right. I like you, Clara. I've prayed since I was fifteen years old for a godly wife, and I think God brought you here for me. I won't stop liking you. I can't."

Tears flooded her eyes. She touched the sleeve of his suit coat. Her voice emerged in a coarse whisper. "You must. I know that I'm not meant to be someone's wife."

Anguish writhed through him. "But why?"

"Don't ask why. Simply trust my word." She swept her fingers across her eyes, erasing the tears. She straightened and assumed a determined expression. "I won't disappoint your mother by refusing to eat with your family, but the day has tired my father. As soon as we've finished eating, we'll need to go home. Will you help Papa, please?" Without waiting for a reply, she clambered down from the seat and darted to the house.

If she hadn't promised Mrs. Klaassen that she and Papa would join them for the strangely worded lunch called Faspa, Clara would have gone home, closed herself in her room, and indulged in a good long cry. Her chest ached so badly, she could scarcely take a breath. But she pasted on a smile and visited with Mrs. Klaassen and the other two women who'd come out to partake of rolls; cold meat; cheese; a sweet, cold, pudding-like soup called *Plumamooss*; and a variety of relishes.

The women gathered in the parlor and the men in the dining room, which should have been enough of a separation for her to distance herself from Titus. Unfortunately, the wide doorway and her position on the sofa gave her a straight view to Titus's chair at the end of the table. His gaze never wavered from her face, and like a magnet, his blue eyes pulled her to meet his gaze again and again and again until she wanted to scream in agony.

The women chatted together about the flavor of Mrs. Klaassen's pickled watermelon rind, a topic that held no interest for Clara. Her ears tuned to the men's talk—especially Mr. Klaassen's booming voice.

"Ezra, Titus tells us you worked as an accountant in Minneapolis."

"That's right." Papa spoke more softly, but familiarity with his voice let her hear him clearly. "At the Minneapolis Bank and Trust Company."

"Very different from farming," another of the men said with a short laugh. "What brought you to Wilhelmina?"

Clara held her breath. Papa wouldn't share her secret heartache—she trusted him—but how could he answer truthfully?

"My wife passed away several years ago. Minneapolis has been lonely without her. Clara Rose and I needed a fresh start. The farmstead in Wilhelmina seemed as good a place as any."

Titus's steady gaze sent prickles of awareness up her arms. She set her plate aside and chafed her forearms, shivering.

The same man who'd asked their reason for coming spoke again. "Too bad you have decided on farming for your living. We have a bank in town, you know, but many of the little towns around us do not. Our banker, Earnest Wiens, is looking for someone to share banking duties with him. No one in Wilhelmina has the knowledge he needs."

Clara tore her attention from Titus to Papa. Interest gleamed briefly in his eyes, but he shook his head. "I'm a farmer now, Mr. Rempel."

The man shrugged and went back to eating.

"Clara?" Mrs. Klaassen's concerned tone pulled Clara's attention from the dining room and Papa's wistful expression. "Don't you care for the Plumamooss? Some people aren't fond of prunes."

Clara forced a smile. "It's very tasty, I'm just. . .full." Full of regret, full of longing, full of dissatisfactions she didn't understand. She stood. "And the hour is growing late. Papa still rests each afternoon, and I've left Rowdy unattended for quite a while. We should go home." Besides, she needed a long cry to rid herself of the strange emotions tumbling through her chest.

Everyone bid her and Papa farewell. Titus assisted Papa into the wagon, and he waved as they drove away. At their beautiful little white-and-green house, Clara helped Papa to his room, let Rowdy run outside for a few minutes, then closed herself in her room for the cry she'd promised herself. But to her great disappointment, the tears did not wash away the longings within her.

Chapter Thirteen

Titus awakened early Monday with a snide question rolling in his mind. So he wasn't supposed to like her, huh? He'd just have to see about that. Ma often bemoaned that Titus had been given the greatest portion of the Klaassen hardheadedness. Once he set his mind to something, he didn't let go. Over the years he'd learned to curb the stubborn tendency when his mind led him toward something he shouldn't have. But Clara was meant to be his wife. He knew it from the depths of his soul. Now it was time for her to accept it.

He pounded down the stairs two at a time and careened into the kitchen. Ma was already there, stoking the stove in preparation for breakfast and Pa's important pot of coffee. He snatched his jacket from the hook, then crossed to his mother, shrugging into the coat as he went.

"Ma, I intend to marry Clara Frazier."

She continued adding split pieces of wood to the tiny flame in the belly of the stove. "I presumed as much, Titus."

He plunked his fists on his hips and shook his head, twisting his lips into a line of scorn. "She has some wild idea that she can't get married, that she has to stay home forever and take care of her father. So I have to convince her getting married doesn't mean she's abandoning her pa."

Ma swished her palms together, closed the door on the stove, and straightened. "Do you know how you will convince her?"

"Other than praying for God to rain some sense into her, no."

Ma laughed. "Are you open to suggestions?"

He nodded emphatically. "Always."

"Good." Her eyes sparkled. "How about you try this...."

Clara was surprised when Titus rode up the lane Monday morning. Even though she'd stood at the window, watching, hoping, she hadn't expected him. After what she had said to him yesterday, she wouldn't blame him a bit for staying away. No other man had returned after she'd stated her intention to remain dedicated to Papa. But there came Titus on Petunia's back, just like always.

Her heart rolled over in her chest, and she dashed to the table to set out another plate.

Papa stumped from the bedroom. "What are we having this morning, Clara Rose?"

"Ham, eggs, and hotcakes with strawberry preserves." The breakfast she'd prepared on Titus's first day with such disastrous results.

Papa gave her a speculative look, but she pretended not to notice and busily spooned sweet-smelling batter into the pan. By the time Titus knocked on the door, a stack of hotcakes waited in the warming hob next to a plate of fried ham and a bowl of fluffy scrambled eggs seasoned with grilled onions.

She poured coffee in the three tin cups on the table while Papa and Titus seated themselves, then she scurried to the stove for the food. As she balanced the plates and bowls in her hands, she tried not to see if Titus watched her. She might begin juggling the items if she glimpsed the same expression on his face as she'd seen yesterday when she left his house. Despite her best efforts, her gaze flicked toward him, and she frowned when she realized he wasn't paying any attention to her at all. He was too busy using a penknife to trim away a hangnail. At her table?

"Titus Klaassen, don't you dare flick a piece of your thumbnail onto my clean floor!"

He looked up, his eyebrows rising. "Oh. Excuse me." He pocketed the knife and glanced across the plates she held.

Her heart began a rapid patter. Would he recognize the significance of the pancakes and preserves?

"Everything looks good, as usual, Miss Frazier."

Miss Frazier? She placed the items in the center of the table, inwardly berating herself for the tremble in her hands. "Yes. Well. . ."

She plopped into her chair. "Pray, Papa, so we can eat."

Papa's lips twitched as he lowered his head. His blessing was short, and his tone held an undercurrent of amusement that tempted Clara to kick him under the table.

Titus echoed his *amen* and reached for the bowl of eggs. "Ezra, I was wondering—"

Clara gritted her teeth. So Papa was Ezra, but she was Miss Frazier? Titus must be carrying a grudge. She wouldn't have expected such a thing from him.

"—do you enjoy playing checkers?"

Papa's eyebrows rose. "Why, yes, I do. I would say next to whist, checkers is my favorite game."

Titus stabbed a forkful of ham. "Whist? What's that?"

"A card game."

Titus shook his head, chuckling. "I'm not familiar with card games. The Mennonites avoid gambling games."

Papa laughed. "I avoid gambling games, too, son."

Clara gaped at him. *Son?*

"But whist is a game of skill and chance. No gambling involved."

Titus smiled. "Maybe you could teach me how to play."

"I would enjoy that, but whist requires four players."

"Oh." Titus cut away another bite of ham and chewed, his expression thoughtful. "Well then, since there are only two of us, I guess we'll have to stick to checkers."

Clara seethed. Only two? He and Papa acted as if she wasn't at the table at all. She thumped her fork onto the wood tabletop. "Excuse me. I believe Rowdy needs to go out."

Papa looked up in surprise. "Rowdy is still sleeping in his—"

Clara glared at him.

Papa gulped. "Never mind. Take him out."

She scooped the sleeping pup from his basket and stomped out the door with him, her nose in the air.

⁕

The week following the painting party proved miserable. The weather was lovely—clear skies and sweet-scented breezes tempted one to spend the entire day outdoors, basking in the pleasure of spring. But Clara couldn't enjoy the fresh air and enticing smells because everywhere she looked, she saw Titus. He was in bodily form in the field, holding tight to the tiller's handles behind the horse, and in spirit everywhere else she looked, both inside and out. She couldn't walk to the chicken house without noticing the white paint and thinking, *Titus arranged that.* While preparing meals, she inwardly questioned, *Will Titus like this?* As she hung clothes on the line, she recalled his caution about the smoky smell. When she worked in her vegetable garden, she squinted at the sun glancing from the wire fence and remembered, *Titus built it.* She even thought of him when she approached the outhouse, astounded at him thinking to make the little necessary dwelling match the house.

For reasons beyond her understanding, he began staying in the evening after supper and engaging Papa in a game of checkers, jackstraws, or twenty questions. The two laughed and carried on like longtime friends, and Clara battled a fierce jealousy as she watched from the other side of the room. Not once did either Titus or Papa invite her to join them, and as the days progressed, her envy grew, as did her confusion. She didn't want Titus to like her. Why, then, did it bother her so much that he ignored her? She didn't understand herself at all.

On Friday evening after Clara cleared the dishes, Papa spilled the jackstraws in the center of the table and then said, "Clara Rose, join us for a game."

She shot a startled look at him. "Me?"

"Why, sure." He seemed baffled. "Three people can play this game."

Then why hadn't she been included on previous evenings? She opened her mouth to decline, but other words spilled from her mouth. "All right."

She returned to her seat between Papa and Titus. She glanced from one man to the other.

Titus held his hand toward her. "Ladies first."

Clara reached for a straw.

Titus stacked his forearms on the table and sighed. "Ezra, I wish you could help Mr. Wiens. He had to turn down a request for a loan this week because he couldn't get out to the property and assess its value."

Two straws rolled away from the one she tried to move. She sat up. "Your turn, Papa."

Papa crouched and examined the pile. "I would be glad to help if I didn't have a field to tend and a crop to harvest." He managed to remove two straws before upsetting the stack.

Titus took his turn. "Even temporarily? While you're unable to work in the field?" He huffed when straws went rolling.

Clara snatched up the single straws from the edges of the pile and then searched for a likely one to slip free.

"Oh, I'm not sure that's a wise idea for me, Titus." Papa chuckled, the sound rueful. "Put me behind a desk in a bank again and I might be tempted to stay."

Clara jerked. Straws shifted. She gaped at her father. "Truly? You'd return to working as an accountant?"

Papa patted her arm. "Now, now, Clara Rose, no need to take on."

She leaned toward Papa. "But I didn't realize you missed your accounting job. I thought you wanted to try farming." Tears clouded her vision, making Papa's image swim. Had she forced Papa into something for which he had no desire?

"Of course I wanted to try something new, or I wouldn't have come here. But wanting to try something new doesn't mean I don't still miss the old." A sad smile formed on his face. "I enjoyed my job at the bank, talking with people every day, helping them. I suppose, even though I like our farmhouse and the openness around us, I will always look with fondness on the years I spent at the Minneapolis Bank and Trust Company."

"Why not do both?"

Clara had forgotten Titus was at the table. At his comment, she jerked and sent her straws into the pile. Straws flew in every direction.

Papa laughed, scooping them back into a pile. "I suppose we'll have to start this game again. Just as well since I wasn't winning."

Clara looked at him pointedly. "You didn't answer Titus's question."

Papa raised his eyebrows. "No. I suppose I didn't."

Clara turned to Titus. "How could Papa do both?"

He scratched his chin, appearing to think deeply. "Well, your farmhouse isn't so far from town that he couldn't go in each day for a few hours at the bank. And if he wanted to raise and harvest a crop out here, he could hire someone to help him. Much the way you hired me." He shrugged. "I could keep coming here. . .if you wanted."

Clara aimed an eager look on Papa. "What do you think?"

Papa pointed at him. "You have your own farm, young man. You've done us a great service by helping during my convalescence, but when I'm on my feet again, you'll need to see to your fields."

"There are four other Klaassen boys plenty big enough to help my pa. Besides, our farms are side by side. It wouldn't be difficult at all to work at both places if need be."

Excitement raised the pitch of Clara's voice. "Do you hear Titus, Papa? Remember what he told us about getting you to church—where there's a will, there's a way. If you want to work as an accountant again, we could find a way."

Papa held up both palms. "You are getting ahead of my thoughts, Clara Rose. Slow down, please."

The realization that Papa missed his former occupation stung her. He'd left Minneapolis for her, leaving behind his house, his friends, a job he enjoyed. She couldn't make him give up everything. She took his hand and squeezed. "Won't you talk to Mr. Wiens? Ask if you could be of help to him?"

"Well. . ."

"Please, Papa?"

Papa rolled his eyes and let out a huff of laughter. "Clara Rose, you know I can't say no when you look at me with those big, pleading eyes." He smiled. "All right. If you will drive me to town tomorrow, I'll go to the bank and talk to Mr. Wiens."

"Hurrah!" Clara's face flamed with the unladylike exclamation. She turned a sheepish look on Titus. "Please forgive my outburst. I'm happy for Papa."

He grinned.

She furrowed her brow. He'd worked as hard as ever this past week, but he'd hardly spoken to her. Maybe he'd rather not be her hired hand anymore. "Titus, did you mean it when you said you would continue to work here?"

He sobered, gazing intently into her eyes. "Do you want me to?"

As aggravated as she'd been with his distant behavior, she wanted to see him every day. Even if she couldn't be anything more than his boss's daughter or, at best, his friend, she wanted him here. She nodded.

Titus aimed his eyes upward and pinched his chin. "Well. . ."

She held her breath.

He looked at her. "I would be willing, but I don't think I could keep doing it without pay."

"Of course not!" Her lungful of air exploded with her answer.

"No, that wouldn't do," he went on as if she hadn't spoken, "unless I was part of the family."

Clara's mouth fell open.

Titus sent a glance across the table to Papa. Papa nodded—one quick, almost indiscernible bob of his head. Titus slipped from his chair and went down on one knee in front of her. He took her hands in his, his grip strong and steady. And dry.

"Clara, our acquaintance is short, but I feel as though you've been in my heart for years. The minute I saw you, I knew you were the one I've waited for. As I've prepared your field to receive corn, I've imagined being here to watch the cornstalks grow tall and to harvest the ears. I've imagined working alongside you and your father, and the imagining feels so right." His dear eyes glowed with love and desire. "Would you allow me to share the rest of your life with you, Clara? Would you become my wife?"

She'd received two proposals before, and her answer had caused the men to storm away. Even if it meant losing yet another beau, she had to be honest. "I love you, Titus, but I love my papa, too. This is his home. I can't send him from it."

"Not even to the addition Ma suggested and Pa helped me plan?"

"W–what?"

He released her to reach into his back pocket and withdraw a folded piece of paper. He laid it flat on her lap and pointed. "See? This is your house. There's plenty of land on the west side to build a two-story addition. The bottom part could be more bedrooms for the children who come along—"

Clara covered her warm cheeks with her palms.

"And the upstairs could be an apartment for your father." He lifted his attention from the paper. "Did you know that in Mennonite families, the grandparents often live with one of their adult children, bestow their wisdom on the grandchildren, and remain part of the family until the day God chooses to take them home?"

Clara's chest fluttered as if a dozen butterflies had been freed from their cocoons. She shook her head in wonder.

"We couldn't start building the addition until the area farmers have their fields planted, but after that, we could host a house-raising and have the walls and roof up in one day."

Clara wouldn't have believed such a thing if she hadn't witnessed last Saturday's transformation of the house.

"So what do you say, Clara? Will you marry me?"

He loved her enough to pour his sweat into her land. He loved her enough to share her with Papa. She hadn't known such a man existed, and here he knelt before her with sweet beseeching in his eyes of sky blue. The Lord had blessed her beyond anything she could have imagined.

She melted from the chair into his embrace. "Yes, Titus. Yes."

Chapter Fourteen

The summer months flew by, hot and humid but so busy and joy-filled Clara sang while she swatted mosquitoes and wiped sweat from her brow.

Her garden flourished, and Maria Klaassen helped her can the vegetables and line her cellar shelves with jars for the winter months. Together they picked apples and pears and dried the fruit on the metal roof of the barn's lean-to. Clara grew to love Maria almost as much as she loved Maria's son. She thanked God nightly for the chance to learn from another mother.

While Clara worked in the garden and house, Titus labored in the field and with the livestock. The pigs gained girth daily, and the corn-stalks grew straight and tall and yielded a bountiful harvest.

Each day, Papa mounted Penelope and rode to the bank, where he quickly gained popularity with the townsfolk. Always cheerful, always helpful, he made himself as much at home in Wilhelmina as he'd been in Minneapolis, and Clara reveled in his happiness.

The first Saturday of August, townsfolk converged for the second time at the Frazier farm and constructed the addition Titus had lovingly planned. On this day, Clara didn't stay in the house but milled among the workers, offering them glasses of cold water from the well and pausing to chat. Watching the walls go up was like watching her life being built strong and secure, and she couldn't wait until the day when she and Titus would cross the threshold as husband and wife.

After the workers departed, Clara roamed the yard, whistling for Rowdy. The pup had grown so much during the summer, losing his baby look and becoming lean and handsome. But as he left babyhood behind, he gained independence, venturing out for hours each day, often returning with a gopher or rabbit in his jaws. Twice he growled at Clara when she tried to take the carcass, and Titus gently warned her to let him be—he was born a wild thing, and she needed to allow him to become what God intended.

She whistled several more times, pausing between the shrill blasts to search the area. He didn't respond to her customary beckoning call, and her heart lurched in understanding.

Titus ambled from the barn, his stride long and his wind-ruffled hair shimmering in the evening sunlight. He crossed to her and slipped his arm around her shoulders. "He isn't coming." Not a question, but a statement.

Swallowing tears, she nodded. She rested her head against his shoulder. "I almost wish I hadn't found him. It hurts so to lose him."

"But you gave him something precious, Clara." Titus tightened his arm, pulling her snug against his side. "You gave him the chance to grow up and live freely. I think God brought him to you to be your company for the time you needed him. But now it's time to let him go."

She sighed. "I'll miss him."

Titus kissed the top of her head. "We both will."

Another month passed before the inside of the addition was finished and Papa moved his furnishings into his little apartment. As he carried his last box of belongings around the corner, he teasingly said, "All right, Clara Rose. Finish planning that wedding. I'm ready for grandchildren."

Clara needed no further prompting. Two weeks later, on a sunny September Saturday, the townsfolk of Wilhelmina gathered at the Mennonite Brethren church to witness the union of Titus Klaassen and Clara Frazier.

Maria had spent weeks tatting a lovely veil in white silk thread, so frothy and delicate, it might have been spun of spider webbing. In the corner of the church's foyer, behind a dressing screen that prohibited anyone from seeing Clara before she walked up the aisle, Maria arranged the veil over Clara's flowing hair, then stepped back and sighed. "Perfect."

Clara stared at her image in the round mirror hanging on the white plaster wall. Yes, perfect. Could that lovely, blushing woman—the one with stars in her eyes—truly be her? The tiny lines at the corners of her eyes, evidence that she was no longer a young girl, mattered not a bit. God had chosen her for Titus.

She nibbled her lip. "Maria, do you think I should wear the veil over my face instead?"

"Nä." Maria cupped Clara's cheeks and smiled. "No hiding today, dear Clara, not even behind a veil."

Clara had no desire to hide. Not today, or any other day for the rest of her life. And why should she? She was loved unconditionally by God. Her father adored her, her new family-to-be had accepted her wholeheartedly, and Titus. . . She sighed, closing her eyes to envision his sweet face, sky-blue eyes, and wavy blond hair. Titus had pledged his life to her. She was no longer the girl who'd lost two beaus but the girl who'd gained the world.

"Hmm." Maria pinched her chin the way Titus did when lost in thought. "You have the bouquet of cornflowers for your 'something blue,' your dress is the 'something old,' and the veil 'something new.' All we lack is 'something borrowed.' Unless you want your mother's wedding dress to serve as the something borrowed as well."

A giggle built in Clara's throat and erupted on a breathy note.

Maria tipped her head, smiling although confusion puckered her brow. "What?"

Clara picked up the thick cluster of delicate blue cornflowers tied with a yellow ribbon and held it against her waist. "I'll be meeting my 'something borrowed' at the front of the church in a few minutes."

Maria's confusion deepened.

Clara touched her arm. "My 'something borrowed' is the most important part of this wedding—it's my groom." Happy tears filled her eyes. "If you hadn't loaned me your son, I'd still be holding myself away from everyone, shamed and lonely. Thank you for letting me borrow Titus. Even more than my 'something borrowed,' he's my answer to prayer."

Maria leaned forward and brushed a kiss on Clara's cheek. "And you, my dear, are his."

A light tap on the screen intruded. Papa peeked around its edge. "Clara Rose, your groom is waiting. Are you ready?"

Joy ignited in Clara's breast. She dashed to him on silk-slipper-covered feet. "I'm ready, Papa." She stepped confidently and eagerly into the life especially designed for her by the Master's hands.

Acknowledgments

Mona Hodgson, Tracey Bateman, and Joanne Bischoff—thank you so much for the opportunity to work with you on this set. It has been a joy and pleasure.

Facebook friend Karen Beams—thank you for naming Rowdy!

Mom—thank you for letting me borrow some of your family names and your love for Minnesota.

My agent, Tamela—thank you for your support and encouragement at all times and in all ways.

Kaisyn and Kendall—thanks for giving Gramma giggle-breaks in the middle of writing this novella.

Finally, and most importantly, God—thank You for Your love even when we choose the wrong pathway and for Your patient guidance that brings us back on track. I couldn't take two steps without You. May any praise or glory be reflected directly to You.

In 1966, **Kim Vogel Sawyer** told her kindergarten teacher that some-day people would check out her book in libraries. That little-girl dream came true in 2006 with the release of *Waiting for Summer's Return*. Since then, Kim has watched God expand her dream beyond her childhood imaginings. With over thirty titles on library shelves and more than a million copies of her books in print, she enjoys a full-time writing and speaking ministry. Empty-nesters, Kim and her retired military husband, Don, operate a bed-and-breakfast inn in small-town Kansas with the help of their four feline companions. When she isn't writing, Kim stays active serving in her church's women's and music ministries, traveling with "The Hubs," and spoiling her quiverful of grand-darlings. You can learn more about Kim's writing at www.KimVogelSawyer.com.

Something Blue

Mona Hodgson

Chapter One

Cripple Creek, Colorado
March 13, 1900

D arla Taggart had no sooner stepped off the platform at the Midland Terminal Railroad Station than second thoughts set her heart to pounding. What had come over her that she believed returning to Cripple Creek was a favorable notion? Especially in the month of March.

Her past.

Adjusting her grip on the handle of her green floral satchel, Darla flexed her toes, then forced one laced-up bootie in front of the other to the edge of Bennett Avenue. She only needed to remain in town long enough to take care of unfinished business and to see if she had a future here.

Darla waited for a wagon and its team of mules to pass, then crossed the main road through town and stepped onto the brick walkway in front of a millinery shop. She'd left Cripple Creek in the middle of the rebuilding process that followed two devastating fires in '96, and she took a moment to look at how the city had changed. Rows of tidy brick buildings and cobblestone sidewalks showed the city's beautification efforts. Empty flower baskets hung from electric streetlamps, anticipating the arrival of spring. Pulling her mantle collar up on her neck, Darla hoped her favorite season held new life for her as well.

A minimal amount of time would be required to walk the extra blocks to the First Congregational Church and the parsonage that harbored the secrets of her failings. But she couldn't do anything about it right now. It was best she start with the boardinghouse and plan to entertain other endeavors when she was refreshed and rested.

At First National Bank, Darla started up Fourth Street and turned left onto Golden Avenue. Brick-lined flower beds full of budding irises framed the walkway in front of Miss Hattie's Boardinghouse, still a bold yellow with white trim. Some things hadn't changed. As Darla took slow steps toward the expansive porch, she couldn't help but hope some things had. She hadn't exactly endeared herself to the woman who had behaved like a mother to the Sinclair sisters. A mother hen, actually. The image her imagination conjured made her giggle.

A tinny but lively orchestral piece poured out of the open window to the left of the door. Darla doubted she'd be heard over the music, but she reached for the brass knocker anyway. The porter would arrive soon with her trunk, and she was in desperate need of a bath and a clean ensemble. After nearly a week on one train and then another, she also craved rest.

Following her third knock, the song faded and the door swung open. Miss Hattie stood on the other side of the threshold. "I hope you haven't been waiting—" Her blue-gray eyes widened with recognition. "Darla Taggart?"

"Yes, ma'am." Darla's words hung in the chilling air.

"What are you doing here, dear?" Miss Hattie tucked a gray curl behind her ear. "I mean to say—"

"I have a reservation for a room."

"Here?"

"Yes, ma'am. I telephoned."

"When?"

"Starting tonight."

A nervous titter escaped Miss Hattie. "I meant, when did you telephone?"

"Oh, of course." Darla rested her satchel on the porch railing and reached for the clasp. "Two or three weeks ago, I think it was. I wrote it down." She'd tucked the note into her handbag. "I spoke to a man."

"You spoke to my husband?"

"You're married?"

"Yes. It was well after you left town. Thanksgiving Day in '98, to be exacting."

Darla glanced at the golden band on Hattie's ring finger. She'd left in the fall of '96. And now it seemed everyone was married but her.

At the sound of footfalls, Hattie glanced over her shoulder. A rather dapper gentleman wearing a gray, single-breasted coat and trousers appeared in the doorway, tapping his earlobes. "My ears are burning."

Hattie wagged her finger at him. "That's because Miss Taggart and I were talking about you."

"All good things, I hope." He smiled at Darla. "Good afternoon, ma'am. Miss Taggart, you say?"

Darla nodded in unison with Hattie.

"A Miss Taggart telephoned for a room. Are you that young lady?"

"Yes, sir. I am."

"You didn't write it in the book." Hattie sounded like an unhappy schoolmarm.

"Oh dear." He smoothed the blue cravat tucked into his vest. "She called on a morning I was sitting Vivian's twins. I'm afraid this grampy wasn't thinking clearly and forgot to record the reservation." He shifted his attention to Darla. "My deep apologies for the mix-up, miss."

"Apologies accepted." Darla rubbed the tension knot forming at the base of her skull. "Do you have a room available?"

Hattie's gaze darted to her husband. "Uh. Yes. We do."

Darla's shoulders sagged. "But you don't have a room for me."

The husband's silvering eyebrows formed an arc above his blue eyes. "If we have a room available, why wouldn't we have a room *for you*?"

Darla sighed. "Because of Kat Sinclair and her Dr. Cutshaw, is my way of thinking."

The man straightened, his shoulders square. "Because of Kat? I don't understand."

It hardly seemed proper for him to use Mrs. Cutshaw's given name. Terribly familiar, even for the husband of Kat's former landlady.

Hattie tugged the sleeves straight on her purple floral shirtwaist. "Miss Taggart used to live in Cripple Creek. At the parsonage."

"Ah, the former parson's daughter?"

"Yes." Hattie moistened her lips. "For a time, she and Kat were interested in the same man."

An understatement where Darla was concerned.

The older woman patted her husband's woolen-clad arm, then

looked up at Darla. "Miss Taggart, I'd like you to meet Mr. Harlan Sinclair."

Sinclair. Darla's mouth went dry. In only the time it took a hen to cackle, things had gone from bad to worse. Hattie had married Kat's father. Pulling her satchel from the railing, Darla heaved a sigh. "I'll make other arrangements for lodging."

"That won't be necessary, dear." Hattie swatted the air. "That was then, and this is now. We believe in fresh starts, don't we, Mister?"

"We do." Mr. Sinclair's smile didn't make it to his eyes, but they held more curiosity than anything else.

After a quick nod, Hattie met Darla's gaze. "Much has changed in the past three or four years." She arched her eyebrows as if she'd meant her statement as a question.

"Yes, ma'am, it has. I have."

"Good. Then it's only water under the bridge, and I say we don't tarry in it. No need to soak good stockings." Hattie took a backward step and waved Darla inside.

Darla's feet didn't oblige. Apparently, second-guessing her decisions related to Cripple Creek was forever to be her path. She hadn't come to cause trouble, but she couldn't promise that her presence wouldn't be troublesome, especially if she didn't get to her diary before someone else did. These two seemed none the wiser. Maybe it hadn't been discovered.

Darla knew why she'd chosen Miss Hattie's Boardinghouse—its proximity to the new hospital, as well as its location up on the Hill and its creature comforts. But could she feel comfortable here knowing Mr. Sinclair, Morgan Cutshaw's father-in-law, lived under the same roof? Knowing that he knew she'd been a thorn in his daughter's side, even if he didn't know any of the embarrassing details? Or at least didn't know them yet.

"Please, Miss Taggart"—Mr. Sinclair took the satchel from Darla—"do come in."

It seemed too late to make other plans, so Darla set her concerns aside and followed Hattie inside. Oak wainscoting lined the entryway. Her gaze settled on a painting that featured a peaceful stretch of a river.

That was what she needed to find. A place that held peace for her. She doubted Cripple Creek could ever be that place, but if she got what she came back for, maybe—

"I must say, Miss Taggart, as the father of four daughters, I've never known a woman to travel so light." Thinly disguising a grin, Mr. Sinclair tipped his head toward Hattie. "Present company included." Her landlady tsked at her husband, wagging her finger at him.

Darla smiled. Mr. Sinclair was a likable man and seemed well suited to Hattie. "Trust me, my father wouldn't count me among any who travel light. I expect the porter to arrive at any moment with my trunk."

"In the meantime, I'll make us some tea." Hattie stopped at the open doorway into the parlor. "We have lots of catching up to do, dear. I want to hear all about your time in Philadelphia. Oh, and your family. . .I want to hear about them, too."

"Missus." Mr. Sinclair paused, apparently waiting for Hattie's undivided attention. "Perhaps we could allow Miss Taggart to see her room and give her a few moments to settle in before the interrogation?" He winked at his wife, then smiled at Darla. "I remember that long train ride. I couldn't wait to get my legs under me and freshen up a bit."

Darla nodded. "I do appreciate your gracious hospitality, ma'am. But a rest would be nice, if you don't mind."

"Of course." Hattie glanced toward the spiral staircase. "You go on up, and I'll bring a cup of tea to the room for you."

"Thank you." Darla followed Mr. Sinclair and her bag to the second floor, all the while wondering about the odds that anyone else in town might share Hattie's water-under-the-bridge sentiment. Especially if her penned flights of fancy had been discovered.

She'd soon find out. Her new job started tomorrow.

───────◆───────

Nearly two hours later, Darla had settled into her room, hung the dresses from her trunk in the wardrobe, and enjoyed a delicious soak in a copper tub. Oh, how pleasant it felt to shed her travel gown and feel clean again! She still looked forward to the long rest that would follow supper, but she wasn't opposed to a home-cooked meal first. The memory of Hattie's culinary skills from dishes sampled at church gatherings drove Darla's steps down the oak stairs and into the dining room.

Mr. Sinclair smiled, standing behind a chair at one end of a long table. "Good evening, Miss Taggart."

She looked up from the four chinaware place settings. "And to you, Mr. Sinclair. Thank you."

A door behind him swung open, and a girl Darla guessed to be age nine or ten sauntered in, carrying a meat-laden platter.

"Cherise, dear, this is our new boarder, Miss Darla Taggart."

Cherise set the platter on a trivet and looked up. "I'm pleased to meet you, Mademoiselle Taggart." A curtain of straight dark hair framed eyes the color of an onyx gem.

Seeing a child in the home, especially one with a French accent, piqued Darla's curiosity. There weren't place settings for her parents, and she seemed quite at home.

Mr. Sinclair stepped around the table and pulled out a chair for Darla. "Our girl is from Paris. We met while I was working there."

"Father"—Cherise glanced up at Mr. Sinclair—"knew my mama and papa. Before they died."

Darla pressed her hand to the chiffon ruffle at her neckline. Mr. Sinclair and Hattie had taken the girl in, leaving Darla with no doubt that she had come to a welcoming home. "I'm pleased to meet you, Cherise."

"And I am pleased to meet you." Cherise slid into the chair beside Darla. "I'm ten. Not as big as you, but I'm glad to see another girl here."

Darla offered Cherise a smile and opened her mouth to say something.

"Coming through." Hattie whooshed into the room with a bread basket that smelled of honey and butter and set it down in front of Darla, effectively interrupting her train of thought as her mouth began to water.

At the sound of Mr. Sinclair's *amen*, dishes started to clatter. Hattie handed Darla a dish of glazed carrots. "Dear, I'm anxious to hear your news."

Darla scooped carrots onto her plate and passed them. "Mother and Father are still living in Syracuse, New York."

Hattie set a slice of pork roast on her plate and handed her the platter. "Still pastoring?"

"He is." Darla reached for her water glass. "And Mother still plays the piano and teaches the children."

"And your brother?"

"Peter is seventeen now. He can tell you all about who the league baseball players are and give you their numbers. And when I last saw him, at Christmas, he was still as ornery as ever."

Hattie tittered. "And your schooling in Philadelphia? You completed your courses?"

"I did. I'm a trained nurse now." Darla scooped a bite of mashed potatoes and gravy onto her fork. "Tomorrow I start my new job at the hospital."

"Oh?"

"Yes. When I completed my courses, I responded to an advertisement for nurses here and sent an application to Dr. Boyd."

Hattie darted a glance at her husband before replying. "Dr. Boyd obviously sent a favorable response."

"He did." A positive reply, in sharp contrast to Mr. and Mrs. Harlan Sinclair's tentative responses to the news of her employment. Was it because they distrusted her? Or were they concerned with how Kat and her doctor husband would respond to her presence in town and at the hospital?

Or did Hattie know more than she'd let on?

"Have you returned to the parsonage yet?" Hattie asked.

"Not yet. But depending upon my work schedule, I hope to see it in the next few days."

"You'll see it Sunday, I expect, if not before."

Of course she'd be expected to attend services at her father's former parish. Part of her wanted to, despite the bittersweet memories, but experience told her the parson's family would be in the sanctuary for the duration of the service. Sunday morning might be the perfect opportunity to retrieve her diary and Gram's cameo pendant from beneath the kitchen floorboards in the parsonage.

Chapter Two

After her best night of sleep in weeks, Darla tucked her folded nurse's cap into her handbag, then pulled her woolen mantle over her white, ankle-length uniform. She carefully set the hood atop her upswept hair, slid her hands into white leather gloves, and opened the front door.

She stepped onto the porch and down the front steps under gray skies. Mr. Sinclair had shoveled snow from the walkway, but a layer still blanketed the flower bed and the street in front of her. Fortunately the overnight snowfall had abated, and she didn't have far to walk.

Taking careful steps west on Golden Avenue, Darla allowed herself to daydream about making a difference in the surgery and recovery wards at the hospital. A mine whistle blew, nearly causing her to lose her footing. She'd been gone from the Cripple Creek Mining District for three and a half years. Long enough to forget the city's morning call to its mine workers.

At the corner, Darla turned left onto Third Street and gazed up at the new three-story brick building that sat atop the hill. The Sisters of Mercy Hospital was conveniently close to the boardinghouse, which was especially handy in stormy weather.

Inside, a stoic woman seated behind a library table directed Darla to the second floor, where she waited across the desk from an empty chair in Dr. Boyd's office. He apparently favored clutter. Books sat two-deep on sagging shelves. Framed photographs lined the top of his desk, and a marble bust of a woman hid the top of a file cabinet.

There was a good chance Dr. Cutshaw would see *her* as clutter. A nuisance from his past. But she would convince Dr. Boyd to assign her to a job that wouldn't require her to cross paths with the doctor from

Boston any more than was absolutely necessary. She was here for something else. Maybe even for someone else.

"Miss Taggart."

The accent was unmistakable. So much for avoiding him.

Darla stood to face Dr. Cutshaw. "I was supposed to meet with Dr.—"

"Dr. Boyd broke his leg two days ago and is at home, recuperating."

That could explain the look Hattie and her husband had shared when she'd told them Dr. Boyd had hired her. They likely knew about the accident and that Dr. Cutshaw would be working in his stead.

He walked toward the chair on the other side of the cluttered desk but didn't sit down.

"I'm sorry to hear that," Darla said, "but Dr. Boyd offered me a job. And I made a very long journey by train from Philadelphia with the promise of—"

Dr. Cutshaw raised his hand, stopping the flow of her words. "I know about the job offer, Miss Taggart, and I have the work assignment for you."

"Oh." Darla thought to seat herself but decided against it. If she had her way, she'd be out of there and in her assigned ward within moments.

Clearing his throat, Dr. Cutshaw pressed his fingertips to the edge of the desk. "First things first, if you don't mind, Miss Taggart."

What could be more important than telling her about the ward where she'd be spending her days? Or nights.

"You need to know that I'm married. To Kat Sinclair, now Mrs. Morgan Cutshaw."

There was her answer—no, she wouldn't be able to live down her past. With or without the diary's content exposed. But she did have a job, and she wished to keep it.

"Yes. You and Kat Sinclair married before I left town."

"And now we have two children."

"Congratulations." Darla swallowed a sigh. She was twenty-one years of age and never married. But that could change if Zachary had waited for her like he said he would.

"Thank you." He lifted a folder from the top of a pile on the desk. "But I wasn't soliciting your congratulations."

She met his pointed gaze. "You have no need for concern, Dr. Cutshaw." She wanted it to be true for both their sakes. That was why she had to get the diary back. Soon.

"Very well, then, let's talk about your assignment." He opened the folder.

"Yes." She removed her gloves. "I told Dr. Boyd I did my specialty training in the operating room. But I'm also good with recovering patients. I'm not very good with children."

"We have several patients who have been discharged from hospital care but still need some looking after. I have assigned you to home-care visits."

She stiffened, and a glove slipped from her hands. "Home visits?"

"Yes. I have three patients who require a visit from you today."

"I won't be working at the hospital?"

"Occasionally, perhaps." Dr. Cutshaw handed her a stack of papers. "When there's no call for home visits. And, of course, you'll come in for your assignments and to turn in your reports. You'll work with Dr. Boyd's clerk, Mrs. Kingston."

"When Dr. Boyd offered me the job, he didn't say anything about having to traipse around town to care for patients."

"I am the one in charge, Miss Taggart."

Indeed. And he'd immediately banished her to the streets of Cripple Creek.

Nicolas listened to the patter of feet and the chatter of his three daughters cleaning up after breakfast. Maria would've been so proud of them. Not one of their girls older than his favorite pair of boots and each had pitched in and done their part since the accident.

"Papa! It's snowing again!" Jaya's voice rose with each syllable.

He lifted his head from the cot, careful not to anger the scabs on his back. He glanced past his daughters and out the window over the dish sink. Big snowflakes tumbled from a gray sky.

"I can't see good. It's too high." Julia, barely seven, darted toward the window by the front door.

"The flakes are so big and fluffy." Jaya faced him, her smile outshining the bare bulb lighting above. "Can we all go outside and make a snowman, Papa?"

He'd like nothing more right now, but—

"Don't be silly." Jocelyn clicked her tongue, ever the big sister. "If Papa can't work or add coal to the stove, he certainly can't play in the snow."

Nicolas swallowed hard against the sadness threatening to settle on him. With the exception of a kindly neighbor or two, he was all Jocelyn, Jaya, and Julia had. Then nearly two weeks ago, in the bowels of the mine, he'd been rendered helpless, and no one could say for how long.

"We can make a snowman as a surprise, and Papa can see it when he feels better and can get up again." His dear Jaya, ever the idealist.

"Perhaps the snowman can wait until Mrs. Nell stops by to check on us." Nicolas laid his head on the cot, facing the countertop where Jocelyn washed a pan and Jaya dried a bowl, his nerves tingling from his bandaged shoulders to his trousers.

"Look! It's an angel." Julia was his dreamer, seeing dancing animals and such in the clouds.

"An angel in the clouds?" Nicolas felt a smile tug at his mouth. "Or an angel in the snowflakes?" After the steam hose broke down in the mine, he'd half expected to see an angel waiting to take him for his reunion with Maria.

"It's a real angel, Papa." Excitement trumped the frustration in Julia's shrill voice. "And she's coming to our door."

"Let me see." The pan made a splash, and Jocelyn marched toward the window. "See her hat? That's a nurse."

"But she's all dressed in white, even the bag she's carrying." Leave it to Jaya to try to smooth any hurt feelings. "She does look like an angel."

Nicolas raised his head but couldn't twist far enough to see through the window on the other side of the door. He hadn't forgotten Dr. Cutshaw's ultimatum. If he wanted to go home, he had to agree to home visits. But he wasn't expecting someone so soon. "Let her in, Jocelyn. Dr. Cutshaw said he'd send a nurse over to change my bandages." With all the speed of a tortoise, he inched his left leg to the edge of the cot.

The door swung open, welcoming in a blast of cold air that set his back to stinging and stopped his progress.

"Please come in, ma'am." Jocelyn was a capable woman of the household, but she was only ten and shouldn't have to fill that role at such a young age.

"Are you certain it's all right?" The voice belonged to a young woman.

"I'm certain, ma'am. My papa is expecting you."

That wasn't exactly true. He'd expected the gruff gray-haired nurse from his hospital ward. Not a young woman.

"Very well, then." The woman who stepped over the threshold did look a bit angelic, dressed in white from her creased hat to her button-up boots. And familiar. When the door clicked shut behind her, she set her leather satchel on a chair, then glanced at the stove on the far wall. "The heat feels good on a day like today. Thank you."

"You're so pretty." His youngest daughter was always generous with compliments.

The woman in white turned away from him, tucked her gloves into a pocket in her mantle and hung it on a peg near the door. "Thank you, Miss..."

"Julia."

"You're pretty, too, Miss Julia." The young woman turned her attention to Nicolas.

He needed to get up. . .to show her he was fine without her help. He was scooting toward the edge of the cot when the nurse raised her hand.

"Please. Stay where you are." She pulled a folder from the satchel. "You are Mr. Nicolas Zanzucchi?"

"I am." He forced himself to lie still. "And you are Miss Taggart. Leastwise, that was your name when you and your father called on us after my Maria died."

"Yes. My name hasn't changed." A slight frown curved her mouth. "I remember our visits."

Nicolas nodded. He remembered being newly widowed with three daughters to care for. And he recalled Miss Taggart's obvious misery at the time. Her father had insisted she join him on his calls in Poverty Gulch. Granted, she was only seventeen then and in school, but Nicolas doubted she'd find even this level of modest company housing any less distasteful.

"Mr. Zanzucchi, I am the nurse assigned to visit you. Here in your home." She glanced around the room, then looked at him. "It is my job to see to your medical needs."

If her name hadn't changed, then she was not married. Except for bandages and a light blanket, he was naked from the waist up. Having her here taking care of him like this wouldn't be right. "I'm afraid I'm not comfortable with that arrangement, Miss Taggart."

Her eyes widened.

"You're too young." And Julia was right—the nurse *was* pretty.

Miss Taggart's shoulders squared, bobbing the little folded hat perched on a pile of chestnut-brown curls. "Let me assure you, Mr. Zanzucchi, that I am old enough to be a trained nurse. Old enough to cross the country on my own. And plenty old enough to change your bandages and help you recover from your burns."

Darla Taggart wasn't crusty like his gray-haired nurse at the hospital, but she seemed no less determined. He drew in a deep breath. "I don't doubt your training or your abilities."

"You don't?"

"No, ma'am." Oh how he wished he could sit up without setting off alarms in his back. He rolled onto his hip bone and peered up at her. "I'm sure you'd do a fine job. It's just that I'm not certain this arrangement would be proper."

"I see." The pink tint on Miss Taggart's face deepened to rose. "I assure you, sir, I am a medical professional and would only do what was necessary to perform my medical obligations."

Nicolas lay back down, resigned to the pain over propriety. His three daughters stood behind Miss Taggart like a row of chicks behind a mother hen, and the image gave him pause.

Jocelyn stepped forward and stood beside Miss Taggart. "We will all be here, Papa."

That was his concern. He was trying to raise his daughters the way Maria would—with proper decorum. What if—

The nurse glanced around. "In addition, Mr. Zanzucchi, we are in the main room of the house."

A valid point. He spent his days on the cot in the main room, not in his bedchamber.

"For your well-being, sir, I believe it best that you set your apprehension aside and let me look after your wounds and bandages."

Nicolas raised his torso onto the ball of his right shoulder so he could look her in the eye. "It doesn't seem I have any choice."

All four of the women, the oldest two with arms crossed over their chests, shook their heads in unison.

"Very well, then. If we're going to give it a try, proper introductions are in order. Or reintroductions, as the case might be." He pointed to his daughters, starting with the youngest. "Miss Taggart, you're already acquainted with Julia, who is seven. The next oldest is Jaya, nine. And the oldest is Jocelyn, age ten, the one who let you in."

"It's a pleasure, girls." Miss Taggart shifted her green-eyed gaze to him. "You won't regret it, Mr. Zanzucchi."

He already did.

She was a trained medical professional. She could do this.

Darla focused on those statements as facts on her way to the chair near the door. She retrieved her bag, then carried it and the spindle chair to the cot where Mr. Zanzucchi lay watching her every move.

He obviously remembered her priggish, dreadful outlook on him and his living conditions when she accompanied her father to Poverty Gulch. Something her father had given up on after only two visits. At the time, visiting the poor seemed a sharp punishment. Something she'd no doubt conveyed to Mr. Zanzucchi, who was now her reluctant patient.

Setting the chair about two feet from the head of the bed, Darla drew in a fortifying breath and opened her patient's medical file. "Mr. Zanzucchi, I will need to remove your bandages and examine your back, but before I do that, I need to ask you a few questions for your hospital record."

"If you must."

"Good. Thank you." But for an occasional wince, she couldn't tell if he was angered by her presence, in pain, or just uncomfortable. His brown eyes weren't giving anything away. She withdrew a pencil from her bag and pulled the first form she needed to complete from the file folder. "I understand Dr. Cutshaw brought you home from the Sisters of Mercy Hospital just two days ago, the twelfth of March."

"Yes, Monday afternoon."

"And you live here with your three daughters. No one else?"

"Not unless you count the possum living under the floor."

Darla lifted her feet from the linoleum with such speed that the folder slid to the floor.

Her patient's baritone chuckle sparked a round of giggles from all three of his daughters.

"Do we really have a possum, Papa?" Jaya spoke with unbridled enthusiasm. "It lives here?"

While Darla regained her composure, Jocelyn set a hand on her hip. "He was teasing."

Darla planted both feet on the floor and met Mr. Zanzucchi's gaze. He'd cradled his head in his folded right arm. A curl the color of Mother's devil's food cake draped his forehead. "I suppose I deserved that. You obviously well recall my visits from four years back."

"I don't know that you deserved it, but it was fun." He peered over the side of the cot. "I do apologize, though. I didn't mean to upset your paperwork."

"No harm done." Darla bent to retrieve the folder. She thought about making a note in regard to Mr. Zanzucchi's lighthearted teasing as a sign of good humor, not something easy to come by in his condition, but she didn't want Dr. Cutshaw to misunderstand her intentions toward her patient.

He straightened on the cot. "Time we got back to your questions, I suppose."

"Yes." Darla found her place in the notes. "The accident that caused the affliction took place down in the Mollie Kathleen Mine?"

His face went slack. "Yes. Two weeks this Saturday coming. I'm a steam drill operator. Or was."

Darla's hand stilled on the page. What was Mr. Zanzucchi to do if he couldn't return to his work in the mine? He had to heal completely so he could provide for his family.

She'd see to it.

"A hose broke, spraying hot steam into the shaft. I jerked around so my back would take the brunt of it." He scrubbed his whiskered cheek. "That's probably more than you needed to know."

Darla shook her head, hoping to rid her mind of the horrid image. "It's helpful for me to know what happened to cause your injuries."

"Your father said he was moving to New York. Is he still there?"

"Yes. Upstate." She looked down at the list of questions. "Has anyone examined your burns or changed your bandages?"

"Dr. Cutshaw changed them himself on Monday. Not since then." He glanced at his daughters, who had busied themselves with various chores. "They have more than enough to do since I'm not able to help."

"Then you understand the risk should you try to do too much?"

He sighed, lifting the curl on his forehead. "The good doctor schooled me in the danger of ripping my scabs." He spoke just above a whisper, no doubt for the benefit of his daughters.

"It seems you're doing a good job of protecting your back."

"I'm trying. But I can't promise how long I'll be able to lie around here doing nothing."

Darla's spine stiffened. "For as long as necessary to assure your complete recovery."

Another sigh of resignation escaped her reluctant patient. "You left Cripple Creek not long after your last visit to the Gulch. You took your nurse's training in the East?"

It was her job to ask the questions, but if asking her a few put him at ease before the examination, she'd happily answer as many as it took.

"I lived with my aunt in Philadelphia and trained at St. Luke's there."

"I have no doubt the refined city holds more opportunity for a young woman such as yourself."

"A young woman such as yourself." Single? Prissy? Scheming? Darla added a period to the page a bit too forcefull,y then looked up. "I'm not the same girl who followed her father around." *Or Dr. Cutshaw.*

"I'm sure not. But why would you choose to return to the wild mountains of Colorado? Alone?"

"I called Cripple Creek my home for most of my childhood." No one needed to know her other reasons for returning. She'd answered enough of Mr. Zanzucchi's questions. She had two more homes to visit today. Other patients to get to know.

Darla closed the folder on the list of questions and stood. If she didn't move this along—

"Forgive me," Mr. Zanzucchi said. "I think I'm a bit nervous. Maria was the one who was sick. Until now, I've never been the patient."

"That's understandable." She set the folder on the chair. "You will get past this, Mr. Zanzucchi."

"If I follow orders."

"Precisely." Darla lifted her leather bag off the floor and set it on the chair. "I'd like to remove your bandages now and take a look."

He flattened onto his stomach against the cot, his arms at his side. Darla opened her bag wide, then took slow steps to the stove, where a kettle of water simmered.

"I have a clean bowl ready for you." Jocelyn pointed to the sideboard. "There. The lye soap is in the dish next to it."

"You already knew I'd need to sterilize my hands?"

"Yes, ma'am. I paid close attention to every word Dr. Cutshaw said to Papa when he brought him home."

Jocelyn Zanzucchi had the body of a child but had assumed the responsibilities of someone much older. While the girl busied herself pulling a towel from a basket at the end of the counter, Darla poured hot water into the bowl.

Her hands thoroughly washed and dried, she went to Mr. Zanzucchi's side and lifted the thin blanket. Cloth strips covered the bandages that spanned from his shoulders to the waistband on his trousers. Myriad footfalls sounded behind her, drawing her attention to three pairs of matching brown eyes.

"I don't want the girls to see. . .any of it." Mr. Zanzucchi didn't move.

"You heard your papa." Darla motioned them away.

"It stopped snowing." Jocelyn placed a hand on Jaya's and Julia's shoulders, directing them toward the door. "Let's bring in more coal before it starts up again. Then we can see to our lessons for school."

When the girls stepped outside and the door clicked shut, Darla turned to her patient. "Unwrapping the cloth holding the bandages in place is going to be the hardest part. I'll need you to raise up off the cot some. Carefully."

"I can do it."

Tucking his elbows under his chest, Mr. Zanzucchi slowly raised his torso. Bent at the knees, he kept his back straight. Darla quickly rolled back the strip of cloth, revealing the crusted gauze bandages. As soon as she pulled the last of the cloth from his back, her patient sank onto the cot with a groan.

She could only imagine what his damaged nerves had to say. She sprinkled some warm water onto the yellowed gauze to soften it, then gently pulled it off, layer by layer. Removing the last layer, she was relieved to find a solid coating of brown scab, though shocked at its extent.

"Does it look as ghastly as it feels?"

Darla pulled the jar of petroleum jelly from her bag. "I'm certain it looks far better than it did when it was buried beneath angry blisters." She traced the edge of the scabs with her fingertips, then gently rested her palm on top of it, checking for any sign of fever. "Actually, there's a solid covering of scabs, with no open wounds, and we want to keep it that way." She spread a light amount of the jelly at the outer edge of the scabbing to keep it soft and prevent pulling. "As difficult as it must be to remain inactive, that's going to be your saving grace. We don't want any rips or tears in the scabbing." As she laid clean bandages atop the scabs, Mr. Zanzucchi relaxed into the cot.

"It appears that you're the right one for this job."

She hoped so, because she wanted to see this man mended. As much as she resented Dr. Cutshaw's assignment mere hours ago, she was now personally invested in the widowed father's recovery.

Chapter Three

D arla had walked the hills and valleys to patients' homes under blue skies for the past two weeks, but not on this Monday morning. In the early hours, winter showed its reluctance to give way to spring, dumping three inches of snow before breakfast.

The temperature hadn't climbed more than a degree or two since she'd left the Zanzucchi home and called on a mother and her fifth baby, this one delivered by Caesarean section. However, the snow had let up, and the sun was clearing the skies, tempting her to take a detour between home visits to stop in at Pfeiffer's Haberdashery. She'd been in town for almost three weeks and still didn't know if Zachary Pfeiffer had married Emily Updike, the banker's beautiful and wealthy niece who had come to town just weeks before she'd left. Chances were high that he'd acquiesced to his father's wishes that he marry someone highly respectable with means. A parson's daughter was hardly considered a good catch monetarily.

Darla sighed. Part of her wished Zachary hadn't married and still wanted to marry her. If for no other reason than to assuage her guilt. But another part of her hoped he had married, so she wouldn't have to think about it anymore.

With or without Zachary, she needed to find a way to move past the shameful things she had done as a rebellious teenager. Which was why coming up with a plan to recover her diary was a priority. That fact spurred her steps toward the First Congregational Church.

The white steeple came into view first. Stopping at the diagonal corner, Darla viewed the place where she'd spent Sundays and many other long days for ten years of her childhood. The white trim on the redbrick building looked summer fresh despite the patches of snow on the ledges and the neatly manicured grounds. It all looked smaller than she remembered. Even the front steps she and Peter had raced up and down didn't appear as high or as wide. It was especially small in comparison to Aunt Cora's church in Philadelphia, which spread a city block.

A glint of color drew Darla's gaze to the windows. Her mind's eye hadn't diminished the splendor of the stained glass. She watched as the afternoon light favored the southern window with sunbeams that made the white lamb in Jesus' arms glow.

Darla waited for an ice wagon to pass, then took careful steps across the slushy street. Her heart pounded as she stared at the tall gloss-white double doors and stained-glass lunette above them. If she climbed the steps and revisited the sanctuary, would she hear Father's voice rise in the heat of a sermon? See Mother's fingers fumble on the piano keys in a painfully slow rendition of "Just As I Am"? Smell wax as she remembered lighting the Advent candles with her friend Betty? Or would the memories carry her to the basement where she'd tasted Zachary's lips and seen the disgust in her father's eyes?

A shiver ran up her spine, and she shook her head. She would save the walk down memory lane for another day. Darla pulled her mantle tighter and tucked the medical bag against her, then walked to the other side of the church. The flower beds Mother had tended lay buried under a fresh blanket of snow, which should bode well for the tulips and irises waiting for spring.

Behind the church building, the parsonage looked much the same, although a paintbrush had recently found its white trim. Snow dappled the rosebushes Mother had planted to line the gravel walkway. Seeing the aspen tree reminded Darla of the time she'd climbed its branches to get away from Peter, only to be startled by a chiding squirrel on the branch above her and tumble to the ground. Mother had given her a second cup of hot cocoa with crème as a consolation. And there was the time Father taught her to play croquet on the lawn. One of her favorite days at the parsonage.

Unfortunately, they weren't all pleasant memories. That was what had driven her to bury her reproachful diary and the cameo pendant she'd intended to wear at the wedding that didn't happen. Why hadn't she thought to hide them beneath the aspens instead of tucking them away under the kitchen floorboards? She couldn't see it in her youth, but Mother was right—she did possess a flair for melodrama. Nevertheless, she needed to retrieve the diary before someone else did. And she didn't wish to raise any more eyebrows or awaken the rumor mill in so doing. She'd come back another time when she was sure the new parson and his family were away.

A door creaked open, and Darla looked up. A woman stood on the parsonage porch cradling a sleeping baby. She offered Darla a warm smile. "Good day."

"And to you."

The woman stepped off the porch, her gaze fixed on Darla's hat. "You're a nurse?"

"Yes, ma'am." Darla took slow steps up the gravel walkway, then stopped in front of the unadorned China rosebush her father had planted for Mother's birthday. "I'm Darla Taggart, the former parson's daughter."

"Oh, then it's especially nice to meet you." A smile lit her blue eyes. "I'm Ida Raines. My husband is Reverend Tucker Raines."

"I'm pleased to meet you, Mrs. Raines." Her new acquaintance looked vaguely familiar, but Darla was certain they'd never met. She'd already left Cripple Creek before Father decided to move and had found his replacement.

"Please call me Ida." She looked back at the parsonage. "I'm already late for tea with family, or I'd invite you in."

"Thank you. You're very kind."

"You know"—Ida's eyebrows arched—"if you'd like to see the house, you're welcome to go inside. I haven't tidied yet, but you could let yourself in and have a look."

Alone. An enticing opportunity. But it was a workday, and she couldn't very well sneak around wearing a nurse's uniform. Besides, she'd rather no one knew she was in the house so as not to draw attention to her activity. "You're kind to offer. I was in the area and wanted to see the place again, but I'm doing home visits and I have patients to call on." Darla pointed up at her nurse's hat. "Another time, perhaps?"

"Of course. You must come by again. Where are you staying? I can telephone you with an invitation."

"Yes. Please do." Darla turned to walk to the street with Ida. "I'm lodging at Miss Hattie's Boardinghouse."

Ida tittered, and the baby squirmed. Without looking away, she patted his bundled chest, quieting him. "That's where I'm headed as we speak. To have tea with Hattie and my father."

Ida was one of the Sinclair sisters. Darla shuddered and nearly lost her footing on the slushy ground. "That's why you look familiar. You're Kat's sister."

"Yes. You know Kat? I guess that makes sense, since she arrived in town a year and a half before I did."

"Yoo-hoo." A short, stout woman waved from the center of the street. "Mrs. Raines."

Darla leaned toward Ida. "I take it Mrs. Wahlberg still likes to keep watch on the neighborhood."

A grin tipped Ida's mouth. "Mostly just the parsonage and the church."

Darla lifted her hand to her mouth as a laugh escaped. "Some things haven't changed."

"I'd say not." They both giggled, and Ida waved at her neighbor. "Good afternoon, Mrs. Wahlberg." The new pastor's wife seemed quite likable.

Darla waved, too. Perhaps she could save herself a lot of trouble and simply tell Ida about the diary and the pendant and ask for permission to retrieve them.

No. Some things were better left a secret and handled privately. She had no desire to invite unwanted questions. And Ida was Kat's sister. She couldn't know what was in the diary.

"We were just leaving," Ida said. "Did you need—"

"Mercy me, it *is* you. Darla Taggart!" The woman's squeal startled the baby, and Ida patted his chest again. "I couldn't be sure from so far away. I'm gettin' old, you know. My eyesight isn't what it used to be."

"Hello, Mrs. Wahlberg. I arrived in Cripple Creek a couple of weeks ago."

"To live?"

"Yes. I'm working as a nurse. In fact, I'm on my way to see a patient now."

"A nurse." Mrs. Wahlberg looked her over from boots to bonnet. "I'd say you've done some growing up while you've been gone."

"Yes, ma'am."

"Good for you, dear. Hmm." Mrs. Wahlberg tapped her fleshy chin. "Two weeks, you say. Funny, I haven't seen you in church." She glanced at the brick building behind them. "It's not that big."

"I haven't been yet. Between a head cold and patients who need tending, I've been busy on Sundays."

"Oh. You know it's not good to—" The baby hadn't quieted so easily this time and let out a wail, startling Mrs. Wahlberg. "Well, we can visit more another time. I won't keep you."

Darla stifled a sigh of relief and smiled at Ida.

"That reminds me." Mrs. Wahlberg raised a gloved finger. "Mrs. Raines, don't forget we're expecting you and the reverend at the luncheon Saturday."

Ida nodded. "It's one week from this coming Saturday, the day before Easter, am I right?"

"I believe you're right. The fourteenth day of April." Mrs. Wahlberg licked her lips. "It appears I'm more than a little anxious for a taste of Hattie's lemon scones."

Darla smiled. She didn't need to share her intentions with Ida after all. Every one of the Sinclair sisters and their families would be occupied elsewhere. Darla said her good-byes and took light steps toward B Street and her next patient.

Saturday, April 14—the day she'd finally reunite with her childhood diary and her grandmother's heirloom cameo.

Chapter Four

Y ou look like you're in awful pain."

Gripping the end of the countertop, Nicolas turned to Jocelyn's voice, watching her dump a bucket of coal into the stove. Concern etched her dark eyes. "I'm afraid you might have hurt yourself. The scabs."

"I'm all right." Or he would be, as soon as he made his way back to the cot. He just needed to be flat again. He didn't know what he'd do if that didn't calm his jumpy nerves. It might have been having the bandages removed—the cold air hitting his scabs again, having ointment rubbed into his back, having the fresh bandage against his skin—or just having a woman so close, but he'd not been able to lie still since Darla Taggart had left the house that morning.

The young nurse had been coming to the house most every day for nearly three weeks. But she had new patients to see tomorrow and didn't plan to return until Thursday. He could blame his increased restlessness the past few days on being confined to the cot most of the time, but after hearing his nurse's laughter today, he couldn't deny it was more than that. He'd found himself hoping he was more than just a patient to Miss Taggart. A notion he needed to avoid like a stagecoach would steer clear of a bandit's hideaway. She was caring and compassionate, and so sweet with the girls, but she was only doing her job. He couldn't afford to let her run away with his heart.

Nicolas set the knife he'd used to peel potatoes on the counter and forced the least-pained smile he could muster to his face. Jaya had stilled the broom. Julia watched him from the table where she rolled bread dough into balls. "Your mama used to say that worry only makes your face wrinkle early."

"I remember." Jocelyn grabbed a handful of her apron and used it to close the chute on the stove. "But you've been restless ever since Miss Taggart left, and I'm afraid you'll make things worse."

She sounded like his nurse. But Jocelyn was only ten and trying to manage the household while watching her father suffer. Nicolas swallowed his sour retort. Perhaps he shouldn't have stood for so long, but—

"I don't think your nurse worries." His youngest ran her hand down her smooth cheek. "She doesn't have any wrinkles."

Julia had forgotten she'd been handling dough and left a trail of flour across her face, and Nicolas couldn't help but chuckle. When he pointed to her doughy hand, all three of the girls started giggling.

His back cramped, and before he could stop himself, he cried out in pain.

The girls quieted, their eyes large as a full moon.

"I'm sorry, Papa." Tears pooled Julia's brown eyes as his own blurred his vision. "I didn't mean to make you hurt."

"It wasn't your fault, sweet pea." He blinked back his tears. "I've been out of bed too long. That's all." He mentally measured the distance between the countertop and the cot—just twelve feet, which right now seemed an insurmountable expanse. *Help me, Lord. Help us all.*

Jocelyn wiped her hands on her apron, then reached for the ties. "Miss Darla told me she was staying at Miss Hattie's Boardinghouse. I'll go get her."

"No. Don't bother Miss Taggart. There's nothing she can do."

"But—"

"I only need to lie down."

The broom thudded to the floor, and all three girls rushed to his side.

"Be careful not to touch his back," Jocelyn said, as she tucked herself against his leg, trying to help support him.

His lips pressed together, Nicolas rested his hand on Jocelyn's shoulder and took a tentative step toward the cot in the main room. The other two girls walked on his left side, supporting his other hand in four little ones.

No one spoke as they shuffled across the linoleum floor, but four sighs punctuated their arrival at the cot.

"Thank you," he said. "I can do the rest."

When the girls stepped away from his makeshift bed, Nicolas lifted one knee and placed it on the cot, then slowly lowered himself to a prone position.

Jaya nudged the pillow under his face. "I'll get you a cup of mint tea."

"Yes." He tried drawing in a deep breath to rid his voice of the strain. "Thank you." The tea would be cold before he felt up to sitting up to drink it, but if it made Jaya feel better. . .

The Lord had indeed blessed him. And as much as it distressed him that his young ones had to take care of him, having them at his side gave him hope.

Darla rested her elbow on the chair arm in her bedchamber. Pen in hand, she tapped the writing desk on her lap. In her wildest dreams, she wouldn't have imagined her first weeks on the job unfolding as they had. And to think she'd been upset with her assignment as a visiting nurse.

It felt particularly rewarding to see a patient in his or her daily environment putting forth effort to recover, to take part in the process. Especially a man like Mr. Zanzucchi, who had suffered a devastating trauma and had three daughters witnessing his struggle and recovery. After nearly three weeks of visiting his home at least every other day, she wasn't sure she could abide being confined to working in a stark hospital ward.

She glanced down at the stationery and the few words she'd managed to pen:

Dear Mother,
Cripple Creek is thriving.

That was as far as she'd gotten, and her ability to concentrate on the letter hadn't improved a whit. The letter would just have to wait. Her mind seemed set on replaying various scenes in the Zanzucchi home: Mr. Zanzucchi's lighthearted teasing about a possum being under their floor when he was clearly in much discomfort. Watching the girls tend to chores or school lessons with the same determination she'd seen in their father.

She needed a distraction, something that would capture her imagination. A good book. She'd seen several books on a shelf in the parlor, including *Pride and Prejudice.* That would surely remove her thoughts from her hesitant and intriguing patient, his sweet and motherless little girls, a diary that was too forthcoming, and the parsonage—and twelve days to wait.

Darla set her writing desk on the chair and stepped out onto the second-floor landing.

She watched as Cherise ascended the stairs, the girl's footfalls creating a lively cadence on the oak steps. Lace accented the flounced collar and cuffs on her pink two-piece dress. She wore her nearly black hair pulled back from her face and secured with a matching bow. Looking at the girl now, Cherise didn't seem to have a care in the world. But Darla knew better, and hers was a touching story, which Hattie had shared with her over a cup of coffee after supper one night.

Mr. Sinclair had worked with Cherise's father on the railroad in Paris. Cherise's mother was sickly most of her daughter's life and had succumbed to her illness when Cherise was seven. Cherise's father had already booked their passage on the boat to America with Mr. Sinclair when a riveted seam on a boiler burst and scalded him. He'd died within the week.

When Cherise caught sight of Darla, she paused on the landing and gave her a polite nod. "*Bonne nuit,* Miss Taggart."

"Good night, Cherise. And, please, call me Miss Darla."

Light from the sconce on the wall accentuated Cherise's round cherubic face. "*Oui.* Mademoiselle Darla."

Darla smiled. "Sleep well." She watched the girl slip into the room just beyond her own bedchamber. At ten years old, Cherise was the same age as the eldest Zanzucchi girl, Jocelyn. Both had suffered loss and heartache. But for Cherise, God had provided a new family through Harlan and Hattie Sinclair. Perhaps he'd give Mr. Zanzucchi and his daughters a fresh start, too.

She sighed. How was it that her mind kept drifting back to Nicolas Zanzucchi and his family? She was his nurse. That was all she was to him. She needed to go downstairs and get that book.

The parlor door stood open, and the warm glow from the fireplace drew Darla inside. Bent over the checkerboard set up between her and her husband, Hattie moved her hand feverishly in an apparent avalanche of jumps.

"Hah!" Her expression triumphant, Hattie looked up. "Darla, dear, you're just in time to hear me gloat."

Mr. Sinclair rose from his chair and stood behind it, a smile tipping his mustache. "Trust me, it's not one of her many charms." He gestured toward the game board. "Perhaps you'd have better luck."

"I came in to borrow a book, if you don't mind."

Hattie waved bent fingers toward the bookshelves. "I don't mind at all. But I see no reason why you couldn't do both. Play a game *and* borrow a book."

Playing would afford her a little companionship. She'd been so busy these first three weeks in town, she'd done no socializing, although her time with the Zanzucchi family felt more like companionship than work.

"You don't play?" Hattie asked.

"I haven't played for more than three years. My aunt liked to play, but once I sank into my studies, I never found time for games."

"Well then, that settles it. It's high time you had a little fun, dear." Hattie arched a thin eyebrow. "You know what they say, 'One who neglects pastime amusement forgets how to play altogether.'"

Darla didn't know that anyone else had ever said that, but her landlady was persuasive. And a little recreation wouldn't do her any harm.

"One game, then."

Hattie's smile bunched her cheeks. "Splendid! I have the black pieces." Her landlady began positioning her game pieces on a printed board. "This will give me a chance to hear more about your house visits."

Darla settled herself at the table and finished setting up the red game pieces.

"You make the first move, dear. Harlan says it's only fair that I let guests go first." Hattie glanced at the deep leather chair where Mr. Sinclair sat with a newspaper. "But I'd hardly consider you a guest. You have a job, and this is your home now."

"Thank you, ma'am." Darla slid a checker forward. "But I don't intend to stay here forever."

"And neither do I." Chuckling, Hattie matched Darla's move. "I have a home on the other side of this life, don't you know."

Nodding, Darla moved a piece two spaces. Her time here had dispelled any doubts she'd had about returning to Cripple Creek or lodging at Miss Hattie's. It wasn't the parsonage, but she *was* beginning to feel at home here.

"It sounds like nurse's training was a lot of work." Hattie slid another piece forward. "You said that with your studies you never found time for games."

"That's right. Between the classes, the homework, and all the medical books on my reading list—"

Hattie blew out a long breath. "No wonder you're still single. I doubt you found a spare minute for romance, either."

The newspaper rustled, and Mr. Sinclair peeked out from behind it. "Go easy on her, dear. Miss Taggart has only been back in town a short time. Starting a new job can be all-consuming."

"*Tsk tsk*, Mister." Hattie shook her head, dislodging a wisp of gray hair from her bun. "Don't you have some stock market to read up on?"

"Yes. I was too busy." Darla studied the game board. "And believe it or not, I wasn't interested."

Her lips pressed together, Hattie stared at the board like a hawk seeking its prey.

"Romantic notions seemed to control every aspect of my life at seventeen, I know," Darla said.

"Like I said when you arrived, dear, that was then, and this is now."

Perhaps it was that easy. Dr. Cutshaw was happily married. By this time, Zachary and Emily probably were also wed. If so, she could let go of the notion that she and Zachary should marry and move on from her past. And she would, as soon as she held her diary, certain it was safe from discovery. As soon as she could be sure her written words didn't see light and cost her her job.

"I dare say, Darla dear, you won't have any trouble finding a good husband in Cripple Creek." Hattie made the first jump of the game and smiled at her. "Not with all the new business owners and bankers moving into our fair city."

Darla studied the board, hoping her concentration would derail her opponent's train of thought.

"You knew Emily Updike, the banker's niece, didn't you?" Hattie asked, undeterred.

"We'd met." Darla braced herself for the inevitable news. Not that she had any real claims on Zachary. Just because he said he'd wait for her didn't mean he was obliged to do so.

"Well"—Hattie jumped another of her game pieces—"did you know that Emily married a couple of years ago?"

"I hadn't heard." Darla focused on a game piece that was in jeopardy. "Since my friend Betty moved from Cripple Creek shortly after I did, I stopped hearing the local news."

There was the answer to that question. Zachary's father had gotten his way, and so had the banker. Zachary and Emily *were* married. Since Zachary had been compliant, he likely co-owned the haberdashery with his father by now. Emily was a better choice of wife for him, anyway, especially if the banker's niece had proven to be chaste.

"Like I said, there are a lot of businessmen moving in from all over the country. And beyond. Emily married a bookkeeper from Chicago."

Not Zachary. Her finger pressed to a red game piece, Darla looked up at her landlady. "I remember talk that Zachary Pfeiffer might marry her."

"Yes, well, she was spending a generous amount of time at his father's haberdashery. Some of us—"

Mr. Sinclair cleared his throat.

Hattie leaned toward Darla. "Let's just say I thought maybe she and Zachary Pfeiffer might marry, but it seems he's not the marrying kind."

Mr. Sinclair poked his head out from behind the newspaper. "Just because he isn't married yet doesn't mean he's not the marrying kind. Some of us just have to work a little harder to find the right woman." He winked.

Zachary wasn't married. For some reason, that fact didn't seem as important to her as it had when she'd first set foot off the train in March.

The question now was whether he still had any feelings for her.

Chapter Five

Darla pulled the stethoscope from her bag and turned back toward the bed where Mrs. Baxter lay recovering from pneumonia. The silver-haired woman hadn't stopped coughing in the five minutes Darla had been there.

"She insisted the doctor let her come home." Mr. Baxter stood on the other side of the bed. "The only way he'd agree was to have someone from the hospital come check on her."

Darla nodded without looking at him. She'd heard the same story on Wednesday, just hours after her patient arrived home. Yesterday, Mrs. Baxter was sitting in a chair and seemed to be feeling fairly well.

"Them mules that roam our streets aren't as stubborn as my woman."

Darla had a wind-up monkey that didn't chatter as much as this man did. Darla swallowed her retort and came up with an idea to distract him. "Mr. Baxter, would you be so kind as to fetch me a cup of hot tea?"

"I suppose I could, if you need one."

"I do. Thank you." When he nodded and shuffled out of the room, Darla drew in a deep breath and bent over her patient. She placed her hand on Mrs. Baxter's forehead. "I don't feel a fever."

"He does like to hear himself talk, don't he?"

Darla nodded as she donned the stethoscope. Pressing her lips together so she couldn't add a comment, she placed the bell on Mrs. Baxter's chest and listened. The woman's heart sounded strong. "I need you to sit up for me. Can you do that?"

Mrs. Baxter huffed a bit while bending her legs and raising up, and Darla detected wheezing that hadn't been nearly as pronounced during her first visit. She pressed the bell to Mrs. Baxter's back and listened to the woman's lungs. "I still hear some congestion in that left lobe, but it doesn't sound much worse." Yet.

Darla removed the earpieces and returned the stethoscope to her bag. "Something has definitely made you feel puny today. I suppose it could be the exertion from the wagon ride home, but the shortness of breath and wheezing have me a little concerned."

Mrs. Baxter flopped back onto her pillow.

"You took the laudanum last night? Did you rest well?"

"I don't like taking anything, but I did." Her patient sighed. "Truth is, it helped a lot. I didn't even hear the mister's snoring."

"Thelma!" Darla and Mrs. Baxter both glanced toward the open doorway where Mr. Baxter balanced a steaming teacup on a saucer in one hand and held a smoking pipe in the other. "Don't be boring this poor girl with our secrets."

"Trust me, Henry. Your snoring is no secret." Mrs. Baxter paused, her breathing shallow. "Not on this street, it isn't. You're the only one who don't seem to hear it."

Her husband huffed, then set the teacup on the bedside table.

Darla gave him a nod. "Thank you."

He raised the pipe to his mouth and took a puff, sending a cloud of smoke over the bed. That was it!

"Mr. Baxter, have you been smoking around your wife?"

"Not while you was here, I haven't," he said. "But today's a different day."

Darla sighed. "That explains a lot."

"It does?" Her patient choked on a cough.

"Mr. Baxter, I believe your wife may be sensitive to your pipe smoke."

"Nonsense. I been smokin' a pipe for all the twenty-three years we been hitched."

Darla did her best to swallow the frustration tensing her shoulders. "Has your wife had pneumonia before?"

"I don't remember."

"I haven't. This is my first time." Mrs. Baxter straightened in the bed. "You're saying it is Henry's fault I'm having trouble breathing?"

Darla took her medical bag from the chair. She had no intention of lingering in the middle of their debate. "Since we don't want a relapse of the pneumonia, Mr. Baxter, you'll need to refrain from smoking in the house or anywhere near her until her lungs are clear."

"I always smoke in my house." He jammed the mouthpiece into his face and took a deep puff, exhaling toward the ceiling. "You women will say or do anything to rob a man of his limited pleasures."

She didn't know whether to laugh or cry at his insolence. "I assure you, Mr. Baxter, Dr. Cutshaw would be just as concerned about you blowing pipe smoke around Mrs. Baxter when her lungs are this compromised."

Mr. Baxter ambled to the door. "I suppose he would."

"That's settled, then." Darla tugged the sleeve on her uniform straight. "I'll stop back by late this afternoon to check on things." She'd added the last part for Mr. Baxter's benefit.

Some home visits weren't as pleasant as others.

Thinking of the more pleasant ones, she'd not been to check on Mr. Zanzucchi since Tuesday. And the day before yesterday felt like a long time ago.

―――――――――◆―――――――――

Fifteen minutes later, Darla crossed Bennett Avenue and stepped onto the curb in front of Pfeiffer's Haberdashery. Zachary wasn't married. One question remained: Had he waited for her?

She took one pace toward the door, then stopped.

She'd told Hattie she'd changed and indicated to Mr. Zanzucchi that she'd changed. Pursuing Zachary and tracking him down at his father's store would signify otherwise. Yes, she and Zachary had once cared for each other and he wasn't yet married, but those no longer seemed good enough reasons for her to pursue him.

Swinging the medical bag at her side, she walked up Third Street, away from her past and toward a destiny of her own making. Her future as a healer. If she was meant to reunite with Zachary, if there was still something between them, it would happen without her being the one to take the initiative.

Darla hadn't yet set her foot on the stoop when the door on the Zanzucchis' tidy company house swung open. Three brown-eyed girls in cotton dresses and simple shawls stood on the threshold looking up at her with expressions of. . .what was it? Relief, perhaps?

"Good morning, girls."

"I'm so glad you're here, Miss Taggart." Jocelyn reached for Darla's hand.

Jaya rocked on her heels. "Me, too."

"And me." Julia's smile revealed a gap in her teeth. She'd lost a baby tooth since the visit on Tuesday.

The girls had been friendly all along, but today they seemed a little too anxious for her visit. "Is something wrong?" Darla followed Jocelyn inside, banging her bag against the doorframe. Mr. Zanzucchi lay on the cot, his head supported by his right arm. He didn't seem in distress in the least.

"He's better now, but Tuesday—"

"After I left?"

He nodded. "I'm fine now."

"What happened?" Darla set her bag on the chair beside the cot, then shed her gloves and tucked them into a pocket on her mantle. After handing it to Jocelyn, who stood waiting, she returned her attention to her patient. "Perhaps that's the wrong question, Mr. Zanzucchi. What did you do?"

"He peeled potatoes." Jaya raised both palms.

The matter-of-fact innocence in the child's statement tickled Darla, and she couldn't help but grin.

Jocelyn draped Darla's mantle on the peg by the door. "He was up too long."

"Papa was stuck there." Jaya pointed at the end of the kitchen counter. "And he couldn't go back to bed."

"But we helped him." Julia's toothless smile made her brown eyes sparkle.

Jocelyn sighed. "I wanted to go get you—may we call you Miss Darla?"

"I'd like that. Yes."

"I wanted to go get you, Miss Darla, but—"

"But I said there was no need to bother you, and I was right." The light blanket was draped across only Mr. Zanzucchi's bandaged back. Stocking feet stuck out below the cuffs of his brown trousers.

"It doesn't sound as if your daughters share your confidence."

"True enough. But do you realize that we haven't even said hello? I couldn't get in a word." He raised his hand in greeting. "Hello, Nurse Taggart. Miss Darla, to some. How are you today?"

Amused. But it might not be appropriate to say so. She had said she was professional, and she needed to remain as such. "I'm well, thank you for asking." She went to the sideboard to wash her hands. Jocelyn already had the bowl of hot water and lye soap ready for her. "It sounds like you've been in a bit of trouble the past couple of days."

"That would be an understatement. Can't even scratch my nose without a guard going on full alert."

She let a giggle escape. "But such adorable protectors they are."

"Please. I can't have you taking their side. I have enough pretty girls giving me grief."

Enough pretty girls. When no one else responded, Darla decided to ignore his comment as well. But drying her hands on a clean towel, she couldn't help but wonder if Mr. Zanzucchi had intended to include her as one of the pretty girls. Or if it was a mere slip of his tongue.

She went to her bag and pulled out the sterile bandages.

Footfalls and faint voices moved the girls toward the window. "It's Mithus Nell!"

"And William," Jaya said.

That was something Darla hadn't yet experienced in her home visits—callers stopping by while she tended to her patients.

Mr. Zanzucchi looked up at her. "Do you know Nell Archer?"

Archer. "Not that I recall."

"Do you have the time to wait a few minutes? The girls adore their *Mrs.* Nell."

"Yes, of course, the treatment can wait."

The girls ushered the guests inside. A young woman close to Darla's age carried a wooden box with a metal clasp. A small boy rode in on Jocelyn's back, giggling and swinging a sack like he was a cowboy and she, a horse.

The woman saw Darla standing beside the cot and stopped. She glanced from her hat to the bandages atop the medical bag. "I apologize for the intrusion." The high cheekbones and the chin made Nell Archer look familiar.

"There's no need to apologize," Mr. Zanzucchi said. "You are always welcome."

"But we've interrupted."

"Only a treatment I'm not especially anxious for." He smiled, then looked at Darla. "Mrs. Archer and her husband, Judson, cared for the girls after the accident. They were a godsend." He looked over at the child trying to lasso Julia with the sack.

"We had fun with the girls," Nell Archer said. "And William loved having them to chase."

"We played cowboys and dolls." The words came out on a whistle through Julia's new gap.

"And checkers," Jaya said.

The visitor nodded and smiled at Darla. "I'm Nell Archer." Her smile reached warm blue eyes. "You look familiar, but—"

"I was thinking you did as well. I'm Darla Taggart." Darla studied the young woman's face. Nell had the same blue eyes, pronounced chin, and dark blond hair as the woman outside the parsonage. Ida. Another Sinclair sister. "By any chance, is it your sister who's married to the new parson at First Congregational?"

"Yes. Ida. There is a mess of us Sinclairs here in Cripple Creek now."

Darla nodded. "Your father married Miss Hattie."

"He did. And you know Kat." She'd said it as a statement of fact, without a hint of judgment.

"Of course. Nell Sinclair. I'd forgotten that you married Judson Archer in a double wedding."

When the sack swung near her, Nell snatched it from little William and handed it to Jocelyn. "We brought cookies, although they're likely in crumbs by now. And I brought you all a game. Mr. Archer made it for you himself." She held the wooden box out to Jaya and Julia.

"That was kind of him." Nicolas laid his head back onto his arm. "The Lord knows the girls need something to do other than guard me."

Jaya flipped the latch and opened the box. "It's checkers!" She did a twirl that set all four of the children spinning and giggling. Jaya was the first to stop. "I get to play the first game with you, Miss Nell."

A frown narrowed the woman's eyes. "Not today, I'm afraid. William and I have a couple more stops before we meet up with Mr. Archer for his midday meal."

When Nell and her son had gone, Mr. Zanzucchi suggested they all have a peanut butter cookie before Darla changed his bandages.

Despite Jocelyn's concerns about her papa, the scabs were intact and there was no sign of fever. Apparently, he'd only angered the nerves and muscles by staying upright for too long. Guessing he'd learned his lesson, Darla didn't say any more about it before returning the leftover cloth strips to her bag and latching it shut.

"Miss Darla."

She glanced up at Jaya, who stood beside the game set up on the kitchen table.

"If you're done taking care of Papa, can you play checkers with us?"

"Yes." Julia clapped.

Darla drew in a deep breath. Without a doubt, this home was her favorite to visit. But she'd done her job here and had already stayed longer than she should have. And she still had other patients to see.

Mr. Zanzucchi raised up onto his forearms. "Do you play checkers?"

"If you count losing to Hattie Sinclair at the boardinghouse as playing, I do."

He chuckled. "Then you'll have to come back another time to play checkers. Sometime when you're not working."

She struggled to hide her stunned reaction to his suggestion but somehow managed to retain her composure and don her mantle.

Julia dashed to her side. "Do you work tomorrow?"

"I don't work Saturday." She shifted her attention to Mr. Zanzucchi. "Thank you for the invitation, but I can't promise I'll be able to come."

She was, after all, a professional. Or had her patient forgotten that? She could understand the girls' enthusiasm. His was puzzling. Unless he, too, could be developing feelings outside their nurse-and-patient relationship.

Nicolas lay in his bed. The position was the same—on his stomach—but the room was different. Quiet darkness had settled over the house on this Thursday night. All three girls had drifted off to sleep, leaving him alone to wrestle with his thoughts. Miss Taggart's attentiveness to his girls the past three weeks. The confident way she consistently tended to his wounds. The tender conversations they'd had about fresh starts—for Cripple Creek following the fires in '96 and for its people. And today. . .the memory of the personal statements he'd made to his poor nurse.

"I can't have you taking their side. I have enough pretty girls giving me grief."

Nicolas scrubbed the whiskers on his jaw. In essence, he'd called her pretty. She was, but whatever had come over him that he would make such a personal and public statement to a young woman who was simply trying to perform her job?

She was right to dismiss his slip of the tongue. She'd busied herself drying her hands. Having trained at St. Luke's, a big university, she no doubt had plenty of experience brushing off the careless remarks of forlorn patients.

And what of his invitation that she return to play checkers sometime when she wasn't working? Whatever happened to his concern that it wouldn't be proper to have a young single woman in the house? Yes, she was especially attentive to his daughters and personable with him, but she was there to accomplish medical tasks. The bewildered look she gave him in response to his invitation said he best not expect her to pay a visit during her off hours.

He'd made the suggestion because his girls enjoyed her company. Nicolas let out a deep sigh. The truth was, he enjoyed her company, too. Who wouldn't? Miss Taggart wasn't just pleasant to look at, but she was also intelligent and good-natured.

Still, it wasn't like him to be so forward. No doubt it was due to the fact that he'd been confined for five weeks. First in the hospital, then in his home. And Miss Taggart had been the first woman to pay him any mind, let alone touch him, since Maria passed. Even the admission that her attention came in the execution of her job as his nurse didn't diminish the fact that it had awakened his need for companionship.

Nicolas lifted his head and squashed his pillow into a ball.

If he couldn't peel potatoes or do any wood carving, he would at least figure out a way to play checkers with his girls. They could play on the floor next to the cot. Or he could sit in the chair with a pillow at his back for a game, two or three times a day.

He needed something else to occupy his mind. Anything to keep him from thinking of Miss Taggart.

Chapter Six

Darla clicked the boardinghouse door shut behind her and stepped out onto a sunbathed porch. Saturday was the perfect day for clear weather—her day off. After breakfast, she'd written letters to Mother and Aunt Cora and polished her white booties. Her clean uniform hung on the clothesline out back.

She descended the steps and picked her way down the slushy gravel walk to the street. As she passed the neighboring houses on Golden Avenue, snow from Monday's storm still huddled in shady pockets here and there, but sunshine reigned and warmed her back.

At the corner, Darla turned right and down the steep street toward company housing. It was a good day to play checkers with the three Zanzucchi girls.

Or was it? As their father's nurse, she would be mixing her job with pleasure. But it hadn't been her idea; it was Mr. Zanzucchi's invitation.

Although Cripple Creek had definitely grown in her absence, it still wasn't such a thriving metropolis that she would never treat friends and acquaintances at the hospital or in their homes. It would be nigh to impossible and quite isolating to never socialize at church and community functions with people who were also her patients at one time or another. Was she not to have any friends or social engagements?

Besides, it was only a game or two of checkers with three girls who didn't have a mother and were suffering the trauma of seeing their father severely injured and rendered helpless for a season. It was the neighborly thing to do, to befriend Jocelyn, Jaya, and Julia and offer the girls a little diversion. That was all she was doing.

At least, that was what she told herself.

On Galena Avenue, Darla walked to the fourth house on the right. Big brown eyes peered out the front window. "Ith her!" The announcement breezed out through the gap between Julia's baby teeth.

Before Darla could knock, the youngest Zanzucchi sister flung the door open, beaming a heartwarming smile. The savory scent of oregano and garlic and the mouthwatering aroma of yeast bread rewarded Darla's senses and made her stomach growl.

"Good afternoon, Julia."

"You did come. Jaya said you would, but Jocelyn didn't think so. And Papa—"

"I did." Darla wasn't sure she wanted to know what Mr. Zanzucchi had to say about it. Stepping inside, she looked at Jocelyn, who stood at the stove with a wooden spoon in her hand. "Is this a good time?"

"It's the best time, Miss Darla," Jaya said.

"Jaya's right. This is the best time." Jocelyn set the wooden spoon in a bowl on the countertop. "We're ready for a break from our chores." She glanced at the table where the other two girls stood. All three of them looked down at the checkerboard, then up at Darla.

Surely they didn't expect her to decide who would challenge her first. She couldn't. Darla glanced at the cot and the man propped up on his elbows. Wavy hair, a mass of dark-roasted coffee richness, dusted the back of his neck just above the blanket. On his forehead, one curl turned up just above his thick eyebrows, and a crooked smile lit his whiskered face.

"Hello, Miss Darla." He'd obviously been listening.

And she'd been focusing on his physical appearance. "Hello."

He seemed to be doing the same thing, though, studying her from the navy-blue shoes to the straw cloche hat on her head. "No medical bag today, I see."

Darla shook her head. "I'm not here in an official capacity. I hope that's all right."

"Yes." The crooked smile returned. "I rather like the day dress."

"It's like the blue sky. And the lace on her neck is like one of those puffy clouds." Jaya spoke with her hands shaping pictures. "Blue is my favorite color."

"Mine, too." Mr. Zanzucchi drew in a deep breath, the expansion of his chest forming a muscled silhouette under the thin blanket. "I'm the one who invited you to return. . .to play checkers with the girls." He hadn't taken his brown-eyed gaze from her. "I didn't think you'd come, but we're glad you proved me wrong."

"Mr. Zanzucchi—"

"Nicolas, please."

"Nicolas, then, and please call me Darla." She glanced at the checkerboard. "I was hoping you could help us decide which of the girls gets to play the first game."

"The oldest," Jocelyn said.

"Th-h baby girl."

Jaya groaned. "I'm none of that. The best player should go first."

Nicolas cleared this throat and looked at Jocelyn. "I think this would be a good time to draw sticks."

Nodding, Jocelyn took a cloth sack from a basket on the sideboard, then pulled the drawstring tight and shook it.

Jaya shook her finger at her big sister. "Don't cheat."

"Miss Darla." Nicolas had laid his head on his arms. "I usually roll the sticks and hold the sack for the drawing. Would you mind doing the honors?"

Darla nodded, then took the sack from Jocelyn, pressed it between her hands, and commenced rolling what felt like three twigs. She loosened the drawstring enough that the girls could reach in and held the sack out to Julia first.

"It's the number two." Darla held the sack in front of Jaya. "You draw next."

Jaya squeezed her eyes shut and pulled out a stick with *One* written on it. She squealed.

"You get to play first." Darla said, and returned the sack to the sideboard where a long loaf of crusty bread cooled, so fresh that steam still rose from it. Seating herself, she drew in a deep breath, sweetened with its aroma. She loved this place. She loved this family. Not in the least surprised by her internal admissions, she focused her gaze on the light and dark game pieces.

"You're our guest, Miss Darla." Jaya motioned to the board, her little hand outstretched, palm up. "So you get to make the first move."

Not just their father's nurse, but a *guest*.

Happier than she'd felt in a long time, she smiled at her miniature opponent and reached for her first game piece.

Nicolas leaned over the table, taking care to keep his back straight. Darla held the bread basket out to him, her green eyes sparkling.

He took the basket from her. He hadn't been able to stop smiling since the moment she'd arrived. "Thank you." For the basket, but mostly for showing up when he was certain she wouldn't.

"You're welcome." She wrapped a noodle around her fork like he'd shown her. "You seem to be doing well. Your back?"

"I feel good, but I know my time at the table is limited."

Darla and the girls nodded in unison, and she rewarded him with a smile he would've thought could heal all his wounds right then and there. Her time with them the past few weeks had gone a long way toward taking his girls' minds off his condition and the necessity to make up for his helplessness.

The girls had each played three games of checkers with her, Jaya coming out the champion. It hadn't been easy convincing Jaya and Julia to clear the table of the checkers game. Until Julia invited their guest to stay for supper, and Darla agreed. It hadn't required any persuasion. His off-duty nurse appeared eager to take part in the activity. In his family's activities.

Spinning another bite of sauce-drenched noodles onto his fork, he looked at the clock on a shelf above the trunk. Darla had been at the house for nearly three hours. Three of his best hours in. . .he couldn't say how long it'd been since his girls had giggled with such abandon. But he could say it had been a long time since he'd smiled this much.

And had he ever had to concentrate so hard on not staring?

The ruffled lace at the collar and sleeves of Darla's dress made for quite the departure from her starched uniform. Frankly, she looked more angelic to him today. Where the uniform gave her the professional appearance she needed as his nurse, the summer sky–blue dress—

"That carving!" Darla pointed to the bas relief above the door. "I admire it every time I'm here."

He followed her gaze, a swirl of emotion revisiting him.

"It's exquisite!"

"Thank you." Nicolas raised his porcelain coffee mug. "It's my favorite."

"Papa made it," Jocelyn said, tearing off another piece from the crusty loaf of bread.

"You did that?"

"I whittle, yes." He took another gulp of coffee. "I'm hoping that someday I can rise up from my ashes."

Her green eyes shimmered with a tenderness that almost made him believe he could be the phoenix in his carving.

"That trunk in the corner," Jaya said, and Darla followed her gaze and nodded. "It's full of things Papa has made." Jaya used her hands for emphasis. "My favorite is the horse."

"I'd love to see them sometime." When he nodded, Darla filled her fork and looked across the table at Jocelyn. "Jocelyn, I'm quite certain this sauce and noodles are the best I've ever had."

"Thank you." His eldest daughter beamed with pride. "I like cooking with my grandmother's recipes. But I have a French girl in my class at school."

"Cherise Sinclair?"

"Yes." Jocelyn nodded. "She always talks about the food back in Paris. I'd really like to learn to cook French style."

"It's one of my favorites."

"It is? Do you think you could teach me?"

"I'm not sure how good of a cooking student or teacher I'd make, but I'd bet we could have fun trying."

The squawk of stressed wagon wheels seemed to impel Julia from her chair to dash to the window. "Mr. Zachary is here, Papa!"

Darla's fork clanged against her plate. "Zachary Pfeiffer?"

"Yes. Zach owns Pfeiffer Coal Operations and sometimes delivers our coal." He set his mug on the table. "And today's the day."

Her brow furrowed, and she ran her tongue over her lips.

"You know Zach?" he asked.

"I did."

As Nicolas watched Darla stand and smooth the embroidered flowers on her bodice, an uneasiness tightened his gut. There was more to this story, and he was certain he didn't want to hear it.

Zachary was here. . .now?

Darla excused herself from the supper table and joined Julia at the door. She didn't plan to go outside, but she did wish to see him. And it was too late to hide the fact that she and Zachary shared a history. Her abrupt response to his name, dropping her fork and practically jumping to her feet, had given at least that much away.

"You know Zach?" Nicolas had referred to him as Zach. The two men were apparently friends, a fact that did nothing to settle her nervous stomach.

Zachary had a coal business? Why wasn't he working at the haberdashery? Did it have something to do with why Emily Updike had married an accountant from out of town? Darla shook her hands at her sides, hoping to release some of her nervous energy. She had so many questions. None of which she wished to ask in front of Nicolas or his girls.

Julia flung the door open. "Mr. Zachary always brings us candy." She'd practically sung the announcement.

He liked children. Or at least he enjoyed treating these three. A sweet gesture that bode well for him, because she favored Nicolas's girls, too.

Ready or not, her reunion with Zachary was going to happen, here and now. Her heart pounding, Darla stood in the open doorway and watched the wagon roll to a stop at the side of the house.

The driver wore bib-and-brace overalls. Not the tailored suit she'd been used to seeing Zachary in when he worked for his father. But it was him, all right. Sandy-blond hair stuck out from beneath a canvas cap. When he climbed down the opposite side of the wagon, a yellow broadcloth shirt stretched tight against his thickset shoulders.

Her mouth suddenly dry, she moistened her lips again. What if seeing Zachary and letting him know she was back in town was one mistake on top of another?

Zachary rounded the back of the wagon, crouching down at girl level and holding up four Tootsie Rolls. Looking up, he straightened and lowered the treats. "Darla?"

When she nodded, he practically bolted up the steps and stopped just short of an embrace. She likely had the smudges on his hands and overalls to thank.

"It really is you."

"Yes. Hello, Zachary."

He plucked his cap off and dropped it on a porch chair. "What are you doing here?"

"She's Papa's nur-th." Julia smiled up at them, a new tooth starting to fill in the gap in her teeth.

Zachary cleared his throat, studying Darla from hair to shoe. "His nurse?" His incredulous tone only tightened the knots in her stomach. "With a dinner napkin tucked into your waistband?"

"Yes." She yanked the napkin free and let it hang at her side. "Just not today." She was friends with Nicolas and his girls, and she'd made a social call. But for some strange reason, she didn't seem able to say as much.

"I didn't know you were in town. When did you come back?"

"It's been a few weeks."

"Weeks?" His blue eyes widened. "I'm not that hard to find."

"My new job at the hospital and doing home visits has kept me busy."

Jaya sidled up to her. "Today she came to play checkers."

"I see." Zachary raked his hair, leaving a blond weed sticking up.

"Do you want to play checkers, Mr. Zachary? We can play it on the floor."

He shook his head. "Not today, Jaya. I have lots of work to do, and you all have supper to finish."

Darla glanced at the candy in his hand, and he quickly distributed it to the three grateful girls who flocked to him.

"I brought the fourth one for Nic. Figured he'd earned one after what he's been through." He glanced inside to where Nicolas leaned on a chair in front of the table, then looked back at her. "I would've brought you one if I'd known you were here."

Was that disappointment or accusation in his voice?

"Hey, Zach." Nicolas walked toward them, his back straight and his brown eyes averted from her. "Buddy, if you brought me candy, I say you need to stop the dilly-dallying and bring it inside."

Darla stepped out of the doorway to let Zachary pass. He shook Nicolas's hand, then gave him the candy.

Nicolas dropped it into his shirt pocket. A pained expression tightening his features, he gripped the edge of a side table and drew in a deep breath. "I'd introduce the two of you, but it seems you already know each other."

"You could say that." The smile on Zachary's face was a little too smug for her comfort. "Yes. Since she was in high school."

"That's when I first met her, too." Nicolas let go of the table. "She's changed some since then."

A sudden flush heated the tips of her ears. Nicolas had no doubt figured out the nature of their past relationship, and they were speaking of her as if she were invisible.

"I wouldn't know about that." Zachary turned and took a slow step toward her. "If you don't have plans for tomorrow evening, Darla, I'd like to take you out to supper."

She avoided looking at Nicolas. Just being in the same room with the two men made her feel disloyal to Nicolas after the wonderful afternoon they'd enjoyed, let alone making social plans with Zachary. But she did have a past with him that she needed to come to terms with. "I'm not working tomorrow. Supper out would be fine."

"Good. It'll give us a chance to catch up." He looked at Nicolas, who seemed to lock gazes with him. "Right now, I have some coal to unload."

And she had some thinking to do.

Chapter Seven

The church foyer was much the same as Darla remembered it, except for the new oak wainscoting and a spindle-back deacon's bench near the sanctuary doors. Folks mingled and chatted just beyond her. Thus far, she'd managed to blend in.

Staring up at the familiar painting of the Lord's Supper above the console table, Darla couldn't remember if she'd ever attended a church without a family member present. Her father didn't pastor a church in Philadelphia, but her aunt had always accompanied her. Today she was on her own. . .with a decade's worth of memories. She and Peter playing hide-and-seek. Mrs. Wahlberg leading the music with her big sleeves flapping like a bedsheet in the breeze. Hearing her father hit the bass notes in the chorus on "When the Roll Is Called Up Yonder." Having her every move scrutinized.

Darla glanced past a mother trying to straighten her son's shirt collar. Seeing the door to the basement brought back the memories of her impulsive teenage years. She'd needed to feel valued, to have someone willing to marry her. Or at least to say he would. How far would she have gone, if her father hadn't come looking for her? She'd asked God's forgiveness, but it seemed impossible to forgive herself for her reckless behavior in those months before she left Cripple Creek. And her reunion with Zachary yesterday couldn't have felt any more awkward if a flock of seagulls had flown into the Zanzucchis' home through the open door.

She'd been having the best time. The checkers tournament with the girls. An Italian supper as if she were part of the family. Hearing about Nicolas's artistry with wood. The promise of French cooking with Jocelyn. But that was before part of her past showed up with a load of coal.

"*You know Zach?*" Nicolas's question had felt accusatory. Even if she was the only one doing the condemning. Maybe if Zachary was willing to marry her, she'd finally feel like she was above reproach.

"Darla."

The voice brought her back to the present, and she turned to face a young woman with high cheekbones and a pronounced chin but about an inch taller than Nell or Ida.

Her rival from four years ago.

"Kat." *Kat Sinclair Cutshaw.* "Hello."

"Morgan told me you were back in town working as a nurse." The warm smile on her face didn't hint at any harbored ill will.

"Yes. I hope you don't mind." Darla bit her bottom lip. "Given my awful behavior when Dr. Cutshaw awarded you with his attention, I'm surprised—"

"That's old news." Kat swept her hand in the air as if to brush away the past. "Truly. I think what you're doing is wonderful."

Wonderful? "You do?"

"Yes. Nell told me she saw you in your nurse's uniform in the Zanzucchi home. Nicolas and his daughters have been through so much." Kat's voice cracked with emotion. "Those girls needed their father home with them. What a blessing that you are here and willing to do home visits." The doctor's wife reached for her hand. "You've made it possible for that dear family to be together."

Her a blessing? Tears stung Darla's eyes. "Thank you for saying that."

Kat looked down at their clasped hands, then met Darla's gaze. "I doubt you'll find any of your patients"—her voice low, she glanced around before continuing—"are as charming as Nicolas Zanzucchi and those girls."

Darla had found Nicolas to be kind and good-natured but hadn't thought of him as charming. Julia, yes. Thinking her an angel and calling her pretty on her first visit.

"Darla." Kat squeezed her hand. "You deserve to find the right man."

Darla couldn't say what she deserved, but perhaps after supper tonight, she'd know if Zachary Pfeiffer could be that man.

———————◆———————

Nicolas tried shifting a little on the cot. He ached all over. Nothing he'd done the last three hours had offered any relief.

Worst of all, he knew the discomfort was his own doing. He wanted to blame Darla Taggart for his restless and careless behavior last night, but his reaction to her familiarity with Zach was his burden, not hers. And now, listening to his girls chattering over the checkerboard only reminded him of his foolishness.

He had no business letting his heart feel something more for the nurse. Her reaction to hearing Zach's name had driven home that fact, as had hearing the two of them make supper plans. She enjoyed his girls' company, but that didn't mean she harbored personal feelings for a widowed father confined to his home. Not just to his home. Mostly to his bed. Because of burns and scabs that could crack on a whim and harbor life-threatening infection.

How could she care for someone so restricted? So dependent on his girls' tending to the family's needs and reliant on her for medical care?

By the time the girls had gone in to bed Saturday night, he'd had all the lying around he could take and set up his whittling tools at the table. Working with his hands again did wonders for his disposition. But after dropping his carving knife on the linoleum and leaning down to pick it up, he'd begun to realize he'd been too active and up too long.

Jocelyn had made it into the kitchen before him that morning and found the half-carved wood and tools on the table. "I hope you were careful," was all she'd said about it. He had been extremely careful, with a pillow tucked between him and the chair spindle. Careful. . .until he forgot and bent over to retrieve the knife from the floor.

Chilled, Nicolas tugged the blanket up over his back. It couldn't have been two minutes since he was burning hot and kicked it off. What had he done to himself?

Darla drew in a deep breath as she stepped onto the curb at the corner of Bennett Avenue and Third Street. Zachary Pfeiffer stood outside the Third Street Café, watching her walk down the slight hill. He'd offered to come to the boardinghouse to fetch her in a buggy, but it seemed a lesser commitment to treat their official reunion more like two old friends meeting for supper.

A lot had transpired in their separate lives in the past three and a half years. For her, much in the past three and a half weeks alone. Although she was curious, she was no longer ready to assume there was anything more between her and Zachary than their past.

As she approached the cloth awning, Zachary doffed his bowler, a broad smile showing off the dimple in his left cheek.

Apparently, wearing the green chiffon gown had been a good choice.

"You're just as beautiful as I remembered you."

He'd said as much yesterday, within earshot of Nicolas. "Thank you."

In sharp contrast to yesterday, when he'd shown up at the Zanzucchis' wearing coal-smudged cotton overalls, tonight Zachary looked much the same as he did when he worked in his father's haberdashery. A brown suit, crisp white shirt, and a narrow royal-blue necktie.

He held the door open for her, his blue eyes dazzling even in the dim light. She'd not been into the café since she'd returned to town but had eaten there a few times with her family on special occasions. The last time being her eighteenth birthday. . .just days before her father determined she would leave Cripple Creek.

Darla swallowed her bittersweet memories and followed her dapper escort and a hostess with a long white braid to a corner table. Settling onto the cushioned chair, she wondered if he'd reserved the back table, knowing they had some rather private things to discuss.

Their hostess clutched two menus to her chest and looked at Darla. "What can I bring you to drink?"

"We'd both like coffee," Zachary said, seating himself across the table from her.

Darla raised her hand, suddenly feeling like a schoolgirl. "I'd prefer a cup of hot tea, if you don't mind."

The hostess gave Zachary a slanted glance, then focused on Darla. "Of course. Would you prefer peppermint or Darjeeling?"

"Darjeeling, please."

Nodding, the older woman handed them each a menu and walked away, her braid swinging.

At a loss for words, Darla glanced at the watercolor painting on the wall beside her. What did she say to a man she'd expected to marry but hadn't seen for several years? Especially to a man presumptuous enough to order coffee without asking her preference.

When Zachary cleared his throat, she met his gaze. "I didn't remember that you don't drink coffee."

"I do drink coffee." Darla straightened the dinner knife in her place setting. "But that's not what sounded good to me tonight."

"Oh." Pressing his lips together, he raked a hand through his hair. "I'm sorry I didn't ask. I suppose I'm just so happy to see you that I forgot my manners."

"It's all right. You can enjoy your coffee, and I'll enjoy my tea."

Nodding, he reached across the table and captured her hand. "I'm glad you came back to me. I've missed you."

Came back to him? Darla looked at their joined hands. He'd apparently also decided she'd be comfortable with physical contact simply because she'd once allowed it. But that was then, and this was now. Wriggling her hand from his, she pressed her back to the cushion of her chair. "I returned for many reasons. Cripple Creek was my childhood home."

"Yes. And now you have your own job here." Leaning forward, he rested his jacket-clad forearms on the table. "But you can't deny I was worth coming back for. We shared something special."

"Pardon me, folks." They both looked up at the hostess, who set a steaming cup of coffee in front of Zachary and a cup of steeping tea on the table for Darla.

Darla forced a smile to her face. "Thank you."

"You're welcome. Are you ready to place your order for supper, miss?"

"Yes, thank you. I'd like tonight's special."

"And you, sir?"

"I'll have the same." He took Darla's menu and handed them both to the waitress.

After she'd sauntered away, Darla wrapped her hands around the teacup, watching the steam rise. She glanced at the nearby tables, satisfied that the other couples were suitably engaged in their own conversations. "I'm not sure I can say that what we had was special. We shared a kiss, Zachary."

His eyebrows arched. "More than once. And if I'm remembering that day in the basement correctly, it wasn't just a peck on the cheek."

An accusatory flush rushed up her neck and into her hairline. She remembered his touch on her bared skin. "It was more than a kiss, and *that* was a mistake."

"It didn't feel like a mistake to me, although I'll agree the timing could've been better." Zachary sat back, his posture softening. "I'm not trying to embarrass you. And I'm sorry if this all seems too forward." He glanced at the nearby tables, then back at her. "All I'm trying to say is that you mean something to me. It wasn't just a moment of passion. I wanted to marry you."

"That's what you said." As he was unbuttoning her shirtwaist. She wanted more from a relationship than just passion—*lust*, her father had called it. Was Zachary capable of a deeper kind of love?

Before she could form a reply, a flurry of activity near the door shifted her attention to a girl huffing out words to the waitress. A lit kerosene lantern hung at her side. When the girl rushed toward her, Darla recognized the white medical bag swinging at her side.

"Jocelyn!" What was she doing out this time of night? Darla's insides clenched. "Your father?"

The girl nodded feverishly, struggling to get her breath. "He's real sick."

Darla snatched her reticule from the seat beside her and jumped up from her chair.

"He's burning up with fever," Jocelyn said, her eyes glistening. "I went to the boardinghouse, but you weren't there."

Darla gave Zachary a backward glance. "I'm sorry, but I must go."

She didn't wait for a reply before cradling Jocelyn's hand and dashing toward the door, a frantic prayer rising inside her.

Chapter Eight

Darla's breath came in fits and starts as she and Jocelyn sprinted, her in heeled shoes, across Bennett Avenue, up the hill, then down to Galena. Darla had taken her medical bag from Jocelyn, but neither of them had spoken since leaving the café. Even if she could manage the breath to speak, there was nothing to say. If Nicolas had a fever, he had an infection. It wasn't good, and she didn't wish to give those words life.

Nicolas's oldest daughter made it onto the stoop first and flung the door open. Darla followed her inside, squinting in the lantern light. The cot was empty.

"Papa's in his bed." Jocelyn pointed to the open door on the left. "I'll close the front door and turn on more light."

Darla rushed into the bedchamber, willing her breath to even out. She set her bag atop the bureau beside the bed and unlatched it. Nicolas lay motionless on his stomach, the bandages on his back exposed.

A bulb hanging in the center of the room flicked on, revealing streaks on the cloth binding his bandages and a deep coloring on his face. He hadn't responded in the least to the light, but his back rose and fell in slow respirations.

Thank You, God.

"Nicolas. It's Darla."

Nothing.

Jocelyn whimpered beside her. "I heard Papa groaning and came in to check on him. He was mumbling. His face. . .it was so red. I knew he had fever, so I pulled the blanket off him. All else I knew to do was to go get you."

"You did the right thing." Darla patted the girl's sagging shoulder. "And don't you worry. There's a great deal we can do." Even as she heard her words, she knew she'd said it to reassure herself as much as Jocelyn.

"I can help." Jocelyn's shoulders squared.

"Good." Darla looked around for a washstand. "I'll need hot water and soap to wash my hands."

"There's water on the stove. I'll put some in the basin for you."

She followed Jocelyn to the kitchen. "I'll need lots of clean cloth or towels. All of them wet. Some real hot. Some cold. I need the hot ones first."

"And an apron."

"Yes." She was so rattled seeing Nicolas like that, she'd forgotten she was wearing an evening dress. "Thank you."

Her hands clean, Darla took a gingham apron from Jocelyn and tied it over her gown before returning to Nicolas's side.

"Nicolas, it's Darla. You're sick, and I need to remove your bandages."

When he offered no help, she tipped him to one side to push the wrapping through beneath him, then tilted him the other way. Like her grandmother was fond of saying, "*Where there's a will, there's a way.*" While she unwrapped the cloth that bound his bandages, heat radiated from his back.

"When I'm done, I'll take a look. But I suspect cracks in the scabbing is the culprit here." When the wrapping cloth lay in a heap on the floor, she carefully peeled the bandages from his back and added them to the pile. Yellow puss oozed from a crack just to the right of his spine. "Yes. We're dealing with infection. But don't you worry, Jocelyn and I are going to beat it. And you're going to help us."

Jocelyn took slow steps toward her, balancing a roasting pan full of steaming hot dish towels. "Papa's awake?"

"Not yet."

The girl set the pan atop the bureau beside the medical bag. "But he can hear you?"

"I'd like to think so." Darla pulled the first steaming towel from the roaster and laid it the length of the split in the scabs, earning a squirm from her patient. Likely involuntary movement but heartening all the same.

"I've been praying." Jocelyn's admission came out on a quiver.

"I have, too." Darla added another sweltering compress. "And we won't stop."

"The towels will help?"

"Yes." As long as she was hoping for the best, she'd start with the hot towels. "We'll use them to soften the scab and draw the infection out of his body. The cold ones we'll lay on his face and legs to fight the fever."

In the three hours that followed, Jocelyn proved to be a capable aide. They'd repeated the procedure with the hot compresses and cold towels time and again. When the fever broke and Darla laid clean bandages across Nicolas's back, Jocelyn refused to go to her bed but laid out a pallet on the floor and fell fast asleep.

Darla pulled a rocker from the main room and sank into it with a patchwork quilt. Pulling the quilt to her shoulders, she rested her head against the chair. All that was left to do was to continue to pray. And wait.

———◆———

Nicolas blinked. The sun entered his bedchamber through a narrow opening between the curtains. At the corner of his bureau, just three feet from his bed, a woman slept in his rocker. Was he dreaming?

He blinked again. Her head resting on a balled-up corner of his mama's quilt, Darla Taggart was sleep-breathing, wearing an evening gown and Maria's gingham apron. His mind fuzzy, he struggled to remember what had happened.

He'd managed to get himself to bed, but the pain. . .Jocelyn came in and said he was sick. That was the last thing he'd heard until the other voice called his name. "*There's a great deal we can do.*"

No, he hadn't been dreaming. He remembered compresses on his back and explanations whispered in his ear. A prayer prayed over him. He reached up and removed a lukewarm cloth from his cheek. Darla had been there taking care of him, bringing him back to life.

Jocelyn popped up from a pallet and knelt between him and the chair, her eyes ringed with redness. "You're awake." Joy floated on her whisper.

"Yes. And I feel better." He patted her face, then pointed to the rocker.

"She came and stayed all night. You had an infection." His daughter's shoulders rose and fell. "I didn't know what to do but to get Miss Darla."

He nodded. "Sunday night? She was out to supper."

"Yes." Her dark eyebrows pinched. "But she said I did the right thing coming to get her."

"You did." There was no need to ask whom she was with at the restaurant. Zach had staked a claim on Darla, inviting her to supper in front of him, and she'd accepted.

It shouldn't matter, but it did.

"Nicolas?" Darla stirred, pulling the quilt off. "You're awake." Her smile rivaled the sunlight filtering into the room. She draped the quilt over the rocker and joined Jocelyn at his bedside. "Thank God, you're all right."

"Yes, and thank you. Jocelyn tells me you were here all night."

She nodded, reaching up to cover a yawn. "Jocelyn and I worked together. She's the best helper a nurse could ask for."

"I like your new uniform." He glanced at the soiled apron. "I doubt those fancy New York designers would think to pair gingham with chiffon."

She dipped her chin and peered up at him. "Your good humor is back. You're feeling better."

He drew in a deep breath and blew it out, wishing he'd been the one who had taken her out to supper.

"We need to get some water in you. Maybe some oatmeal. And then I'd like to check your back and the bandages one more time before I leave."

He nodded. He'd let her treat him this morning, but she'd obviously given her heart to Zach years ago, and this should be the last time he let her touch him. Even in a professional capacity.

For both their sakes.

Chapter Nine

Lord God, we are most grateful to you for sparing that dear father's life again." Hattie's voice cracked, echoing the sentiment quaking Darla's insides. "Thank You, Lord, for gifting our Darla with good training."

Our Darla.

"And for bringing her back to save Nicolas."

For bringing her back. Apparently, Hattie believed God had a part in bringing her here. Not the diary or the cameo pendant. Not Zachary. Not her need for forgiveness. Not even her desperation to understand and resolve her past behaviors. Had God truly brought her here?

Her head still bowed, Darla wiped a tear from her cheek before it could spot her uniform.

It did seem that God had redeemed her misguided notions about Nicolas and his little girls when she'd met them in that one-room cabin in Poverty Gulch. Returning had given her a chance to get to know the Zanzucchi family, and in so doing, to better know herself. She didn't feel like her past with Zachary had been resolved or those questions answered, but thanks to her time caring for others, she now had a better idea of what she wanted.

"Amen." Hattie's benediction brought Darla back to the prayer just in time to join the chorus of *amen* that followed.

Even though the question of God's true purpose for bringing her back to Cripple Creek still hung in the air unanswered, the *amen* certainly was a fitting closure to her prayers for Nicolas, and Jocelyn's prayers for her ailing papa. God had answered them. Yesterday morning Nicolas had eaten a bowl of oatmeal and drunk a cup of coffee. She'd left satisfied that they'd beaten the infection and he was on the mend.

"Dear, would you start the egg mess on its journey?" Hattie nodded toward the bowl of scrambled eggs parked in front of Darla.

"Yes, of course." She scooped eggs into the serving spoon, taking care to include generous portions of bell peppers, onions, and diced ham in her *mess*. She looked forward to these hearty morning meals. And couldn't help but wonder if Nicolas and the girls would enjoy egg mess.

"I'll happily take the first two or three biscuits." Mr. Sinclair set one steaming biscuit on his breakfast plate, then another.

Hattie's smile reached the crinkles that framed her blue-gray eyes. "Don't forget to share, Mister."

"Oh, I'll share." He winked. "Eventually."

As Darla passed the bowl of eggs to Cherise and took the plate of potato cakes from Hattie, she couldn't help but pray for the kind of love Hattie and Harlan Sinclair shared.

"Are you all right, dear?" Hattie covered her hand like a mother hen would shelter her chick with a wing.

"Yes, ma'am. I feel better than I have in a very long time." Darla patted the knobby hand resting atop hers and met Hattie's tender gaze. "Thank you."

"We love having you here." Hattie reached for the bread basket. "You will see Nicolas and the girls today?"

"Yes." Darla stopped her fork midair. "I'll go check on Rose and her baby, then see Mrs. Baxter. From there, I'll go to the Zanzucchis' home." Those visits always required more time, or at least, they'd earned more time. Visiting Nicolas and his girls gave her something to look forward to at the end of her workday.

She'd scooped the last bite of potato cake into her mouth when the new doorbell rang, and Mr. Sinclair rose to answer it. She'd barely had time for a sip of tea before he returned.

"You have a caller, Miss Taggart."

"I do?" She set her teacup in the saucer. Perhaps Dr. Cutshaw had someone to add to her list of home visits.

"It's Mr. Zachary Pfeiffer."

"Oh." She wiped her mouth with her napkin and stood. "I'm afraid

I left our supper quite abruptly the other evening."

"I told Mr. Pfeiffer you'd meet with him in the parlor. Is that agreeable?"

"Yes, thank you." Standing, she glanced at Cherise and Hattie. "Please excuse me."

When Darla walked into the parlor, Zachary stood in front of the hearth, looking at a small marble bust of President Lincoln from the mantel. He'd traded in the suit for a clean pair of bib-and-brace overalls.

"Good morning," she said, walking to the back of the settee. Since their supper on Sunday had been cut short, she needed more time with him in order to determine if there was more to her feelings for him than infatuation and regret; more to his interest in her than physical attraction. Since she didn't have time for all of that this morning before work, determining the true nature of their relationship would have to wait. Perhaps he was there to arrange another supper.

Zachary returned the memento to the mantel and faced her, his eyes widening. "You weren't wearing that the other day."

She'd not pinned on the hat yet, but the rest of her uniform was in place, including her white button-up boots. "No. But I did tell you I'm a nurse."

"Yes." He lifted one eyebrow. "A nurse who makes house calls in day dresses and stays for supper. I remember."

Her shoulders tensed. He'd seemed happy to see her Saturday. Now he was upset because he'd found her visiting the Zanzucchis? Her mouth suddenly dry, she moistened her lips. Whom she chose to share supper with was her business. But she *had* abandoned him in the restaurant night before last. He had a right to be disappointed that their reunion had ended so abruptly. He deserved the benefit of the doubt.

"I'm sorry I had to dash out of the café Sunday night."

"And dash off, you did."

"Nicolas is my patient, and he was gravely ill."

Zachary took a slow step toward the settee. "Everything is all right, then? At the Zanzucchi house?"

"Yes. Thank you."

"I'd hoped to hear from you." Zachary shifted his weight from one leg to the other. "If not that evening, certainly yesterday."

"I should've telephoned or sent a message, but I was up most all night Sunday, and I was tired."

"You were at his house all night?" His volume had increased with each word.

She pinched the oak frame on the back of the settee. "When one of my patients is sick and needs me, I'm on duty."

"Of course." His posture softening, he strolled around the settee. Stopping directly in front of her, he brushed her cheek.

His touch made her flinch.

"And if I needed you? You'd be in a big hurry to get to me?"

"I've changed." And it didn't seem he had. They'd passed notes before or after church. Met secretly. Kissed. Touched. Conversing had never interested him. That didn't seem to have changed. It was doubtful that marriage was truly on his mind then or now. "Zachary, the things I want in life have changed."

"I find it hard to believe that *everything* has changed." Threading their fingers, he drew her in closer.

She was pulling away to escape his kiss when her landlady sauntered in carrying a silver tray with two steaming teacups.

"I brought tea before you have to rush off to work." Hattie set the tray on the table in front of the settee.

Zachary gave the bib on his overalls a tug and looked Darla in the eye. "You know what I want. And it isn't tea."

"I can offer you tea and conversation." She looked down at their clasped hands. "Nothing more."

He let go and glared at her. "You're saying that now you're too good for me?"

"I'm saying that was then, and this is now."

Hattie cleared her throat. Her hands balled at her hips, she pinned Zachary with a steely gaze. "You heard her. Need I fetch Mr. Sinclair?"

He huffed. "I was just leaving."

Hattie's nod was sharp. "You will show yourself out, then?"

Shoving his hands into his pockets, he spun toward the entryway. The thud of the front door released Darla's tears.

How could she have been so naive? Zachary was not what she wanted. *Who* she wanted.

Hattie embraced her, then walked her to the settee and pulled a handkerchief from her skirt pocket. "A cup of tea will help." When they'd sat down, Hattie lifted a cup from the tray and took a sip. "Mmmm. One lump of sugar and a dash of cream. Just the way I like it." A grin added a twinkle to her blue-gray eyes.

"Just the way I like it." Her landlady hadn't brought that second teacup in for Zachary. Her friend likely knew more than she'd let on about their relationship four years ago and had come in to chase him off, to liberate her from the past as much as to free her from Zachary's present notion that nothing needed to change.

Darla patted her eyes dry and smiled. "Thank you." She could see why the Sinclair sisters liked lodging at Miss Hattie's Boardinghouse. Having a mother hen *did* come in handy.

Breathing in the fresh air and feeling the warmth of the morning sun through the thin blanket helped some. Jocelyn and Jaya had carried his cot out while Julia made sure his steps toward the door matched hers—small, slow, and careful. The infection and fever had left him feeling weak, but the pain had diminished significantly, and he was gaining strength, little by little. Quite the wonder that sixty hours earlier he'd been in a fever crisis with a nurse camped at his bedside, fighting for his life.

And not just any nurse. Darla Taggart, dressed in a fine gown. She'd given up her supper out to don an old apron and deal with open wounds and puss.

Seeing her nestled in his mother's quilt, asleep in the rocker he'd made, had added to the longing. The same notions he'd experienced watching her play checkers with the girls and having her seated across the supper table from him—before Zach showed up and her breath caught at the mere mention of his name.

Nicolas sighed. He couldn't afford to feel something more for her, and that meant he couldn't have her so close. It wasn't just his heart at stake, and he didn't want his girls to believe she could be more to them than his nurse and their friend. He couldn't continue to allow Darla to endear herself to him or to his daughters. Not when her romantic attentions were clearly focused on Zach. She had a history with him, and what woman wouldn't prefer a man who didn't have a ready-made family? A man who could do something besides lie on a cot.

Raising his head, he glanced toward the dirt street in front of company housing. The matter should be settled by now, and Jocelyn should return from the hospital soon.

Jaya looked up from the grid where she played hopscotch with Julia. "Is Miss Darla coming today?"

He drew in a deep breath. "Dr. Cutshaw will send someone else to tend to me."

"But I wanted to show her the dog you made." Julia's bottom lip stuck out past her button nose.

"She has other patients to see."

"She liked the bird," Jaya said.

He remembered their conversation about the phoenix above the door. The awe that lit her green eyes at the sight of it, and the admiration that followed when she learned he'd carved it and why.

Jaya left her game and joined him at the cot. "Miss Darla wanted to see what else you made."

Yes, she'd said she wanted to look through the trunk full of carvings after supper that day. The day things changed.

Julia pressed her little hands to his arm. "She can see 'em when she comes to play checkers."

"Yes." Jaya nodded. "Or when she comes to teach Jocelyn how to cook French food."

He'd forgotten about the French cooking lesson. He needed to tell them. Nicolas raised up on his elbows. "Miss Darla won't be coming here anymore."

"But I thought she liked us." Jaya bit her bottom lip.

"She does." They'd already given their hearts to her. He'd seen it on Jocelyn's face when he'd given her the message for Dr. Cutshaw. He reached out and cupped Jaya's cheek. "Miss Darla does like you. She enjoys your company—all of you girls—but she has a job and work to do elsewhere." *And someone else to eat supper with.*

The frowns on their faces made his heart ache. They all needed a distraction.

"Let's go inside and have one of the scones Mrs. Nell brought us." He slid his left leg off the cot and eased into a standing position. "I can sit in my chair until Jocelyn returns and can help with the cot."

He wrapped the blanket around his shoulders and accepted a helping hand from Jaya and Julia.

They were nearly to the stoop when he heard footfalls behind them. He glanced over his shoulder, expecting to see Jocelyn. Instead, a nurse wearing white from head to toe smiled at him. Her white medical bag swung at her side as she approached the cot.

"What a good idea to spend some time outside today! It's lovely out."

He nodded. Neither the weather nor any of God's breathtaking landscapes could be as lovely as her. Backlit by the sun, her chestnut curls glowed like a dawn.

"Mith Darla!" Julia ran to hug the nurse's leg, seeming to forget she was needed to help him.

"You're here!" Jaya's voice rose.

"I am here. And it looks like my patient is faring well."

"Much better," he said. "Thanks to you."

She awarded him with a smile, then looked around. "Is Jocelyn inside?"

"I sent her on an errand. She should be back soon."

Darla looked at Jaya and Julia, then met his gaze. "Do you need my help getting up the steps?"

"No." The flutter of her eyelashes told him he'd spoken too abruptly. "Thank you. But we can manage." She wasn't supposed to be here, and now he would have to tell her so. But how?

Julia dashed back to him and grabbed his hand.

"All right. The least I can do is help with the cot." Darla tipped the metal contraption on its side and folded the legs.

"Thank you." At the top of the steps, he pushed the door wide open with his foot and stepped inside, one daughter leading, one following.

Julia held the door open with her free hand. "Papa said you wouldn't be coming anymore."

"What?" Darla stopped just shy of the doorway, not two feet from him.

The question of how he would tell her had been decided for him. He braced himself on the armchair.

"You told them I wouldn't be coming to your home anymore?"

Jaya nodded. "He said someone else would tend to him."

"Someone else?" She set the edge of the cot across the threshold and looked up at him. "Is that true?"

"Girls, now would be a good time for you to work on your school lessons," Nicolas said, his shoulders tensing. "In your room."

Jaya tugged Julia's dress sleeve and pulled her toward the bedroom the girls shared.

While his resolve battled his feelings, Nicolas drew in a deep breath. "It's true. I sent Jocelyn to the hospital this morning with a note for Dr. Cutshaw, asking him to find a replacement."

"But why? I thought we were getting along well." Darla's voice caught. "Did I do something wrong?"

He leaned forward. "You spent the night here."

She jerked herself upright. "You're questioning my virtue?"

"That's not it."

"Then what *are* you talking about? I am your nurse." She pointed at her uniform. "It was *my job* to see to your medical needs."

"Yes. But it wasn't your job to tend to me during your off hours." Wincing, he lowered himself into the chair. "Not while you were dressed like a princess and out with a man you care for."

Her mouth dropped open. "With a man I care for?" Darla carried the cot inside and set it up with abrupt movements. "None of this should surprise me." Her steps heavy, she returned to the doorway and faced him. "You don't approve of me having supper with Zachary. As if you, or he, have attained some sort of ownership of me."

Nicolas fought a twinge of remorse. It was true that he didn't like the fact, but his decision was based upon release, not upon a sense of ownership. "I doubt Zach was pleased that you rushed off, that you stayed the night here."

"Papa? Miss Darla?"

Nicolas looked at the doorway, where Jocelyn stood at the bottom of the steps, her eyes wide.

Darla turned her back to him. "I didn't hear you, Jocelyn. Did you deliver your father's message to Dr. Cutshaw?"

"Yes, ma'am."

Darla stepped aside, letting the girl past. "Did the doctor respond?"

"He did. That's what took me so long." Jocelyn handed a folded piece of paper to Nicolas. "He asked me to wait while he wrote you a reply." She looked at Darla. "He said he would send another nurse out later this afternoon."

"Then I'd say it's settled. I'm no longer needed here." Darla dipped her chin and rushed out the door.

Her hasty descent down the steps made Nicolas wish he could follow her and tell her not to pursue a relationship with anyone else, least of all Zach. But he had no right to do so.

———————◆———————

Nothing was settled. Tears streamed Darla's face as she practically ran away from the company house on Galena. Just about everything was less settled than it had been when she'd stepped off the train in Cripple Creek.

How could she have been so gullible? Still? Had she not learned anything about men in the past four years?

Zachary had left the boardinghouse that morning in a disrespectful huff because he didn't get his way. She had to have been wearing blinders to think she'd seen a future in what they'd once shared. A kiss. A touch. Mere physical attraction. Well, his flattery might have been enough in her teenage years, but she was no longer the girl who swooned at a man's notice. She wanted more. Love. Commitment. A relationship that ran deep.

A barrage of images flashed in her memory. Nicolas. The contentment on his face watching her play checkers with his girls. Sitting across the supper table from him. Waking up in the rocker to the sound of his voice. Seeing him outside walking toward the stoop. He'd endeared himself to her with his quick wit, grace in the shadow of sorrow, strength in the midst of pain, tenderness toward his dear daughters, and attentiveness to her. She'd allowed herself daydreams about the possibility that he could see her as more than his nurse. That he could care for her.

But everything had changed the day her past showed up at the company house with a load of coal. Nicolas apparently knew Zachary's reputation as a lothario. And because of her association—past and present—with him, Nicolas had decided she wasn't a suitable companion for his daughters, let alone someone he could ever care for in a romantic sense.

He'd told Jaya and Julia she wasn't coming back, making it crystal clear he meant to break all ties with her. If they'd had any chance for a deeper relationship, it was gone.

Darla stopped at Golden Avenue to catch her breath. She pulled Hattie's handkerchief from the pocket in her uniform skirt and blotted her face. After the way she and Hattie had dismissed Zachary that morning, she didn't expect him to come around anymore. And now she didn't have to waste any energy pondering how Nicolas felt about her. Saturday, she'd have her chance to retrieve what she'd squirreled away under the parsonage kitchen and put some of her shame where it belonged—in flames.

If only she could still see herself rising out of the ashes like the triumphant phoenix Nicolas had carved.

Chapter Ten

Just after eleven o'clock on Saturday, Darla stood three blocks away, watching the gravel walkway between the church and the parsonage, and pressed the carpetbag of tools to her side. The day of Mrs. Wahlberg's luncheon had finally arrived.

Within the hour, she'd have the diary in which she'd recorded her flights of fancy along with the schemes and the lies she told while trying to win Morgan Cutshaw's heart from Kat Sinclair. Not long after that, she'd recorded her impure feelings and lurid thoughts toward Zachary. She would also hold in her hand the cameo her grandmother had bequeathed her, the heirloom she hoped to wear on her wedding day.

After this week, a wedding day seemed an irrational and distant dream. The only man she could see herself with had fired her.

Movement outside the kitchen door of the church returned Darla's attention to the present and quickened her pulse. Was she ready? Could she really sneak into someone's home and take up a floorboard? Someone she'd met and liked. Someone who had invited her in, and offered to show her the place.

She was only reclaiming what was hers.

Ida's husband stepped out of the shadows and walked to the house. It wasn't time yet. Darla drew in a deep breath, willing herself to calm down.

Three long days had passed since she'd last seen Nicolas, Jocelyn, Jaya, or Julia. Sitting in the rocker at his bedside that night, she'd actually wondered if maybe God had brought her back to Cripple Creek to find true love with Nicolas. Apparently not.

Ten minutes later, Reverend Raines strolled the gravel walkway past

Mother's roses and out to the street with Ida at his side, pushing a red pram. Darla moved closer to the church property, watching the parson and his wife walk down First Street with their baby son. Satisfied they were well on their way to the luncheon and no one was watching her, she took quick steps across the side yard and onto the porch.

She pressed her shaking hand to the knob. She hadn't thought about what she'd do if the door wasn't open. Aunt Cora and her neighbors in Philadelphia had started locking up their homes. But the knob turned freely, and she pushed the door open. Fortunately, the folks in Cripple Creek hadn't yet adopted the habit.

Darla hurried inside and clicked the door shut behind her. She thought to indulge herself with a quick look at the parlor and the other rooms she'd occupied most of her growing-up years, but not knowing how long her task would require, she didn't dare take the time. This was her chance to seize her past and put it behind her.

The entryway led to the dining room, past the furniture her father didn't want to haul to New York. The walls in the small kitchen wore a new coat of pale yellow paint. But it was the flooring that captured her attention. The new parson and his wife hadn't given in to the linoleum craze. Not only had the door not been locked and the flooring unchanged, but the board she'd buried her diary and the pendant under was still free of furniture.

A mixed sense of reverence and fear fueled her steps toward the corner between the sideboard and the wall. Kneeling in the corner, she pulled the claw hammer and the pry bar out of her bag. Hopefully, she wouldn't need the latter. She bent over the board with the claw hammer and started to lift.

"Stop where you are!"

Jerking around, Darla dropped the hammer and raised her hands like the hooligans did in dime novels. "Ida."

Her boss's sister-in-law stood near the icebox, brandishing a closed parasol as if it were a cudgel. "You're the one making all that noise?"

Darla nodded, searching for any words that could adequately explain her actions.

"I'd forgotten to get this." Ida lowered the parasol to her side but didn't take her gaze from Darla. "I heard strange sounds but didn't, for the life of me, expect to find someone squatting in the corner of my kitchen."

"I'm sorry." Darla stood, smoothing her gray walking skirt. "I didn't mean to—"

"I said you could come by for a look at the place, but. . ." Ida glanced from the bag on the floor to the hammer and the cockeyed board. "What are you doing?"

"When my family lived here, just days before I went to live in Philadelphia, I hid two things under a floorboard." Darla pointed to the corner. "I didn't think about my family one day moving out of the parsonage."

"When we met the other day, why didn't you tell me about this? I would've given you permission."

"I should've, but—"

"I would've been nosey." A smile warmed Ida's blue eyes.

Darla released a sigh of relief. "It's my diary and a cameo pendant my grandmother gave me."

"Those are personal items. No wonder you kept quiet." Ida walked over to the corner. "Did you find them?"

"Not yet. I was just starting to pull up the board. It seems there might be new nails in it."

Ida knelt on the floor in her luncheon gown and set the parasol down. "We'd better see to it, then." She picked up the pry bar and caught a corner of the board, enough for Darla to get under it with the hammer. The nails slowly surrendered, and the board peeled back.

Darla drew in a deep breath and reached down into the darkness. Nothing but dirt and cobwebs. "They're not here." She wiped the webs on her skirt.

Groaning, Ida bent over the hole. "This is where you buried them?"

"I'm sure of it."

Ida shrugged. "I suppose my husband might know something about it."

Darla's stomach clenched.

"I'll ask him. Another time." Ida stood and glanced up at the wall clock. "Right now, I'd best go before he comes looking for me. I left him and the baby at the corner."

"Mrs. Wahlberg will never let you hear the end of it if you're late for her luncheon."

"You know her well." Nodding, Ida pulled her parasol from the floor. "You'll fix the board before you leave?"

"Yes. And thank you." Darla rose to her feet and gave Ida a hug before the gracious woman dashed out of the kitchen.

Darla sank to her knees. Now what?

Hattie believed God had a part in bringing her back to Cripple Creek. If that was the case, His plan didn't coincide in the least with hers.

Chapter Eleven

Ten days without having seen Darla Taggart had proven to be a challenge. Now it was day eleven. Friday. Nicolas glanced up at the wall clock, counting pencil taps. Twenty taps in the last ten seconds.

The replacement nurse looked up, her pencil pausing in midair. "Dr. Cutshaw is pleased with your progress, Mr. Zanzucchi." She perched on the rocker, her sturdy black shoes barely touching the linoleum. "Now that the majority of the scabbing is gone, so is the risk of infection."

Nodding, Nicolas couldn't help but be distracted by the wrinkles in the woman's faded white uniform. Mrs. Alexander had visited three times in the past nine days. She wasn't sweet by any stretch of his imagination, but neither was she severe. Competent enough but not very engaging. And she'd made it clear the first day that she wasn't there to visit with his girls.

She wasn't someone Julia would mistake for an angel.

She wasn't Darla.

That shouldn't surprise him. He'd never met a woman like Darla. And he'd had the privilege of glimpsing the before and after. The impudent teenager who couldn't wait to leave the Gulch and the compassionate grown woman who played checkers, noticed his carvings, and looked as if she belonged in the rocking chair snuggled beneath the patchwork quilt.

The woman he'd pushed away.

Mrs. Alexander's all-too-familiar throat clearing dragged his gaze to the permanent frown on her face. "From the looks of things"—she glanced from his shirt collar to his pull-on boots—"it seems you're returning to your daily life."

"Yes, ma'am." This was his chance to prove that he no longer required her services. "I've been up and about doing light chores every day for the past week." He glanced at the kitchen table, where the girls were seeing to their studies. "We all walked to the school yesterday." Julia looked up, giving him a missing-tooth smile. "And come Sunday, we'll be going back to church."

Still smiling, his youngest daughter nodded.

"Very well." Mrs. Alexander added notes to her paperwork. "Then it's only a matter of days before you can resume your full duties in the mine."

He squirmed on his spindle chair, straightening his legs, then bending them again. For six weeks, he'd been incapable of doing any more than lie around and need care. He was more than ready to resume his role as a healthy father and neighbor. But was he ready to return to the mine? The darkness, the heat, the constant danger?

Could he return?

The pencil tapping resumed, a miniature steam drill pounding at his temples. He'd only taken the job at the mine because, at the time, it was work readily available to Italian immigrants and he had a family and another baby on the way.

"Did you hear me, Mr. Zanzucchi?"

Nicolas straightened and pressed his shoes to the floor. "I apologize. I seem to have much on my mind distracting me, ma'am."

"Indeed." She sighed, her slate-gray eyes narrowing. "It might put your mind at ease to know that you'll soon be earning your full wage again. I'm signing off on your rehabilitation." She scribbled what he guessed was her signature, then looked up at him. "I expect Dr. Cutshaw will clear you to return to work on Thursday."

"This coming Thursday?" He had only five more days aboveground?

"Yes. I will send notification to Mr. Gortner at the mine." She gripped the chair arm and pushed herself into a standing position. "If you'll excuse me, I'll take my leave."

"Of course." He followed her to the door and held it open for her. "Thank you. Please pass my greetings on to Henri."

Mrs. Alexander glanced back at the table where the girls watched with wide eyes. "The best of luck to you and your family."

Luck had nothing to do with it. He stood on the stoop enjoying a breath of fresh air, watching his replacement nurse walk out to the road. It had been God's grace that had seen him and his girls through losing Maria, the accident at the mine, the infection. . .all of it. And it would only be the grace of God that could power his next steps.

Nicolas turned toward the sound of wheels grinding the rocky spring soil. The coal wagon rolled toward his house with Zach in the driver's seat.

Zach brought the horses to a stop in front of him and glanced up the road at Mrs. Alexander. "Your new nurse?" He swung out of the seat and down the wheel.

"She was."

Letting out a low whistle, Zach lifted the wheelbarrow from its hooks. "Your decision? Or Darla's?"

"And why is that your concern?"

"Because we're friends," Zach said.

Nicolas watched him unload a few shovels full of coal into the barrow. "My decision."

Zach shook his head. "Then you're not as smart as I thought."

Something they agreed on. He met Zach at the coal chute and lifted the door with his boot. "You and Darla?"

"After she finished high school, we talked about getting married. Then she moved away." Zach dumped the load of coal through the chute. "But anything we shared got lost in the growing up. You were right—she's changed."

Nobody had to convince Nicolas of that. He'd seen it for himself.

"And given the choice, Zanzucchi, she'd choose you."

Nicolas chuffed out a breath. He'd sent her away, and she'd left with nary a word. *Then I'd say it's settled. I'm no longer needed here.*

He'd never felt so unsettled as he had watching her leave that day. She was needed. He needed her, and not as his nurse. Perhaps it was time he gave her the choice Zach talked about.

When Zach drove off, Nicolas turned back toward the house. All three of his daughters stood on the stoop, their armed crossed.

"We want to talk to you." Jocelyn and Jaya spoke in chorus.

"And me, too." A curl danced above Julia's brown eyes.

Nodding, Nicolas made his way into the sitting room and slid onto the rocker. "I'm listening."

Seated on the sofa across from him, Jaya and Julia both looked at Jocelyn. It seemed the role of spokesman fell to the oldest. Jocelyn lifted her chin. "We think you made a big mistake."

Nicolas drew in a deep breath and let it out. "I think I did, too."

"You do?" Sunlight played across the freckles on Jaya's nose.

"Yes, I do."

Surprise creased Jocelyn's brow. "We're talking about Miss Darla."

"That's who I'm talking about."

"You've been sad ever since she left."

He nodded. "Yes. I have."

Julia's little shoulders slumped. "We have, too."

"Papa." Jaya straightened. "We like Miss Darla."

"I like her, too." Admittedly there was more to his feelings than that, but before divulging them, he'd have to find out if there was even a chance she would speak to him.

———————◆———————

Darla ran her fingers across the embroidered cotton mull. She and Mother used to stitch, but she hadn't sewn since starting her nurse's training. If she did take up stitching again, it would be fun to sew dresses for little girls. Her fingers strayed to the next bolt. The solid blue chambray would make a nice shirt for Nicolas.

She sighed. It would only be fun if the man were speaking to her. Since ten days had passed without a word from him, that didn't seem likely.

She slipped her hand into the pocket of her afternoon dress. It was high time she thought of something else. *Someone else.*

"Miss?"

Startled by the gruff voice, Darla spun around, nearly colliding with the beak-nosed owner of the dry goods store.

"Did you want me to cut some fabric for you?"

"Yes, please." Darla let her fingertips touch the various fabrics she'd admired. "I'd like three yards of this cotton mull with the yellow embroidery. Three yards of the green plaid. Three yards of the blue calico." She pointed to the bolt directly in front of her. "And two yards of the chambray beside it."

Her purchases made, she continued walking up Bennett Avenue, slowing her steps in front of Russell's Grocery and Produce. Clutching her paper-wrapped bundle of fabric, she wandered from the barrel of carrots to a gunnysack of yellow onions, then past trays of mushrooms and garlic. Cherise had shared her grandmother's recipe for chicken fricassee. But for the same reasons Darla didn't need the fabric she'd purchased, she had no need of groceries for a French cooking lesson. This time, she'd resist the temptation. The material she could use for other purposes. But living at the boardinghouse, she had no cause to cook. Not when Hattie and Cherise did such a fine job of it.

Since she had nothing better to do on her day off, she decided to stroll down to First Street, then make a loop up to Golden on her way back to the boardinghouse.

The small building that had belonged to the clock maker was devoid of any signs, so she stepped up to the windows. The shop was empty. What a shame. It would make a good workshop and store for another craftsman. A photographer. A silversmith. A cobbler.

Or…an artist who made wainscoting and rocking chairs and carved trinkets his daughters enjoyed and bas reliefs that captured her imagination. The empty shop would be perfect for Nicolas.

If he didn't want to return to the mine. If he was interested in making a business out of his whittling. He was a courageous man. Something she'd seen in those first several visits in his home.

Darla shook her head. She probably needed to see to her own business before sticking her nose into someone else's. Someone who had dismissed her. Her diary wasn't where she'd left it, and the contents could turn up when and where she least expected, claiming her job and the place she was building for herself in Cripple Creek.

While her thoughts collided with one another, she stepped away from the building and turned to continue on her way.

"Miss Taggart!"

She turned back toward the center of town, where a young man waved from the corner. It was the postmaster's son, Archie. Perhaps a letter from Mother or Aunt Cora awaited her? The teenage boy rushed toward her with one hand hidden behind him.

"My father said he'd seen you walking west on Bennett."

Cripple Creek was still a small town if the postmaster could track one's moves on a busy street. "You were looking for me?"

"Yes, ma'am. My father received a message for you. And a gift."

"He did?"

A grin bunched the freckles across his cheeks as he presented his other hand like a platform, holding a small cloth sack and a folded slip of paper.

Who would be sending her a gift? Perhaps Zachary had second thoughts about his behavior in Hattie's parlor.

"They came from Nicolas Zanzucchi."

Her heart skipped a beat at the sound of his name. "They did?"

"Well, his girl Jocelyn delivered them to the post office. But she made us promise to make sure you understood the note and the present were from her papa."

Darla squeezed her eyes shut for a second to reject unbidden tears, then leaned over his hand and pulled the drawstring sack open. Her breath caught, a breath sweetened by the scent of several chocolates. Creams. Truffles. Mint patties. The teenager appeared as light-headed over the gesture as she felt. "These are from Rosa's Confectionary. You're sure they're meant for me? From Mr. Zanzucchi?"

Archie nodded, slowly and deliberately. "I think he's sweet on you."

She might have used the note to fan herself except that she wanted to maintain the appearance of composure, even though her insides were doing flips. Smiling, Darla reached into her leather pocketbook for a coin for Archie and tucked the sack of candy into her skirt pocket. "I suppose I should read the note and see what is necessary." She unfolded the page and began reading, silently:

Dear Miss Taggart,
    Should you refuse my request, I would not hold it against you. I have done nothing to deserve your audience. But I would ask for

another chance to earn that right.

If you see fit to allow me to redeem myself, please come to see us at your earliest convenience.

No matter your decision, please accept this sweet token of my remorse.

Nicolas was sorry for thinking the worst of her. . .for sending her away. No, he was remorseful. He'd missed her, too, she was sure of it.

Darla blinked. Two words had been erased from the end of the sentence. She held up the paper for a closer look. *"And affection."*

"Yep, he's sweet on you, all right," Archie said.

Oh dear, she'd read that last part aloud.

She nodded, then pressed her lips together and returned her gaze to the page.

With all sincerity,
Nicolas Zanzucchi

When she heard herself sigh, she folded the note and pressed it into her pocketbook. She handed the coin to Archie.

"Thank you." He reached up and slid it into his shirt pocket. "Did you need me to deliver a response to Mr. Zanzucchi?"

"No. Thank you." She'd see to it herself.

The boardinghouse could wait. She needed to return to Russell's Grocery and Produce.

Chapter Twelve

"Papa, do you think Miss Darla will come?"

Nicolas crowned his first king, then looked across the checkerboard at Jaya. "I hope so."

Julia bounced onto her tiptoes beside the table where he and Jaya played checkers. "We really want her to come."

He'd wanted to deliver the note and sweets to Darla personally but thought it best to leave the choice to see him up to her.

"She will come. You'll see." If only he shared Jaya's childhood confidence.

"If she does come, who is going to open the door?" he asked.

"You are." Julia pointed at him.

"That's right." He captured her finger, rewarded with a little-girl giggle.

"We won't forget." Broom in hand, Jocelyn bent and pressed the dustpan to the floor.

"We'll wait in our bedroom until you say to come out." Jaya jumped two of his game pieces, then looked up at him. "I know she'll come because she really likes us."

Sighing, Jocelyn stepped out onto the stoop and emptied the dustpan onto the ground below. She practically floated through the door with a grin brightening her face. "Miss Darla will come because she *really likes* Papa."

Embarrassment warmed his neck. When had his daughters become matchmakers? "I don't want you girls to be too disappointed if things don't turn out the way you want them to."

"She'll come. You'll see." Jocelyn returned the broom and pan to the corner. "A girl just knows these things."

"A ten-year-old girl?"

"I turn eleven in two months."

Nicolas sighed. He had allowed himself to believe that Darla might be developing an affection for him. When he'd learned that she'd stayed at his bedside until she was sure he was on the path to recovery, he'd found it even easier to imagine.

He and his girls were all hopeless romantics. And he couldn't help but pray that Darla was, too. And that she liked chocolate.

When Nicolas swung the door open, Darla nearly lost her footing and dropped her packages. He'd shaved and trimmed his mustache. Dressed in fresh trousers and a forest-green shirt, he also wore a smile that could melt the truffles in her pocket.

"You came!" His enthusiasm matched that she had received from his girls on previous visits. Girls she didn't see or hear. "Where are the girls?"

"They're in their room doing schoolwork. I arranged for us to have some privacy."

Darla let a few seconds pass before breaking the silence. "Thank you for the chocolates and the note."

"You're welcome." He looked down at the two sacks. "You brought groceries?"

"I promised Jocelyn a French cooking lesson."

"Ah, yes. Please come in." When he reached for the sacks, his thumb brushed her wrist, sending a warming tingle up her arm.

She set her bundle of fabric on the chair near the door, then followed him to the kitchen table, where he set the sacks.

"Are these favorable to sitting for a few minutes?" he asked.

"Yes."

"Good."

It was good. Because the last thing she wanted to do was to deal with groceries, cook a meal, or even turn her gaze from this brown-eyed man who had invited her back into his life. Nicolas had a healthy glow about him, and his eyes sparkled with vitality.

"I'm glad to see you're doing well," Darla said.

"I am. Thank you." He glanced at the kettle on the stove. "I brewed some mint tea. Would you like a cup?"

"That would be nice. Thank you."

He carried a steaming teacup and saucer to the sitting room and set it on a small table beside the rocker she'd sat in the night she'd kept watch over him. When she seated herself, Nicolas went to the spindle chair across from her.

"Thank you for this chance to redeem myself, to tell you why I so abruptly asked Dr. Cutshaw for a replacement." He reached up and brushed his hand through the rich brown curls cascading over his forehead. "When you showed up here for the first time, I was hesitant to accept the arrangement for you to be my nurse."

Darla nodded. She started to reach for her teacup but decided against it. "You said I was too young. But I thought you'd moved past that hesitation."

"I had." He drew in a deep breath. "Until Zach arrived and your breath caught at the mention of his name."

Her mouth suddenly dry, Darla moistened her lips.

"Despite my best efforts, I had begun to care for you. But you were my nurse, and you'd only seen me injured, sick, lying on a cot. Not nearly as appealing as a man who is strong and runs his own business."

Darla leaned forward. "Admittedly, there was a time when my interest in a man ran shallow, but that is no longer the case."

"I know that now." He blew out a deep breath. "But *that day*, I could tell from your reaction to him and his to you that the two of you were, or had been, close. I assumed you were interested in pursuing a future with him. I didn't want to interfere, so I thought it best to let you go."

A noble gesture that had caused her to lose sleep. "I was at supper with Zachary that night to sort out and resolve my feelings. Any closeness he and I shared was in the past."

"So Zach informed me."

"You spoke with him about this?"

"He delivered coal earlier today, and your name came up in conversation." A sweet grin tipped Nicolas's mouth. "He said that anything you two once had got lost in the growing up."

Darla wasn't sure how much growing up Zachary had done, but she breathed a sigh of relief anyway. She apparently didn't have to concern herself with him causing a scene.

"That's not all he said."

Her neck warmed, and she braced herself to hear the worst of it.

"Zach said if I was willing to let you get away, I wasn't as smart as he thought I was, and that if given a choice, you'd choose me." He leaned forward. His forearms resting on his knees, he looked her in the eye. "Is that true?"

"I did choose you." Tears stung her eyes, and she blinked them back. "I'm here."

The chocolate-melting smile returned to his face. Nicolas did truly care for her. But he didn't know all he needed to know about her.

"In my note, I asked you to accept the candy as a token of my remorse," he said.

"Yes. And affection."

His eyes widened, and he nodded. "I didn't erase it because it wasn't true. It is true. I tried to erase it because I wasn't sure how my apology would be accepted. And I didn't want to narrow my chances by laying bare my deeper feelings. I—"

She raised her hand to stop him. "There's more you need to know before you can allow yourself to have true affection for me."

"Darla, the past doesn't matter to me. Like Paul said in his letter to the Philippians, I want to forget about those things that are behind us and reach for what lies ahead of us."

"Please. Let me tell you."

He relaxed against the back of the chair.

She took a deep breath. "I was a snappish teenager who didn't appreciate being the parson's daughter. I didn't like the way some people watched me and seemed always ready for me to step out of line, a line they had drawn. I grew tired of their lofty expectations."

"That sounds understandable."

"Yes, well." She lifted the teacup to her dry mouth and took a sip. "Unfortunately, my rebellion led me to seek male attention. Yes, Zachary. But first was a doctor who had just arrived in town from Boston."

"Morgan Cutshaw?"

"Yes, and he's now my boss. That's one of the many strange turns of events I've experienced since my return to Cripple Creek. Another being Miss Hattie having married Kat Sinclair Cutshaw's father. My landlady is now the stepmother of the woman I wronged."

Nicolas stood. "I think I will grab a cup, if you don't mind."

She motioned toward the kitchen, grateful for a short break before telling the worst of it.

Nicolas returned to his chair with a steaming mug of tea. "Sorry for the interruption. You were saying?"

"Yes." Darla set her saucer on the table beside her. "Dr. Cutshaw had grown fond of Miss Kat Sinclair, but his lack of interest in me didn't stop me from pursuing him. To the point of being deceitful and intentionally trying to come between them. I really was terrible to Kat."

"You were yet a child, just becoming a woman. We've all done things in our youth we're ashamed of. Have you seen her since you've been back?"

"I have. At church."

"And does she hold the past against you?"

Darla shook her head. "She said the trouble between us was old news."

"Well, then. I don't see—"

"I kept a diary about that shameful time in my life. I buried it under a floorboard in the parsonage just days before my father sent me to Philadelphia to live with my aunt and go to nurse's training." She leaned forward and lowered her voice to a whisper. "He'd found Zachary and I in the church basement. We were. . .uh, kissing."

His gentle nod told her she needn't say any more about that.

"Part of the reason I came back was to retrieve the diary and a pendant that had belonged to my grandmother."

"And have you?"

"No." More tears stung her eyes. "I should've told the parson and his wife about it, but I didn't." She sniffed and blotted her eyes. "Instead, I snuck in while they were away, and Ida returned to the parsonage for her parasol while I was trying to pull up the board."

"What did she do?"

"After my confession, she grabbed a pry bar and helped me. But my things were no longer there." Darla bit her bottom lip. "So you see, it was me all along who needed redemption. Not you."

"We all need redemption." Nicolas rose from his chair and walked toward her, knelt in front of her, and took her hands in his. "You seem to be the only one in town who can't accept the fact that you've changed. Everyone else you've mentioned seems to have extended grace. Isn't it time you accept God's forgiveness, forgive yourself, and reach for those things in front of you?"

Darla nodded, glancing down at their joined hands. Yes. It was time.

The aroma of a simmering creamy chicken stew and a fresh loaf of French bread perfumed the house. The woman he loved wore the faded gingham apron again, this time over a pink dress with lace and black-and-pink trim. Knowing how she'd struggled then and now had endeared her to him all the more.

Darla sat in the rocker in front of the open trunk while the girls took turns unwrapping his carvings and handing them to her. He couldn't help but stare as she examined each one, admiring the detail.

"I like this one a lot." Julia held up a playful kitten, stroking its wooden fur.

Darla added a miniature stallion to the collection on her lap and took the kitten. "I can see why you like it. She's cute—like you." She poked Julia in the belly. When giggles spilled out, tears filled Darla's eyes again, but he could tell they were joyful tears.

She may have thought God had brought her back to resolve her past with Zach and to retrieve her belongings from the parsonage, but he believed God had brought her to Cripple Creek to rescue him and his family.

Jaya lifted a small shelf from the trunk. "Did Papa tell you he has to go back to work?"

Darla looked to where he knelt on the floor at the end of the trunk, a frown narrowing her green eyes. "At the mine?"

He nodded. "Yes. According to Mrs. Alexander, the doctor's release is for this Thursday."

A deep sigh rounded her shoulders. "What if you didn't return to the mine?"

"I have thought about it, but—"

"I'm sure there are many other things you could do."

"I suppose with all the new buildings going up, if I'm healed enough, I could hire on as brick layer. But those crews tend to travel from town to town."

Her eyes widening, she glanced down at the carvings on her lap then up to the phoenix. "What about your woodworking? I saw that the watchmaker's building is empty. You could open a shop."

"My own shop for whittling?"

"It looks to me like woodworking means more to you than a mere hobby might."

"Papa did the wainscoting at the church," Jocelyn said. "And Miss Hattie's, too."

Jaya set the shelf on the floor. "And that bench in the foyer. You made that, too, Papa."

Darla nodded. "I think you'd have more work than time to do it."

"I think that's a wonderful idea." Jocelyn looked at him, her eyebrows raised. So did Darla and the little ones, as if waiting for his response.

Of course he liked the idea, but he couldn't say it would be realistic for him to think he could quit the mine and start a business. "I appreciate the votes of confidence." He met Darla's gaze and smiled. "We'll see. I'll think about it."

Jocelyn pressed her hand to Darla's knee. "I'm so glad you came back, Miss Darla."

"I'm glad I did, too." She patted Jocelyn's hand.

"Me, too." Julia leaned against Darla's other leg, and she stroked the little one's curls. *Like a mother would.*

"That makes five of us," Jaya said.

Nicolas nodded, tears pooling his eyes. *Five of us.* He liked the sound of that.

Chapter Thirteen

Hattie's modern stove was far newer and bigger than the one in the company house. But Darla couldn't imagine being happier than she had been yesterday, cooking for the Zanzucchi family with Jocelyn at her side. Never had she laughed so hard as when Nicolas and his girls decided eating a French meal required using a French accent. Her time with them made her miss her brother, Peter, and Mother and Father. But she couldn't fathom making the long train ride to New York any time soon, and she doubted they had any notion to come clear across the country.

Now she stood in the boardinghouse kitchen with her landlady, stirring cranberry sauce for a meal that was likely to be almost as special as the chicken fricassee. The two elderly sisters boarding at Miss Hattie's had gone for a buggy ride to Victor. Cherise was spending the day with Kat and her children. And Nicolas's three girls were playing at Nell's house for the afternoon.

Hattie looked up from the meat platter on the countertop and glanced at the small pot in front of Darla. "About ready?"

Darla lifted a spoonful of sauce, watched the sauce flow back into the pot, and nodded.

"So are the pork chops. The potatoes should be getting close." Hattie resumed her task of filling the platter.

Darla reached to the back burner and gave the roasting potatoes another stir.

"It's so kind of you and Mr. Sinclair to host us. Thank you!"

"It's our pleasure, dear." Her landlady and friend set the last pork chop in the center of the platter.

With the saucepan and ladle in hand, Darla drizzled the cranberry sauce over the meat. "It will be especially pleasurable for Nicolas and me to eat supper in the company of other adults."

Hattie tittered. "You mean with another couple, don't you?"

She and Nicolas were a couple. They had both admitted to feeling they belonged together that Saturday when she'd played checkers with the girls and stayed for supper. Darla set the empty saucepan and wooden spoon in the sink. "Just don't pinch me. I don't want to wake up from this dream."

Last night, after she and Jocelyn succeeded in preparing their first French meal, she had shared her chocolate with the family and beat Nicolas at checkers. When the girls were tucked in, he'd walked her home to the boardinghouse. Inside, she'd had a long conversation with Hattie before retiring to her room to dream about the possibilities that lay before her.

Still, she'd feel better if she could cut the nagging tie to her past. Her diary. But Nicolas was right. Diary or no diary, she needed to trust God with her past as well as with her future.

While Darla framed the pork chops with the roasted potatoes, Hattie poured the honey-glazed carrots into a cut-glass bowl. They both hung their aprons on a hook inside the pantry. When they swept into the dining room, carrying platters and bowls, both Harlan and Nicolas stood, the latter looking positively delicious. He wore a gray tweed jacket over a white shirt and blue string tie. His free-spirited curls cascaded above warm chocolate-brown eyes. Kat Sinclair had been right—she wasn't likely to find a patient as charming as Nicolas Zanzucchi. Or a man as compassionate and courageous as this widowed father of three girls. This was the man she loved.

Harlan took the bowl from Hattie and set it on the festive cherrywood table. "We hesitated to appear too hungry or anxious, but we didn't vacillate very long before seating ourselves."

"Darla and I are glad to hear you're hungry."

Darla added the platter of pork chops to the mouthwatering spread.

"That is a lot of food, and it all looks delicious." Nicolas smiled at her and pulled out the chair beside his. "A feast."

"And rightly so." Seated, Hattie pulled the napkin from her place setting. "We have much to celebrate."

They did have much to celebrate. Nicolas had recovered, and they were now a couple. And this afternoon she was spending time with him somewhere other than the company house.

Following Harlan's brief prayer, they each began filling their plates and passing the serving dishes around the table.

Nicolas started the meat platter on its rounds. "I'm eating especially well this week." He held the platter while Darla scooped a pork chop and potatoes onto her plate. "The girls do well enough, but I'm sure you heard Darla and Jocelyn prepared a French meal for us yesterday. The food was *magnifique*, as Jocelyn would say."

Darla loved the joyful sound of his baritone chuckle.

A few minutes later, a knock on the front door quieted their conversation, and Harlan started to stand.

The door clicked shut, and a happy baby's chatter filled the entry. "Father? Hattie?"

"Ida and Joshua." Harlan settled back onto his chair and speared his last bite of potato. "We're in the dining room, Ida."

———————◆———————

Darla set her fork on her plate. Ida had probably only come to visit her father and Hattie, but she couldn't help but hope she'd one day bring news from her husband concerning the whereabouts of the diary and pendant.

Ida walked into the room with Joshua perched on one hip. A flour sack dangled from her other hand. "I've interrupted your supper." Nicolas had stood, but Ida waved for him to be seated. "I apologize for my poor timing."

"No need." Hattie pulled her napkin from her lap. "Would you like a plate?"

"As you can see"—Harlan tipped his head toward the full table—"we still have ample." He scooted his chair back and reached for the baby.

"No, thank you." Ida settled Joshua on his grandfather's lap, then smoothed the bodice on her lavender dress. "I ate earlier. Before Tucker went to put the finishing touches on tomorrow's sermon."

"Then you're just in time for dessert." Hattie patted the chair beside her. "Darla and I made peach pies."

"I'd like that. Thank you." Ida walked around the table and paused beside Darla. "But first, I brought you something."

Darla stood with weak knees.

A warm smile lit Ida's blue eyes as she pressed the sack into Darla's hand. "Tucker found the loose board and your things. He put them in a box and kept it behind some theology books on the shelf in his office in case someone came to claim them one day."

Darla gripped the sack as if her life depended upon it and pulled Ida into an embrace. "Thank you so much."

Nicolas stood beside her, his gaze tender. She drew in a fortifying breath, then untied the drawstrings and freed the box. Ida retrieved the sack, and Darla lifted the clasp on the box.

Gram's little velvet jewelry case lay nestled beside the diary, just like she had left it. She bent and set the box on her chair. Her hands shaking, she lifted out the diary. The double-granny knot she'd tied around it nearly four years earlier hadn't been disturbed. A sigh of relief punctuated her silent prayer of thanksgiving.

She reached for Nicolas's hand, then looked at the others. "Will you excuse us?" When they nodded, she led him through the kitchen door to the coal stove.

"Like you said, it's time I truly let go of the past and embrace my future." She gripped the diary with both hands, then looked at the stove. "Will you help me?"

"I'd be honored." He grabbed the towel from its peg beside the sink and wrapped it around the handle on the coal chute. When he opened the chute door, the acrid smell of burning coal stung her nostrils. She set the diary on the edge of the chute then pushed it into the miniature inferno. When the dry cardboard lit, she slammed the chute door on her past and looked up at the man she wanted in her future.

"Will you go for a walk with me after some of your peach pie?" Nicolas asked.

"Yes." She'd gladly follow this man anywhere, but he'd piqued her curiosity, and she wouldn't be able to down her dessert fast enough.

Chapter Fourteen

Nicolas made a deliberate effort to take shorter, slower steps. Darla was doing a good job of keeping up, but her fashionable narrow skirt wasn't suited for his anxious stride down Bennett Avenue.

When they reached the corner at Second Street, he slowed down enough to cup her elbow and guide her across. Their destination wouldn't remain a surprise much longer. "Any minute now—"

"The watchmaker's shop!" She looked at him, her eyes widening. "That's where we're going?"

He nodded. Her smiles quieted the commotion around them, and he wouldn't live long enough to get his fill of them.

"What a great idea to look at it together. Even if we can't see very much." Off she went, her narrow pale blue skirt twisting with each step.

At the glass door, he pulled a keychain from his trouser pocket and dangled a key from it.

She stepped back from the window. "You have the key?"

He placed the key into the lock, unable to believe the extraordinary turn of events himself. "As it turns out, I had supper with the owner today." He pushed the door open and motioned for her to lead the way inside.

Darla took slow steps over the threshold. "Hattie owns this building?"

Stifling a chuckle, he followed her inside. He loved that Darla had the confidence to think first of a woman owning a business building in a mining town. "Actually, it was her husband who bought it from the watchmaker's heirs."

"Oh. All of this came to pass in the few minutes you two were waiting for Hattie and me to serve supper?"

"Yes. And the best part of it is that Mr. Sinclair said he had me in mind when he signed the papers two weeks ago. I'm thinking of renting it from him."

Darla's emerald-green eyes glistened behind a pool of tears. She squared her shoulders, her rounded chin jutting out. "What's there to think about? You are a gifted artist. Don't you want to pursue your craft, to have your own business? If you opened a woodworking shop, you wouldn't have to go back to the mine."

Emotion threatened to clog his throat, and he swallowed hard. "I knew what I wanted to do, but I can't begin to tell you how good it feels to have someone beside me again who cares." He watched a tear slide down Darla's cheek and brushed it away. "I'll go tell them at the Mollie Kathleen Mine first thing Monday."

"That's wonderful news! The girls will be so happy to hear it. I know I am."

He strolled to the middle of the showroom. The walls were faded except where clocks had hung, and the building had gaslights, which would have to be changed out. "Mr. Sinclair said he's having electricity brought in. It needs a little work, but—"

"The five of us working together could whip it into fine shape in no time at all."

"I was hoping you'd say that." He winked.

Blushing the color of a summer sunset, she gazed at the back corner. "I can't wait to see you standing at a lathe back there. Crafting chair spindles and table legs. Making animal carvings. And of course, your impressive wall carvings."

He reached for her hand and squeezed it. "That's what I love about you, Darla Taggart. You're a dreamer."

Her eyes glistened. "You do?"

"I do." He glanced at the closed door in the center of the back wall. "Uh, there's more to see." He led her past the few boxes scattered on the floor and opened the door into a room about half the size of the front one with shelves on two of the four walls. "This would make a good supply room. Wood. Tools. Items waiting for pickup or delivery."

"It's seems so perfect."

He nodded. The only thing missing was a kiss, but that would come. Soon, if he had a say in it.

———◆———

Darla watched Nicolas examine a storage cabinet just inside the back door. He'd been walking through the shop like a child in a candy store, full of wonder—running his fingertips across the surfaces. She loved that he was just as ready for a fresh start as she was.

He loved her. She'd seen it in his eyes when she showed up at his house with the groceries. When she suggested he didn't have to return to the mine, that he could pursue woodworking. She'd seen love in his eyes when she surrendered the diary to the burning coals and stepped into his embrace. She was a dreamer, and in this moment, she was dreaming of walking into the shop full of his wooden kittens and birds rising up out of the ashes, and living as his wife in the apartment upstairs. She glanced at the staircase just inside the storage-room door.

"Mr. Sinclair said the apartment has two bedrooms. I'm guessing it's comparable in size to the company house. Only with stairs." He glanced from her hobbling skirt to the staircase. "Do you think you could make it up there?"

"Certainly. I want to see it all." She'd make the climb, if she had to crawl. She didn't want this dream to end.

Fortunately, there was a smooth wooden railing on either side of the staircase and the steps weren't deep, so she had no trouble ascending as long as she wasn't in a hurry.

At the top, Nicolas unlocked another door and pushed it open. They stepped into a sparsely furnished sitting room with light coming from an alcove window that overlooked the street. The perfect niche for reading or sewing, and it was opposite an open kitchen with a good-sized dining table in the center.

Nicolas went to the bedrooms and met her in the sitting room. "It comes complete with a toilet room between the bedrooms."

"It's a nice layout and seems very comfortable." She did a slow spin, taking it all in. "A certain rocking chair. Some quilts and curtains. That's all it needs."

He crossed his arms and looked around. "It needs a woman's touch."

"Yes." Heat rushed up her neck and into her face. She wanted nothing more than to be that woman.

Nicolas ran his finger along the inside of his collar as if it were suddenly too tight. "Would you mind sitting for a minute?" He looked at the caned chair beside the small potbellied stove in the corner.

She sat down and looked up at him.

"I was going to speak to you on the porch at the boardinghouse, but this building in the heart of town now seems like a better time and place."

They had been speaking all afternoon, had they not? "A better time and place?"

"To discuss our future." He reached into his jacket pocket and pulled out a small satin box.

"Oh!" Good thing she was seated, because she was sure her legs wouldn't have held her.

Kneeling, he held the box in front of her and opened it.

Her breath caught at the sight of the rings. A pale blue sapphire graced a gold band with silver accents. Beneath it, a gold wedding band. A matched set. "They're beautiful."

"My papa's papa gave the rings to Nonna Zanzucchi when they married." He lifted her hand from her knee. "Miss Darla Taggart, I may have loved you from the moment you lost that first checkers game to Jaya, but I know I love you now. And those days without seeing you showed me that I don't want to live apart from you."

Tears of joy streamed down her face.

"Would you do me the honor of being my wife and the mother to my girls? Would you marry me and wear this ring of eternal love and commitment?"

"Yes!" She reached up and brushed the cascade of curls on his forehead. "I may have loved you before I read those words you tried to erase—*and affection*—but I know I loved you then. Yes. Let's be married." Leaning forward, she pressed her lips to his and experienced a sweetness she'd never known.

———————◆———————

Twenty minutes later, she and Nicolas reunited with the three girls on Nell and Judson's porch. Nell was inside pouring them all some lemonade while Nicolas leaned against a post. Darla rested the hand without an engagement ring on the railing and looked at her soon-to-be family. Jocelyn sat at a small metal table with a book, while Jaya and Julia knelt beside a playful beagle.

Darla cleared her throat, careful to keep her left hand hidden in her skirt. "Your papa and I have some very big news." She quickly had their undivided attention and glanced at Nicolas, then back at them. "Your papa won't be returning to the mine. Instead, he will rent the watchmaker's building from Mrs. Nell's father and open a woodworking shop."

"Oh." The smile on Jaya's face faded. "I thought maybe you were getting married."

Jocelyn closed her book. "When I saw the sappy looks on your faces, that's what I thought, too."

Nicolas stepped up beside Darla. "It's all true. I am going to have a woodworking shop, and I'm not returning to the mine." A grin filled his face. "And. . ."

With that cue, Darla displayed her left hand. All three girls gasped.

"Miss Darla has agreed to marry me."

A chorus of cheers erupted. While the girls encircled them, Nell spilled out the open door with William toddling behind her.

"Papa and Miss Darla are getting married!"

"What wonderful news!" Nell leaned over the top of Julia and pulled Darla into a warm embrace. "Congratulations to the both of you."

Yet another member of the Sinclair family had come alongside Darla and the Zanzucchi family, cheering them on. God had indeed brought her back to Cripple Creek for so much more than she'd planned. She brushed Nicolas's arm and breathed another prayer of gratitude.

Chapter Fifteen

Darla wouldn't have thought it possible that six weeks could fly by *and* drag at the same time. But they had. She'd prepared to wed the man of her dreams in a flurry of activity that included cleaning the apartment above the shop, setting up the displays of Nicolas's carvings, sending several telegrams to her parents to arrange for their trip west, and sewing parties with Hattie and the Sinclair sisters. But at the end of each day, when she returned to the boardinghouse alone, it seemed time stood still and May 27 would never arrive.

But this day had already been worth both the rush and the wait. Starting with breakfast at the boardinghouse with Father, Mother, and Peter. Attending the Sunday service with her first family seated on one side and her new family on the other. She and Father were once again under the same roof. This time, when past mistakes and hurts returned to weigh her down, the truth in Hattie's words echoed in her heart. *"That was then, and this is now."*

As she stood in the foyer beside her father, she couldn't be more ready for now, with the past in its rightful place.

Father reached for her hand and laid it on his arm, as if to punctuate that fact. "I couldn't be more proud of the woman you've become, Darla May."

Tears threatened to spill over, and she blotted her lower lids with the embroidered handkerchief her mother had loaned her for the ceremony. "Thank you, Daddy." Pressing her hand to his arm, she raised up onto her tiptoes and kissed him on the cheek. "I'm so glad you're here."

"I am, too." His voice wavered, but his arm was steady.

She pressed her hand to the blue agate cameo she wore—her something blue. "I've learned a lot since my return, but nothing so profoundly as I have learned that God works in mysterious ways."

"Indeed He does." A chord sounded on the piano, and they looked at each other. "Are you ready?"

Darla gave him a slow nod so as not to upset the exquisite old cap and veil Mother had brought from her side of the family. "I'm ready."

The foyer doors swung open, and the tune began. A sea of smiling faces greeted them as Darla practically glided down the center aisle toward the man she loved. Nicolas wore a borrowed tailcoat and top hat with the blue chambray shirt she'd stitched for him. The span in his smile made the wait seem a distant memory. Nell's husband, Judson, stood beside him.

Darla took a deep breath. Mother smiled at her from the piano bench, her hands dancing across the keys. Peter reached out and squeezed her hand. Mrs. Wahlberg choked back tears as she passed, which Darla remembered her doing at all weddings.

At the front, Darla took her place between Nicolas and Ida, her new dearest friend and matron of honor, while Father stepped around them and behind the pulpit. Her heart racing in the nearness of her soon-to-be husband, she looked out at the little girls who sat in the front row with Hattie and the Sinclair family. Her girls. Jocelyn wore a dress made of the cotton mull with the yellow embroidery. The green plaid dress was a perfect match for Jaya. And Julia looked like a summer sky in her blue calico. They each beamed smiles as vibrant as the stained-glass windows framing this occasion.

When Father pronounced them married, Nicolas reached into his pocket and pulled out a small wooden figurine. An angel with its wings spread. He pressed it into her hand as he bent toward her ear. "Julia was right the first time she saw you arriving at the house—you are an angel. My angel sent from God."

Tears of matchless joy stung her eyes. "And you, Husband, are my phoenix, sent to lift me out of the ashes with you."

Their first kiss as husband and wife sent shivers up Darla's spine, and she was sure she heard fireworks overhead. *Mrs. Nicolas Zanzucchi.*

Yes, God did indeed work, and in truly mysterious ways.

Married forty-two years to her leading man, **Mona Hodgson** from Arizona lives in the Southwest where trees have arms instead of branches and salsa is a staple. When Mona isn't writing or speaking, she's playing Wii games with her Arizona grandson, spending time with her mom, picnicking, texting her sisters, or chatting via Skype with her grandchildren in Africa. Mona is the author of nearly forty books, including her Sinclair Sisters of Cripple Creek series, *The Quilted Heart* omnibus, and *Prairie Song*, Book 1 in her Hearts Seeking Home series. Her children's books include bestseller *Bedtime in the Southwest* and *Real Girls of the Bible: A 31-Day Devotional*. Mona's writing credits also include several hundred articles, poems, and short stories, which have appeared in fifty different publications. She is a speaker for women's groups, Christian women's retreats, book clubs and reading groups, schools, and conferences for writers and librarians.

Also available from Barbour Publishing

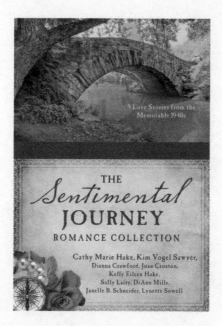

*Nine romances set during the
turbulent era of World War II.*

Wherever Christian books are sold.